AMERICAN ROYALS IV: REIGN

ALSO BY KATHARINE McGEE

American Royals
American Royals II: Majesty
American Royals III: Rivals
Inheritance (A Prequel Novella)

REIGN

AMERICAN ROYALS IV

KATHARINE McGEE

Random House New York

Text copyright © 2023 by Katharine McGee and Alloy Entertainment
Jacket art copyright © 2023 by Carolina Melis

Visit us on the Web! GetUnderlined.com

Educators and librarians, for a variety of teaching tools, visit us at RHTeachersLibrarians.com

Produced by Alloy Entertainment
alloyentertainment.com

Library of Congress Cataloging-in-Publication Data
Name: McGee, Katharine, author.
Title: Reign / Katharine McGee.
Description: First edition. | New York: Random House, [2023] | Series: American royals; IV | Audience: Ages 14 and up. | Summary: In an alternate America, Beatrice, Samantha, and Jefferson struggle to determine what they really want and how much it is worth when weighed against the crown.
Identifiers: LCCN 2023003810 (print) | LCCN 2023003811 (ebook) | ISBN 978-0-593-42974-7 (hardcover) | ISBN 978-0-593-71021-0 (international) | ISBN 978-0-593-42976-1 (ebook)
Subjects: CYAC: Kings, queens, rulers, etc.—Fiction. | Princesses—Fiction. | Princes—Fiction. | Siblings—Fiction. | LCGFT: Alternative histories (Fiction) | Romance fiction. | Novels.
Classification: LCC PZ7.1.M43513 Re 2023 (print) | LCC PZ7.1.M43513 (ebook) | DDC [Fic]—dc23

The text of this book is set in 11.2-point Goudy Old Style MT Pro.
Interior design by Michelle Crowe

Printed in the United States of America
10 9 8 7 6 5 4 3 2 1
First Edition

To all the readers who have been with me
on this journey: this book is for you.
Thank you.

PROLOGUE

BEATRICE

The sound of a door swinging open, and a sharp intake of breath. "I'm sorry, Your Lordship. I didn't realize you'd slept in here again."

Who was that? Beatrice tried to open her eyes, but her body felt impossibly heavy. She blamed the champagne from last night. She'd only had a couple of glasses, but that was more than she usually drank.

"Please, call me Teddy." A steady voice, warm and soothing as honey.

"Would you like me to call building services and request a cot? Surely you don't want to keep sleeping on that couch."

"I don't mind, really." A sigh. "Yesterday I saw her eyebrows twitch. I didn't want to leave, because what if she woke up and I wasn't here?"

"Perhaps Her Majesty was dreaming, sir," the other voice said gently. "Would you mind if I checked her vitals?"

There were shuffling sounds, and the cool sensation of fingers on Beatrice's forearm. "I love you so much, Bee," someone was telling her. "Please, wake up. . . ."

"Bee, wake up." Connor knocked softly at her door. "Your father is looking for you downstairs."

Beatrice blinked. Dawn crept at the edges of the heavy curtains, illuminating the cedar bed frame, the stone fireplace in one corner. They were at her family's mountain house in Telluride.

She sat up abruptly, hair tumbling around her shoulders, as the past few days crashed over her in vivid detail. She and Connor had been caught in a snowstorm, stranded in a cabin in Montrose—where everything had changed.

Beatrice creaked open the door, her heart leaping when she saw Connor. "My dad is already up?"

"He asked if you wanted to go for a walk." Connor glanced toward the staircase, then leaned over to brush a quick kiss on her lips.

She forced herself to slip back into her room and dress in warm layers of snow gear. When she emerged, her eyes met Connor's again, and they exchanged a secret smile.

The house felt heavy with the drowsy, contented silence that always follows a late night. While the New Year's Eve party had been at Smuggler's, a members-only club in town, Beatrice saw the aftermath of the celebrations everywhere—Sam's platinum bangles scattered on a side table, where she'd drunkenly slid them off her wrist; a row of half-empty champagne flutes, their rims marked with lipstick.

King George IV was seated at the kitchen table, his hands curled around a mug of coffee. He looked up sheepishly at her arrival.

"Sorry if this is too early, Bee. I just thought . . . you're usually the only person who wakes up when I do."

"I was already up," Beatrice fibbed.

"Want to go for a walk?" her dad asked, as if they were heading out on their usual morning jog through the capital, rather than facing several feet of fresh snow. But then, he'd never been held up by something as prosaic as weather conditions.

Outside, Beatrice took a bracing breath, relishing how

the cold air felt inside her lungs. Their snowshoes traced soft whispers over the snow.

"Thanks for coming." Her dad turned onto one of the on-mountain trails that wound between the trees. "I always love starting the new year outdoors, where I have space to think about everything I've accomplished in the previous year, all my victories as well as my mistakes."

"You hardly ever make mistakes!" Beatrice protested, immediately defensive on her father's behalf.

He smiled at her outrage. "I'm not too proud to admit when I'm wrong. And as a leader, it's important to listen to your critics—especially the ones you disagree with the most."

"You make it sound so easy." Beatrice's heart sank at the thought of all the criticism constantly directed at *her*—because she wasn't fashionable like Princess Louise of France, because she held back her emotions, which made her seem aloof and unreadable. *Be more like Jeff,* those people exclaimed on message boards and late-night talk shows. As if Beatrice could just flip a switch and become her brother, who won everyone over with easygoing charm.

Sometimes, at her weakest moments, Beatrice wondered whether things would be easier if those people's wishes had come true. If Jeff had been born first, giving America yet another king instead of its very first queen.

"Beatrice, look!" Her dad pointed a few yards to the right, where a trail of small footprints disappeared into the trees. "She might still be close by. Let's keep an eye out."

"It could be a *he,*" Beatrice noted.

"It could," George conceded, "but I think it's a female. Male foxes don't venture into the cold as much. They aren't as fierce." He glanced over, smiling softly. "That's one of the many reasons you will be a great queen, Beatrice."

She shook her head slowly. "I am many things"—intellectual, serious, dedicated—"but fierce isn't one of them."

"Your convictions are fierce, and you will need that. This job isn't an easy one. You have to be the stabilizing force beneath a rotating carousel of senators and judges, a constant amid the changing times."

Beatrice shivered, and not from the cold. "You're being very philosophical this morning, Dad."

Something like regret flitted over her dad's expression, but it was gone before Beatrice could parse it out. He chuckled. "You're right, this is too serious a conversation for the morning after a New Year's party. Speaking of which," he added, "you and Teddy were enjoying yourselves last night."

"Um, right," Beatrice fumbled to say. "But we haven't been dating very long."

She and Teddy had been going on dates to appease the media—or more accurately, to appease their parents. Beatrice had to admit that she felt relaxed with Teddy. She had come to consider him a friend, and she didn't exactly have those in spades.

"I'm not saying you should rush into anything," her dad agreed. "But I worry about you, Bee. I don't want you to be lonely in this role."

"I'm not lonely! I have you."

Her father drew in a breath to reply—but then, behind a distant veil of trees limned in frost, Beatrice saw the flash of a red foxtail.

"Dad, look!"

She grabbed instinctively for his forearm. He stilled, his smile echoing her own, as they both watched the fox peer at them with suspicious eyes.

"Her pulse is picking up."

"What?" Beatrice exclaimed, and the fox darted off. She

sighed and released her grip on her dad. "Why did you say that?"

"Say what?" Her dad leaned against a tree, fiddling with one glove as if adjusting it, but Beatrice realized that he was stalling. He had moved more slowly than usual this morning, which she'd attributed to the cold, but now she wondered if it was more.

"Bee, I miss you," he went on.

"Dad, are you okay? Why are you saying that?" She took a step forward, her brow creased with concern—

"I miss you, Bee. I love you so much."

She opened her eyes and blinked. A fluorescent light came into disjointed focus. A beeping noise, the low hum of machines. A face bent over hers, handsome features creased with concern.

What was Teddy doing here?

"Bee? Thank god!" Teddy's hand grabbed hers, the feel of his skin startling and familiar at once. "Dr. Jacobs!" he cried out, blue eyes never leaving her face. "She's awake! Hurry!"

Where am I? Beatrice longed to ask, but her mouth couldn't form the words. She tried to search the room for Connor, because surely he was nearby, but her eyelids felt so heavy, and everything was so bright, and it hurt. . . .

Before she could force the images and sounds to make any kind of sense, her mind slid into darkness once more.

DAPHNE

Hundreds of people craned their necks as the doors to the throne room swung open. The trumpets blared, and then he stepped forward—the most important man in the country, possibly in the *world*. Acting King Jefferson.

Daphne Deighton allowed herself a brief moment of satisfaction. To think that after everything that had happened, after all the ups and downs of their relationship, she was finally here: higher than she'd ever imagined she might soar. Standing next to Jefferson while the senior peers of the realm swore him homage.

According to protocol, the dais should have been reserved for members of the royal family. But when the Lady Chamberlain had pointed this out, Jefferson had simply stated that Daphne would be up there with him, and that was that.

After all, the only person who outranked him was currently in a coma.

An equerry began to unfurl the ermine-trimmed robe of state, but Jefferson made an impatient gesture, letting the robe whip out behind him. When Beatrice appeared in public, she always walked slowly, like a bride processing down the aisle. Not so her younger brother. As Jefferson strode forward, light gleamed on the crimson of his ceremonial blazer, the white sash of the Edwardian Order, the burnished gold of the Imperial State Crown. He looked like some conquering hero from a long-ago era, a figure from a painting sprung to life. He looked every inch a king.

Daphne could practically hear the sighs of the millions of Americans who were watching the live coverage of this event, and imagining themselves in love with her boyfriend.

The room echoed with the sounds of rustling fabrics as everyone bowed or curtsied. Daphne tucked one leg behind the other and sank exquisitely low, letting her skirts ripple around her. She held the gesture for several beats longer than necessary, eyes downcast, so that the photographers could capture the flattering image. She was well aware that she looked resplendent today, her deep green gown emphasizing the vivid green of her eyes.

Jefferson proceeded up the steps, and then—his jaw set with regret, or perhaps with disbelief—he sat on the throne, his hands curling over its armrests.

Lord Ambrose Madison rose heavily from his chair and made his way to the microphone. As hereditary Queen's Champion, he would serve as today's master of ceremonies.

Daphne watched him, her face pleasantly neutral, though her body seethed with resentment. She hated the Duke of Virginia, but she hated his daughter, Gabriella, even more.

"Sirs and ladies," Lord Ambrose intoned, his chest puffed up with arrogance, "I present to you Jefferson, your Acting King, who serves in the place of Her Majesty Queen Beatrice. Long may she reign."

"Long may she reign" rumbled through the throne room.

The duke nodded approvingly. "May we all now swear him our service and fidelity in the name of Our Sovereign Queen, for as long as he shall hold this office on her behalf. We shall begin with His Highness the Duke of Manchester."

It was strange to have Jefferson's uncle Richard taking such an active role; normally these ceremonies didn't need to stretch so far down the royal family tree. But Washington family members were in short supply right now, with Beatrice on life support and Samantha missing in action. Samantha and her boyfriend, Lord Marshall Davis, had run away together a month ago—and no one knew if they ever planned on coming back.

Richard ascended the steps of the throne and knelt before his nephew, then recited the Oath of Vassal Homage.

"I, Richard, Duke of Manchester, solemnly swear that I am your liege man. I will honor and serve you in faith and in loyalty, from this day forward, and for all the days of my life, so help me God."

"I humbly and gratefully accept your service," Jefferson replied evenly.

One by one, the lords and ladies of the realm all made their way to the throne, knelt before Jefferson, and swore the same vow. First came the Old Guard, the members of the thirteen original dukedoms that had been created in the wake of the Revolutionary War. Lord Ambrose Madison went first, looking as pompous and insufferable as ever. Then came the Duke of Boston; his son Teddy had renounced his rights to the dukedom, so he wasn't in attendance. And then the rest of the Old Guard: the Dukes of Dover and Plymouth, of New Haven and Roanoke. They all looked stiff with formality in their court dress, some of the older generation even wearing breeches or white gloves.

Next came the rest of the dukes, then the marquesses and earls, until over an hour had passed and they had finally reached the lowly baronets.

Daphne's father should have been up there, swearing his fealty to Jefferson like the rest of them, except that he'd been stripped of his title a month ago, as punishment for his so-called "ungentlemanly behavior." He'd been caught gambling in Vegas—on the odds of Daphne and Jefferson getting married.

Now everyone in America knew the sordid truth. Wherever she went, people stared at her with judgmental—or worse, *pitying*—looks. Even the media, who had always adored Daphne with an obsession that bordered on worship, had turned on her. Worst of all was their new nickname for her: the Poker Princess.

Everyone assumed that Jefferson would break up with Daphne soon enough. Surely someone from such a tacky, déclassé family could never date a prince. But Jefferson loyally pretended not to hear the gossip.

He would do anything for the woman he thought was the mother of his child.

The strain was wearing on Daphne, but she knew it was worth it. People were wrong when they whispered that she wanted to marry a rich, well-connected man.

Please. She hadn't braved years of social warfare and left scorched earth in her wake just to marry a rich, well-connected man. She had done it for *the* rich and well-connected man, the only one in America who really counted.

Now all she had to do was marry into the royal family, even though no commoner had done it before.

Daphne looked down into the throne room, and her eyes locked with those of Gabriella Madison. Gabriella's mouth curled into a sneer, color flushing her cheeks. Daphne relished the fact that she was standing up on the dais while Gabriella was lost in the crowd. It was always nice looking down on one of your archrivals.

Daphne's other sworn nemesis, Nina Gonzalez, wasn't here today.

Earlier this year, Nina had pulled an elaborate and deeply cruel con on Daphne, pretending to be friends so that she could get close and try to break up Daphne and Jefferson. And like a stupid, naïve fool, Daphne had *let* her.

She wouldn't make that mistake a second time. She knew better than to believe in friendship anymore.

Friends became eyewitnesses to your weaknesses, your secrets. Friends could weaponize your vulnerabilities against you.

Gabriella looked away from Daphne with evident frustration. For now, the two of them were locked in a stalemate. Gabriella knew that Daphne had sold photos of herself to the tabloids, and Daphne had a video of Gabriella doing cocaine. Neither of them dared to act, for fear of the other sharing what she knew, but Daphne had a feeling that their cease-fire wouldn't last forever.

She glanced back to where Jefferson was still accepting homage, reciting those same words over and over. As each person knelt before the throne, he studied them with calm focus, showing no signs of impatience or weariness.

Daphne knew better than to voice this thought aloud, but lately she'd caught herself wondering: What if Beatrice never recovered? What if *Jefferson* was America's future?

What if she wasn't just a future princess, but a future queen?

"Jefferson!" Daphne stepped into the Green Room: the vast chamber where the royal family gathered after public appearances, which also happened to be decorated in various shades of green. She noted with distracted pleasure that she matched the room perfectly, her dress set against the background as if she were a figure in an eighteenth-century painting.

Jefferson turned from where he'd been staring out the window and smiled. "Hey, Daphne. Thanks for standing up there all afternoon. I'm sure it wasn't easy on you, given . . ." He trailed off before saying *the baby.*

She closed the distance between them, her heels sinking pleasantly into the lush carpet. Jefferson reached for her hands and tugged her closer, lowering his mouth to hers.

Usually their kisses were all sparks and fire and roving hands, but today it felt different: lingering, and soft, and tender. Not a frantic teenage kiss fueled by hormones, but the type of kiss that a man gave the woman he loved.

When they pulled apart, his eyes darted to her stomach, which was as flat as ever. "Ready to share our news?"

"As ready as I'll ever be," she murmured.

A month ago, at the closing banquet of the League of Kings conference, Daphne had told Jefferson that she might be pregnant. She had been desperate, trying frantically to keep him from breaking up with her after he'd kissed Nina earlier that night.

Ever since, she'd been pleading with Jefferson to tell their parents—the crucial first step in her plan. The sooner she could nudge them into a public engagement, the better. She could only keep up her fake pregnancy for so long.

"Jeff! You were wonderful out there!" Queen Adelaide exclaimed as she swept into the room. Belatedly, she remembered to curtsy to her son—which she didn't normally have to do, but circumstances were far from normal these days.

Jefferson cleared his throat. "Thanks, Mom. Actually . . . there's something I need to talk to you about."

With impeccable timing, a footman materialized in the doorway. "Your Royal Highness. Mr. and Mrs. Deighton are here, as you requested."

Mr. and Mrs. Deighton. It was still jarring hearing her parents referred to by the common form of their names.

Daphne's parents entered amid curtsies and bows and murmured pleasantries. They were dressed nicely, though not in gowns and ceremonial wear like Daphne and the Washingtons, because, of course, they hadn't been at the ceremony. It was only for people with titles.

Daphne's eyes cut to Queen Adelaide, who treated the Deightons with her usual courtesy; she was too well mannered to act like anything had changed. Still, Daphne swore she caught a fleeting hint of distaste on the queen's features.

"Thank you all for coming," Jefferson began. "Daphne and I have something to announce."

Peter Deighton took a seat on the damask couch, clearly afraid to speak. *He* should *be afraid*, Daphne thought spitefully. He'd already lost their family's title through his stupidity and carelessness; they couldn't afford any more of his mistakes.

Daphne's mother sat next to him, tucking her legs elegantly to one side. Even with a grown daughter, she was still frighteningly beautiful, her lips as red and her hair as blond as they had been in her days as a runway model. She flashed Daphne a knowing glance, and then her eyelashes swiftly swept down.

"Jeff? Is everything all right?" Queen Adelaide asked, a note of concern in her voice.

Jefferson hesitated. "Daphne and I . . . She's . . . I mean . . ."

Daphne held her breath and said nothing. She sensed instinctively that the news needed to come from him, not from her.

"We're having a baby," he finished.

Here goes nothing, Daphne thought, terrified yet at the same time oddly thrilled. This was what she did best. Lie. Improvise. Act.

"Oh, *Jeff*." His mother's voice broke on the words.

To Daphne's shock, the queen rushed to her feet, tugged Daphne upright, and threw her arms around her.

Daphne tentatively returned the hug, and felt Adelaide's thin frame shaking with sobs.

"I'm sorry, Your Majesty," Daphne hurried to say, but Jefferson's mother pulled back. The queen was crying and laughing at once, her face a confused mess of pain and joy, as if all her emotions had mingled together, leaving her exhausted and . . . happy?

"Sorry?" Adelaide repeated. "Why on earth would you be sorry?" She sighed. "Oh, young love. No matter what else is happening, it always finds a way, doesn't it?"

"Mom?" Jefferson seemed alarmed.

"This is entirely out of order and improper, especially given your recent . . . troubles," Queen Adelaide announced, with a vague wave at the newly common Deightons. "But it's been so long since we had a baby at the palace. To think that soon enough we'll hear little feet pattering up and down the hallways! That's how Jeff learned to walk, you know," she said, clutching Daphne's hand. "He used to toddle up and down the hall, waving at the guards, watching them salute each time he passed. He was the most adorable baby." Her voice shook a little as she added, "I only wish George were here."

"I know," Daphne said soothingly, willing herself not to smile. This was going even better than she'd expected.

"Daphne!" Her mother stepped forward to join the collective embrace. Her arms circled her daughter a bit awkwardly, as if she wasn't quite sure how this hugging thing worked. "I can't believe it! Why didn't you tell us?"

"I was afraid you might be upset," Daphne murmured.

Rebecca was doing a remarkable job of feigning surprise and motherly concern. She'd already known, of course. There was no one else Daphne could have shared her plan with, no one else she trusted to help; and she didn't trust her mother, not really. Rebecca could be relied upon for now, as long as her fate was tied to her daughter's interests. But Daphne knew her mother's loyalty was only ever to herself.

"People are going to talk." Queen Adelaide stepped back, wiping at her eyes. "We'll have to rush your wedding as much as possible."

The ensuing silence was deafening. Those two words seemed to reverberate through the room—words that had the power to make or break Daphne's entire future. *Your wedding.*

Jefferson had gone pale. "Wedding?"

Daphne noticed that her parents were careful to say nothing; they were very still, like two people holding their breath at the blackjack table, waiting to see if their monumental gamble had paid off.

Well, she wasn't the Poker Princess for nothing, was she?

"Of course you're getting married," Adelaide said briskly. "What else do you plan on doing? Living in sin?"

Jefferson reached for Daphne's hand. "Mom, we're a bit young to be discussing marriage."

"If you're old enough to have a child, you're certainly old enough to take on the responsibility of marriage," the queen countered.

Jefferson's grip on Daphne's hand tightened. "It's not *living in sin* anymore. This is the twenty-first century; people don't expect us to rush into anything."

"What are you 'rushing into,' precisely? You've been dating for four years."

Some of the conviction had drained from Jefferson's voice. "Mom, that's not the—"

"You are a *Washington*." The queen stood taller now, her voice ringing through the space with authority. "You are not some rock star who *knocked up* his girlfriend—forgive my crude phrasing," she said absently, with a brief glance at Daphne. "You are a prince and the steward of this family's legacy, and this situation is problematic enough already. My first grandchild will not be *illegitimate*. Especially when that child might—"

She broke off, but Daphne could fill in the end of the sentence. *Especially when that child might rule someday.*

With Beatrice on life support and the whole complicated situation with Samantha, Jefferson might actually become king.

The prospect was so dizzying that, for a moment, Daphne didn't even register the queen's other words, about how the situation was *problematic enough already.* This was, presumably, her tactful way of saying that her future daughter-in-law was currently the butt of national jokes, her family a gross embarrassment.

Slowly, Jefferson turned to her. "Are you okay with this, Daph?"

She and the prince had been dating for four years, and Daphne had spent all four of those years imagining Jefferson's proposal. Sometimes she'd pictured it at a black-tie function, Jefferson sinking to one knee as crowds watched with bated breath, and she would accept to tumultuous applause. Other times she'd imagined that it would be just the two of them on a romantic mountaintop somewhere, her hair artfully mussed by the wind as he slid a ring onto her finger.

Never in all her imaginings had Daphne dreamed that Jefferson would ask her to marry him because his mother had forced him to.

He hadn't even sunk to one knee or said the proper words. All he'd asked was *Are you okay with this?*

Oh well.

"Of course I'll marry you," Daphne assured him. "I love you."

Queen Adelaide broke into a relieved smile. "It's settled, then. We'll need to set a date—I think we can plan something in eight weeks' time, perhaps even six if we hurry. Time is of the essence, of course."

Right, because if Daphne were *actually* pregnant, she would begin to show soon.

"What about New Year's?" she heard herself suggest.

To ordinary people, New Year's Eve was about champagne flutes and sequined dresses and kissing someone at the countdown. But Daphne had always thought of it as a liminal state, a transition point where the old, stale, mistake-ridden past gave way to an unknown future. It was a moment of change, of excitement.

"A new year, new beginnings," Daphne added, and the queen's expression softened.

"That's a lovely sentiment."

Moments later a footman was sailing into the room, holding a tray of crystal flutes brimming with champagne. Daphne almost reached for one before remembering that she was supposed to be pregnant.

"To Daphne and Jeff," the queen exclaimed, and everyone lifted their glasses in a toast, repeating her words.

Daphne didn't have a glass to lift, but it didn't matter. A heady sense of satisfaction coursed through her.

After all her years of hard work, she would be a princess at last.

NINA

"I don't belong here," Nina Gonzalez announced as she and her friend Jayne walked into the auditorium.

Ranged in the seats below were several dozen kids in skinny scarves and even skinnier jeans. They laughed easily, stretching their legs onto the seats in front of them, passing bags of gummy candy to one another.

Jayne snorted. "Same. No way am I actually doing this show. I just couldn't handle the puppy-dog eyes Rachel would give me if I didn't come."

Rachel Greenbaum, their third roommate, was one of the student producers of this year's winter play: *A Midsummer Night's Dream*. She'd been hounding them about auditions for weeks, and would have considered it a personal betrayal if they didn't at least show up.

"Nina! Jayne!" Rachel broke away from a few of the theater kids and hurried toward them. "Thank you guys for coming!"

"I'm really just here for moral support. I don't expect to get a part," Nina assured her.

Rachel met her gaze meaningfully. "With that attitude, you definitely won't. Come on, Nina, weren't you just saying that you want to shake things up?"

Nina had to admit that she could use a distraction. It still felt surreal that Beatrice, who'd been like an older sister to

Nina in so many ways, was on life support. Meanwhile Samantha, Beatrice's younger sister and Nina's best friend, had gone *missing*. And that wasn't even including the mess Nina had gotten into with Prince Jefferson, Samantha and Beatrice's brother.

Earlier this fall, Nina and Jeff had tried to be friends— and only that. But Nina hadn't been able to help it; she'd fallen back in love with Jeff. He'd said he wanted to give their relationship another try, only to end up with Daphne. *Again.*

"You're right. I'm done thinking about Jeff, and I mean it this time." Nina tried to smile. "Though it would be easier if I didn't have to see his name every time I open a newspaper. Maybe I should move to England. Or Canada," she added ruefully.

"Not a bad idea," Rachel agreed. "Speaking of which—"

"Rachel!" one of the other producers called out, and Rachel sighed.

"I should get going. But good luck! I can't wait to see your auditions!" she told them, before going to rejoin the others.

In spite of herself, Nina smiled as she began watching the auditions. She wasn't usually excited about Shakespeare— she'd rather read a Jane Austen or Brontë novel—but she did have a soft spot for *A Midsummer Night's Dream*. It was pure mischief, the characters tangling together in such hopeless ways and then finally untangling.

"Nina Gonzalez," one of the directors called out. Nina headed onstage, accepting the typed papers he handed her.

She'd expected a declaration of love, if only because this play was full of them, but the text surprised her. It was Helena's exhortation to Hermia when she discovers her best friend's betrayal.

"Nina?" Rachel prompted, after a long silence.

Nina cleared her throat and began to speak. "'Lo, she is one of this confederacy! / Now I perceive they have conjoined all three / To fashion this false sport, in spite of me. / Injurious Hermia!'"

There was a roar in Nina's ears, or maybe it was just the roar of her words gaining momentum. Unexpected tears blurred her vision. Suddenly she wasn't in the auditorium anymore; she was back in that hospital room, meeting Daphne Deighton's gaze, realizing how much Daphne hated her.

Earlier this fall, she and Daphne had joined forces against Lady Gabriella Madison, a spoiled, self-centered aristocrat who'd set out to hurt them both. They'd started to thaw toward each other, had shared secrets and vulnerabilities. After a while, Nina was fool enough to think she and Daphne might be friends.

Nina didn't have any other friends like Daphne: friends who understood where she came from. Samantha would move heaven and earth for Nina, but she'd still been born to the royal life, while Nina existed outside it. And as fantastic as her college friends were, they didn't get it either. Daphne was the only one who knew what it was to live on the royal periphery. With Daphne, Nina had felt *seen*.

"'Is all the counsel that we two have shared, / The sisters' vows, the hours that we have spent, / When we have chid the hasty-footed time / For parting us—'"

Nina broke off, voice breaking, and closed her eyes for a moment. When she continued, her final words came out in a whisper.

"'O, is all forgot? / All school-days' friendship, childhood innocence?'"

Daphne had been playing Nina the entire time: the way she played Jeff, and the media, and everyone in her life. Their friendship had never been real. So why did its loss still hurt so much?

Nina blinked and took a dazed step toward the wings, muttering a thank-you, but the director's voice halted her progress.

"Wait! You still have to do a partner read."

Before she could refuse, a young man stepped out onto the stage. He moved with a self-important swagger, as if he really was wearing a Shakespearean doublet and jerkin, rather than a crew-neck shirt and skinny cashmere scarf. "'O Helena!'" he proclaimed, launching right into their scene.

Nina felt, rather than saw, the auditorium erupt in feverish whispers at his arrival.

"'O Helena,'" he repeated, "'goddess, nymph, perfect, divine! / To what, my love, shall I compare thine eye?'"

He was undeniably gorgeous, with sculpted cheekbones and tousled blond hair, his blue eyes hidden behind dark-framed glasses. Right now those eyes were trained on Nina's with a pleading, hopeful expression—as befitted the declaration of love he was reciting—but there was a knowing glint there, too, as if he expected Nina to realize who he was. She tried, and failed, to place the slight accent in his voice.

This boy was clearly the theater kids' anointed star. Nina wondered how many people in the audience he had hooked up with.

She glanced down at her paper. Someone had reordered the lines of this scene into a more rapid conversation. "'O spite! O hell!'" she cried out, with genuine frustration. "'I see you all are bent / To set against me for your merriment!'"

The young man stepped forward, and recognition nipped at the edges of her consciousness. *Had* she met him before?

His voice lowered into something seductive. "'O, how ripe in show / Thy lips, those kissing cherries, tempting grow!'"

15

Nina froze. His hand had strayed upward, as if to stroke her face, and she wasn't sure whether she would lean into it or pull away. Everything slowed, fell still. The glow of his eyes turned molten, and as his fingers brushed her cheek, an involuntary gasp escaped her.

She stared down at the paper for her next lines. "'If you were civil and knew courtesy, / You would not do me thus much injury.'"

His face was very close to hers as he replied, "'O, let me kiss / This princess of pure white, this seal of bliss!'"

In a single dramatic motion, the stranger dipped Nina back as elegantly as a ballroom dancer and lowered his mouth to hers.

For a moment Nina was frozen with shock. This boy was holding her entire weight on one arm with apparent ease, *kissing* her. Through the soft fabric of his sweater, she felt the contours of his body, the way his arm cradled the base of her spine.

She twisted, making an outraged sound deep in her throat, and the boy quickly swept her upright. He bowed to the audience with a flourish, grinning. Nina couldn't see through the blinding stage lights, but she heard cheers and delighted whistles from the onlookers.

Heart pounding, she stormed off the stage and out the exit doors to the hallway.

How *dare* he kiss her without warning, without permission— and kiss her in a way that made her feverish and tingly all over? It didn't mean anything, of course. It was just that she hadn't been kissed since that night in the gardens at Bellevue with Jeff, all those weeks ago, and she hadn't realized quite how much her body craved human contact.

"Wait a second!" the boy called out, jogging to catch up with her. "Are you okay?"

"I'm *fine*." Nina tried to brush past him. She'd only taken a step before she was yanked abruptly backward.

"Seriously?" Nina stared down at the edge of his cashmere scarf, which had caught on the zipper of her tote bag. The fabric snapped taut between them like a leash.

"My apologies." The boy was grinning again, that vibrant, dazzling grin. Clearly he found everything in life a source of deep amusement.

Nina was seized by an irrational urge to keep going and let his stupid scarf unravel in her wake. She took another step forward, forcing him to shuffle along next to her.

"As much as I love being dragged about like a fish on a line," he drawled, "this is a bit much. Do you mind?" He gestured to her bag as if asking for permission to touch the zipper. Right, because he needed her go-ahead for *that*, but not a kiss?

"Are you serious?" Nina gave the scarf a frustrated yank, which only succeeded in fastening it further. "Why do you wear this thing, anyway? It's too skinny to keep you warm. And it makes you look like a pretentious jerk." Apparently her filter had dissolved up there onstage, along with her dignity.

He unwound the scarf from around his neck. "Maybe I am a pretentious jerk. And I have other ways of keeping warm," he added with a wink.

Nina fumbled with the fabric and finally unhooked it from her bag. The scarf fluttered down, forcing her to catch it. "Here," she said ungraciously, but he didn't reach for it.

"Great job in that scene, by the way. You were amazing."

She couldn't take it anymore. "What made you think it was okay to kiss me like that?"

He lifted an eyebrow indolently. "Have we kissed? I usually remember kissing girls like you."

"What?" she spluttered, pointing wildly back toward

the door. "Just now, in the audition! You treated me like a human prop!"

He seemed genuinely puzzled. "You're upset about the scene? That wasn't me kissing you; that was Demetrius kissing Helena." A light danced in the boy's eyes as he added, "Trust me, Nina, when you and I kiss, it'll be far better than a bit of improvisation."

She wondered angrily how he knew her name, until she remembered the adhesive name tag on the front of her shirt. Somehow he'd gotten away with not putting one on, and she hated that it left her at a disadvantage.

"There is no *when*. There will be no kiss." She spun on one heel and started back toward the exit, with faster steps this time.

He trotted to keep up. "You say that now, but we have weeks of rehearsals ahead of us."

"I wasn't actually trying out. I mean—I don't expect to get a part." Why was she telling him any of this? She shook her head, flustered. "I'm only here because my roommate is one of the producers, and she bullied me into showing up."

"Really? I thought you were a great performer."

A *performer*, Nina thought bitterly. It was an apt descriptor, in some ways. Hadn't all her years at court taught her how to be false and artificial, to put on a show? After all, that was what the royal family did best—pretend that things were normal even when the world was falling apart around them.

"So you're not a theater major?" the boy pressed. If only to stop thinking about the Washingtons, Nina answered.

"English major."

"Of course." He gave a knowing smile. "Let me guess, nineteenth-century fiction. You're all cotillions and corsets and Heathcliff brooding on the moors."

She said nothing, because his assessment was all too accurate.

"Look, you're clearly upset. Can we talk about this more?" he went on. "Where are you headed? I'll walk you."

Her grip on her tote bag tightened. "That's really not necessary."

"It's getting dark. You plan to walk across campus by yourself?"

"I do it all the time!" She shook her head, exasperated. "You can spare me the gentlemanly overtures, okay?"

He barked out a laugh. "I assure you, Nina, I'm no gentleman."

Something in his tone gave her pause. "Sorry, have we met?" she asked bluntly. "Were you in my Brit Lit class last year?"

He studied her for a long, slow moment, and she shifted beneath the weight of his gaze. Then he let out a breath. "I'm James. I just started at King's College this semester."

"Well, goodbye, James." Nina took a few steps past him, and this time he made no move to follow. Belatedly, she realized she was still holding his scarf, and gritted her teeth.

"This is yours," she forced herself to say, turning around.

"Keep it. It looks better on you anyway. As I'm sure most things do," James replied. She wondered if his flirtation was automatic, as reflexive to him as breathing. "And good luck with the audition—not that you need it." He grinned. "You're the type of actress that Old Bill wrote this part for."

"Did you just call Shakespeare *Old Bill?*" Nina almost shouted, but James had disappeared back through the door to the stage wings.

She crumpled his expensive navy scarf into a ball and held it over the trash can—yet she couldn't bring herself to throw it away. Not something so wonderfully soft. It felt like butter against her skin.

Nina stuffed it into her tote bag, then headed brusquely outside.

She wished she could tell Sam about this exchange. She wished she'd *heard* from Sam, but so far there had been nothing, not even an anonymous postcard.

Wherever her best friend had gone, Nina hoped she was okay.

SAMANTHA

Princess Samantha Martha Georgina Amphyllis of the House of Washington leaned out the side of the small fishing boat, trailing her fingers in the ocean.

"Careful," snapped Brad, his eyes half closed, and she shifted back. In her old life, no one would have barked at Sam like that—at least, no one except her family and her best friend, Nina. But Sam was very far from her old life right now.

The ocean really was beautiful this time of day, the water as ink-dark as the sky, the horizon an indistinguishable blur in the distance. Sam and Brad weren't far out enough to hit the major swells; she could see the coast to her left, the waves cresting magnificently before crashing and hissing over the sand. Flecks of volcanic ash made the beach incandescent in the predawn light. She wondered which beach Marshall and his new friend Kai had driven to this morning, and whether Marshall would reappear grinning and exuberant, or covered in coral scrapes from a fall off his board.

It was amazing how many hours he could spend in the water. He taught surfing lessons every afternoon—he'd amassed a surprising number of clients in the month since they'd arrived, from excited ten-year-olds to high schoolers who were thinking of getting into competitions. Sam wasn't surprised at his popularity; Marshall had always been at ease with other people. If only his family could see that. They'd been telling him for years that he wasn't good enough, because of his dyslexia.

When they had first arrived on Molokai, Sam had felt a bit aimless, uncertain what to do while Marshall was busy surfing. Until one morning when she and Marshall had wandered over to the docks in search of fresh ahi, and she'd stumbled across Brad.

"Hey, kids," he'd called out, his voice gravelly. "Either of you looking for a job? I could use an extra pair of hands."

There was no telling how old he was; he was as tanned and wrinkled as a raisin, with a shock of white hair and a perpetual scowl. Though Sam suspected that underneath his gruff exterior, Brad was a complete softie.

"I can help," she heard herself offer. "I'm a quick study."

Brad assessed her, his eyes sharp beneath bushy white brows. "Be here at four tomorrow morning," he said at last.

Sam had come out on the boat every day since. She'd forgotten how much she loved being on the water: the sea spray cooling her face, making her lips taste like salt; the way her muscles burned with satisfied exhaustion at the end of each day.

When one of the lines pulled taut, Sam jumped up and began tugging it in, hand over fist. The cord burned against her palms, which had grown callused over the last few weeks. Not very princess-like, she thought in amusement, but her hair was worse.

Their first day in Hawaii, she'd insisted they stop at a drugstore for hair dye and scissors. She'd sheared off her wavy brown hair, which used to fall below her shoulders, and dyed her ragged pixie cut a platinum blond. She'd toyed with doing a wilder color, like neon blue, only to decide it looked too memorable. She was trying to *avoid* notice, after all.

She hadn't expected how light her head would feel without her long ponytail, as if she'd shed years of expectations and judgments along with her hair.

Sam hauled in the last of the line, then wrangled the barramundi into the crate, where it flopped back and forth.

"Well done," Brad told her, and she stifled a grin. He was judicious with both his praise and his criticism, a bit like Sam's dad had been. The thought sent a pang of longing through her.

"Time to head back?" she asked. The sunrise was beginning to gild the water, casting its surface with the pinks and golds of dawn. When Brad nodded, Sam pulled the chain on the motor and it kicked to life.

Usually Brad was content to sit in silence, but this morning he cast her a curious look. "So, Martha."

From the way he said it, she sensed that he knew it wasn't her real name—and for the first time, she wondered if he recognized her. Would he have said something if he did?

"You ever going to tell me what you're running from?"

Just our positions, our families, and the entire world. It felt like America had poked a thousand vicious holes in Sam and Marshall's relationship, one ignorant comment or headline at a time, until the joy they felt at being together began to deflate.

Brad sighed at her obstinate silence. "Whatever it is, you're going to have to go back and face it eventually."

"Not if I stay here forever," Sam quipped.

"I don't think you will. You have too much energy for this tiny, remote corner of the world. Even if there are things out there that scare you."

Sam studied Brad—his tanned, weathered features, the lazy baritone of his voice. Was this what she and Marshall would become if they stayed here? Their lives would stretch on and on into the future, one long tapestry of surfing and sunsets and hamburgers on the water, punctuated by the occasional reminder of everything they had left behind. Of the families they had walked away from, in order to give their relationship the breathing room it needed. Would it really be enough?

It had to be. She and Marshall couldn't be together back home, not without pain and heartache, and she couldn't live without him. So here they were.

As they pulled up to the dock, Sam noticed a familiar figure standing there in a wet suit, grinning.

She hopped out of the boat and hurtled toward him, and Marshall folded her into a hug. Sam let her arms loop up around the back of his neck as they melted into a kiss.

They kissed right there on the dock at dawn, and no one catcalled or shouted or took a photo to post online. No one told them that they were disgusting or admirable or hateful or the future of America. They were just two young people, kissing because they wanted to. Such a simple thing—such a monumental thing.

This was what they'd traded their former lives for: freedom.

When they finally pulled apart, Marshall leaned his forehead against hers. His wet suit was damp, causing goose bumps to trail down her arms.

"You smell like the ocean, Scott," she said, using the name Marshall had adopted in Hawaii.

"*You* smell like fish, Martha." He laughed, then nodded toward the parking lot. "I already loaded your bike in the car. Want to head home?"

"Would you mind if we went into town instead?" A shard of loneliness had wormed its way into her chest, and she wasn't sure how to dispel it on her own. She blamed Brad and his pathological truth-telling.

"Of course," Marshall agreed.

Town was really just a small grid of streets with a few hundred residents. This was the most remote part of Molokai, which in itself was the most remote island of Hawaii. There wasn't even a newspaper, just a monthly newsletter printed on computer paper, which reported local headlines like THE THREE SISTERS CAFÉ NOW SERVES DINNER or MALLARD DUCK

SPOTTED AT THE CORNER OF WOODHEAD AND FREMONT. IS THIS YOUR DUCK? There was no mention of Hawaii's Queen Liliuokalani, let alone international politics.

Sam tried not to think about the problems her absence must be causing for her siblings. She knew that Beatrice would understand; they'd talked about it at the League of Kings banquet, and Beatrice had agreed that Sam should follow her heart. But she'd never gotten a chance to explain her motives to Jeff.

Sam imagined that the royal PR machine was scrambling to explain her absence, probably claiming that she was taking some time off for vaguely termed "personal reasons." People would be buzzing with speculation, saying that she was in rehab, or hiding a pregnancy, or that she and Marshall had broken up and she was a crying mess. The one thing that none of them would guess was the truth.

"How were the waves?" Sam asked as they wound down the empty road.

A goofy, excited grin stole over Marshall's face. "Kai and I agreed it was the best day yet! Seriously, Sam, we've got to get you out there soon. I have a beginner lesson at two."

"That's okay. I'll sit outside with my book. It's going to be a gorgeous day." Though, to be fair, it was always a gorgeous day here.

"You're still reading that fantasy series, right?" Marshall asked. "What book are you on now, three?"

"Four! Alina just betrayed her fiancé, and Luke is getting back from his quest. And there are these mysterious prologues that I don't know how to interpret! I keep wanting to text Nina, but . . ." Sam trailed off without finishing the sentence.

Before they landed in Hawaii, she and Marshall had both turned off their phones, which they had then stuffed in the back of a suitcase—and kept there, wrapped in a pair of old socks, as if they were bombs that might detonate. They had no idea if the palace could use their phones to track their location in Hawaii, but they weren't taking any chances.

Sam hadn't told Marshall about all the times she'd snuck into that closet and fished out her phone, her thumb hovering over the power button. The need to turn it on was like an itch she couldn't scratch. If only she could text Nina and Beatrice, just to let them know she was okay.

But the moment she did that, the life she and Marshall had built could evaporate like smoke.

It was safer if Nina knew nothing. No texts, no emails, nothing that could incriminate her when the palace came asking questions, as Sam knew they would. Still, Sam's chest ached at the silence between them. She hadn't gone this long without talking to Nina since they were seven. It felt like half of her internal monologue had abruptly shut off.

She and Marshall headed through the doors of the only coffee shop in town. After they ordered lattes from the guy behind the counter, Sam glanced around the empty tables—and her heart skipped. An abandoned newspaper lay near someone's empty coffee mug.

She stepped closer, and saw that it was a week-old copy of the *Honolulu Star*.

"Sam," Marshall warned, momentarily forgetting her fake name, but Sam was already thumbing through the pages, which were covered in crumbs and coffee stains.

When she reached the section on world news, Sam froze. The headline was so nonsensical, it must be a mistake: ACTING KING JEFFERSON ACCEPTS HOMAGE FROM AMERICAN PEERS.

"You okay?" Marshall asked.

Sam stared down at the letters, willing them to rearrange themselves. "This newspaper thinks Jeff is the king," she said slowly.

The barista set their lattes on the counter. "Acting King," he corrected her, and shook his head. "That poor family. The number of accidents they've had, almost makes you wonder if they're cursed."

"Accidents?" Sam repeated, her voice rising. "What happened to Queen Beatrice?"

"She's hurt or something. Who knows." The barista spoke with complete detachment, because to him, Beatrice was just a figure from a magazine, more abstract than real. He had no interest in what happened to her.

Sam looked back down at the newspaper, which was shaking; her hands had begun to tremble. Marshall took her by the elbow and led her to a table in the far corner, their lattes abandoned. Sam felt nauseous as she continued to read: *After Queen Beatrice's car accident last month, there is still no update on her condition. Prince Jefferson has accepted recognition from the American peers in a formal ceremony of homage. . . .*

"Oh my god," Sam heard herself say, over and over. "Oh my god, oh my god."

Marshall looked stricken. He still had a hand on her back, tracing slow circles over her shoulder blades, but for once she hardly felt his touch. "I'm so sorry," he croaked.

Sam lifted a tear-streaked face to his. "Marshall, this is my family! I have to be there. I can't—I don't—" She swallowed, turned to him, though they both already knew what she would say. "I have to go back."

Half an hour later, Sam sat cross-legged on the bedspread, Marshall's computer poised in her lap—because, in typical Samantha fashion, she didn't have her own laptop with her. "I found a plane," she announced. "It's not *Eagle III*, obviously, just some random rental plane."

Until now, she hadn't known that you could book private planes on the internet. Apparently all you needed was a search engine and a credit card. Except . . .

She frowned, distracted, and entered her credit-card information a second time. CARD NOT VALID still flashed across the screen. "It's not accepting my card."

"Your accounts are probably frozen. Here, use mine," Marshall offered, pulling a black card from his wallet.

Sam hesitated. "What if it gives away our location to your parents?"

"It won't. I got full control of my accounts when I turned twenty-one," Marshall assured her.

Sam bit her lip but accepted Marshall's credit card. "Thank you. I'll pay you back once I figure everything out."

Marshall glanced around their cottage, which looked like a hurricane had torn through it, beach towels and flip-flops strewn about. "Can I help you pack? My stuff's all ready."

Sam looked up at that, and realized his suitcase was zipped and waiting near the door. She shut his laptop and set it aside.

"Marshall . . . as much as I would love for you to come, don't you think it makes more sense for me to go alone?"

His eyes widened. "Your sister is in the hospital. Of course I'm coming."

Sam forced herself to shake her head. "You said it yourself: *my* sister is the one in the hospital. I'm the one who needs to visit her. My family will let me come back to you afterward," she said gently. "What about yours?"

They both knew that once Marshall's grandfather discovered Marshall's location, he would stop at nothing to bring his grandson home.

Marshall sank onto the bed next to her. "They can't keep us apart forever. What are they going to do, lock me up?"

"Of course not. But they can ruin the life we've built here," Sam reminded him. "They can out us. We won't be Martha and Scott any longer."

Sam hadn't anticipated all the ways that their shared anonymity would bring her and Marshall closer. They were both growing and changing, discovering new things about themselves, and the best part was that they were growing together. Their lives had become intertwined by the things most people probably took for granted: Going on quiet walks. Cooking for themselves. Learning how to *budget*.

Marshall's features were etched with sorrow. "I don't know if I want to be here without you, Sam."

"I'll come back, I promise. Just let me go home, see for myself how Beatrice is doing. I promise I won't tell anyone where I was, no matter how much they ask," she added fiercely. "I won't blow your cover."

He sat with that for a moment, the only noise the ceiling fan stirring lazily overhead. "I hate the thought of you facing this alone. I don't want to ask it of you," he said at last.

"You didn't ask. I offered. There's a key difference."

Of course Sam wanted her boyfriend with her right now. If she'd loved him any less, she would have *begged* him to come back so that she could lean on him through the trials ahead.

But Marshall was building something in Hawaii, growing in confidence and self-reliance. If she pulled him away from it now, he might never find it again.

Loving someone, Sam realized, was more complicated than songs and novels made it seem. People always wanted to talk about the *falling*-in-love part, the rush of hormones and giddy excitement and breathless kisses. But being *in* love, sharing a life, meant so much more. You loved someone knowing all their scars and vulnerabilities and flaws. You loved someone even when they hurt you; more than that, you *let* them hurt you, because the last thing you wanted was to become a burden on that person—another weight pressing on their shoulders, when they already carried so much.

"Call me when you get there, okay? I'll buy a burner phone first thing tomorrow and text you the number," Marshall pleaded. "Promise me you'll send constant updates."

Sam didn't trust herself to speak right now, so she shifted on the bed, curling her fingers in Marshall's hair and dragging his mouth down to hers.

Marshall growled as they fell back onto the comforter and Sam tugged his shirt up over his head. How many mornings had they lain in this bed, kissing lazily, telling each other old anecdotes and listening to the distant crash of waves? They had been so oblivious to reality, absorbed wholly in each other, as if the rest of the world had paused while they were here.

But reality had ground on without them, and they couldn't ignore it any longer.

Sam trailed kisses along Marshall's jaw, wrapping her arms around his torso as if she might fuse them right here to this spot. If she had to say goodbye—if this was their last time together, at least for a while—then she would make it count.

4

NINA

"I'm so glad you came today. You were overdue for a party. A *real* party," Rachel amended, "not some sorority tailgate or stupid League of Kings banquet."

Nina smiled. The fact that Rachel, a die-hard royal enthusiast, had called the most exclusive gathering in the world *stupid* was a testament to her undying loyalty.

She cast an amused glance around the backyard, where students in frayed jeans and ripped tees jostled in blithely sweaty proximity. Music blared from speakers in one corner; a group of students whom Nina recognized from an a cappella group had climbed onto a plastic folding table to sing along.

This was Tudor House, one of the old "pass-down houses," which were handed from one generation of King's College seniors to the next. With neon murals scrawled over its walls and a mismatched scattering of boho furniture, Tudor House had a reputation among the artsy crowd. It reminded Nina of a club Sam had dragged her to last year, when she and Jeff were newly back from their world tour—some place on the east side with a punk-rock band. The memory stabbed a dagger of worry between Nina's ribs.

"Should we head inside? My friend Ella is in there. She says they have Jell-O shots," Rachel explained, typing on her phone.

Nina shook her head. "I need to get some air. Catch up with you later."

Before Rachel could protest, Nina pushed her way through the sunshine-drenched backyard until she reached a gravel path to the driveway. Dozens of cars were parked there, bumper to bumper, so that the cars at the back were hopelessly boxed in. A staircase led up the side of the garage to what looked like a separate apartment.

Nina sank onto the bottom step and leaned her head into her hands with a muffled groan. Even here, at a college party with cheap beer and indie music—the complete opposite of a black-tie royal gathering—Nina still couldn't go ten minutes without thinking about the Washingtons. She was *always* thinking about them, because her life had long ago become enmeshed with Sam's.

Yet it hurt to think of Sam these days. Nina missed her best friend, and worried about her, and, even worse, thoughts of Sam invariably led to fear for Beatrice—lying there like a rag doll in the hospital bed, surrounded by a tangle of tubes—which led to thoughts of Jeff, America's Acting King. The one person Nina really, really did not want to think about anymore.

When footsteps sounded behind her, she was oddly unsurprised to hear James's voice. "Mind if I join you?"

She glanced over her shoulder at him. "You really need to stop following me."

"You certainly have a high opinion of yourself," he said cheerfully. "What if I just came out here for a bit of fresh air?"

"You arrived at the party and came straight out here, to the driveway, where I'm sitting alone. That's not coincidence; that's stalking."

"Ahh," James said in a low, significant tone. "You noticed that I wasn't at the party earlier. You were *looking* for me."

"I was trying to avoid you," she amended, but she wasn't actually convinced that was the truth.

The sunlight danced over James's silhouette, glinting on the beer bottles in his hands. Nina lifted an eyebrow.

"You claim you weren't looking for me, but you have *two* beers," she couldn't help observing.

He looked down. "So I do," he said, as if he'd forgotten that he was holding a bottle in each hand. "They were both for me, but the chivalrous thing to do is share, isn't it?" He handed one to her and started to leave.

Nina sighed. "You may as well sit down."

James grinned and sank onto the step next to her, clinking his bottle to hers. Nina bit back a smile. She didn't want to like him, but he had an irrepressible energy that made it hard not to.

A silence settled around them, punctuated by laughter and the hum of conversation from the backyard, the bass's low pulse thumping like a heartbeat.

"When I heard about a party at Tudor House, this wasn't quite what I imagined." James leaned an elbow on the step above them.

"What did you expect, Elizabethan ruffs and court jesters?"

"At the very least a gabled roof and charming English garden. The only thing Tudor about this place is the number of people crammed into a small space."

"The party has hours to go. We might still get a banishment or beheading."

"In that case, I may stick around." There it was again: that hint of an accent, maddeningly unplaceable.

"I can't decide where you're from," Nina declared. "You don't sound European."

"I traveled a lot when I was younger, with my parents. I picked up a hodgepodge accent along the way."

"So what brought you to King's College?"

He considered the question with surprising thoughtfulness. "I wanted a change, and this was as much of a change as I could get away with," he said at last. "My family expects a lot of me. Getting far from home . . . it's a way to escape the attention, for a little while, at least."

That much Nina understood. Her parents were the best, but they were still parents, and could hover too closely over her life.

"If you don't like attention, why did you audition for the play?" she ventured.

James winked, the moment of seriousness evaporating. "Maybe I auditioned because I heard you were auditioning."

Nina rolled her eyes. "You said it yourself: we'd never met before the audition."

Something deepened in his gaze, but it was gone before Nina could fully decipher it. "What about you? Did you come to King's College to get away from home, too?"

"Hardly. My parents live half a mile from campus."

James spun the beer bottle on the steps, a restless gesture that reminded Nina of Sam. "You like having them nearby?"

"It's the best. They give me space to do my own thing at school, but if I need to go home for any reason"—*like needing to cry in private because my royal boyfriend broke up with me,* Nina thought—"then I can go sleep in my own bed, eat a home-cooked meal. My mom is the only one of us who can cook," she added. "My mamá can't make anything but toast, and even that she usually burns. She works at the Ministry of the Treasury."

"Sounds like you're very close," James said quietly, perhaps a bit enviously.

"What about your family? What are they like?"

"Oh, they're glad I'm here," he replied, which wasn't really an answer to her question. "Since you're an expert, though, Nina, I'd love to hear your advice about King's College. Anything I should know?"

"Didn't you go on a campus tour before you arrived?" Nina asked, and he shrugged.

"Just a virtual tour. I'm here for the semester on an exchange program." Before she could ask what school he'd come from, James flashed that roguish grin. "Come on, pass along some of your wisdom. What's the best place to eat off-campus?"

Her reply was automatic. "Mulberry's, but *never* at happy hour. It's way too crowded. You want to go late-night for their cheese tots."

"Cheese tots," James repeated slowly.

"Tater Tots covered in cheese."

"Yes, I'm familiar with the concept," he agreed, amused. "I just didn't take you for someone who would recommend cheese tots."

"Try them and you'll see," she promised.

"Fair enough. Should we go tonight?"

Behind them, the gate to the backyard creaked open, and Nina blinked. What was she doing out here, making vaguely flirtatious plans with a boy she didn't particularly like?

Yet she didn't *dislike* him, not the way she'd expected to. At the very least she'd become curious about him. And some unnamed force—the beer, or loneliness, or perhaps the way he smiled at her—seemed to have pinned her in place, right here on the concrete step, in spite of the fact that she was still angry about that kiss during the audition.

Nina hadn't been kissed by anyone but Jeff in so long. He had wound his way into her life, taken up residence in her thoughts and dreams, and she wasn't sure how to shake him loose. For years she had adored him and resented him, back and forth from one extreme to the other, and whether it was love or hate, her heart had always *belonged* to him.

Maybe she should kiss another boy, if only to banish the specter of Jeff that haunted her.

James shifted, and for a wild moment Nina wondered if she'd said that last thought aloud.

She sat back quickly, tucking her hair behind her ears.

"Nina." James's voice dipped low. She sensed that he was watching her very carefully, guessing the thoughts that whirled frantically through her head. "I'm not going to kiss you unless you ask me to."

"You certainly have a high opinion of yourself," Nina replied, though it lacked the sarcasm she'd intended.

She wanted to feel his mouth on hers again, and in the enchanted haze that had woven itself around them, it made sense. Before she could second-guess herself, Nina lifted her mouth to his.

James kissed her back eagerly. He seemed to crackle with heat, his palms singeing her through the fabric of her shirt. He tugged her forward and Nina found herself on his lap, her weight balanced easily on his thighs.

Nina had never expected to feel this again—the white-hot rush that used to blaze through her whenever she kissed Jeff. She'd thought that feeling was extinguished when they broke up. Yet here it was, and with a boy she barely knew. Who would have thought.

Dimly, she heard a buzzing from the purse at her feet. She ignored it, focusing on the feeling of James's hands skimming over her arms, down the sides of her torso to settle around her waist. He knew how to kiss a girl, that much was certain.

Nina wasn't sure how far things would have gone if her phone hadn't immediately started buzzing again. Whoever was calling, they were insistent.

She broke away from the kiss and grabbed her bag, ready to silence her phone—but when she saw the name on caller ID, she went utterly still.

It was Sam.

She stood, heart racing. "Sorry, but I have to take this. My best friend is—" Nina broke off before revealing too much. "She needs me."

James looked like he wanted to say something, then thought better of it. "Of course. I'll catch up with you later," he told her, as casually as if she hadn't been wrapped around him just seconds ago.

Nina waited until his steps had retreated before she accepted the call, lowering her voice. "Sam?"

"Thank god, Nina! I was worried you wouldn't answer!" Her friend sounded close to tears.

"Where are you?"

"Currently somewhere over Orange. I'm in a plane. Wi-Fi calling," she explained distractedly. "I should land in about five hours."

"Are you okay? Is Marshall with you? Where have you been?" The questions tumbled out of Nina rapidly, like gunfire. Before Sam could even answer she kept talking. "Sam, we've missed you so much. Everything is a mess. Beatrice is—"

"I know," Sam interrupted, voice breaking. "I'm heading straight to the hospital."

"I'll go with you," Nina assured her.

"You don't have to do that."

Nina cast one last glance toward Tudor House. If Sam wasn't arriving until this evening, Nina could go back in there and find James—but after hearing Sam's voice, she felt too rattled to do anything but wait for her friend.

It had been a mistake to kiss him, anyway. She didn't even know anything *about* him.

"Of course I'm coming," she told Sam. "What else are friends for?"

5

DAPHNE

"Daphne?" A preteen girl detached herself from her parents and started forward.

Daphne automatically flashed a smile. "It's lovely to meet you . . ." She paused, and the girl jumped to provide her name.

"Lily. Omigod, I *cannot* believe I'm meeting you in person! My friends and I are *obsessed* with you." Lily fumbled for her phone, and Daphne widened her smile, expecting the girl to request a selfie—but Lily held the screen toward Daphne.

"Look, I was you for Halloween this year!"

"I'm honored," Daphne said slowly. She had to admit, the costume was impressive: Lily had re-created the peach-colored dress Daphne wore to the Royal Potomac Races last year, complete with the matching fascinator. And was that a knockoff signet ring on her finger?

Then Daphne blinked, registering what Lily was holding in her other hand—a deck of cards.

In case anyone didn't recognize the costume, the cards would have explained it. Lily had gone to Halloween as the Poker Princess.

A photographer nearby cleared his throat. Acting on auto-pilot, Daphne angled herself and Lily toward the camera. She forced herself to keep smiling, even as anger pounded through her body.

God, she really *was* a national laughingstock, if twelve-year-old nobodies were mocking her at Halloween.

"It was lovely meeting you," Daphne murmured before Lily could say anything else. "Enjoy the Fall Festival."

Daphne strode across the palace's back lawn, which had been transformed into an autumn carnival, with face-painting and bobbing for apples and a petting zoo. Waiters in crisp uniforms served apple cider and popcorn and the Washingtons' famous cherry tarts. The guests, mostly parents with young children, were commoners, invited through a charity organization or their local mayor's office.

Like the palace's spring and summer garden parties, the Fall Festival was one of those "ordinary people events" so crucial to the monarchy's survival. By opening their home to all these strangers—giving people a glimpse into the most closed-off and exclusive institution in the world—the Washingtons secured people's love.

Normally Daphne thrived at events like this. But today the crowds were staring at her with confused disbelief, as if they didn't understand why she was still here, and it was getting harder to keep her smile from slipping.

"Daphne!" Anju Mahali, Beatrice's Lady Chamberlain, bustled toward her. "Have you seen His Royal Highness?"

Daphne nodded toward an empty stretch of lawn near the orchard, where Jefferson was throwing a football with a couple of elementary school boys. He looked almost too wholesome to be real, with his warm smile and perfect jawline, wearing a sweater beneath a puffy vest. The only thing missing was a golden retriever, Daphne thought, just as Beatrice's yellow lab, Franklin, came bounding up. Jefferson ruffled the dog's ears good-naturedly, teeing up the perfect image for the photographers without even trying.

"Your Royal Highness!" Anju called out. "May I have a word?"

When Jefferson jogged over, Daphne came to join them. Anju shot her a look but clearly decided it wasn't worth protesting.

"Your sister is on her way."

For a wild moment, Daphne thought Anju was talking about Beatrice. But Jefferson understood at once.

"Sam is back?"

"Air traffic control just called. She's on a private plane, scheduled to land in several hours."

Daphne watched the storm of emotions that played out on Jefferson's features, relief giving way to hurt and something that might have been resentment. He turned and started briskly toward the palace. "Can we keep it from the media?"

"So far, yes."

They were all crossing the lawn with quick steps, nodding distractedly at everyone who bowed or curtsied or waved shyly as they passed. An aura of royalty seemed to set them apart, circling them like a halo.

Anju hesitated. "There's one more thing, Your Royal Highness. . . . Your other guest just arrived as well."

Other guest? Daphne shot Jefferson a puzzled glance, but his mouth had softened into an almost-smile.

"Ethan is here? That's great."

Daphne stumbled at the mention of Ethan, and Jefferson held out a hand to steady her, oblivious to her turmoil. "Daph, can you keep Ethan company while I talk to Anju?"

"Sure," she said weakly, her mind fumbling to keep up. Ethan was back? And Jefferson hadn't thought to mention it?

Of course, Jefferson had no idea of the complicated, twisted history between his fiancée and his best friend. And Daphne intended to keep it that way.

She had only just regained control of her breathing when an all-too-familiar figure trotted down the palace's back steps.

"Ethan!" Jefferson said eagerly. "I'll catch up with you and Daphne in a few, okay?"

He and the Lady Chamberlain started toward the palace, leaving Daphne and Ethan alone.

"Hey, Daphne," Ethan said in an irritatingly casual tone.

Her eyes darted over him, taking in every detail of his appearance. He'd cut his hair shorter, and there was a Band-Aid on the back of his hand. His eyes looked lighter than she remembered, the irises more amber than brown.

"What are you doing here?" she asked coolly.

His eyes were locked on hers. "What do you think? I'm here for the wedding of the century."

"You . . . he . . ." Daphne swallowed. "Jefferson told you?"

Ethan shrugged. "I'm the best man."

Of course he was. Somehow, Daphne hadn't considered the fact that she would be in a wedding where she'd slept with the best man. She hated how tawdry and clichéd it made her feel.

"You plan on being in Washington until New Year's?" she demanded, crossing her arms over her chest.

"I didn't realize you were having a New Year's Eve wedding." When Daphne nodded in confirmation, Ethan chuckled. "How typically Daphne. You want everyone in America to start the New Year thinking about you."

The remark startled a laugh from her. Ethan's eyes sparkled in surprised pleasure.

They were acting almost normal around each other. At least, as normal as could be expected given how they'd left things nearly half a year earlier, before Ethan went to Malaysia. Daphne had shamelessly thrown herself at him: told him that she loved him, begged him to stay.

And Ethan had walked away.

Of course, so much had happened since then. She'd won

42

Jefferson back, and *kept* him, despite Nina and Gabriella's attempts to break them up. She was practically a princess.

"Daphne." Ethan hesitated, the amusement fading from his gaze. "I heard about everything. Are you okay?"

She shifted her weight with a sigh. They were still standing outside, but far enough from the festivities that no one could overhear.

"I didn't realize the news of my family's disgrace had made it to Malaysia."

"I'm sorry. I know this has been tough on you." There was no hint of Ethan's usual irreverence.

She kicked one heel back and forth in the grass. "My dad really messed up this time."

"He did, but I'm not sure I blame the guy. I would bet on you too," Ethan said softly. "Every time."

Daphne looked up sharply. Ethan's eyes had settled on hers, light glinting in their depths.

No. This was too dangerous. She knew better than to be alone with Ethan, not after everything that had happened between them.

"I have to go." She turned and started back toward the party, fixing her perfect princess smile to her face once more.

Later that evening, Daphne sighed, leaning her head against the tinted glass of the palace's courtesy car.

She hadn't gotten a moment alone with Jefferson until after the festival. When she finally found him, he'd smiled: a weary, automatic smile that didn't reach his eyes. "Hey, Daph. Are you okay if we move up the engagement announcement?"

"Of course."

She'd expected him to say more, but he had just kissed her on the forehead.

The driver cleared his throat, stirring her from her thoughts. "Miss Deighton?"

Daphne looked up—and cold panic set in.

The street crawled with media vans. Reporters stood before the Deightons' townhouse in hastily applied red lipstick, talking eagerly into their microphones. The news vans' spotlights made the area as blindingly bright as the stage of a rock concert.

Oh *no*. Had something else come to light, something even worse than her father's behavior?

What if Gabriella had finally violated the terms of their unspoken truce, and told everyone that Daphne sold her own photos to the tabloids?

"Park down the block, please," Daphne managed.

There was an alley behind all the townhouses on this street, too narrow for a car. Daphne pulled up the hood of her jacket and walked down the alley as fast as she could, stumbling around the occasional stray tricycle or hissing cat. When she was safely at her family's back gate, she entered the code on the electronic keypad and slipped inside.

Then, her hands shaking, she pulled out her phone.

Its screen was lit up with dozens—no, hundreds—of messages and missed calls. Blindly, Daphne clicked on the only name that mattered.

I'm sorry, Jefferson had written. *I tried to hold the announcement until tomorrow, but Anju overruled me. She had to tell the press about us to distract them from thinking about Sam. Call me when you can?*

Daphne tapped over to her web browser and, as she had done countless times before, searched her own name. The screen immediately filled with headlines, all variations on

PRINCE JEFFERSON, OFFICIALLY OFF THE MARKET! or THE ROYAL
WEDDING WE'VE ALL BEEN WAITING FOR!

She clicked on the first link, which led to the palace web-site's official press release: *His Royal Highness Prince Jefferson is delighted to announce his engagement to Miss Daphne Deighton. The wedding will take place in Washington in the coming months. Both families are thrilled by the joyous news.*

Typical of a Washington Palace press release, short and to the point.

The panic that had seized Daphne released its hold, and blissful relief flooded through her chest.

At long last, it was really happening.

Daphne could have hugged Samantha for coming home unannounced. The media must have gotten wind that something was going on, because a good reporter could always sniff out a story brewing. So, to keep the press from digging into Samantha—to keep Samantha hidden as long as possible, while they figured out a way to handle her—the palace had thrown out the news of Daphne and Jefferson's engagement. Daphne was a human smoke bomb, sent out to distract the media with glitter and wedding gowns while the palace dealt with its prodigal ex-princess's return.

Things were working out even better than she could have planned.

SAMANTHA

When Sam stepped onto the plane's staircase, a black SUV appeared at the edge of the jetway. Moments later, it pulled up before her, and one of the back doors flung open.

"*Sam!*"

Then Nina was sprinting forward, throwing her arms around Sam in a fervent hug.

Sam stopped trying to hold back the tears. She stood there, hugging Nina, letting it all wash over her in a wave of regret and self-recrimination.

When they pulled apart, she dabbed at her eyes. "I didn't know you were coming to meet my plane."

"She insisted on it," another voice cut in. Sam looked over to see Beatrice's chamberlain, Anju, who shot her a level stare. "Welcome back, Samantha. We're all glad you finally decided to rejoin the land of the living."

Sam followed Anju and Nina into the car. As they headed out into the city, she kept staring in shock at the skyline, so different from the golden seclusion of Hawaii. It seemed impossible that the world looked so normal—people streaming in and out of the metro, office buildings honeycombed with light from employees working late, cars honking as if nothing was wrong. As if the entire world hadn't been brutally, viciously upended with Beatrice's accident.

"Thanks for coming to get me," Sam told Anju, who was

perched in the front seat. "We're going straight to the hospital, right?"

"Visiting hours are over for the day." Anju sounded genuinely sorry as she added, "I promise you can go first thing in the morning. Her Majesty's condition is still unchanged, so a few hours won't make a difference."

But they'll make a difference to me, Sam thought, her heart aching. Aloud she said, "Can't they make an exception, just this once?"

Anju hesitated in a way that made Sam suspect the hospital had already made a lot of exceptions, perhaps for their mom, or Teddy.

"I'm supposed to take you straight to Loughlin House," the chamberlain told her.

"To Grandma Billie's?" Sam asked, confused. Then comprehension settled in. "You don't want anyone to know I'm in town, do you?"

Anju sighed. "Samantha, do you have any idea what people are saying about you? That you're suicidal, or on drugs; that you and Marshall eloped, or that you're pregnant. You're not pregnant, are you?" she added. "Because I really can't deal with another pregnancy right now."

Sam blinked. "*Another* pregnancy?"

"Never mind," Anju said quickly. "But please, come to your grandmother's house for a little while, just until we figure out how we're handling everything."

Nina, who had been watching their conversation, wrapped an arm around Sam's shoulder. "Anju, what if Sam stayed the night at my place?"

"*Yes*," Sam said automatically. Much as she loved her grandmother, she would rather be with Nina right now.

Anju twisted her torso so that she was staring back at both of them, and narrowed her eyes. "You want Samantha to stay with you at King's College?"

47

"She's done it before—"

"Oh, fantastic," Anju muttered, which Nina ignored.

"And both of my roommates have signed NDAs. We'll be very careful, I promise."

♛

Half an hour later, Sam was in Nina's common room, watching her friend bustle around making powdered hot cocoa.

She glanced around the room: at the desks scattered with laptops and photos, the calendar tacked to the far wall with notes written in colored marker. A shelf in the corner served as a makeshift pantry, stocked with granola bars and cans of diet soda. On the wall behind her hung a poster of the new Mr. Darcy, from the most recent *Pride and Prejudice* remake.

"I met him, you know. At Aunt Margaret's film premiere," Sam remarked, gesturing to Darcy.

She knew she was stalling, but to her relief, Nina let her stall.

"What was he like?"

"Sadly, he was a pretentious jerk."

"Sounds like he was well cast, then." Nina handed Sam a hot chocolate, in a mug that was printed with tiny cartoon cheetahs, and Sam took a grateful sip.

It wasn't until they were both seated on the L-shaped couch that Nina cleared her throat. "Sam . . . are you going to tell me where you've been?"

"I'm sorry, but I can't. Marshall is still there," Sam added quickly. "He wanted to come with me, but I told him not to. Once he's in America, his family will take over his life again."

"You really love him, don't you?"

When Sam nodded, Nina let out a breath. "Makes sense. You're only ever this protective of the people you really love."

Sam struggled to explain. "Being away, off the grid . . . it's been good for Marshall. He's become so confident there, and so happy; I can't let him walk away from that. Once he does, there's no going back."

"What about *your* family? Have you talked to them?"

"Not yet. You were the only person I called from the plane." Sam stared into her hot chocolate as she added, "Everything I need to say to Jeff and Mom is better said in person."

"You'll see them tomorrow," Nina assured her. Her phone pinged, and Nina glanced down at the screen, distracted.

Sam had a sudden thought. "Has Jeff said anything to *you* about it?"

"To me?"

"I thought you two were friends again, right?"

"We were," Nina said slowly. Her eyes were still fixed on her phone, making Sam wonder if she was texting a guy. "But . . . um . . ."

"You hooked up again, didn't you?" Sam guessed.

Nina looked up sharply. "No! I mean, we kissed *one* time, the night of the League of Kings banquet, but that was it. We're done now."

"I don't think you and Jeff are ever done." Sam's mouth lifted in a hint of a smile. It was just so comfortingly familiar, being back with Nina, teasing her about Jeff. It made the world feel temporarily *right*, just for a moment.

"This time I think we really are done." There was a funny note in Nina's voice as she held her phone toward Sam. "Look."

Sam blinked at the headline on the news website: PRINCE JEFFERSON AND DAPHNE DEIGHTON ENGAGED AT LAST!

"This is just another clickbait rumor."

"Look at the press announcement," Nina insisted. Sam followed the link, and swallowed when she saw the announcement on the palace's official website, stamped with the royal coat of arms. This wasn't a joke.

"Oh my god. Are you okay?" she asked Nina.

Her friend made a strangled, almost amused noise. "You're the one whose sister is in the hospital, remember? That's a way bigger problem than my ex-boyfriend getting engaged to someone else." She seemed to pause over that word, *engaged*, as if she couldn't quite believe it.

"I can't understand why he's doing this, especially after he kissed you as recently as the League of Kings!" Sam scrolled through the article without actually reading it. "What is he thinking? Beatrice is in the hospital!"

"He's probably doing this *because* Beatrice is in the hospital."

It was a surprisingly cynical comment from Nina, but she had a point. The palace's PR team were experts at deploying happy stories when they needed to distract the media from anything negative or damaging.

And now that Beatrice was hurt, there would be a whole different kind of pressure facing Jeff. Their mother had probably pressured him to get married, to secure the all-important line of succession. After all, that was what had happened to Beatrice when their father was diagnosed with cancer: he'd asked Beatrice to announce her engagement to Teddy, to reassure America of their family's future.

"We need to go talk some sense into him! Just because Beatrice is hurt, it's no reason to rush into a wedding."

Nina laughed weakly. "*You* go talk sense into him. I refuse to venture anywhere near that situation. Even if he is marrying someone who doesn't love him."

"Okay, that's a bit harsh," Sam protested. "I know Daphne can be a lot. But she genuinely cares about Jeff."

Nina seemed like she was biting back an angry protest. It made Sam doubt her claims of being completely over Jeff.

"Oh, before I forget—" Nina dug into her bag, then tossed Sam a set of keys. "I've had Albert all this time. You left some stuff in the backseat, too. A laptop, an old hoodie, a pair of spin shoes . . ."

Albert was Sam's nickname for her lemon-yellow Jeep, which she'd lent to Nina before the League of Kings conference, since Nina didn't have a car.

She placed the keys back in Nina's palm. "That's okay, you keep Albert. He's a little flashy for going incognito, and according to my family, I'm not even in town."

Her words sounded mournful, even to her own ears.

Sensing her mood, Nina leaned back and reached for the remote. "Should we watch the hot-but-terrible new Darcy and see what we think?"

"Absolutely," Sam agreed. If only for a little while, she wanted to hold off the tidal wave of emotion that threatened to crash over her.

"I'm so sorry, Bee," Sam whispered, alone in Beatrice's hospital room the next morning.

The figure in the hospital bed was a pale shadow of her sister, like a pencil sketch that someone had blurred and smudged. A breathing mask was fastened over Beatrice's nose and mouth, and various tubes and IVs were hooked into her arms. There was something almost translucent about her skin, as if Sam might be able to peer through her eyelids and see the dreams flickering over her brain.

At the sound of voices moving down the hall, Sam looked up. She knew who was coming. Only one person in America was always at the center of a crowd, the planet around which the rest of the world quietly orbited. The monarch—or, in this case, the Acting King.

The group turned the corner, and a half dozen conversations fell silent as everyone saw her through the glass windows. Sam realized, belatedly, that she was wearing the same clothes as yesterday, like in her old walk-of-shame days. Her cheeks grew hot.

Jeff spoke softly, and the people around him darted off in all directions like a school of fish.

"Jeff," she exclaimed, the moment he stepped into the room. "I can't believe . . ."

She started toward him, only to pause at his expression.

"Well, *we* can all believe it because we've had to," Jeff said wearily. "We've been living with this for weeks while you were off drinking rosé in the Maldives."

At his words, she flinched. "I'm sorry. I didn't know."

"*Didn't know?*" he repeated, disbelieving. "Where *were* you, Sam?"

"We sort of . . . went off the grid." She fumbled for something she could tell Jeff without betraying Marshall's trust. "We needed to be far away, to get some space."

"Right," Jeff said slowly. His eyes traveled to her hair, then her tanned, freckled arms. "You and Marshall needed *space*, because everything has been so unbearably *hard* on you. Because no one in history has been under the kind of pressure that you two have suffered."

"I'm not—"

"News flash, Sam, you're not the only one under pressure. *Pressure* is wondering if your older sister has taken her last breath! *Pressure* is taking an indefinite leave of absence from college while you rule in your sister's place, because America is already hanging on by a thread, and what other choice do you have? *Pressure* is trying to keep those thoughts to yourself so that no one realizes how totally unequipped you are to deal with it all!"

He broke off, frustrated, and Sam was suddenly aware how

much older her brother looked. The habit of command had settled over him, carved new lines around his mouth.

"I'm so sorry. I never meant for you to go through this alone," she whispered.

"But I did go through it alone, Sam. We've all been calling and texting you for weeks without a single reply."

"My phone has been off! I thought it was better this way. I never imagined . . ."

Jeff looked away. "I tore apart my room at Bellevue looking for a note from you. I kept thinking, surely Sam has left me some kind of explanation, or at least a goodbye. You wrote a note for Beatrice, after all, and Anju said you texted Nina." His jaw tightened as he glanced swiftly back up. "You never even thought of me, did you?"

"I'm sorry." Sam knew how utterly inadequate the words were.

Her brother turned toward the window. "I looked for you, you know. Even after Mom and Aunt Margaret and Anju all said to stop, that you would turn up when you wanted to be found, I kept looking."

Sam felt like something had splintered in her chest.

Jeff laughed hollowly. "Do you have any idea how many false sightings there have been of you? You've been spotted at a club in Tel Aviv, buying healing crystals at a voodoo shop in New Orleans, working a fishing boat off some island in Hawaii. I had a team chasing down all the leads that sounded plausible, but they always came up empty-handed."

Sam's throat was closing up; she swallowed. "I know I didn't make this easy on you, but it's so clear that you've done a fantastic job managing things. I'm really proud of you, Jeff."

"It's all Daphne. She's been helping me navigate everything."

"About Daphne . . . I saw the news," Sam said quickly. "You don't have to do this, you know. Don't get married just because Beatrice is hurt and you think you have to."

"You don't know what you're talking about," Jeff protested, but there was an undercurrent of hesitation in his voice, if only for a moment.

She spread out her hands in a conciliatory gesture. "Look, if you and Daphne want to get more serious, that's great. Why don't you move in together? Don't run off to the altar just because of Beatrice."

They both glanced at the hospital bed, where their older sister lay quietly breathing.

"All I'm saying is, you shouldn't feel pressured to rush anything," Sam finished. "You're not alone anymore, Jeff. I'm back now, and this is all my responsibility anyway. You and Daphne should slow down. You can go back to school, to normal life—obviously, things won't be normal, but . . ." She trailed off at the look on Jeff's face.

He swallowed. "Sam, you can't take over. You're not Beatrice's heir."

"Of course I am. You were her Regent during the League of Kings conference, but I'm older." She tried to sound teasing, the way they used to, as she added, "Remember, I beat you by four minutes?"

"Yes, but—"

"Then it's settled. I can take over from here."

"Sam, you're not the heir anymore! You're not a princess at all!"

His words rebounded cruelly through the room, so utterly bizarre that at first Sam couldn't process them. It was as if Jeff had spoken in German. The sounds just didn't fit together right.

Her reply came out hoarse. "What do you mean, I'm not a princess?"

"You were missing, okay? No one had any idea where you were. No one knew when, or *if*, you planned on coming back."

"Beatrice knew! I left her a note!"

Sam glanced at her sister as if hoping Beatrice would chime in, but of course, Beatrice just lay there, quiet and still.

"We all saw that note. Anju did her best to keep it a secret, but Lord Orange knew about it," Jeff explained, naming Marshall's grandfather. "He's really angry with you both. He must have told a few other peers, because pretty soon word got around that you and Marshall had run off together. So the Senate put forward a motion to strip you of your titles, and the House of Tribunes approved it."

"What?"

"You're no longer Her Royal Highness, the Princess Samantha. You're just . . . Sam."

Sam braced a hand against the wall, trying to regain some semblance of balance. The world had gone wildly off-kilter. "You stripped my titles because I was gone for a month? Don't you think that's an overreaction?"

"I didn't do anything; Congress did." Jeff's face colored as he added, "You do remember the branches of government and separation of powers, don't you?"

"Oh, come on!" Sam burst out. "Congress may have voted on it, but you *let* them! If you'd spoken up, they would have stopped!"

"*You* let them, Sam! You wrote a statement of renunciation right there in your note to Beatrice! 'I need to stop being the Princess of America'?" Jeff lifted his hands into vicious air quotes, reciting her note back to her. "'I'm choosing love over duty'? Come on, Sam, what else were we supposed to think?"

As swiftly as it had come, her rage seeped away, leaving nothing but an aching sorrow in its wake.

"This is the Duke of Orange's fault, isn't it," she said heavily. Marshall's grandfather had done this to punish them. He'd adamantly opposed their relationship, and now he was taking revenge.

Jeff shook his head. "I think he voted in favor—almost all the dukes did, especially the Old Guard—but the Duke of Virginia authored the bill."

Lord Ambrose Madison? Sam blinked, trying to remember if she'd ever spoken to the squat, unpleasant man beyond a few polite words. What could he possibly have against her?

"I wish you'd said something, separation of powers be damned." She suddenly felt exhausted on a bone-deep level. "When I said I needed to get away, I meant that I needed to leave *for now*. I wasn't trying to walk away *forever*."

"How was I supposed to know that?" Jeff demanded.

Because we're twins, she longed to scream. *Because you always knew how I was feeling before.*

For most of their lives, she and Jeff had been able to communicate without speaking. Sam would wake up from a nightmare as a small child and find that Jeff was already coming into her room to comfort her, trailing his stuffed bunny on the floor. Or in middle school, when the clique of mean girls said something mocking or cruel, Sam would look up a few minutes later to see Jeff and Ethan outside the window of her classroom, beckoning her to come play hooky because Jeff "had a feeling she needed it."

They had always shared an implicit understanding, as if some invisible twin mechanics clicked between them, keeping them quietly in sync. Until now.

"Sam." Jeff reached a hand toward her, then seemed to think better of it. "Can you stay at Grandma Billie's for a while? Just until we figure out how to break the news that you're back."

Her voice wavered. "I've lost my title, and now you don't even want me at home?"

"It's not about what *I* want; you know that. If you need money, you can talk to Anju," Jeff added uncomfortably.

"Need money?" Sam repeated.

"Since your allowance has been cut off."

Well, at least she knew why her credit-card accounts were frozen. That money belonged to the Princess Samantha, who'd been written out of existence with a stroke of the congressional pen.

One of the aides waved at Jeff through the window, and he nodded.

"I'm sorry, but I have to go. I'll come meet you at Loughlin House later, okay?"

Sam could only nod as he headed back into the hallway. The group of assistants materialized as if from nowhere, falling into step alongside him and immediately peppering him with questions.

When they were gone, Sam collapsed into the chair by her sister's bed, hanging her head in her hands.

If only Beatrice could wake up and make everything right. Her sister had always been the peacemaker among the Washington siblings, the one with a calm mind and steady hand. There was a blade of steel beneath Beatrice's softness, unwavering enough to withstand any force bearing down on her. Beatrice was resolute when it mattered. That was what made her such a good queen.

Sam often felt like she was the opposite: sharp on the exterior, with an angry, prickly shell that hid the sensitive beating heart beneath.

Maybe she should just go back to Hawaii. At least everything felt simple there.

"Oh, Bee. I've really made a mess of things."

It felt a little silly, talking to Beatrice when she probably couldn't hear, but it was better than silence.

"Remember when you told me to 'go all in' on my relationship with Marshall? Well, I did. We ran off together to Hawaii. I chose love over duty, just like we talked about."

Was it her imagination, or did Beatrice's hand move? Sam grabbed it, wrapping her warm palms around Beatrice's cold one, willing her sister back to health.

"I left you a letter, actually; you may have gotten it before you—before your accident. I had no idea," she hurried to add. "I've been gone for a month, and I never knew you were here, hurting. I hate that I abandoned you."

With each word, Sam felt the weight pressing down on her chest lighten a bit. So she kept talking.

She told Beatrice everything that had happened since the League of Kings final banquet. She described Hawaii and the boat and the funny little kitchen with its red tiles, her efforts to cook breakfast that had ended in burned toast, and nearly a burned house. She off-loaded her worries about Jeff and her insecurities about the future. It was such an overwhelming relief to let the words pour out, to admit her flaws and short-comings to the one person who would always forgive her.

Sam had no idea how long she sat there, holding tight to her sister, but eventually the words ran dry. She closed her eyes and leaned forward, holding Beatrice's hand to her fore-head as if asking for a benediction.

She couldn't leave.

No matter how much simpler things were in Hawaii, no matter how desperately she missed Marshall, she couldn't go back. She might not be a princess anymore, but she was still Samantha Washington—and she would stay here and fight for her family.

"I'm not going anywhere," she whispered, still clutching tight to her sister's hand. "But it's not the same without you. Wake up, Bee—please. I miss you. We all need you."

7

BEATRICE

"Wake up, Bee. Please."

"Just five more minutes," she said automatically, snuggling closer to Connor.

This had become their morning routine lately: Connor would stir first, only for Beatrice to drag him back under the covers and ask for more time.

She kept telling herself that they should stop, that the next time Connor snuck into her room she would send him away. There was no possible future for them, and they both knew it. Yet Beatrice, who had always lived by logic and reason, found herself acting irrationally.

She and Connor might not have forever, but she could give them right now.

"I miss you," he murmured, which was strange.

"Miss me? I'm right here." Beatrice tucked her head into Connor's shoulder, letting her hands trace over his tattoo. She was getting braver, now, about touching him—though he was still wearing his boxers, because she wasn't ready for that, not yet.

She felt the rumble of Connor's voice in her chest as he replied: "We all need you."

"What are you talking about?"

"Bee . . ."

She squinted, disoriented. The lights were too bright, oversized fluorescent bulbs glaring down at her.

"Bee?"

Samantha was in a chair next to her bed, looking disheveled as usual, mascara ringing raccoon circles around her eyes. And what had she done to her hair?

"Oh my god." Sam's hands flew to her mouth in momentary shock; then she stumbled to her feet and began shouting hoarsely. "Doctor! Someone! Come quick—Beatrice is awake!"

Beatrice tried to sit up, but her body felt so heavy, her legs and arms and especially her eyelids. It was a colossal effort to keep her eyes open. She felt them fluttering shut, sleep wrapping its tendrils around her, as soft as falling backward into a bank of snow.

She forced herself to look up again, and saw that Samantha was still staring at her with a shocked sort of awe. "Thank god," Sam breathed. "We were so worried, Bee."

Something was very wrong. Beatrice nearly laughed at herself for that thought: of *course* something was wrong. She was in a hospital.

"Why am . . ."

"Shhh," Sam admonished. "You were in an accident, but everything is fine. Now that you're awake, it's all going to be fine."

An accident? Beatrice cast her mind back, but she couldn't remember anything. Her mind felt spongy and strangely porous, as if her memories were droplets of water, impossible to separate from one another. Images flickered before her: Teddy standing next to her at a party, both of them making polite, empty conversation; her father's face, lit by the flickering firelight of his office as he said how proud he was of her. But she couldn't sort the memories into any kind of sense.

"Did I . . . fall?" The words were muffled under a plastic breathing mask, but Sam must have read the movement of her lips, because she shook her head.

"It was a car accident."

Beatrice's chest seized in fear. If it was a car accident, had Connor been driving? Was he hurt? The machines next to her bed beeped more quickly, registering her elevated pulse.

Before she could ask, a sea of people in scrubs and white coats rushed through the door, wielding medical instruments and clipboards, nearly tripping in their haste.

"Your Majesty, I'm Dr. Jacobs. I've had the honor of managing your care while you've been here at St. Stephen's," said a man with glasses and white hair. He began removing the breathing mask over her nose, grinning in a likeable and decidedly unprofessional manner. "I have to say, I'm thrilled to see you awake. Now, please just take it easy while we perform a few basic tests."

Beatrice nodded, too shaken to point out that *Your Majesty* was her father's honorific, not hers.

The doctors tried to shoo Samantha from the room, but when Sam said she wasn't going anywhere, they gave up and let her stand to one side. Beatrice's eyes kept darting curiously to her sister. She was grateful not to be alone, of course, but it wasn't as if she and Sam were particularly close. She wondered if Sam was here because their parents had insisted upon it. She didn't look like she'd been out partying, in her leggings and faded vintage T-shirt, but there was something rumpled and stale about her, as if she'd spent the night in a stranger's bed. Why couldn't she have packed a bag with a fresh change of clothes? There were showers here in the VIP section of the hospital. But then, Sam had never really acted the part of a princess. Which was why Beatrice had to be princess enough for both of them.

The doctors examined her eyes and her ears, asked her to flex her fingers and toes, fired questions at her like *What is your mother's maiden name?* and *What country is Paris in?* Beatrice obediently did as they asked, mind whirling. The sky outside the window was a cheerful robin's-egg blue, the capital's sky-line oddly comforting, its slate and stone roofs dwarfed by the twin domes of Columbia House and, farther, the white stone bulk of the palace.

"Teddy is on his way," Samantha offered while the doctors were adjusting Beatrice's IVs. "He's going to be so mad he missed your waking up! He's been here practically every moment since you were hurt."

Beatrice swallowed, hardly listening. "I . . . was anyone else in the car with me?" The question came out raspy and weak.

Dr. Jacobs winced sympathetically. "Just the Revere Guard who was driving, Your Majesty. I'm sorry to say that he died on impact."

No no no. "I . . . was it Connor?"

"I believe his name was Shane Bartlett."

Beatrice's relief was so acute, she gasped out loud. Sam shot her a strange look. "What made you ask about Connor?"

Beatrice blinked. "I'm worried about him. Do you know where he is?"

Sam went very still. "Bee," she said slowly, using the old nickname from when they were children. "What's the last thing you remember?"

Dr. Jacobs cleared his throat. "Please, Your Roy—I, um, Samantha. Don't press her. We will be conducting a series of mental tests over the coming days—"

"I don't remember the accident," Beatrice cut in. "Where was I going, anyway?"

The doctor ignored her question. "It's perfectly normal not to remember the accident. You suffered extensive damage to both sides of your cerebral cortex. Really, it's a miracle to see you awake and answering questions so coherently," he added, and smiled. "Though I have to say, I'm not surprised to see you so recovered. You have a remarkably strong will and determination."

"Does that mean I can go home?"

He hesitated. "We need to keep you here for observation until we're fully assured of your recovery. But don't worry, we'll have you back out there in no time."

Beatrice splayed her hands over the hospital blankets. Her nails were filed into perfect half-moons, her cuticles pushed back; she wondered absently whether someone had been giving her manicures while she was unconscious.

"Where is everyone?" she asked.

"Jeff will come as soon as he can. And Mom is already on the way," Sam added. Beatrice started to ask about Dad, but before she could get the words out, Teddy Eaton appeared in the doorway.

"Oh my god. *Bee*," he whispered, voice breaking on a sob.

Then, to Beatrice's shock, he strode forward in a few swift steps and folded his arms around her, closing her in a hug. He paused a moment, then leaned over and brushed a kiss on her brow.

There was so much emotion folded into that gesture, tenderness and relief and a tight-leashed fury, that Beatrice had no idea what to make of it. She held herself very still.

"I can't believe it. Thank god," Teddy kept saying, over and over. He turned to Samantha, and a warm smile creased his features. "Sam. Nice hair. I almost didn't recognize you."

"That was kind of the point," Sam said ruefully.

He shook his head. "I can't believe I missed it; I've been here the whole time—"

"I know, and I'm so grateful. The doctors told me you hardly left—"

"I should have known she would wake up for you!" Teddy's smile illuminated the whole room. "What did you say, Sam?"

"Oh, I just asked for her advice about all the problems in my life. Never a shortage of drama when I'm around, is there?"

Teddy nudged Sam's shoulder playfully. "You don't want the drama but the drama finds you?"

Beatrice glanced back and forth between them, bewildered. Their energy wasn't at all flirtatious; if anything, it reminded her of the way Sam and Jeff used to tease each other. But didn't Sam once have a crush on Teddy?

Beatrice supposed she must have moved on to someone else. Sam's energies were too wild and restless to stay fixed on any one point for long.

"Dr. Jacobs." Sam's voice was surprisingly resolute. "Can you finish up these tests later? Teddy and I need a moment with Beatrice, alone."

The doctor started to protest, only to fall silent at something in Sam's gaze. He nodded to her, bowed to Beatrice, then left the room.

When the door had shut behind him, Sam turned back to Beatrice. "Bee. What's the last thing you remember?"

Teddy threw out a protective hand. "We don't need to interrogate her; she just woke up."

"I wouldn't ask if it wasn't important."

He hesitated, then looked to Beatrice. "Bee? What do you remember?"

A dizzy feeling snaked up her spine. Trying to remember . . . it was like stepping into a vast darkness without being able to see her steps. She might fall off an edge at any moment.

"Do you remember the League of Kings?" Sam prompted.

"What about it?" Beatrice asked, to hide her confusion.

"Did you enjoy it?"

"It's not meant to be a party; it's *work*, Sam. But, yes, I enjoyed parts of it."

"She sounds pretty normal to me," Teddy joked, resting a hand on Beatrice's shoulder in a casually affectionate gesture. What was he doing?

Sam ignored him, eyes fixed on Beatrice. "What was your favorite part of the conference?"

"I don't know! The stables at Chenonceau are pretty wonderful. I borrowed one of their horses and went on a few early-morning rides." She narrowed her eyes at Sam. "Why are you asking about the League of Kings, anyway? It was years ago."

Silence. Beatrice looked up and realized that Teddy was no longer smiling.

"She's lost weeks," he said softly.

Sam shook her head. "Maybe more."

"What do you mean, I've lost weeks?" Her voice was scratchy; Sam heard it and handed her a cup of water from the bedside table. Beatrice took a small sip, feeling perilously close to tears. She hated not being able to control every situation, and this was as out of control as she could ever remember being.

Teddy fell to one knee by the bed, like a figure in a medieval court painting, and took her hands in his. "Bee—do you remember our wedding?"

"We got *married*?" The words burst from her lips with a strangled cry. Teddy flinched at her tone.

"No. I mean, we were supposed to, but . . . it didn't happen."

She stared at him, disbelief and fear warring in her chest.

"Do you remember Walthorpe?" he asked softly. Beatrice shook her head. Something gleamed in Teddy's eyes; he quickly blinked it away.

This was all too much, too fast. She stared out the window, at the sunlight dancing over the familiar roofs of her city, feeling more alone than she could remember.

"I want Mom and Dad," she confessed, her voice small.

Teddy sucked in a breath. Sam made a sound in the back

of her throat, a sort of low animal cry. Beatrice watched them, a sick, ominous feeling twisting in her gut.

Somehow, she sensed her sister's next words before Sam spoke them.

"Bee," her sister breathed, "Dad is . . . He . . ."

Teddy took over. "We lost your father. I'm so sorry, Bee." He squeezed her hands, and Beatrice was too stunned to even register the contact.

This couldn't be real. She would wake up and find herself in bed with Connor once more, and this whole exchange would turn into the silvery cobwebs of forgotten nightmares.

Except she knew deep down that it *was* real. Dreams were never this cruel and cold and unforgiving. Dreams made sense, while real life, as Beatrice knew too well, could be brutally senseless.

"How long have I been unconscious?" Her voice sounded faraway and distorted to her own ears, as if she'd stuck her head in a fishbowl.

"A month," Teddy said heavily. "But it would seem that you've forgotten much more."

Beatrice wanted to scream and cry and beat her chest. She wanted to wail like a small child who'd skinned her knee on the playground. She wanted to punch something, or someone.

Yet she did none of those things, because she was Beatrice, and she had always held her emotions on a very tight leash.

"What happened?"

"Dad had cancer," Sam said, understanding the question. Beatrice nodded and closed her eyes.

"I'll give you two a moment." Teddy looked at her with anguish in his eyes, but Beatrice couldn't bring herself to care. She didn't even say anything when Sam came forward to wrap her arms around her and pull her close.

"I'm sorry, Bee. I hate that you have to lose him all over again," she murmured.

Beatrice leaned back, extricating herself from Sam's grip. She already knew the answer to this question, yet she had to ask it anyway.

"If Dad is gone, that means I'm . . ."

"You're the queen now," Sam finished for her. "And a damn good one, by the way."

Beatrice focused on breathing, in and out, in and out. The enormity of her grief, and shock, was being held at bay by a flimsy barricade of self-control. She couldn't let herself consider the unbearable depth of her loss, not until she had the space to grieve properly—or at least to grieve alone.

Her father was gone. Beatrice had always known this day would come, but she'd assumed it was something she would face in the distant future, when she was an adult with decades of experience. She certainly didn't feel like much of an adult right now. She was as lost and achingly confused as she'd been as a little girl, when she woke up in an unfamiliar bedroom—which happened all the time when her family was on a royal tour—and lay awake, listening for the familiar rumble of her parents' voices as they returned from whatever event they'd been to that evening.

But there was no one to reassure her now, unless you counted Samantha, and Beatrice knew better than to rely upon her sister. Sam might mean well in the moment, but she never followed through on her promises. She was too erratic, always chasing her latest impulse or infatuation.

"Where's Connor?" she asked, and Sam shot her that look again.

"He's not a Revere Guard anymore. You let him go."

"I wouldn't have done that," Beatrice insisted.

"Bee . . . you and Connor ended things."

Beatrice's heart skipped and skidded in her chest. Samantha

knew about Connor? She considered denying it, but felt too flustered to lie right now.

"How did you find out?" she asked instead.

Samantha looked awkward. "You told me, Bee."

"What? No." Sam was the last person with whom Beatrice would share something this sensitive, this explosive.

Sam laid her hand on Beatrice's. "You may not remember, but you love Teddy now. The two of you—"

"*Stop it!*" Beatrice pressed her hands over her ears. "Just stop! Leave me alone, okay? You're such a liar!"

Sam opened her mouth as if to say something else, then seemed to think better of it. "I'll give you some space. I really am sorry," she added, forlorn.

When Sam had left, a nurse knocked tentatively at the door. Seeing Beatrice's tear-streaked face, she gasped. "Your Majesty, is everything all right?"

Of course it's not all right, Beatrice wanted to scream. *I just woke up from a coma and my father is dead and I'm apparently Your Majesty!*

"I need my phone" was all she said aloud.

The nurse, who'd been sorting bottles of medication, fell still. "Dr. Jacobs wanted you to recover in peace. I know he's worried about you reading the news."

"I'd like my phone, please," Beatrice repeated. Despite the politeness of her tone and the *please*, there was no mistaking it for anything but a direct order.

The nurse retreated into the hallway, returning a few minutes later with a plastic bag labeled HER MAJESTY. "Your personal effects, from after the accident," she mumbled, before quietly shutting the door behind her.

Beatrice sorted through the bag with a dazed sense of wonder. Her thin evening bag contained nothing but a lip gloss and comb, which was no surprise, since Beatrice didn't exactly need to carry a wallet or ID. She opened a smaller pouch to find a stack of pavé diamond bracelets, a pair of droplet earrings, and two rings.

A diamond engagement ring, presumably from Teddy, and a heavy signet ring. Not the one Beatrice usually wore as Princess Royal, but a grander one—one that she was used to seeing on her father's finger, because it belonged to the monarch.

She stuffed them back into the pouch and zipped it shut.

Her phone still had a sliver of battery left; someone must have turned it off when they put away her belongings after the accident. Beatrice watched its screen come to life and frowned, because this wasn't her phone. The quilted navy case was hers, but she didn't recognize the home screen—

Except it was her phone. It must be, because the photo on the home screen was of her and Teddy.

Beatrice's grip tightened until her fingers turned white beneath their nail beds. She tried to study the image abstractly, the way she used to in art-history class.

She and Teddy seemed so *happy* in the picture. They were both laughing, their eyes bright. The photo was a selfie, spontaneous and carefree, which was surprising in itself because Beatrice never took selfies. The sky behind her and Teddy was an impossible blue, palm trees swaying in the background. Wherever this was, it wasn't at the Washingtons' beach house on the Virginia shore.

It was surreal, looking at a picture of herself that she didn't remember taking. Again Beatrice felt like she was caught in a dream, maybe in someone else's dream. The cool hospital air seemed to settle around her, lifting the hair on her arms.

Then her eyes snagged on the calendar app in the corner of her home screen, and she forgot all about the mystery photo. Today's date was November 15.

The reality of it crashed over her then, in a way it hadn't before—that she truly had lost nearly a year of her life.

Her fingers shook as she flicked open her contact list,

ignoring the tiny blue bubbles alerting her to thousands of unread messages and emails. That could wait, all of it. Beatrice dialed a number, holding her breath.

She was immediately greeted by a three-tone alert. "We're sorry," a robotic voice informed her, "but the number you have dialed is disconnected or is no longer in service. Goodbye."

Beatrice stared at her phone in disbelief. Connor had changed his number.

She longed to call her dad, but apparently that wasn't possible either.

Finally, the threads of Beatrice's self-control began to snap. She closed her eyes, let her head fall against the thin hospital pillow, and cried.

NINA

"Disguise is a powerful and recurring theme in Shakespeare's works." Professor Larsen paced the front of the lecture hall, twirling a piece of chalk in his hands. "In *King Lear*, for instance, there are noblemen posing as servants, and daughters who disguise their true intentions. . . ."

Nina's pen scribbled over the page as she summarized the professor's thoughts about disguise. If only King's College offered a class on *that*. She could use a lesson or two in hiding her intentions—the sort of thing that everyone at court seemed to do as easily as breathing.

Especially Daphne, who apparently had no qualms about marrying someone she didn't even love. Someone who deserved so much better.

"Nina!" whispered the girl next to her, a fellow English major named Blair. She was one of the student producers of the show, along with Rachel.

Reluctantly, Nina paused her note-taking, and Blair brushed her bangs back from her face to lean closer. "So, you and the prince? Congratulations! Were you surprised?"

Nina stared at her, stunned. Had Blair heard about Jeff's engagement and somehow thought that he was marrying *Nina*?

"You're mistaken. There's no news about me and the prince," she whispered.

Was this how it would be for the rest of her life? People would recall that she'd dated Jeff and wonder if they were getting back together, or if Nina was crying jealous tears about his engagement, or forget the difference between Nina and Daphne altogether. Would she always be tied to him, even though they hadn't been allowed to date publicly when they were *actually* together?

"Before we leave today's class, I have an announcement," the professor said, interrupting her thoughts. "I'll be leading the spring study-abroad program at Oxford."

The room buzzed with excitement; Professor Larsen held up a hand for silence.

"The program is open to ten students each semester. The admitted students will take classes at Oxford, and, more importantly, will each work on an independent study under the close supervision of an Oxford professor." He smiled. "Applications are very competitive, as many of you know. There will be a reception and info session soon for those of you who'd like more information."

Nina's heart skipped. Of course she'd heard of the English department's semester abroad: it was the most coveted program at King's College, and impossible to get into. Most of the three hundred English majors her year would apply, and the school only accepted ten. She'd heard that if your GPA was below a 3.8, they wouldn't even consider you.

Nina filed out of the lecture hall along with the rest of the class, blinking as her eyes adjusted to the brightness. It was one of those deceptively warm fall days that made everyone shed their coats and sprawl out in the sunshine. A group of students sat cross-legged on the steps of a fountain; farther ahead, an admissions tour was heading toward the chapel. Nina heard the student tour guide pointing out the statue of King Edward III. Back when she and Jeff were dating, she used to think that statue looked a bit like him. Now she resented it for reminding her of her ex.

Not that it was particularly easy to forget about Jeff. He and Daphne were currently on the cover of every magazine and website in the country.

Nina reached for her earbuds, ready to head back to her dorm and check on Sam, who was still staying with her. She'd come back from the hospital yesterday with big news—apparently Beatrice had woken up, but didn't remember most of the past year. "Can I crash with you a few more days? Just until I clear things up with Jeff," Sam had asked, her voice small.

"Of course," Nina had replied, trying to ignore her mounting nervousness. The longer Sam stayed, the greater the risk of her being found out. Jayne and Rachel would never tell, but what if someone else caught sight of her?

Nina's eyes drifted to a guy walking a few yards down the path—and her heart skipped. It was James. She couldn't see his face, yet Nina *knew* it was him, with the sort of instinctive certainty that comes from having kissed someone.

"James!" she blurted out before she could think better of it.

He glanced over his shoulder and grinned, pausing so that she could catch up. "Nina. Hey."

Her eyes drifted, unbidden, to his mouth. She didn't even know his last name, yet she knew how his hands felt around her waist, how he tasted. It threw Nina's mind into a tailspin of confusion.

"How's your day going?" he asked as she fell into step alongside him.

"It's good so far." She hesitated, then added, "I just wanted to say, about the Tudor House party . . . I had to go help out my friend. That's why I left without saying goodbye." She squirmed, wishing he would interrupt and make this easier. "I didn't want you to think that you'd scared me off."

James shrugged. "I wasn't worried. I get the sense you don't scare easily."

"I guess not." The truth was, Nina felt constantly scared— of falling short of her parents' expectations, or, worse, her own expectations. Of regrets. Of failure. But she liked the idea of this other Nina, the one who lived without fear.

"So does this mean I get a redo?"

Nina glanced over and met James's eyes. They were the warm blue of the ocean on a cloudless day, the type of blue you could sink into and drift all the way to the bottom. It took her a moment to register what he'd said. "A redo?"

"Can I take you out? On a date," he added, as if he needed to be explicit.

The statue of King Edward III seemed to be staring at Nina, handsome and aloof and judgmental—reminding her of her royal ex-boyfriend, who'd just gotten engaged to someone else.

"All right," she heard herself say. "I mean, yes. I'd love that."

James nodded toward the edge of campus. "Great. Shall we?"

"I . . . right now?"

"Yes, right now. I'm not waiting for the next party at Tudor House, hoping to catch you before you run off on a mysterious errand." He held out a hand to indicate the sunshine. "Besides, this is the perfect weather for the Broken Spoon. Unless you'd rather get Mulberry's cheese tots, obviously."

Nina fell in love with him, just a teensy bit, for knowing to suggest ice cream on a first date.

"Definitely not. You don't want those cheese tots before midnight," she agreed.

They headed onto Market Street and into the neighborhood adjacent to campus, filled with fast-casual restaurants and coffee shops.

74

As they walked, Nina noticed that people kept glancing their way. She couldn't blame them; James was undeniably gorgeous, with his chiseled features and roguish grin, blond hair glinting in the sun. There was something self-aware in the way he walked, as if he expected everyone to be looking at him, and the force of his ego was so massive that they all *did* look at him.

"What did you think of that class?" James asked. "To be honest, *King Lear* has never been my favorite of the tragedies. I'm old-school and prefer *Romeo and Juliet*."

"*Romeo and Juliet?*" Nina made a face, then registered his words. "Wait—you're in Dr. Larsen's Shakespeare class, too?"

"I just joined."

"They let you do that mid-semester?"

"I got special permission." Before she could ask for details, he deftly changed the subject. "That Oxford program sounds incredible. Are you applying?"

Nina shook her head. "I don't think so."

"The girl who lives and breathes Jane Austen? Why not?"

Because she could never do something like that. The farthest Nina had ever traveled was to the Caribbean with the Washingtons one year at spring break.

"I don't want to go that far from home," she told James. He didn't know her well enough to hear the lack of conviction in her voice.

They pushed open the door of the Broken Spoon, and a bell chimed inside. The chalkboard menu overhead advertised today's selections, mostly inventive flavors like lemon poppy seed or Boston cream pie. Nina ordered a scoop of strawberry, then chuckled when James asked for a waffle cone of triple brownie batter.

"Triple brownie batter? That's a lot of chocolate."

"So?" James asked, paying for their ice cream despite Nina's protests.

"So, nothing should be that chocolatey. It's a chocolate overload."

He placed a hand on the small of her back to guide her gently from the store. She felt a little jolt of electricity at the contact.

"Why don't you try for yourself." James held out his cone in amused challenge.

Nina hesitated, wondering if it was too girlfriendy to share his ice cream cone—but then, they *had* already kissed. She smiled and took a bite, only to pause at the sound of her name.

"Nina!"

Rachel was stepping out of the stationery store down the street. When she saw that Nina was with James, her eyes widened—just as Blair followed her out of the store and noticed the exact same thing.

"*Omigod*, our two leads are already vibing!" Blair clapped in glee. "I *knew* we were right to cast you two! Nina, you *seriously* have a type," she added meaningfully.

Nina's stomach swooped. *Our two leads?* She glanced over at James, whose brow was furrowed as the directors hurried toward them—Blair beaming, Rachel looking unmistakably guilty.

"You actually put me in the show?" Nina demanded when her roommate was closer. "I told you that I didn't want to do it!"

"But, Nina, you were so good. How could we *not* cast you?"

"Who am I playing?"

"We posted the cast list earlier today; I'm surprised you haven't seen it." Rachel fumbled in her bag and withdrew a printed sheet of computer paper.

Nina's eyes skimmed over the names. *Hermia—Annie*

Gleason; Lysander—Kevin Straithairn; Helena—Nina Gonzalez; Demetrius—Jamie Stuart . . .

Wait a second. *Stuart?*

"Your Royal Highness, you're going to be *amazing* as Demetrius," Blair gushed, twirling a lock of hair around one finger. "We almost cast you as Bottom because he has the most lines, but I insisted that Demetrius was the right fit. It's a much more *physical* role, and of course, it's so *romantic. . . .*"

Nina thrust the cast list toward Rachel and walked off without another word, tossing her uneaten strawberry ice cream into the trash.

Everything clicked into place with brutal logic. Blair's earlier comment: *So, you and the prince?* The furtive glances people shot James wherever he went. His expensive and understated wardrobe, his cryptic references to his parents, the easy confidence with which he entered a room—that wasn't just because he was attractive, but because he was royal. Jamie Stuart, the Prince of Canada.

Another prince.

"Nina, wait!" James hurried after her, and as childish as it was, Nina quickened her steps. She ducked blindly into a makeup store, weaving between rows of glimmering lip-gloss tubes. A salesgirl with electric-green eyeliner took one look at Nina's expression and darted into the back.

Some part of her had known James would follow. He caught up with her by a display of mascara wands and reached for Nina's forearm, tugging her to a stop.

"Why didn't you tell me who you are?" she demanded.

He glanced around the empty store and lowered his voice, though they were alone. "I assumed you knew, at first."

"Because you expect everyone to recognize you?"

"Because we've *met* before, Nina. At the League of Kings banquet."

Oh. The memory crashed over her in sudden, vivid detail. James had bumped into her on the terrace late at night and asked her to dance, but then Nina had seen Jeff—had gone into the gardens and *kissed* Jeff—which promptly obliterated everything else from her mind.

That night felt so far off now, so detached from reality. The Nina who'd fallen for Jeff a second time, who'd let herself dream that they might finally have a future together, felt like a distant memory.

"I remember," she said softly.

Something glimmered in James's eyes. "To be fair, I wasn't wearing my glasses that night. Like Clark Kent in disguise."

"You were wearing a wolf pelt, if memory serves."

"It's a fur vest, and you have to admit it's better than most ceremonial outfits. The Albanians' bronze helmet with goat horns?" He shook his head. "That thing looks heavy."

He almost coaxed a smile from Nina, but then she shook her head. "I'm sorry I didn't recognize you at first, but James—Jamie—" She faltered, not sure what to call him. "You should have told me."

"Would you have gone out with me if you'd known?"

"No," she admitted, because he deserved the truth.

"Then I don't regret it," he declared. "Look, Nina, when I saw you onstage and you acted like we'd never met, it was a blow to my ego. But it was also . . . kind of nice. I wanted a chance to get to know you on my own terms, without all the royal drama getting in the way."

Nina knew the royal drama all too well.

"I can't believe there's *another* prince at King's College," she muttered.

"My father insisted that I do a study-abroad program here. He pulled some strings so that I could come straight from the League of Kings conference and start mid-semester. I didn't really want to come, but . . ." Jamie shrugged. "At least I'm

78

not attracting the same publicity that I do at home. You Americans don't seem to care about foreign royals nearly as much as you do about your own."

"There's a media ban on campus, because of Jeff," Nina said absently, her mind spinning.

Study abroad—it explained Jamie's presence on campus, but not in Nina's life. How utterly surreal that her path would cross that of not just one but two princes.

Unless it wasn't a coincidence at all, and those princes were connected.

She crossed her arms over her chest. "What are you doing, Jamie?"

"Trying to get passing grades and have fun, the same as everyone else in college."

"I meant, what are you doing with *me*? Did you ask me out because of Jeff?"

"What does Jeff have to do with it?" he asked, but she'd seen him flinch at the name. Nina felt both vindicated and saddened that her suspicions were right.

"I saw the tension between you two at the League of Kings conference. You obviously know he's my ex-boyfriend—did you ask me out hoping someone might snap a photo and it would upset him? Because I have news for you: he's engaged and doesn't care what I do!" Nina's voice had risen in volume; she lowered it self-consciously. "Is that why you tried out for the play, because you knew I'd be there?"

"How would I have known that?" Jamie asked, bewildered. "When we met at the League of Kings, I had no idea that you were *at* King's College, let alone that you would turn up at a Shakespeare audition."

"I'm not stupid, okay?" Nina felt dangerously, foolishly close to tears. "I used to date a prince, and now another prince appears out of nowhere and kisses me at a party, and I'm sup-posed to believe that those two things aren't connected?"

"*You* kissed *me!*"

"That's not the point."

Jamie ran a hand through his hair, frustrated. "You're best friends with Sam, you go to palace events all the time, and you're surprised that the guys who keep asking you out are princes? That seems pretty logical to me, Nina," he observed. "How is an ordinary guy supposed to meet you when you're on the royal circuit?"

"You're telling me you just *happened* to ask me out, and it had absolutely nothing to do with Jeff?"

Jamie hesitated, and she made a disgusted noise.

"Stop!" he exclaimed, before she could storm off. "Okay, fine, Jeff might be the reason I knew who you were, but he has nothing to do with the connection between us! Come on, Nina, do you honestly think I'm using you as—what? Emotional sabotage?" He shook his head. "Who would even do something like that?"

Daphne would, Nina thought darkly. A small, sad part of her wondered if Daphne had ruined her—turned her into a mistrustful version of herself, one she didn't recognize.

"I don't know what to think," she muttered.

Jamie sighed. "Maybe it just takes someone as confident as a prince to see how awesome you are."

Nina's heart beat erratically in her rib cage, scrambling her thoughts. She wasn't sure whether she wanted to melt into Jamie's arms or kick him in the shins. It took all her self-preservation and willpower to do neither.

She wanted to believe Jamie; but even if he was telling the truth, and had no ulterior motives, what did it matter? She'd already been out with a prince once, and look how that had ended. What was it Blair said earlier? *Nina, you seriously have a type.*

The tabloids wouldn't phrase it that nicely if they learned she'd been hanging out with Jamie. They would call her a prince chaser, a tiara tramp, a gold-digging, fame-obsessed commoner. No one liked a social climber, and they would paint Nina as the worst social climber of all.

She was almost to the door when Jamie's voice stopped her in her tracks.

"Are you really not doing the play?"

Nina looked back at him over her shoulder. "I don't think so."

His next words chased her onto the street, echoing in her head long after she'd reached the comparative safety of her dorm room.

"That's too bad, Nina. I hadn't pegged you as a quitter."

DAPHNE

"Don't worry, Daphne. Everything will be fine," Jefferson promised, with a slightly nervous glance around the examination room. He kept looking at the anatomical posters on the walls, then awkwardly away again.

Don't worry. What a useless thing to say. Daphne worried constantly. Worry was a strong motivator, the force that kept her aware of threats and dangers from all fronts.

"I know." She shifted, crinkling the medical paper that the nurse had draped over her legs. She was still wearing her green silk top from this morning's interview, her face caked with full TV makeup—her lips a little redder than normal, her foundation a few shades too dark.

"I'm sorry we had to rush and do the interview today." Jefferson sighed. "This whole thing with Sam, and now Beatrice . . ."

"I'm just so relieved that she's okay. It's a miracle," Daphne said quickly.

Jefferson had been back and forth from the hospital ever since his sister woke up. Daphne had only seen Beatrice for a few minutes, long enough for the queen to congratulate her on the upcoming wedding.

Thankfully, Beatrice's recovery hadn't stopped the engagement interview. If anything, it was further incentive for the palace to put out some good news, at least until they were ready to announce that the queen had woken up. Daphne couldn't help wondering whether Beatrice was as fully recovered as she pretended to be.

She and Jefferson had done the interview live this morning, in one of the sitting rooms at Washington Palace. Dave Dunleavy, the friendliest of the reporters on the royal beat, had tossed them softball questions about Jefferson's proposal— the official story, that he'd proposed months ago over a candlelit dinner at home, was far more romantic than the truth—and had cheerfully asked for details about the wedding planning. He made a point not to mention Daphne's parents, or her commoner status, as if this was all happening in a romantic vacuum.

The only strange moment had occurred when Dave asked Jefferson, *When did you know Miss Deighton was the one?*

Jefferson had replied, with utter seriousness, *Daphne has been part of my life for so long, I don't know how it would feel to live without her.*

She wasn't sure what to make of that answer. On the surface, it sounded like a sweeping, swoon-worthy romantic declaration. Yet if you listened hard, you might notice that there was no mention of love. Only of shared history, of lives that had become so enmeshed and intertwined that there was no easy way to tear them asunder.

Daphne's fingers itched to scroll through her phone, see what new comments had popped up in the last half hour. She'd stolen a quick glance on the drive over and was relieved to see that she still had a loyal army of supporters; #TeamDaphne was still active.

But she had plenty of critics now, too. They had become vocal after her father's scandal—as if her family's fall from grace had broken a shield that used to protect her, and now anything was fair game—and from the look of things, they were having a field day with this morning's engagement interview.

They rounded up plenty of evidence of her unworthiness: body-language experts who analyzed her posture and said she was lying (well, she was); fashion critics who called her outfit "totally cringe"; die-hard royalists who protested that she "just didn't deserve" Jefferson, whatever that meant. Someone had even unearthed her mother's decades-old swimsuit catalogs, from her days as a model. *Daphne's mom was a total skank!!* they wrote. *Like mother like daughter. #TackyDaphne*

A commoner princess. She was something entirely new, something the likes of which the world had never seen. Which was why she had to be excruciatingly careful about her behavior. She had to act more princess-like than a princess by birth, more royal than the Washingtons themselves, or the entire fairy tale she'd spun around herself would fall apart.

She stretched out her fingers, and the facets of her ring, a cushion-cut diamond on a simple platinum band, sparkled in the morning light.

There was a knock at the door, and a woman with shoulder-length gray hair strode inside. "Your Royal Highness, Miss Deighton, I'm Dr. Carlisle. I apologize for the delay; I came straight from the hospital." She chuckled. "Babies tend to arrive on their own timeline."

"Thank you so much, Dr. Carlisle. It's a pleasure to meet you," Daphne replied, with a nervous smile. This entire practice had shut down their offices for the morning so that Daphne and Jefferson could visit the doctor in private, and the staff had all signed NDAs. Still, she needed to get the doctor on her side.

Her entire future was riding on how the next fifteen minutes would go.

"You believe you're at eight weeks?" Dr. Carlisle nodded at Daphne to put her legs into the stirrups and lean back, which Daphne did.

"I'm not entirely sure, but I think so." Daphne hesitated. "Will you be able to see much on an ultrasound at this stage?"

"We should be able to see the baby's head and torso, and the beginnings of some tiny arms and legs. May I?"

Daphne sucked in a breath. "No need to be anxious," Dr. Carlisle added kindly, lifting the hospital paper. The entire room fell silent as she began moving the ultrasound probe.

This was going to happen eventually, Daphne reminded herself. She'd maintained the fiction of her pregnancy for an admirably long time, thanks to Jefferson's trusting nature, and the old-fashioned nature of the monarchy as an institution. And, of course, her own quick thinking.

"It's too early to tell whether it's a boy or girl, right?" Jefferson sounded nervous, yet a bit excited, too. Guilt wedged into Daphne's chest, which she did her best to ignore.

"Too early." Dr. Carlisle moved the ultrasound wand, studying the screen with ferocious intensity. "Can you shift down a little?" She helped Daphne nudge her hips lower and adjusted the angle of the ultrasound wand.

Daphne knew what to say next. "Is everything okay?"

"I'm just having trouble finding your little one. Baby is playing hide-and-seek! Don't worry," the doctor said absently, "it's common this early in the pregnancy, given how tiny the embryo is."

Daphne arranged her features into an expression of concern. She kept darting glances at Jefferson, who seemed increasingly worried—and confused—the longer the doctor went without saying anything.

Finally Dr. Carlisle sat back with a sigh. "Please give me a moment."

She retreated into the hallway, then returned with two unfamiliar doctors in lab coats. Each of them took a few minutes with the ultrasound machine, frowning down at it in the mounting silence.

"Miss Deighton, why don't you go ahead and sit up," Dr. Carlisle said at last. Daphne obeyed, trying not to wince at the stickiness of the ultrasound gel, and pulled the crinkly paper across her lap.

"I'm not sure how to say this . . . ," the doctor began, at a loss. She'd probably never imagined that she would have to tell an Acting King that his fiancée had been mistaken about a pregnancy.

"Is something wrong with the baby?" Jefferson asked quietly.

"There is no baby." Dr. Carlisle winced and tried again. "Miss Deighton, I'm afraid you're not pregnant."

For a fraction of a second, Jefferson's face flooded with unmistakable relief, but then it was gone. He grabbed Daphne's hand and laced his fingers in hers. "Are you saying that Daphne had a . . ."

"It's possible the pregnancy ended in miscarriage, yes." Dr. Carlisle was choosing her words very carefully. "But given how thin your uterine lining is, Miss Deighton, it's more likely that you were just mistaken. Your BMI is so low that you might have stopped getting your period because you're underweight." She kept talking, saying something about the benefits of healthy fats: avocados, almonds, the occasional piece of dark chocolate.

As if Daphne could afford to eat chocolate. Didn't anyone understand that she had throngs of paparazzi chasing her these days? People who made it their mission to get a photo of her looking sweaty, or disheveled, or, best of all, pudgy.

Dr. Carlisle seemed to realize that no one was listening, because she trailed off and swallowed awkwardly. "I'll give you two a moment alone," she added, gesturing her fellow doctors out into the hallway.

Once the door closed behind them, Daphne looked uncertainly at Jefferson. He still stood there, holding on to her hand, leaning his weight against the examination table.

"I'm sorry," she said, breaking the silence. "I didn't— I mean, I really thought—"

"Daphne, stop. You have nothing to be sorry for."

She waited for him to say something else, about how there was no need to rush the wedding now that there was no baby on the way, or, worse, that they should call off the engagement altogether. Instead his eyes met hers.

"How are you feeling?" The question was clunky and surprisingly vulnerable. "I mean—are you okay?"

Daphne should have been immune to regret by now, yet a sudden pang of it shot through her.

She stared at Jefferson's handsome features, his jaw clean-shaven from this morning's interview, his dark hair haloed by the fluorescent lighting of the exam room. "I'm okay," she replied, but it came out a whisper.

Jefferson stepped closer and folded her into his arms, causing the medical paper to crinkle awkwardly between them. Daphne was surprised to realize that he was shaking with emotion. The tidal wave of it all suddenly crashed over her, and she felt it too, a sense of loss—not for the baby that had never existed, but for some key part of herself. Some last piece of integrity in her relationship with Jefferson that she had quietly, remorselessly, traded away for . . .

For her future, she reminded herself. For *their* future.

"I'm sorry," she repeated, a single tear trailing morosely down her cheek.

Jefferson nodded, his expression unreadable.

"Should we get going? I'll tell Anju to call the car."

She had been prepared for worse—for accusations that she had been careless, that she should have done bloodwork or seen a doctor earlier. She'd been so afraid that the wedding might not happen anymore. Jefferson was a college-age boy, after all; they could be engaged for several years if they wanted, take the next step when things were more settled.

Except that Jefferson wasn't a boy anymore, was he? At some point over the past year, he had grown up. He was the type of man, now, who held himself to his promises. He had just gone on live TV before the whole world and said he would marry Daphne, and he would do it, even if the whole reason that he'd made that decision was gone.

She got dressed and pulled open the door, only to pause when she saw that her phone was flashing with a new email. Daphne flicked over to read it—and her stomach twisted.

From: UNKNOWN SENDER <12345@webmail.com>
Subject: (NO SUBJECT)

Come on, Daphne. Why are you getting engaged to Jeff when we both know you don't love him? Break off the engagement or I'll tell everyone what you did.

"You okay?"

Jefferson was waiting near the exit, watching her with a concerned frown.

"Of course." Daphne tried to slip her phone back into her purse, but her hands shook, and she dropped it. The phone shattered on the floor, its screen fragmenting with a thousand small cracks.

"Oops! Clumsy me." She hurried to grab the phone before Jefferson could read the incriminating email.

I'll tell everyone what you did. Which secret was this person talking about? Daphne had so many of them: sleeping with Ethan, hurting her friend Himari, selling photos of herself to the paparazzi, sabotaging Nina and Jefferson, threatening

Gabriella. Faking a pregnancy, in a last-ditch effort to keep her hold on Jefferson.

Everything felt slow and sticky, as if Daphne had fallen into a nightmare and couldn't move. She was being black-mailed by an anonymous stranger. How ludicrous, how awful, how utterly fitting.

It was possible that this email was nothing, just a scare tactic from a rogue reporter who wanted to spook her into action. But something about the tone made her think otherwise. *We both know you don't love him.* That sounded like someone who *knew* Daphne, personally.

Someone like Gabriella.

Whatever secret this person was talking about, Daphne couldn't let it be revealed. She was skating on thin ice as it was. If the media got wind of any more reasons to scorn her—if Jefferson ever found out a fraction of what she'd done—she could lose everything.

10

BEATRICE

There was something comfortingly familiar about having her makeup done before a palace press briefing, as if things were almost normal again.

Beatrice snuck a glance at the mirror. Her tailored red dress hung looser than it used to; she'd apparently lost weight while she was unconscious. The makeup artist had hidden her pallor beneath a layer of bronzer and was now dusting color onto her cheekbones. Tissues had been stuffed into the neck of Beatrice's dress to protect the fabric, making it look like she was wearing a ruffled Victorian collar.

If only the room were less crowded. Anju sat nearby, glancing nervously from her tablet to Beatrice and back again, and Teddy stood resolutely to Beatrice's right. She was still baffled by his presence. According to Anju, he'd been at the palace ever since they came back from their non-honeymoon, though to her relief he was staying in a room several hallways down from hers. She knew she'd have to face him eventually, but so far Beatrice had managed to avoid seeing him alone.

Jeff was here, too, as well as Beatrice's mom. Apparently Samantha had been MIA for a month, and now that she was back, she'd ignored their family's requests to stay at Loughlin House and was living at King's College with Nina. How typically Sam.

Beatrice tried not to think about the aching space where

her father should have been. The shock of his loss kept hitting her over and over. She would be fine one minute and then something would spark a memory, and the grief would hurtle toward her, as fast and unrelenting as an oncoming train.

She had moved out of the hospital yesterday. Dr. Jacobs and his staff were still monitoring her with round-the-clock care, but at least she was home.

Except that the palace didn't feel like home, not in the way it used to. It was suffocating and at the same time eerily empty. Beatrice's eyes kept darting to the things that had changed—new curtains hanging in one of the rooms, familiar faces gone from the security team. Especially the one face she was longing to see.

How was she supposed to pick up the pieces of her life when it felt like someone *else* had been living that life for the past year?

According to Dr. Jacobs, Beatrice's injuries had caused retrograde amnesia, a loss of short-term memory (though she found it hard to believe that almost an entire year counted as "short-term"). She remembered her first twenty-two years of life—her family members, her college roommates, her favorite books and her multiplication tables and who was the current Secretary of State. Her *general* knowledge was just fine. It was her *personal* memory of the past year that seemed to have vanished.

She wished she could talk about this with someone. It didn't feel fair to put anything more on Jeff's shoulders when he'd already carried so much lately. There was her mom, of course, but Beatrice didn't want to unload this on her, either.

So Beatrice did what she always did: she folded her emotions away and buried them down deep. If she could pretend hard enough that everything was fine, maybe it would be.

The makeup artist gently tapped the corner of Beatrice's

eyelid with a brush, and Beatrice closed her eyes. At least Lilian and her silent signals hadn't changed in the past year.

"Your Majesty, are you sure you're ready for this?" Anju ventured. "I can postpone until next week—or at least make it an exclusive with Dave Dunleavy instead of an open conversation with every reporter in town."

"I'll be fine," Beatrice replied, eyes still closed.

To her surprise, Teddy spoke out in agreement. "Of course you will. You're an old pro at these; you could do a press briefing in your sleep."

Beatrice was startled into looking up at him. His blue eyes were fixed on hers with resolute purpose. It calmed the frantic beating of her pulse, as if his certainty was contagious.

In truth, she'd never liked addressing the media like this. She felt more at ease in one-on-one meetings, when she could look people in the eye and have something resembling a conversation. Big press conferences made her feel like a performer thrust onto a vast stage, alone, without really knowing her lines.

But she knew this was the right call. Doing an exclusive interview with Dave Dunleavy, as Anju had suggested, was the easy way out—and Beatrice's father had trained her to face challenges head-on.

Jefferson took a step forward. "Do you want me to go up there with you? We could make it a joint press conference, field the questions together."

"Thanks, but I should do this on my own," Beatrice assured him.

She was so proud of what Jeff had accomplished in her absence, especially given that his role within the monarchy had, until now, consisted of social interactions and "fluff" photo ops. Jeff was the Washington sibling sent out to play pool on a royal tour or sample peaches at a farmer's roadside stand; even in elementary school he'd been tasked with escorting the children of visiting diplomats to miniature golf or water parks. Actual governance was something new to him.

Beatrice hadn't been all that surprised when Jeff told her that he and Daphne were getting married in less than two months. "Do you want to slow things down?" she'd offered, but he'd just shaken his head and said the date was already set. They didn't speak of it again, and didn't need to. Beatrice understood why Jeff and Daphne had agreed to rush their wedding—to give the media something to salivate over while their queen was in a coma—just as she knew the reasons that they needed to move forward with the date they had set, even after Beatrice had woken up.

Americans may have accepted one canceled royal wedding, but they wouldn't be so forgiving a second time.

The makeup artist dusted powder over Beatrice's nose, then stepped back to survey her work. Anju gave a satisfied nod and began pulling the tissues from Beatrice's collar.

"If you're ready, Your Majesty, it's time."

All too soon, Beatrice was walking onto the stage in the Media Briefing Hall, with its intimidating wooden podium. She forced herself to keep her head high despite the blinding camera flashes, because, as her grandmother always used to say, only celebrities embroiled in a sex scandal looked down.

"Good afternoon, everyone," she began, but the microphone screeched with angry feedback. She winced apologetically.

"I'm so glad to be back and addressing you all again." A sea of unfamiliar faces stared up at her from the folding chairs below. Were all the reporters on the royal beat strangers now, or was her memory failing her? The lights were just overbright, Beatrice decided, squinting down at their blurred features.

She delivered her prepared speech, explaining how grateful she was for the care she'd received at St. Stephen's Hospital and for the prayers of millions of Americans, how she was recovered from her injuries and ready to resume her duties, and how excited she was for her brother and Daphne—because if they were going to get engaged as a human smoke screen, then she might as well play that to her advantage. Finally she cleared her throat and attempted a smile.

"Are there any questions?"

Every single reporter shot a hand into the air.

Fear snaked down Beatrice's spine. She was expected to call upon each reporter by name, to turn the press conference into a witty repartee of question-and-answer. Her father had always been so good at that. She swallowed against her rising panic and scanned the crowd for a friendly face, exhaling when she saw Dave Dunleavy in the front row.

"Mr. Dunleavy," she said into the microphone.

He stood and bowed. "Your Majesty, we were all thrilled to hear that the Queen's Ball would take place in the new year. Can you give us any hints of who might receive a title?" His smile let her know that the question was meant as a friendly softball. "Perhaps Miss Deighton, or Mr. Eaton?"

"Teddy?" Beatrice blurted out, startled. But he was already titled; he would inherit the Duchy of Boston someday. Unless . . .

Unless he'd renounced his rights out of loyalty to her.

He would have to do such a thing as king consort, but had Teddy gone ahead and relinquished the dukedom *before* they were married?

She realized that the silence had stretched out to an uncomfortable point and gave a nervous laugh: the one she used when someone had caught her off guard, which wasn't often. "Mr. Dunleavy, you know better than to ask me about matters that are best kept secret. I can't reveal the list of Queen's Ball honorees until it is published." She looked back out over the crowd. "Next?"

A reporter in a navy skirt suit jumped to her feet like a wind-up toy. Beatrice nodded, mind racing as she tried to remember the woman's name. "Yes, Miss . . ."

Her hands grabbed the sides of the podium in a death grip. God help her, she simply had no clue who this woman was.

"Helen Crosby," the reporter supplied, seeming hurt. "Your Majesty, you should know that we were all so impressed with the bill you championed at the League of Kings conference. Now that you're back in the office, what will you do to further its goals?"

Beatrice shot a panicked glance at Anju, who was standing in the wings. They'd spent the last day in a flurry of briefings on legislation and economic updates, yet Anju had never thought to recap the League of Kings conference? Anju was mouthing something, but Beatrice couldn't tell what it was. *Children?* Had Beatrice proposed some kind of global children's health initiative?

"I remain committed to global reform. Thank you for asking," Beatrice said, well aware that it was hopelessly vague. "Of course we will all continue the work we began at the conference, for the good of children everywhere."

The room felt suddenly stifling. Everyone was glancing at her with a puzzled expression, or whispering to one another, wondering if she had slipped up—and what it meant. She felt color rising to her face but forced herself to keep going.

When the press briefing was finally over and everyone rose to their feet, Beatrice fled into the hall. Her breath was coming fast and shallow, her throat hot with restrained tears—

She nearly collided with someone and drew to a startled halt. What was Lord Ambrose Madison doing at the palace?

"Your Majesty. Welcome back." He bowed, though the gesture was so cursory that it bordered on disrespect. Beatrice couldn't help marveling at his phrasing, the way he'd welcomed her to the palace as if it belonged to him. She'd never much liked the Duke of Virginia or his daughter, Gabriella, who was as coldly arrogant as her father.

And she couldn't forget that Ambrose had authored the bill stripping Samantha of her titles. Not that Beatrice was defending Sam's actions—it was hardly responsible of Sam, running off into the sunset like that—but hadn't Congress overreacted by removing her HRH?

"I hadn't expected to see you today, Your Grace."

"I came to your press conference, of course," he replied stiffly.

"Are you a member of the media now?" Beatrice said it like a joke, though her smile was edged.

The duke scoffed. "Please. As hereditary Queen's Champion, I'm entitled to attend all your press briefings." His voice was overly loud as he added, "I'm certainly glad that I did."

As if Queen's Champion were a real position. They both knew it was wholly ceremonial, the sort of thing that involved wearing an oversized plumed hat and standing onstage, reading names off a heavy paper scroll. No one actually expected Lord Virginia to *monitor* the queen.

"Well, thank you for your support." Beatrice tried to make it sound like a dismissal, but instead of leaving, the duke fell into step alongside her, uninvited.

"Your Majesty, I was startled to hear that you're already returning to work. I know I speak for my fellow congressmen when I beg you to slow down."

"You mean your fellow members of Congress," Beatrice corrected him. She sensed that he'd used the outdated term on purpose, as if the female members of Congress weren't even worth a mention.

Ambrose ignored her remark. "It might be best if we formalized the current situation."

"Current situation?"

"With Jefferson as your Regent. You're so delicate, and you've been through so much over the past year, between the loss of your father and the accident. You need to focus on your health."

His tone was slick with what he probably hoped sounded like avuncular concern, but Beatrice knew it for what it was—condescension.

"Let your brother carry the burden of government for you. You may think you've recovered, but after severe accidents, it's best not to push yourself too hard." He chuckled. "We wouldn't want you hurting yourself because you'd returned to work on a whim!"

Of course. When a man wanted something it was a need, but a woman's desires were merely a *whim*.

That thought sprang into Beatrice's head without warning, surprising her. It reminded her of someone, though she wasn't sure who.

"I appreciate your concern, but I'm the best judge of my own recovery," she insisted.

"You didn't seem recovered during that press conference. You seemed rather shaky."

When Beatrice kept walking, Ambrose reached out to put a hand on her forearm—as if he needed to physically restrain her, or warn her. To remind her of her place.

Beatrice jerked her arm away.

"Your Majesty, it's come to my attention that you're under the care of Dr. Malcolm Jacobs. A specialist in cognitive and neurological trauma."

"I was in a *car accident*. Of course I saw a specialist." Beatrice's words came out cool, though panic spiked in her blood again.

"So you're saying you suffered no mental damage? Your mind is exactly the same as it was before the accident? Because," he pressed, "I must remind you that you are required by law to inform Congress if there is something we need to know about your health. Specifically anything that prevents you from adequately performing your duties as queen. If you fail to do so," he added, "Congress can remove you from your position."

"Excuse me?" Beatrice felt heat creeping up her neck.

"The Constitution states in article one, section twenty-four that if the king is unfit to carry out the duties of his office, Congress can remove him from said office by a majority vote. At which point the heir apparent will—"

"I'm aware what the Constitution says. I was asking why you're threatening me with the unfit-to-rule clause," Beatrice interrupted.

"Threatening you?" Ambrose chuckled. "I would never do such a thing. Our families have been friends for three hundred years." A sour expression darted across his face as he glanced back toward the Media Briefing Hall. "You know, I always hoped that Gabriella might be the one to marry your brother. Just think . . . an alliance between the Madisons and the Washingtons. What a powerful couple they would be."

"It's not the nineteenth century anymore. I think we can stop talking about royal marriages as alliances."

"But isn't that precisely what you and Theodore have?"

He spoke the words carelessly, as if they weren't shockingly intrusive.

How dare you, Beatrice wanted to cry out, and *It's none of your business,* and strangest of all, *It's not like that between us.* Because it was exactly like that . . . wasn't it?

Why was some part of her ready to insist that she loved Teddy?

"Thank you for your concern. I'm grateful to have such a *dedicated* Queen's Champion." Beatrice nodded in the direction of the front door. "A footman can show you out."

Ambrose's expression darkened at the brusque dismissal.

"I'll be watching for your recovery," he said ominously, and stormed off.

Beatrice waited until he'd disappeared around the corner before drawing in a breath. She felt like her dress was tightening around her chest, her bobby pins digging tiny claws into her skull.

"Your Majesty?"

Through monumental force of will, Beatrice rearranged her features into something resembling a smile. She was relieved to see that Anju was alone.

"The press conference went well," Anju began, with forced cheerfulness. Beatrice didn't bother acknowledging the lie.

"Anju. If I ask you for a favor, can you keep it confidential?"

"Everything between us is confidential, Your Majesty."

"Thank you." Beatrice let out a breath. "I want you to help me track someone down. A former Revere Guard of mine, actually. His name is Connor Markham."

Anju seemed startled by the request, but nodded. "I'll start looking right away."

Maybe if Beatrice talked to Connor, the bewildering events of the past year would begin to make sense. Maybe then her memories—elusive, half-formed thoughts that melted away each time she reached for them—might start coming back.

11

SAMANTHA

"Give Jeff some time. I'm sure he'll come around," Marshall insisted.

Samantha nestled into Nina's couch, pressing the phone tighter to her ear. "I don't know, Marshall. We've never fought like this before."

She wasn't even sure if *fight* accurately described what had happened between her and Jeff. She'd come home to find that her entire life had imploded, including—or, rather, especially—the relationships she'd always taken for granted.

Thank god she still had Marshall. The moment she'd emerged from Beatrice's hospital room a few days ago, Sam had been relieved to find a text from Marshall's new burner phone. She'd immediately called him and shared everything that had happened since her arrival in Washington: Beatrice's memory loss, Jeff's anger, his engagement—and Congress's decision to strip her of her royal status.

"Jeff probably isn't thinking clearly right now," Marshall said. "He should have stood up to Congress when they removed your titles. That wasn't fair of him, or of them."

"Thank you for saying that," Sam murmured.

Neither of them mentioned the fact that Marshall's position as future Duke of Orange was still safe—that Sam was the only one who'd been punished by this. But then, she was more famous, and had a much bigger title to lose.

For better or worse, being a princess had shaped Sam's entire life. She had enjoyed it at times and hated it at times, but whether she was basking in it or grappling with it, her status had always been a part of her. Even in Hawaii, living under a false identity, she had assumed that she could go home and reclaim her old life when she was ready.

And just like that, it was gone.

"At least now your family can't be upset that you're dating a princess, since I'm not one anymore," Sam pointed out, striving for levity.

Marshall didn't laugh. "Sam . . . you know this wasn't how I wanted anything resolved. Not without you getting to *choose*."

She stared at the oak tree outside Nina's window, its limbs gently lifted by the wind. "I know."

Her royal status had been one of the many obstacles to their relationship, because a member of the royal family couldn't marry a duke or duchess. It was a conflict of interest.

Well, Congress had solved that problem for her.

"Oh, and I forgot to tell you—the tabloids coined a new word for my situation," she added. "*Samcelled*. As in Samantha was canceled."

Marshall groaned. "I didn't think it was possible for their puns to get worse, but they keep proving me wrong."

"Enough about me," Sam decided. "How are things on Molokai?"

Marshall clearly sensed that she needed a distraction, so he launched into a story about how he and Kai had encountered a pod of dolphins while surfing yesterday. "You'd never believe it, Sam! They weren't scared of us at all; they swam right up next to our boards. I ducked my head underwater and could hear them clicking to each other. . . ."

Sam closed her eyes, letting the low rumble of Marshall's voice steady her. It was a poor substitute for the real thing—she wanted to throw her arms around him, bury her face in his neck, feel the weight of his body against hers. But even hearing him on the phone helped settle the queasy anxiety that had had plagued her since she'd learned of Beatrice's accident.

When Marshall finally said he had to go, Sam could barely squeak out a goodbye. Her throat was burning. She started to toss aside her phone—only to pause at the BREAKING NEWS alert on her home screen. *The palace has confirmed Queen Beatrice's recovery! Her Majesty is expected to give a press conference today, sharing all the details. . . .*

Beatrice was giving a live press conference? *No, no,* Sam thought, this was a terrible idea. Why couldn't her sister have done a taped interview instead, something much safer and easier to control? She was doomed to slip up and reveal the extent of her memory loss.

Sam hurriedly changed into jeans, sunglasses, and one of Nina's King's College sweatshirts, pulling the hood low over her brow. She ducked into the hallway outside Nina's dorm room, where she nearly collided with Caleb, her Revere Guard.

"Oh my god, Caleb!" Her smile was flustered but genuine. "Have you been here the whole time?"

"Off and on. I wanted to make sure your cover wasn't blown."

Sam watched as he tucked a bag of M&M's guiltily into his pocket. It looked like Nina had paid him a visit.

"I need to get to the palace. Can you help?"

Caleb cleared his throat. "I have been instructed to take you nowhere but your grandmother's house, and to tell you that if you refuse to go there, I can no longer serve as your Guard. Since you are now a private citizen and not a working employee of the Crown, you're no longer entitled to security at the taxpayers' expense."

Sam should have known that her family would try to scare

her into compliance. And perhaps she was being stubborn, or difficult, but she couldn't bear the thought of letting them stuff her behind the high stone walls of Loughlin House as if she'd been excommunicated.

"Never mind, I'll figure something out," she started to say, but Caleb shook his head.

"I'll still bring you to the palace, of course. Just wanted you to know what you're up against. And, if you plan to keep going incognito, I have some advice."

Going incognito—was that what she was doing? Sam guessed so.

"I'm listening," she told him.

"Your hair is a huge help; don't dye it back. You're already good at using hoodies," he added, nodding to how she'd pulled the hood of Nina's sweatshirt low over her face. "Baseball caps work great, too. Glasses are surprisingly effective. I can get you some other disguises if you'd like—mustaches, false chins, pregnancy bumps . . ."

"I don't think a pregnancy bump would help my cause," she said drily, and Caleb smiled.

"Fair enough. The main thing is to avoid eye contact. People are inherently self-absorbed; half of them walk through life staring at their phones these days anyway. If you're somewhere crowded like a metro car, just keep moving, and look down. You'll be fine."

"What if I used a British accent?" Sam asked, speaking in what she liked to think of as a plucky Eliza Doolittle voice.

Caleb was visibly fighting not to laugh. "Maybe stick to the haircut."

Sam hurried down the corridor in the direction of the Media Briefing Hall, marveling at how eerie the palace felt without the usual bustle of tour groups. It was too quiet, like being on a school campus when everyone had gone home for the holidays.

When she heard voices coming from around the corner, Sam started forward, hoping to find Beatrice—but it was Jeff, and their mother.

"Oh, Sam." Queen Adelaide rushed forward, pulling her daughter into a hug so tight it nearly crushed the air from Sam's rib cage. "I've been so worried about you."

"I'm sorry, Mom." Her words were muffled into her mom's chest.

Adelaide took a step back but didn't let go. She kept a hand on Sam's elbow, as if afraid that the moment she released her, Sam would sprint off into hiding again. "Why haven't you gone to Loughlin House? It's so much safer there than Nina's dorm room!"

"Can I please just come home?" Sam replied. The question was plaintive and raw, causing her mom to shift her gaze uncomfortably.

Jeff let out a heavy breath. "It's not that simple. With everything going on . . . we need some time before we can figure out how to handle your return."

"I didn't realize I was something that had to be *handled*," Sam shot back.

Her mother flinched. "Please, Samantha, just until after the engagement party. Then we can find a way to ease you back into things, okay? It's simpler like this, I promise."

When her mom's meaning had sunk in, Sam drew in a breath.

"You and Daphne are having an engagement party?" she asked Jeff. He flushed, but nodded. "And I'm not included because I'm not *royal* anymore?"

"Sam, it's not really up to me, okay? It's a state occasion—"

"I've been to hundreds of state occasions," she reminded him, but Jeff cut her off.

"That was before!"

Before she'd run off, and lost her HRH, and become the black sheep that her family no longer knew how to handle.

Sam retreated a step, then another. "Fine. I'll get out of your hair."

"Sam, please," Jeff started to say, but she turned and ran off, just as everyone apparently expected her to do. She took the stairs two at a time and hurtled down the hall to her room—her old room, she supposed, since she wasn't welcome here anymore—and threw clothes into a suitcase, just wanting to get *away*, out of this nightmare world where nothing made sense and no one seemed to care about her. She had become a ghost in her own life.

It wasn't until she reached the door that led to the royal family's private garage that Sam remembered her car was still parked at King's College, in Nina's student spot.

She slumped against the back of the door and pressed her hands to her eyes, fighting an onslaught of tears.

"Are you okay?"

The young man who stood before her wore the palace valets' uniform of navy pants and a white shirt, but Sam would have recognized him anywhere. "Oh my god," she said slowly. "*Liam?*"

A light danced in his brown eyes, which glowed with mesmerizing flecks of green. "I wasn't sure you would remember."

She wiped quickly at her eyes and stood up straighter. "As if I could forget breaking out of the palace in a garbage truck."

"Garbage-truck joyrides, you never forget your first," he deadpanned.

Sam had met Liam the night she and Jeff graduated high school. He'd helped her sneak out of the palace and taken her to his band's concert—and then Sam had left on her gap-year trip the next morning, and never saw him again.

They had kissed that night, too. It felt a bit like cheating, that she was standing here remembering the feel of Liam's lips on hers, but she couldn't help what she'd done before she and Marshall started dating.

"What are you doing at the palace? I thought you quit," Sam asked, then winced. She hadn't meant for Liam to know that she'd gone looking for him.

When she and Jeff came back to town, she'd discovered that Liam no longer worked in the kitchens. She'd even dragged Nina to Enclave, that venue on the east side where his band had played—this time with her security team's knowledge and a tedious sweep of the space beforehand—but there was no sign of him.

"Our band headed to the West Coast," Liam explained. "Things didn't work out, obviously. I came back to Washington a month ago."

Right after she and Marshall had fled to Hawaii.

"It's good to see you. I mean—I'm sorry that your band didn't make it. But I'm glad you're okay." She eyed his uniform as she added, "And you're a valet now?"

He grinned. "I finally got promoted from garbage duty. The hours are more flexible, which is a huge help. Some of your snobby guests tip in hundred-dollar bills."

Sam refrained from pointing out that the guests who tipped that way might hope that Liam wouldn't just take them home, but would go home *with* them.

He reached for a set of keys on a hook. "So, am I taking you to Loughlin House? We get alerts on our phones," he added, when Sam glanced at him in surprise. "A notification already went out to the palace drivers, asking if anyone could take you there."

Sam shook her head. "I'm not going to Grandma Billie's. I just came out here to hide from my brother."

"I used to hide from my brother all the time," Liam replied, as if that was completely reasonable. "Did he do anything in particular?"

Sam huffed out a breath. "He let himself get pressured into this whole wedding, and now he doesn't want me at his engagement party. And on top of that my sister suffered severe head trauma and doesn't remember the past year! Sorry," she added belatedly, "please don't tell anyone that."

"Of course I won't tell." There was a beat of silence; then Liam smiled wryly. "Man, I thought my band had a lot of drama."

Sam chuckled. It seemed to loosen something in her chest, and she realized it was the first time in almost a week that she'd laughed.

"So if you aren't going to Loughlin House, where am I taking you? Back into hiding?"

"I wasn't in hiding." Sam hated that phrase. It made it sound like she'd committed a crime, like she'd been forced to slink away out of shame and fear.

Then again, fear had played a large part in her decision, hadn't it?

"I'm not going back," she went on, in a softer tone. "I'm just leaving the palace. I can't stay here now that I'm not a princess."

"What are you going to do, lease an apartment?"

"I can't afford an apartment."

"I find that hard to believe," Liam remarked.

Sam tugged her purse off her shoulder "This is all the money I have in the world."

He watched, clearly torn between amusement and shock, as she opened her hot-pink wallet and withdrew a tangle of old receipts, a punch card from her favorite taco truck on Molokai, and a few stray bills.

"You don't have a credit card?"

"I've been cut off from my bank accounts. That money belongs to the royal family, of which I'm no longer a part." Sam tried not to reveal how much it hurt to say that.

Liam cleared his throat awkwardly. "I'm sure you have better options, but you're welcome to crash with me and my housemates." When Sam hesitated, he hurried to add, "It's a coed house. Not just guys, I mean."

If the Washingtons were upset that Sam had gone to Nina's, they would be absolutely livid—not to mention appalled—at the prospect of her "crashing" with a palace employee.

Which was probably why Sam felt so tempted to say yes.

She'd felt isolated ever since she came back. Beatrice had literally forgotten her; Marshall was thousands of miles away; Nina was living her own life at school and didn't need Sam's drama.

But here was someone offering to help: making her feel a little less alone.

She looked back at Liam. "Your housemates wouldn't mind?"

"We always have friends coming and going from our place. It's like a revolving door of people who need to couch-surf."

That sounded perfect.

"Are we taking the garbage truck?" Sam asked, and Liam chuckled.

"I wouldn't have it any other way."

12

DAPHNE

Daphne removed her silken headband and set it on her vanity, which was scattered with moisturizers and makeup brushes and a silver eyelash curler that gleamed in the waning light, making it look eerily like a weapon. And really, these things *were* her weapons—the tools she wielded against the world.

Ever since that ominous email, she'd been on edge, jumping at every question from Jefferson or stray camera flash. At least the wedding was still on track. No one even mentioned the ultrasound appointment. The entire so-called pregnancy had been swept under the rug as if it had never happened, as if Daphne and Jefferson really *were* so carried away that they were rushing the wedding for love alone.

The only person who'd brought it up, strangely enough, was Queen Adelaide. When she saw Daphne after the fateful appointment, she had pulled her into a hug and murmured, *I'm so sorry. But don't worry, you're young; you have lots of time to be a mother!* And she must have spoken to the doctors, because now she was constantly trying to feed Daphne, scooping second helpings of potatoes onto her plate or passing her almonds when they were in the car together. It was endearing, actually.

Daphne smiled through it all, but she couldn't stop thinking about that email.

It had to be from Gabriella. In the middle of the night

Daphne would lie awake scrolling through Gabriella's social media, past kissy-face selfies and photos of Gabriella flouncing into parties wearing jumpsuits and heels. She studied every picture with furious intensity, searching for some clue as to how she could get Gabriella off her back.

Part of her longed to call her old best friend, Himari, if only to think this through with someone, but Himari had moved to Japan. Fleetingly, Daphne let herself think of Ethan, who'd sent a few cryptic messages over the past few days. Messages she had studiously ignored.

A noise sounded at her window, and Daphne froze. Had the paparazzi broken into her family's *yard*?

The tapping came from the side window, the one that overlooked the narrow strip of holly trees that ran between the Deightons' house and their neighbors'. Holding her breath, Daphne ventured over—only to gasp in mingled relief and outrage.

"Ethan!" She fumbled to open the window. "What are you *doing*?"

"You haven't answered any of my calls or texts." He spoke as if it were completely normal to throw pebbles at her window, like a character from some romantic comedy.

"How did you get in here, anyway?" she hissed.

Ethan ignored the question. They both knew that it wasn't the first time he'd snuck into or out of her family's house.

"Can we please just talk?" Ethan took a step closer, vulnerability flashing across his face. "I wouldn't ask if it wasn't important."

Against her better judgment, Daphne relented. "Fine."

She shut the window and angrily unzipped the high-waisted dress she'd worn to a charity event with Jefferson earlier. In her frustration she flung her necklace across the room and it broke, scattering pearls over her floor like teardrops.

Great. Now she would have to hunt them all down and have the necklace restrung.

When she stepped outside in black leggings and a puffy dark jacket, Ethan was waiting for her. "Let's go," he said brusquely, which was when Daphne noticed the motorcycle parked in the alley behind her house.

She retreated a step. "Since when do you have a motorcycle? You can't seriously expect me to get on that thing!"

Ethan held out a spare helmet. "Do you have a better suggestion? Maybe we should walk back through your side yard and wave at the paparazzi out front?" He nodded at the alley. "There's no one this way. And even if there was, they wouldn't recognize you. You look like you plan on robbing a bank," he added, eyeing her all-black ensemble with a smirk.

Daphne rolled her eyes but tucked her hair into a knot, then buckled the helmet under her chin. "I don't see why you get to drive and I have to be the passenger."

"I'm happy for you to drive if you have a motorcycle license," Ethan said pleasantly. When she didn't reply, he patted the seat behind him. "Hop on, Daph."

Her body blazed with tiny flames of anger. It felt shockingly liberating, being so openly furious with him, not having to act polite or *sweet*.

She climbed onto the back of the bike, looping her arms as lightly as she could around his torso.

"You need to hold on a little tighter if you don't want to fall off." There was an unmistakable note of laughter in Ethan's voice, as if he was tempted to remind her that they had touched in far more intimate ways than this.

"Don't get any ideas," she muttered.

The motorcycle leapt forward, and she gritted her teeth in surprise. But as Ethan drove through the familiar streets, turning corners with practiced ease, Daphne felt herself slowly relax. She'd never seen the capital from this vantage point before.

There was a cold mist in the air. It smudged golden halos around the streetlights, made Daphne's eyelashes feel damp and heavy. Ethan's motorcycle cut past evening buses, past cars full of people who had no idea their future princess was in the next lane, on a motorcycle.

Daphne was oddly unsurprised when Ethan turned onto the campus of Forsythe Academy, the private school he and Jefferson had both attended. She should have known he would bring them back here, to where it all began.

"Interesting choice of venue," she observed, once he had pulled up to the elementary school playground and killed the engine.

Ethan shrugged. "I figured we'll see anyone coming a mile away."

Daphne studied the playground the way a general might assess the terrain before battle. She had to admit, Ethan was right. The playground's open spaces meant that no one could hide and eavesdrop, and it was only accessible by bike paths. No paparazzi cars could drive by with a long-range lens.

As she glanced around, Daphne felt something in her soften. This playground was a little kid's dreamland, with multiple slides and three different jungle gyms and an enormous painted elephant with a saddle on top. A wooden ladder led up its tail.

"Jeff and I used to climb that elephant all the time," Ethan remarked, following her gaze. He pointed to a spot on the ground a couple of yards away. "There used to be a tree here, but they cut it down because of Jeff."

"What?"

"He climbed from the elephant into the branches of the tree, then jumped from the tree onto the roof, where he rescued generations' worth of lost baseballs. Seriously, I think he tossed down thirty of them." Ethan smiled at the memory. "His protection officer was livid, but Jeff didn't care. From that point on, his second-grade street cred was astronomical."

"That sounds like Jefferson." Daphne couldn't help thinking that it was easy to be fearless when, for your entire life, someone had held out a safety net to protect you from falling.

She crossed her arms over her chest, trying to get things back on track. "Okay, Ethan. What's going on?"

"I was hoping you could explain this."

He clicked over to his email app and held out his phone.

Daphne's stomach twisted as she saw the message in his inbox, so similar to hers. The same anonymous email address, the same empty subject line. Almost the same message, though it had been tweaked for him: *Ethan, I know what you and Daphne did. You need to break up the royal wedding or I'll tell the world about you.*

She read the words once, twice, a third time. A chill danced over her skin, and she thrust the phone toward Ethan as if it were a live grenade.

"Are you suggesting I *sent* that email?" she asked, incredulous. "Why would I threaten you and demand that you break up my wedding?"

Ethan threw his hands up. "I don't know! To undermine me? To make Jeff think I betrayed him, and draw him closer to you? I don't pretend to understand how your demonically brilliant mind works."

If she didn't know better, Daphne might have thought that last sentence was a compliment.

"I didn't send it. In fact . . ." Before Daphne could think better of it, she'd pulled out her phone, then scrolled to her own cryptic email. "I got basically the same message."

Ethan's expression darkened as he read it. "So, whoever is behind this is blackmailing us both."

"Apparently so." Daphne snatched her phone back and stuffed it in her bag, face reddening.

"What should we do?"

"*We* are not doing anything, because there is no *we.*"

Ethan's brows drew together. "You're just going to ignore this?"

"Absolutely not. I'm going to handle it."

"On your own."

"Yes, on my own! It's how I do most things."

"And how's that working out for you?"

"Just fine until you came back!"

Ethan made a disbelieving sound in the back of his throat. "Look, Daphne, I don't like this any more than you do, but we both have too much at stake. This person knows what we did to Himari."

His words gave her pause. "Is that how you read it?"

"How else would you read it?"

"That she knows about *us.*" Suddenly Daphne couldn't make eye contact with him. "That I cheated on my boyfriend with you; that you betrayed your best friend."

"What makes you think it's a she?"

"It's Gabriella."

Ethan retreated a few steps and sank onto a swing, closing his hands around the cold metal chains. Daphne hesitated before taking the swing next to him. She yanked out her bun and tossed her hair angrily over one shoulder, then kicked against the ground so that her swing lurched back.

"Gabriella Madison?" Ethan asked slowly. "That doesn't make sense. I hardly know her."

"She's going after *me.* You're just caught in the cross fire." Daphne leaned forward, and Ethan started swinging just a little bit higher than she was. Typical.

"If it's really Gabriella, then we have to work together on

this. We don't stand a chance against the Madisons on our own," he pointed out.

"Ethan, you and I are *incapable* of working together! We don't even trust each other!"

He was silent for so long that she felt compelled to look over and meet his gaze. When she did, his expression was uncharacteristically serious.

"I trust you, Daphne."

She started to reply, something flippant or caustic like *You should know better,* but the words died on her lips. Ethan was looking at her in a way that rattled something deep within her.

"I trust you," he said again, "and you know that you can trust me. The one thing you and I have never done is lie to each other."

Daphne realized, a bit stunned, that he was right. She'd spent her entire life lying, by innuendo and omission and, when necessary, outright falsehood. Yet she and Ethan had never dealt in anything but the truth.

Her swinging slowed.

Things between them were so complicated. Over the years they'd been antagonists, lovers, allies, keepers of each other's darkest secrets, and, in their own strange way, friends. Or at least, two of a kind. They were both outsiders who wanted to belong.

Maybe they could team up one last time, just to free themselves of this threat.

"If we do this, I'll need some kind of leverage over you. Otherwise how would I know you aren't working with Gabriella to double-cross me?" she added, at Ethan's confused look.

"Double-cross you? Why would I do that?"

"It's what *Nina* did!"

She was gratified by the surprise on Ethan's face. "What do you mean?"

Suddenly, the whole awful story came spilling out of her: how she and Nina had teamed up to take down Gabriella, how Nina had betrayed her. It was a relief to finally share this with someone after months of keeping it bottled up inside.

"You really think Nina was playing you?" Ethan asked, when Daphne had finished talking.

"I do."

She'd seen Nina and Jefferson together in the gardens that night—the same night that Nina's scholarship had been reinstated, while Daphne's life had nearly fallen apart.

"It just doesn't sound like Nina," Ethan murmured.

Daphne twisted the metal chain of the swing as realization struck. "But it makes sense! How else would Gabriella have known about you and me? Nina must have told her!"

Ethan's eyes widened. "You told *Nina* we hooked up?"

"No, of course not! She figured it out. She's observant and smart, I'll give her that," Daphne said grudgingly.

She thought back to that confrontation, in the aftermath of Beatrice and Teddy's almost-wedding. Nina had looked at her with dawning comprehension and said, *You're in love with Ethan, aren't you? You've always loved him.* And Daphne hadn't denied it.

Well, it might have been true back then, but it wasn't anymore.

Nina had clearly shared all this with Gabriella, who'd decided it was too juicy a secret not to make use of.

Ethan kicked a sneaker against the shredded rubber underfoot. "I talked with Nina once or twice while I was abroad. She never mentioned any of this."

A strange annoyance prickled in Daphne's chest at the thought of Ethan video-chatting with Nina. "She wouldn't exactly have bragged about it, would she?"

"I just feel like I would have noticed if she'd changed that much."

"We all changed while you were gone. Including you," Daphne said pointedly. "Speaking of which, since when do you drive a motorcycle?"

"Since it was the easiest way to get around Malaysia."

"You've come a long way from your blue beach cruiser." Her words were surprisingly soft, almost nostalgic.

For most of high school, Daphne and Ethan had been the only ones in their group of friends without a car—because, of course, they were the only ones who came from families without massive bank accounts. Sometimes they rode their bikes home from school together, since their routes were the same until they parted ways on Wright Street.

Daphne was struck by the memory of a time they'd been caught in a downpour. Ethan had taken off his windbreaker and draped it over her head in a futile effort to keep her dry, and the two of them had ended up standing there in the rain, soaked through and laughing at how ridiculous it all was.

"I'm still not convinced that the emails came from Gabriella," Ethan insisted. "We should track who sent the email."

"How?" Daphne scoffed. "Do you have a hacker on staff I don't know about?"

Ethan's mouth lifted in a half smile. "Not on staff, exactly, but I know someone. We'll figure this out."

That *we* seemed to echo across the deserted playground, though Ethan had spoken it quietly. Daphne felt it then: the echo of their old friendship stirring between them.

"If we're really going to work together, I have some ground rules," she decided. "Neither of us does anything without the other's approval, and we can both call this off at any time. And we only communicate in person. No texting. I can't afford a paper trail."

Ethan nodded. "Fair enough. But if you're going to impose rules, I think I'm allowed a rule of my own."

Daphne gestured for him to go ahead, and he planted his

feet on the ground, abruptly stopping the movement of his swing.

"We can't hook up again. It's too risky."

A tension stretched out between them, as if they were holding opposite ends of a rubber band and tugging it to its tautest point. Daphne was unnervingly aware of everything: her heart beating against her ribs, the distant rumble of traffic, the weight of Ethan's gaze on hers.

She forced herself to laugh, breaking the strange moment. "In your dreams, Ethan."

"In my dreams, or yours?" He was smiling his light, irreverent smile again. "After all, it wouldn't be the first time."

"Just take me home now, please." Daphne started marching toward the motorcycle before Ethan realized that she was smiling, too.

13

SAMANTHA

"You live on the east side?" Sam asked as Liam exited the freeway onto Donovan Street. Walk-up apartments were wedged between neon-lit bars, tattoo parlors, and bodegas. Colorful murals sprawled over the walls, bright with messages like LOVE IS ALL YOU NEED or DON'T LET THE CROWN GET YOU DOWN. Sam blinked, wondering if she'd misread that one, but it was already behind them.

"You could also say that I live in Tribedo. The triangle below Donovan," Liam clarified. When Sam frowned in confusion, he added, "You know Donovan Street is the edge of the gentrified section, right? Above Donovan it's all hipster boutiques and coffee shops with oat milk. Down here in Tribedo it's . . . well, it's not," he finished.

Sam had never heard that nickname before; but she was realizing that there were many things about her city she didn't know.

She pulled out her phone and shot Marshall a quick text: *I'm not staying at the palace, long story. Call me later?*

It was still early in Hawaii; surely she would catch Marshall after his morning surf lesson.

"Ah, here we are. Home sweet home." Liam pulled up the driveway of a ramshackle old house, a Victorian wood-frame with a second story that drooped wearily above the first. The wooden railings were carved with whimsical scrollwork and painted a color that had probably once been purple, or maybe blue, but was now a dingy and peeling gray.

Liam insisted on carrying her suitcase up the front steps. Sam followed, wondering how it had come to this—her family shuffling her aside as if she were a sordid secret, forcing her to couch-surf with people she hardly knew.

Well, she would show everyone that she could stand on her own two feet. She was still Samantha, and she was a force to be reckoned with, with or without a title.

Liam glanced over before opening the door. "I should warn you, this isn't the palace. . . ."

"It's perfect," Sam assured him, stepping inside.

The living room held a mishmash of secondhand furniture: the coffee table scattered with half-open bags of barbecue potato chips and the remnants of a pizza, scarves and winter coats thrown over the backs of chairs with abandon.

A blanket on the couch moved as the boy who'd been napping beneath it sat up. "Hey, Liam," he mumbled, rubbing blearily at his eyes. Then his glance drifted to Sam.

"Sorry, have we met?"

She paused for a moment, still not used to the whole not-being-recognized thing. "Nice to meet you. I'm Martha."

A part of her still expected this stranger to cry out in sudden recognition and snap a picture with his phone, but he just shrugged. "Cool. How long have you guys been . . . ?"

He trailed off meaningfully, and Sam felt her cheeks reddening.

"It's nothing like that, I'm just—"

"Martha's crashing here for a while. I told her it was okay," Liam cut in. "She can take Jesse's old room, right?"

"You'll have to clear out Jessica's second closet," the guy on the couch warned.

Sam looked from one of them to the other, trying to keep up. "How many people live here, exactly?"

"Aside from me and Ben," Liam began, nudging the guy on the couch, "there are Amber and Talal—they pay the most rent so they get the biggest room. Then there's Jessica . . . Leah, but only sometimes . . ."

Sam was nodding along, wondering how she would possibly keep track of all these people, when Ben asked, "Where did you guys meet?"

"Martha came to one of our shows, way back before LA," Liam answered.

"Ahh. A groupie," Ben teased. Sam rolled her eyes, and he laughed appreciatively. "So, Martha, what do you do?"

It took her a moment to realize that he was asking about work. "Oh . . . I'm between jobs at the moment," she said evasively. Some part of her must have wanted to share a real truth, because she heard herself add, "I was living at home before this, but my family kicked me out."

"Whoa." Ben sounded impressed by this. "You must be really rebellious."

I just spent too many years dancing on tables and making trouble, then fled the country and lived under a fake name in Hawaii while my sister was in a coma.

"They don't really understand me," Sam said quietly.

Ben was still frowning at her face. "Has anyone ever told you that you look like Princess Samantha?"

Sam shrugged, though her heart had picked up speed. "I've heard that before, yeah."

"Liam totally had a thing for her." Ben chuckled, and Sam saw Liam's face redden. "He claims that he actually talked to her once, and she wasn't nearly as much a spoiled brat as she seemed."

Liam took a step toward the hall, still carrying her suitcase. "Come on, Martha, I'll show you Jesse's old room."

Sam hurried after him, her mind still spinning from Ben's words. Liam had told his friends about her? And also—

121

"Do people really think I'm bratty?"

"Not at all," Liam said, too quickly. "Or at least, um, not any brattier than any other princess?"

Sam sighed. "It's okay. I've seen the headlines about me."

They walked in silence for a few moments. Then Liam cleared his throat. "What you said, about your family not understanding you—I know what that's like. My parents were so upset when I got serious about the band. They wanted me to become an accountant, just like the two of them. They met at their accounting firm thirty years ago, and they both *still work there.*" He sighed in a way that was both amused and frustrated. "Parents, always trying to turn us into little replicas of themselves, ignoring the ways that we are completely different from them."

"That's really insightful," Sam told him.

She of all people knew how complicated families could be: how you could love them and resent them all at once; how you could be grateful to them for shaping you into the person you'd become, and at the same time feel desperate to break out of the mold they had cast you into.

"Sometimes I worry my parents are right, though. That I should give up music," Liam said gruffly. "I'm not exactly a rock star."

"Don't do that." Unthinking, Sam reached for his wrist, forcing him to pause. She quickly let go. "Don't second-guess yourself. You're so talented."

Somehow the silence that followed his words was stranger than the touch had been. Liam was the first to break eye contact. He stepped toward a pair of French doors, smiling.

"Maybe you should take your own advice, *Martha*. Don't let your family, or anyone else, make you feel like you're not good enough."

Before she could answer that, he threw open the doors,

revealing a small space with floor-to-ceiling windows. Boxes labeled JESSICA ALBRIGHT in Sharpie bubble letters were stacked in the middle of the room; Liam unapologetically began shoving them to one side.

"This was supposed to be a dining room, but I mean, who actually *uses* a formal dining room? Sorry, I'm probably asking the wrong person," he added wryly.

Sam tried to hide her trepidation. Where was the closest bathroom? "I've never slept in a dining room before," she said warily.

"Here, I'll help you set up the air mattress," Liam offered, which was when Sam noticed a giant plastic thing in the corner.

She watched in mute fascination as Liam unfurled it, then pressed a button. The mattress began filling with an angry whirring sound. Liam looked up to meet Sam's gaze, his hair falling into his face, and grinned.

"You've never set up an air mattress before, have you?"

"Of course I have. I'm just distracted by how unbearably loud yours is," Sam fibbed. Before Hawaii, the only mattresses she'd ever slept on were real ones, handmade in Sweden out of cotton and thick-spun wool and layers of very expensive horsehair.

Liam reached for a set of sheets and began tugging one corner over the edge of the air mattress. Sam tried her best to help, ignoring how intimate it felt for Liam to be setting up the place where she would sleep. He obviously didn't think it was weird, and for all Sam knew, maybe it wasn't. Hadn't he said that they had guests constantly coming in and out of this house?

A clamor of voices made them both look up. Liam rocked back on his heels, grimacing slightly. "That's the main drawback of this space—you hear everything in the living room."

"Are those the rest of your housemates?" Sam stood, raking fingers through her cropped hair. "Can you introduce me?"

"I don't know if this is a great time. We're all about to go out," Liam began, but Sam cut him off.

"A night out sounds like *exactly* what the doctor ordered."

As it turned out, the group was headed to Enclave, the very same bar where Sam had snuck out to see Liam's band on her graduation night. When they headed through the side entrance, Sam saw that it was just as she remembered: dimly lit and smelling faintly of beer. A pre-concert anticipation buzzed in the air.

I should bring Marshall here, she thought, which only made her sadder, because she might never get the chance to.

She turned to Jessica—Liam had introduced them earlier, at which point Jessica had apologized for all the clothes, and urged Sam to borrow whatever she wanted. "Should we stake out spots near the stage?"

Jessica shot her a concerned glance. "Liam didn't tell you? We all work here."

"At Enclave?"

"Amber is the sound tech, Leah and I are bartenders, Talal works security, and you already know that Ben and Liam are in the band." Jessica reached up to pull her glossy dark hair into a ponytail. "It was how we all met, actually."

"That makes sense." Sam's eyes darted around the venue, which was filling up by the minute. Instinctively she pulled her fedora lower over her brow. "Well, I'll just find a spot, and—"

"Jessica!" An impatient-looking woman strode toward them. "I need you to work your section plus Deborah's tonight; she just quit. God, this is not the night I wanted to be under-staffed. It's a sold-out show." She closed her eyes and pressed her fingers to her temples, groaning.

"A sold-out show? Good for Liam," Sam exclaimed, before she could think better of it.

The woman glanced over, then looked at Sam for a beat too long, her eyes studying Sam's face. "Sorry, have we met? You look so familiar . . ."

"I'm a friend of Liam's," Sam said quickly.

"Well, new girl, how well can you open beer bottles?"

Sam blinked, and the woman threw out a hand to indicate the venue. "This is going to be a rough night for us without enough bartenders. Are you looking for work? As of now, we're hiring."

The old familiar sense of adventure crackled through Sam. Work as a bartender for the night? There were a million reasons it was a terrible idea.

"I'd love to," she declared.

She'd *been out* to bars plenty of times in her life. Surely she could handle being on the other side of things for once.

After that, the night passed in a blur of beer bottles and shouted demands, of credit-card receipts and customers whining when she got their drink orders wrong. Sam felt like she was running from one crisis to the next, she and the other bartenders elbowing past each other as they navigated the length of the bar. Her feet hurt in her strappy heels and she sliced her hand chopping limes and the cut stung when she accidentally got vodka on it.

It was exhilarating.

Whenever she could catch her breath, Sam stole a proud glance at the stage. Liam's band really was good. Their music seemed to echo the pulse of her heartbeat, its emotion raw and vulnerable yet somehow strong, too.

Eventually, the room dissolved in hoarse shouts and applause, and the houselights went up.

Sam blinked, wishing she could look at her phone to check the time; wasn't this bar open until two a.m.? Had it really gotten that late? She focused on handing over the last few receipts, waiting as security slowly shuffled everyone out of Enclave, the stage lights dimming and then going off.

"New girl, you did okay tonight." The manager peeled some bills from a stack and handed them to her.

Sam fought back a smile. The cash felt almost hot in her hand, as if it radiated its own energy. This was the very first money she'd ever earned on her own—or at least the first American money. And it felt somehow more momentous than everything Brad had paid her back in Hawaii, because she was doing it here, on her home turf.

"Who wants a drink?" Liam came to stand behind her and Jessica, throwing an arm around each of their shoulders. "I'd say we've earned one."

"Isn't the bar closed?" Sam asked.

Liam laughed appreciatively. "It's closed to the general public, but we work here. We're just grabbing our closing drink." He took a few beer bottles from behind the bar and began handing them out. The rest of the bartenders and security staff started gathering around: a much smaller group than had been in this room half an hour ago, yet the space vibrated with noise as everyone struggled to be heard over one another.

"I'm telling you, the way people responded to 'Not This Time'! I told you that song was a winner—"

"Did you see Jenna in the audience? She and Nat are back together—"

"No! *Again?*"

"We need to stock more bar mops behind the bar, it's getting way too stressful halfway through shift—"

Someone plugged their phone into an aux cord; Amber kicked off her shoes and began twirling a slow circle barefoot, laughing deliriously until Talal came and swept her off her feet. Sam felt a sudden rush of affection for them all.

"So? You really worked behind the bar tonight?" Liam asked.

"It went great. No problems at all," she assured him before he could ask if she'd been recognized.

Perhaps that was the strangest thing about the entire night: that no one had realized who she was. It might have been the dim lighting, or the haircut and fedora, but Sam suspected that a huge factor was the fact that she'd been behind the bar rather than out in the crowd. Everyone had been so focused on getting their drinks and returning to the concert that they'd hardly glanced at her face—had looked through her, not *at* her.

"Hey, Martha!" Jessica called out, holding the phone that was plugged into the speakers. "What's your favorite song?"

A giddy exhilaration coursed through Sam. Her entire life, people had made snap judgments about her—had decided what they thought of her before they even met her. It was such a relief to interact with someone without a host of preconceived notions and opinions in the way.

She hesitated a moment, then went to Jessica, who obediently passed her the phone. Sam kept scrolling until she found what she was looking for.

The opening notes of the song—a vibrant guitar riff, intercut with a saxophone—echoed through the room. A few people let out shouts of excitement or began laughing. "Do you remember . . . ," the entire room sang at once.

As the song built through the chorus, everyone's voices drew out the last vowels: "Never was a cloudy dayyyy!"

Liam laughed approvingly. "I should have known you had good taste in music. Here's to that," he added, holding up his beer bottle to Sam's.

Sam clinked her glass to his. "And to new beginnings," she told him, smiling.

14

BEATRICE

"Who is this?" Anju clicked to bring up another image on the projector.

Beatrice immediately recognized the person in the photo, though Anju was trying to trick her, using a picture of this young woman in leggings instead of a tiara. "That's Princess Louise." *My friend*, some part of her wanted to add, but she pursed her lips and said nothing.

This had happened a few times lately—a voice emerging from the depths of her, chiming in with a fact or opinion that left her conscious mind bewildered. Dr. Jacobs had assured her that it was a good sign.

He didn't know how unsettling it felt: as if there was the ghost of another Beatrice, the one who'd gotten in the car accident, tangled within her.

She sighed and looked back up at the screen. She had been in this sitting room for an hour while Anju quizzed her on a collection of photos. According to Dr. Jacobs, seeing images of the people in her life would help reawaken the neural pathways that had fallen dormant.

At least it was more interesting than yesterday's activity, when Anju had forced her to review vocabulary words. They had started at the fourth-grade level, then quickly made their way upward once Beatrice started using terms like *Ruritanian* and *grandiloquence*, hoping to make it stop. Delighted, Anju had switched tacks and started quizzing Beatrice in French and German, all of which she'd passed with flying colors.

If only she could summon her own memories as easily as she could vocabulary words in foreign languages.

Anju clicked to another slide. "And who is this?"

The young man in the photo looked familiar, with bright blue eyes, thick blond hair, and broad shoulders. A memory hovered at the edge of Beatrice's mind, as if someone was waving a Polaroid photo maddeningly out of reach. . . . She saw a cozy sectional couch, a video-game remote in her hand; and, perhaps most strangely of all, she felt a buoyant joy in her chest, the sort of carefree childish joy she hadn't felt in a long time. . . .

Beatrice closed her eyes, willing the snapshot to come into clearer focus, but it had already dissolved.

She looked back up to see Anju watching her carefully. Her gaze turned to the young man in the image once more. Come to think of it, he looked a lot like Teddy.

"That's Teddy's brother," she guessed. "Lewis?"

"Very good!"

Beatrice squirmed guiltily at the thought of Teddy. He'd been trying to see her ever since she'd come back to the palace, but she'd managed to avoid him thus far, cowardly as it was.

"Anju," she asked abruptly, "have you made any progress on finding Connor Markham?"

Anju's brows drew together, but she quickly smoothed her expression. Perhaps she'd started to suspect why Beatrice was asking about him.

"He seems to have left the capital, and I can't find a forwarding address. I'm happy to outsource this to a private investigator, or ask around among the other Guards, but I was under the impression that you wanted this to stay between us."

"Yes," Beatrice said quickly. The last thing she wanted was some PI digging through her history with Connor. "Just keep searching, and let me know once you find anything. I think we're done for today," she added, and Anju nodded in understanding.

Beatrice stood, her mind spinning with half-formed thoughts. At first it had felt strange to be in the palace without Connor, but so many things were off-balance right now—the loss of her father, the disorienting fact of being queen, the wary scrutiny with which the media was studying her. Connor's absence was just one small part of the *wrongness* that seemed to confront her at every turn.

She stepped out into the hall, only to slow at the sound of jangling up ahead. Moments later, Teddy turned the corner, a yellow lab trotting along after him.

Beatrice wanted to turn around, pretend she hadn't seen him, but a cautious smile had already risen to Teddy's face. And the dog leapt toward her so eagerly that Beatrice couldn't help going to meet him, kneeling down to rub her hands behind her ears.

"Hello there." Beatrice chuckled as the lab covered her face with sloppy kisses. "Who are you?"

When the silence had stretched for a beat too long, she looked up at Teddy. He cleared his throat awkwardly. "This is Franklin, Bee. You and I adopted him together."

That was when she noticed that Franklin's dog tag was monogrammed with two simple letters: *BR*. Her monogram—Beatrice Regina.

"We got a *dog*?" The words came out in a whisper.

"He's more your dog than mine. Probably because you slip him treats all the time." Teddy hesitated. "He's really missed you. I was going to bring him by sooner, but I figured that with everything else going on, you didn't have time to . . ."

To take care of a dog she didn't remember.

"We were about to go on a walk, if you want to come?" Teddy added hopefully. "We can take the wheelchair."

"No."

Franklin whined and nudged her leg as if he understood her rejection. Something in Beatrice melted a little, and she sighed. "I mean, no wheelchair. I need to build up my strength."

She was already second-guessing that decision when they reached the steps down to the gardens. Teddy held out a hand, but Beatrice ignored it, clutching the iron handrail so tight that it left a red mark on her palm. She made it to the bottom of the steps and started gratefully onto the path, her shoes crunching over the gravel.

Franklin's tail twitched eagerly back and forth, until Teddy bent down to let him off his leash. The dog yelped in excitement and took off running.

Beatrice kept waiting for Teddy to say something, but he didn't. He let her stroll along in contemplative silence—which should have been relaxing, since silence was what she wanted. But it unnerved her a little that he seemed to sense that. When had Teddy become so attuned to her moods?

They passed a marble plinth where a statue of King Edward I used to stand, and Beatrice paused. In its place was a statue of a woman with long hair, her skirts twisting around her legs as she stared into the distance. She wasn't smiling, yet there was something unmistakably playful about the arch of her eyebrows.

Beatrice stepped forward, wincing a little at the unsteadiness in her legs. The plaque beneath the statue read QUEEN EMILY I, 1830–?, R. 1855–1855.

Emily, the one other woman who could claim to have been Queen of America, though she ruled for only a single day before she mysteriously vanished.

Beatrice had always accepted the general historical opinion that Emily was assassinated in a political coup, despite the romantics who claimed she'd run away from it all to live with a commoner. It had always sounded like fantasy to Beatrice.

Though she had to admit, it didn't sound as outlandish as it used to, now that Samantha had done something similar.

"When did they replace the statue of Edward I?" she wondered aloud.

"You did that," Teddy said softly. "You said there were more than enough statues of Edward I around this city, and it was time we recognized some other people for a change. Especially the women and people from marginalized backgrounds who had been erased from history."

The statue of Emily seemed to be staring at her with a bold confidence that Beatrice didn't share. She sighed. "It's nice to know I did some good things while I was queen."

"Don't use the past tense. You're still queen," Teddy protested.

"Except I don't feel like much of a queen."

Beatrice turned aside, and as she did, her knees gave way beneath her. She started to collapse—

Teddy swept forward and caught her, bracing his hands beneath her elbows, pulling her ever so slightly closer to his chest.

For a split second they stood suspended like that, as immobile as the statue behind them. Despite their stillness, Beatrice's heart was pounding, every nerve ending in her skin flaring to life. She saw the rise and fall of Teddy's chest beneath his jacket, his breath as unsteady as her own.

Panic laced through her, and she stumbled back as if scorched.

"I'm sorry," Teddy stammered. "I didn't—I wasn't—"

"It's fine," Beatrice said tersely.

She saw a stone bench a few yards away and started toward it with ponderous steps. Teddy stayed close, but didn't make another move to touch her.

When she lowered herself onto the bench, Beatrice drew in a ragged breath. The air burned in her lungs. "Look, Teddy, I just can't do this."

He was silent in the long, drawn-out way that meant something. When she finally looked up, his expression was pained. "What do you mean?"

She tore her gaze away. She stared everywhere else—at Franklin, running in circles farther down the path; at the wintry skies overhead; anywhere but at the piercing blue of Teddy's eyes.

"You and me. I don't . . . ," she fumbled, unable to finish the sentence.

"I know you don't remember, Bee. It's okay." There was something so soothing in Teddy's voice, something about the way he said *It's okay* that made her want to believe it really *was* okay, despite all evidence to the contrary. "You'll get your memories back," he added.

"What if I don't?"

Teddy was undaunted. "I want to help. We can look at photos of things we did together, visit the places we went. I know it might take a while, but if we jog your memory, it'll come back—"

"*Stop!*"

The word had burst out of her, just one short syllable, but it might as well have been a gunshot. Teddy broke off abruptly, and she winced.

"I'm sorry, but I don't remember, okay? The things that happened between us . . . it's like they didn't happen for me. Right now I just need to focus on getting better."

She couldn't handle any of it right now—the expectant, hopeful way Teddy was looking at her; the weight of a one-sided history. There was too much to process without adding another person's emotional burden to the mix.

"Are you saying you want to break up?" Teddy's question came out hoarse.

Yes, she should have replied. An unthinking, automatic *yes.* Yet the word didn't come.

"I'm asking you to stop trying to repair a relationship I can't remember." She shook her head. "With everything that's happened, with Jeff and Daphne's wedding coming up, we can't afford any more upheavals. Can you please just act like my fiancé for a while longer? We can figure everything out after Jeff's wedding. But I can't do this," she added helplessly. "Not right now." *Not while Congress is threatening to have me deposed.*

Teddy was deadly still. The echo of her words seemed to ring between them, hollow and cruel, and Beatrice felt a sudden pang in her stomach.

Somehow, inexplicably, she felt protective of Teddy's feelings. Which was especially confusing since *she* was the one who had hurt him.

"Of course," Teddy said at last. His voice was different, as if all the joy had been vacuumed out of it, and his eyes were flat and emotionless too. "I won't say anything romantic again."

A bleak silence stretched between them. Beatrice told herself it was better this way. They needed to establish a clear boundary before Teddy got his hopes up.

If she didn't remember their past, how could Teddy possibly expect to share her future?

15

DAPHNE

"I can't believe I agreed to ride your motorcycle again." Daphne quickly withdrew her arms from where they'd been wrapped around Ethan's torso and stepped onto the curb, tugging her hat lower over her hair.

"Please, you love the bike," Ethan insisted. "It's a manifestation of all the reckless things you won't be allowed to do anymore once you're a princess."

Daphne shot him a look, wondering just what he meant to imply by reckless and forbidden things, but then she took in their surroundings and faltered.

A deserted-looking office building stared down at them. "Are you sure this is the right place?" she asked dubiously.

"Yep." Ethan started toward the lobby, and she trotted to keep up.

"How do you even know a hacker?"

"Ray and I go way back. We were on the same T-ball team in elementary school, actually." Ethan pushed open the door to the staircase, flicking on a switch that illuminated the fluorescent lights overhead.

"This feels like a murder scene in a horror movie," Daphne said under her breath. Ethan ignored her.

They emerged into a half-finished office space. Paint buckets and empty water bottles were scattered over the subfloor, and the walls were open in places, with insulation fluffing out of them like cotton candy.

"This is Ray's office?"

A laugh sounded behind them, light and airy like the pealing of bells. Daphne whirled around and saw an Asian American girl leaning against a worktable. With her simple black top and jeans, her hair pulled into a ponytail, she looked utterly normal—forgettable, even.

"The office isn't mine," the girl announced. "We're just borrowing it for this meeting. The owners aren't moving in for months; they'll never know." She nodded to the open walls. "Plus, we know it's not bugged, so that's a plus."

"Wait. *You're* the hacker?" Daphne asked, comprehension dawning.

The girl rolled her eyes. "I assume you were expecting a guy?"

"You said his name was Ray!" Daphne whirled back to face Ethan.

"Rei. *R-E-I*," he corrected, fighting back a laugh.

"It's a Korean name." Rei jumped up to sit on the table and swung her legs back and forth. "Ethan. You didn't give Daphne any context on me? I'm a little offended."

"I know better than to tell anyone your story. I don't want to end up being accosted in a dark alley." Ethan came to stand next to the table, and Rei nudged him with her boot.

"Don't threaten *me* with a good time."

Daphne stared at them. She couldn't remember the last time she'd seen Ethan so at ease, his body language relaxed, even playful. The knowledge that some strange girl had brought out this side of him was profoundly irritating.

"Thanks for meeting us, Rei," she said, a bit coolly.

The other girl nodded. "I hear you need my help tracking the source of an email."

"Is that something you normally do?" Daphne fumbled. "Or, really—*what* do you normally do?"

"I deal in secrets."

"What *kind* of secrets?"

"The expensive kind." Noticing Daphne's frustration, Rei relented. "Look, I help people spy on their exes, change their school grades, fake vital documents. I don't steal," she added solemnly.

"How do I know you won't tell anyone about this?"

Rei waved her hand in a dismissive gesture. "I have better things to do than to break your story to the tabloids. Now, come on, show me your email. I've already seen Ethan's."

Daphne pulled her laptop from her bag and, with some trepidation, handed it over.

Rei slid off the table and opened the laptop to the incriminating email. "May I?"

When Daphne nodded, Rei began typing at lightning speed. Daphne was mesmerized by the sight of her purple manicure flying over the keyboard, issuing commands that made the computer turn into something alien, a black screen with strange letters and numbers illuminated in incomprehensible sequences.

"What does—" she began, but Ethan reached for her in warning. The contact startled Daphne into silence. She quickly jerked her hand away.

A few minutes later, Rei stretched her arms overhead, blinking as if waking from a trance. "As I expected, this is the same firewall as Ethan's email. Someone is harassing you both," she warned, "but I'm not going to figure out who on your puny little laptop. I need real horsepower for this one. More than even *I* have."

"What do you mean?" Daphne asked, but Ethan understood at once.

"How much?"

"A few thousand? I'll need to rent a private server bank to get enough computing power."

"We'll work on it," Ethan promised.

Rei nodded distractedly. "This is one of the most intense encryption systems I've seen. It's either government, or someone incredibly wealthy and paranoid about security," she added, talking more to herself than to them.

"That makes perfect sense!" Daphne exclaimed. "The Madisons would have access to the government's digital security. Plus they have plenty of money, and secrets to hide."

"Daphne thinks the emails were sent by Gabriella Madison," Ethan explained, in response to Rei's confused look.

"A duke's daughter?" Rei looked intrigued. "Why would she blackmail you like this?"

"Because she's an awful person, and she hates me."

"She can't be the only one."

Daphne looked up sharply, but exhaled when she saw the teasing smile on Rei's lips.

Ethan chuckled appreciatively. "I knew you two would get along."

"If that's what you call it," Daphne shot back, though strangely enough, she found that she trusted Rei. People who insulted you to your face rarely bothered to stab you in the back.

She turned to Rei, an idea forming. "Can you remotely hack a personal computer?"

"Depends on whose computer. Are you asking me to hack Gabriella?"

"Daphne, no," Ethan cut in.

She scowled at him. "We're wasting time tracking this email. We should be focusing on Gabriella, find some way to take her down!"

"Out of the question," Ethan insisted. "If she finds out,

she'll try to hurt you. I don't want you messing with the Madisons."

Daphne decided it wasn't worth fighting about—at least, not right now. "Fine."

He looked startled by her acquiescence, then turned back to Rei. "We'll be in touch soon with the money."

Rei withdrew a pair of business cards from her pocket and handed one to each of them. "My personal number is off-limits," she told them, with a pointed glance at Ethan. "If you need to reach me, use the contact form on this website. Request a fiftieth-anniversary cake."

Daphne stared blankly at the card, which advertised MELINDA'S GOURMET BAKERY in a cheerful blue font. "What?"

"Use the contact form on this website," Rei repeated. "It's heavily encrypted, so it's safe. I'll get your message immediately."

"What do you do if someone stumbles across this website and *actually* orders a fiftieth-anniversary cake?" Daphne couldn't help asking.

"I order them a cake from somewhere else," Rei said, as if it were obvious. "I would never ruin a fiftieth anniversary."

When they were back outside the abandoned office building, Daphne glanced over at Ethan. "You said that you and Rei played T-ball?"

"Yep. She was the best third baseman in the league, until she got kicked out for throwing a punch."

"Why am I not surprised," Daphne muttered. "And how did she get into all this . . . illegal activity?"

"The usual way. Her legal options didn't work out."

Daphne started strapping her helmet under her chin, then hesitated. "Did you two ever . . . ."

Ethan looked at her with a teasing expression. "Are you jealous?"

"Of course not," she sniffed. "Just want to know the context, since you didn't give me any before."

He grinned. "Well, for *context's* sake, Rei and I are just friends."

It was darker than it had been when they drove over here; the afternoon sun cast long shadows over the streets, making Daphne wish she'd brought a heavier jacket. As they exited the highway and began to cross midtown, she slowly became aware of a car on their tail.

It was a nondescript black SUV, the sort of car Daphne could drive past without ever really noticing. Except that this one had been trailing half a block behind them for several minutes now.

"Ethan," Daphne muttered, but he'd already seen.

"Don't worry, I'm on it." He revved the motor and the bike leapt forward eagerly.

The car behind them picked up speed, too.

She could feel it now: someone was taking a picture. Call it intuition, but Daphne had always been able to sense when a lens was aimed her way; it was part of what made her so good with the paparazzi. She ducked her head into Ethan's shoulder to hide her face.

They were approaching a traffic circle. Her fingers tightened in the fabric of Ethan's jacket as he whipped around, then cut down the second exit toward the museum district. Perhaps fifty yards ahead of them, a traffic light turned to yellow.

Daphne sensed what he was about to do before he even started accelerating. He pushed the motorcycle to its top speed, glancing both ways as he shot through the intersection like a bullet.

The SUV tried to follow, only to nearly collide with a truck. Daphne heard the screech of brakes, the chorus of angry horns erupting behind them, and let out a breath. They were safe.

It was another few minutes before Ethan finally turned onto a quiet side street and slowed to a purr.

He glanced back over his shoulder. "You okay, Daph?"

She wasn't sure whether it was the rough concern in his tone, or the fact that he'd called her *Daph*—but something about the moment felt sharply intimate. Her heart was pounding from a wild mixture of shock and adrenaline.

"I'm fine. Thank you for getting us out of there." She hesitated, then added, "Did they have a camera?"

"Just a phone, I think."

That was a relief. A real camera, especially one of the long-lens ones the paparazzi used, might have gotten a clear photo, but not a phone.

"Then we're in the clear."

Ethan nodded and turned around, setting back out into the darkening streets.

As they approached Herald Oaks, Daphne felt her torso pressing against Ethan's back, her body molding against his in a way that felt oddly steadying. His words echoed in her mind. *Don't worry, I'm on it.*

Jefferson had told her the same thing at the doctor's office, the day of the ultrasound—*don't worry*, he'd assured her, *it will all be okay.* Somehow the sentiment felt different when coming from Ethan.

Perhaps because Ethan, unlike Jefferson, understood what Daphne was actually afraid of.

"What was it like in Malaysia?" she heard herself ask.

"Hot. And humid."

"You know that's not what I was asking."

The sun was setting in a glorious liquid glow over the horizon, glinting on the rooftops. Daphne had never lived anywhere but here—in Washington, the city of energy and ambition, a city fueled by millions of people all chasing their own wants.

She wondered, suddenly, what it would feel like to leave.

"I liked Malaysia, but I was lonely." Ethan's voice rumbled back to her, barely audible over the hum of the bike. "There were things about home that I really missed."

Daphne's pulse echoed in her ears again. Probably an after-effect of that car chase.

"Lonely, you? And here I thought you hated everyone."

"Nah, just you," he replied easily. "Why did you ask about Malaysia, anyway? Are you thinking of leaving Washington?"

She laughed. "Of course not. Why would I leave? Washington is the center of the world, and everything I ever wanted is right here."

"Of course it is," Ethan agreed flatly.

They didn't speak again for the rest of the ride.

NINA

A hum of voices emanated from within Chancellor's Hall, the rotunda at the center of the humanities buildings. Nina stood frozen before the wooden double doors, where a sign read ENGLISH DEPT. OXFORD EXCHANGE PROGRAM: INFO SESSION.

She hadn't been planning on showing up today. Then, as the clock inched toward four p.m., she'd found herself changing into a navy sheath dress—ignoring that it was the sort of thing Daphne would wear—and crossing campus to the reception hall.

She was just gathering information, Nina reminded herself, and pushed open the doors. Showing up at an info session didn't mean she had to *apply*.

The room was even more crowded than she'd expected, students cramped together so tight that some of them had spilled into the study carrels in the neighboring room. Nina's heart sank a little. It looked like every last English major her year had shown up, plus several upperclassmen—though the ones with green name tags, she realized, were students who had done the program in years past. From the look of things, Nina had missed the official question-and-answer session; a projector on the far wall flashed through pictures of students walking through Oxford's iconic cloistered courtyards or smiling on field trips to London.

Nina grabbed a pamphlet from the information table, filled

out a name tag, and stuck it to her dress. Then she started into the crowds, figuring she should at least talk to one of the program's alumni, hear what it was like firsthand.

A professor with wavy gray hair and an intelligent gaze stood nearby, surrounded by half a dozen jostling students. Something about her made Nina look twice, and then she nearly gasped, because the woman's name tag read DR. ELIZABETH LYTTON, OXFORD UNIVERSITY.

Hadn't Nina read an essay by a Dr. Lytton for her paper on *Emma* last month?

Nina forced her way through the throngs of students, hovering nearby until Dr. Lytton finally turned to her.

"Dr. Lytton, it's an honor to meet you. I recently cited your academic paper on *Emma*."

The professor was clearly pleased that Nina had made the connection. "And what interests you about the Oxford program, Miss Gonzalez?"

Nina realized, in that moment, that she wasn't simply curious about the program. A small but fierce part of her longed to do it—to go somewhere new, test the boundaries of her own abilities. She wanted to be *brave*.

"I'd love to focus on nineteenth-century fiction," she heard herself say.

"Ah, yes. A Jane Austen enthusiast." From the dry way Dr. Lytton spoke, Nina suspected that she wasn't the only student to have made that claim this afternoon. *Those students aren't like me*, Nina wanted to cry out; *they just watched the new* Pride and Prejudice *and liked seeing Darcy in a clinging wet shirt! I'm the real deal—I read biographies of Jane Austen in my spare time!*

Instead, Nina blurted out, "I'm also playing Helena in an on-campus production of *A Midsummer Night's Dream*."

Interest gleamed in the professor's eyes. "An actress? And what do you think of Shakespeare?"

Despite her initial misgivings, Nina had shown up to the

first couple of rehearsals. She told herself it was out of loyalty to Rachel, and *not* because she was curious about Prince Jamie. Honestly, she was doing her best to avoid him.

She and Dr. Lytton spoke about the production for several more minutes before another student came to hover near the professor. Nina said goodbye, heart pounding through her smile, before she walked toward the exit and let out a breath.

"That looked like it went well."

She looked up, startled, at Jamie's voice. He stood nearby, holding a paper plate full of snacks from the refreshments table.

"What are you doing here?" she asked.

"I was in the area and saw the free food. You Americans have such a funny relationship with ranch dressing," he mused. "Am I really supposed to dip *celery* in it?"

"It's a choose-your-own adventure situation." Nina started toward the door and was unsurprised when Jamie tossed his plate into the trash and followed.

They headed into the quadrangle at the front of campus. Nina was still taut with adrenaline from her conversation with Dr. Lytton, so when Jamie gestured to the fountain at the center of the lawn, she decided, *Why not?* and went to sit next to him.

"I'm glad you're considering the Oxford program. What changed your mind? The same things that changed your mind about the play?" he added, voice devoid of his usual irreverence.

Nina ignored his comment about the play, leaning her palms back on the fountain's rough stone surface. "My friend Ethan studied in Malaysia this year. I talked to him a few times while he was abroad, and I could tell how much he loved it." She'd learned a lot more from those conversations—like the fact that Ethan, Nina was pretty certain, still loved Daphne—but that wasn't worth mentioning.

The truth was, Nina was ready to go somewhere new. She wanted to meet people on her own terms, without her romantic history or her entanglements with the Washingtons overshadowing things.

"Oxford is beautiful. You'd love it. Plus, there's a far better nightlife than you'd expect," Jamie added with a wink.

Nina knew he was being flippant but rolled her eyes. "Studying abroad isn't just about drinking."

"You're right. It's about the people you meet."

Nina was grateful when her phone buzzed, shattering the moment. She pulled it quickly from her purse and saw a new message from Samantha: *I promise I'm fine!*

Last week, when Sam hadn't come home and instead texted that she was crashing with "my friend Liam," Nina had been so worried she'd almost called the palace. Who was this so-called friend, and why didn't Nina know anything about him? She had always feared that Sam's impulsive streak would get her into trouble.

Call me soon! I want to make sure you're okay! she replied, then looked up to find Jamie watching her.

"Sorry," she mumbled. "I'm just . . . It's my friend."

"And how is Sam doing these days? Back in town, I assume?"

Nina looked up sharply at his words.

"You knew that Sam was back, didn't you? That night at Tudor House, when you acted like you didn't know who I was!"

"I didn't *act* like anything," Jamie insisted. "But you're right, I knew who you were, so when you said you needed to help your best friend, I figured that Sam had come home."

"And you didn't tell anyone."

Jamie might be full of himself and insufferably charming, but he was trustworthy when it came to the things that mattered. The realization sank into Nina's chest, warm and solid like a stone.

He shrugged and changed the subject. "You've been really good in rehearsals. I still can't believe this is your first time acting."

"At least, my first time since the skits Sam and I used to perform as kids. I usually wrote the script and she was the star." Nina shook her head fondly at the memory. "What about you—did you act in high school?"

"It's nothing like Shakespeare, but I did children's theater with a volunteer group. We performed at elementary schools where most of the kids had never seen live theater before." Jamie grinned. "I played the crab in *The Little Mermaid.*"

"Not the prince?"

"Where's the fun in that?"

Nina glanced over at him, curious. "So you didn't have any problems getting permission for the play? I mean, isn't it a security risk?"

There had always been stringent regulations when the twins were involved in extracurriculars, which for them had usually meant sports. Heightened security at their games, no photography, and, strangest of all, no mascots (the big costumes were too easy to hide a weapon in). Since the twins had attended the same small private schools since kindergarten, their classmates were used to it. But Nina had no idea what rules were in place for Jamie, a future king studying abroad in a foreign country.

"By that logic, everything is a security risk. Being onstage isn't that different from any of the royal appearances I do back home," Jamie replied. "You're right in guessing that my dad doesn't approve, but only because he thinks theater is a waste of time."

"I'm sorry."

Jamie shrugged. "Oh well, there are more embarrassing royal hobbies. At least I'm not starting a vanity tequila company like Prince Juan Carlos. I mean, have you seen the bottle?" Jamie added, eyes twinkling. "It's so ridiculous. The cap is shaped like a crown."

"Remind me to order that next time I want tequila shots," Nina joked. Then, after another beat of silence, she asked, "What's your dad like?"

"He changed a lot after the divorce." When Nina stared at him in surprise, Jamie hesitated. "You didn't know?"

She didn't follow other royal families all that much; even if she *had* read the tabloids, which she tried her best to avoid, the foreign royals got minimal coverage compared to the Washingtons.

"We don't have to talk about it," Nina said quickly.

"It's okay, I'm used to it by now." Jamie seemed to be striving for a lighthearted tone and failing. "My mom fell in love with her tennis instructor. Tale as old as time, right?"

"I'm sorry," Nina breathed.

His eyes drifted downward as he continued. "My parents only dated for four months before they got engaged. My mom was swept along in the fairy tale of it all, but for my dad, it was the real deal. Even after he caught her cheating, he begged her to stay with us, but she wanted a divorce. She and Henri got married. They live in Nova Scotia with my three half siblings."

"And your dad never remarried?" Nina asked gently.

Jamie shook his head. "The thing is, Dad is still in love with Mom. He's sort of old-fashioned in that way: once he gave her his heart, it was hers forever, and that was that. Game over. If I hadn't been born, he could probably have forced himself to marry someone else for the sake of the succession," Jamie said heavily. "Instead it's just the two of us. And I know that in his heart Dad still thinks of her as his wife, in spite of the divorce, in spite of the fact that she's out there living another life."

It struck Nina as deeply tragic, and misguided, yet also

loyal in a way that people never were anymore. As if Jamie's father lived by a code of integrity practically forgotten in the modern age. And poor Jamie, to feel abandoned by his mom and then have to fill so many roles for his father: being his successor and also his entire family unit. That must have put him under a tremendous amount of pressure.

"Funny enough, this place—Washington—is the last time my parents were together and happy, before it all fell apart," Jamie went on. "I was twelve."

It sparked a clang of recognition in Nina's mind. "Wait a second. I remember you!"

"Ah, you've finally recalled our magical encounter in the gardens at Bellevue?"

"No! I mean, yes, I remember that—but now I remember when we were *kids*. You used to come see Jeff and Sam during the summers, didn't you?"

Jamie nodded. "I joined my parents on their annual state visit to Washington. They were pretty close with Adelaide and George back then," he said. "We would stay for a couple of weeks."

It struck Nina as a very unique form of power, something only another royal could do, to refer to the Queen Mother and the late king by their first names. She had known them since she was a kid, and even she had never dared call them anything but Your Majesty.

Looking at Jamie now, she marveled that she hadn't made the connection. Of course this was the same blond, impish boy who'd joined the twins in all their schemes. "Didn't we sneak down to the docks one time and try to steal the royal barge?" she recalled.

"We almost succeeded! We had it unmoored and halfway out into the river before we got caught."

"And we were flying a pirate flag!" Nina and Sam had found it in one of the upstairs closets, stashed alongside pumpkins and Halloween decorations. Sam had instantly decided that they would commandeer the royal barge and sail down the river in true pirate style.

"Alas, the pirate joyride was too good for this world. May we mourn it in peace," Jamie said somberly, and they both laughed again.

It was bittersweet, recalling events that were so saturated with the memory of Jeff. Nina couldn't stop feeling angry at him and Daphne for not realizing how epically mismatched they were. She could only hope that one of them would call off the wedding.

"We should steal the barge again sometime," she said, looking back up at Jamie. "Or, you know, go on the grown-up version of a pirate-ship joyride."

"I believe you Americans would call that a booze cruise," Jamie pointed out.

"As long as we're not driving."

Jamie seemed a little surprised by her reply, and really, so was Nina. But she was so tired of keeping herself withdrawn. She'd spent too long being angry—at Daphne, at Jeff—and she had thought of her anger like a shield, protecting her heart. Except the shield had become impossibly heavy and begun to drag her down.

Maybe it was time she let someone in.

17

DAPHNE

A week later, Daphne stared around the ballroom at Washington Palace, which was as crowded and glittering as she had ever seen it. She should have been thrilled: this was her engagement party, the culmination of everything she'd spent years working for. In her narrow-waisted white dress with blue embroidery, her hair swept into an updo, she looked like she was already a princess.

But the reality wasn't *quite* as flawless as she'd dreamed. She still caught a few of the guests, the high-ranking dukes or foreign ambassadors, staring at her with mingled confusion and distaste. They were clearly wondering what Jefferson was thinking, tying himself to the daughter of a disgraced former baronet when he could have had any woman in the world. *She's pretty, sure,* Daphne could almost hear them whispering to one another, *but that doesn't mean he should* marry *her*.

Not to mention, she was still dealing with the ominous messages from Gabriella.

Another had landed in her inbox this afternoon, from the same anonymous address. Daphne kept looking across the ballroom at Ethan, wondering if he'd received one, too; she'd texted him before the party but he hadn't answered. She wished she could march over and ask him outright. Instead she'd spent the night standing here with Jefferson, greeting the endless stream of guests who came over to offer their congratulations.

Finally, one of the guests stepped aside, and Daphne glanced across the ballroom to where Ethan was staring at her.

She jerked her head toward the exit. Ethan seemed to sigh in resignation, though Daphne was too far away to be sure. She mumbled her excuses to Jefferson and his mother and headed into the hallway, where Ethan was already waiting.

"What is it?" he asked, but Daphne shook her head. No way would she risk anyone overhearing.

She waited until they were halfway down the hallway before throwing open the door to a linen closet, its shelves stacked with dozens—no, hundreds—of sheets and pillowcases, all stitched with the royal crest. Some part of her registered that it was close quarters, but she was too hyped up on anxiety and adrenaline to worry about that right now. At least they were safe in here.

"Gabriella sent another email this afternoon," she hissed. "Did you get one, too?"

Ethan hesitated. "I did. But, Daphne, I'm still not sure it's—"

"I know, I know, you don't think it's Gabriella. Just *look*."

Daphne fumbled with her clutch, a tiny thing covered all over in pearl embellishments. She pulled up her email and passed her phone to Ethan.

From: UNKNOWN SENDER <12345@webmail.com>
Subject: (NO SUBJECT)

Why are you getting married when you're in love with the best man? After everything you've done, you should know better. Call it off, Daphne.

All evening Daphne had been replaying the words in her mind. This wasn't written by some stranger, a random paparazzo or internet stalker who'd never met her. This was someone who knew her—who despised her.

Ethan was quiet. "She says you're in love with me?" His words lifted at the end, turning them into a question.

"I told you, that's what Nina thinks." At Ethan's look, Daphne rolled her eyes. "Of course Nina thinks that! It justifies her own desire to get Jefferson back—because if I'm in love with someone else, then I *deserve* to be steamrolled out of the way. How typically Nina, that she would need to be high-minded and idealistic even when destroying someone."

They were both leaning close, hovering over her phone screen. Daphne felt suddenly aware of every inch between them.

Ethan was the first to take a step back. "I see."

"Anyway, I have the money." Daphne pulled out her wallet, which was much fatter than normal. It had been slightly nerve-racking, carrying around this much cash. "Three thousand exactly."

"Do I want to know where you got this?" Ethan asked, tucking the bills into his pocket.

"Are you suggesting I did something illegal?"

"You've broken laws before."

Daphne decided to ignore that. "I sold some clothes, okay?"

"Ah," Ethan said meaningfully. "And I take it people pay above market value for clothes that were owned by a princess-to-be?"

"They would, except I never tell them. I don't exactly want tabloid headlines about how I'm selling off my wardrobe." It would make her look pitiful, and there was nothing Daphne hated more than other people's pity.

"Anyway, please just go convert this to cryptocurrency or whatever you need to do. I don't want to be involved," Daphne added quickly. The sooner they paid Rei, the sooner Rei could hire extra servers and hack that firewall.

"I'm pretty sure Rei takes cash." Ethan sounded amused.

Before Daphne could reply, footsteps sounded outside the door to the linen closet. Ethan's head snapped toward the noise.

Then, in a single motion, he closed the distance between them and pushed Daphne against the wall, behind an open shelving unit of sheets. His mouth landed on hers with brutal swiftness.

She should cry out, or slap him, or push him away. Yet her body didn't seem inclined to do any of these things.

It was as if Daphne drifted outside herself, forgetting every core tenet of her being—who she was, what she wanted—and let herself melt into Ethan. Her mouth opened on instinct, deepening the kiss. Her arms were still pinned back against the wall, but she didn't care.

She'd forgotten how readily they fit together, how good it felt to be tucked up against him. Every inch of him so achingly familiar, so infuriating, so intoxicating.

Dimly, as if from a great distance, she heard a male chuckle. "Whoops. Looks like this room is, um, taken."

Then the door shut behind the intruder, and Ethan pulled away. Daphne sucked in a breath, stunned.

What had just happened? And why had she *allowed* it to happen?

"I'm sorry." Ethan met her gaze, though he looked nervous. "I heard the footsteps and figured this was our best option. At least it would make them go away quickly."

"The best option?" Daphne's voice came out hoarse. "You *wanted* us to be caught making out?"

"All they saw was me! Why did you think I pushed you so far back against the wall? I hid you behind this stack of towels!"

"They're *sheets*," Daphne hissed, though through the haze of her anger she realized that Ethan was right. She looked down at the tulle frothing up around her knees like whipped cream. Somehow, in that split second between the sound of footsteps and the door opening, Ethan had thought to kick her voluminous skirts behind the shelving unit. Whoever was standing in the door would have seen Ethan's body leaning against someone—and almost certainly heard the soft noises Daphne had been making—but there was nothing to identify the mystery girl as her.

He had protected her, strange and unexpected as it was.

Daphne edged around him, tugging her skirts impatiently after her. She resented the tension that still pulsed between them, thick as smoke.

"It's fine," Daphne snapped. "Just forget it ever happened, okay?"

She straightened her gown and cracked the door open a sliver, glancing in both directions down the hallway. When she felt certain the coast was clear, she headed back toward the party.

Luck was clearly not on her side tonight, because the moment she entered the ballroom, Gabriella stepped into her path.

"Daphne, hello." Gabriella reached for the diamond necklace at her throat and toyed with it idly, twirling it around her finger as if it were a plastic children's toy.

"Gabriella." Daphne started to brush past, but Gabriella's next words stopped her in her tracks.

"Where did you disappear to? It's not like you to leave your own party. If I didn't know better, I'd say you were *up to something.*" There was an emphasis on those last three words that would have been almost comical if Daphne weren't shivering from apprehension.

"If you must know, I was in the ladies' room."

"Nice try, but I was just in there."

Well, fine. If Gabriella wanted war, then war she would get.

Daphne laughed as if her enemy had said something outrageously funny, drawing them to one side of the ballroom. To everyone else, they probably looked like two friends sharing a secret. "You really need to stop stalking me, or you'll regret it," she warned.

"I'm trying to make you realize how out of your league you are. Dating a prince is one thing, but marrying one? I blame myself, honestly. I should never have let things between you and Jeff get as far as I did. But I was in France"—a slight accent laced Gabriella's voice with those words, deeply pretentious and artificial—"and honestly, I just assumed he would sleep with you until he got bored. I never imagined he would take it so far as to get *engaged*."

Daphne stood up straighter. "Even if you did manage to break us up, which you won't, he's not going to date you."

"I don't care. At this point I'd settle for getting rid of you."

"How charming," Daphne said flatly.

"Honestly, Daphne, you're lucky that Beatrice woke up and redirected the tabloids' attention. But I'm not worried." Gabriella smiled cruelly. "It's only a matter of time before your parents do something stupid again. Then the Poker Princess will be back in the headlines where she belongs."

There was something distinctly proud, almost proprietary, about the way Gabriella spoke that last sentence.

"Gabriella." Daphne's voice was ice-cold. "Are you the one who invented that nickname?"

Gabriella gave a slow, mocking clap. "I was wondering when you'd figure it out! My first suggestion was Dicey Daphne, but for some reason they didn't use that one. Oh

157

well." She leaned forward, eyes glowing. "Promise me you'll enjoy it while it lasts. After all, this is the only time in your life that anyone will ever call you Princess."

Daphne knew she should be outraged, or afraid, yet all she felt was a hollow sort of sadness. "Why are you like this? What did I ever do to you?"

Gabriella blinked as if the question didn't make sense. "Isn't it obvious? You reached too high."

You reached too high. Even after all this time, those words hurt Daphne in some deep, vulnerable place that she never let anyone see.

She squared her shoulders and forced herself to smile. "I'm not reaching, Gabriella. I'm climbing. You said it best, I'm a social climber, and I will keep being one—right until I climb over you, all the way to the very top."

Gabriella flounced off with an angry sniff. Slowly, and with some trepidation, Daphne angled herself away from the rest of the ballroom and pulled out her phone.

She'd saved the website for Melinda's Gourmet Bakery after Rei handed her the fake business card. It was the work of a moment to fill out the contact form, writing her name and *Fiftieth Anniversary Cake* in the subject line.

Later that night, when Daphne was seated at her vanity wiping off her makeup, her phone rang from UNKNOWN CALLER. She fumbled to answer it. "Rei?"

"Hi, Daphne. What can I do for you?"

Rei's tone was brisk, no-nonsense. Daphne liked that about her.

"I need you to hack the Madisons' home network. I'll pay your going rate," Daphne added quickly. "But this is important."

There was the sound of clicking keys. "You want me to stop working on the firewall behind your threatening emails?"

"Can you do both? Consider this a side project for me," Daphne pleaded.

"I see." Rei's voice lowered meaningfully. "Ethan doesn't know."

"Look, do you want my money or not?"

Rei chuckled. "Easy there. I'm on it, okay? I'll invoice you later."

"Thanks," Daphne began, but the other girl had already hung up.

Daphne stared at her phone in shock, shaking her head. Fine. She would negotiate with hackers who navigated the dark web, would sell more of her wardrobe to pay for it, would do whatever it took to rid herself of Gabriella.

If Gabriella wanted to fight dirty, then so would she.

18

BEATRICE

"Your Majesty, it's wonderful to see you again." Lady Francesca de León paused on her way out of the ballroom to curtsy.

Beatrice forced a smile. "I'm glad to be back."

"If I might have a moment of your time, there was something I wanted to discuss," the noblewoman—and senator—went on.

Right now? Beatrice thought wearily. Jefferson and Daphne's engagement party was limping along to its conclusion. After hours of being on her feet, dodging questions when she didn't know the answer, and fumbling to hide her memory loss, Beatrice was ready to unhook her tiara and fall into bed.

"Were you able to take a look at the final draft of my proposal?" Lady de León was saying.

"Your proposal," Beatrice repeated awkwardly. "Can you . . . remind me which proposal this is?"

Lady de León seemed hurt. "My nationwide initiative for women's small businesses. We spoke about it extensively earlier this year."

"Of course!" Beatrice cried out. "I'm so grateful that you're helping to support female business owners. And I hope your proposal has a special allowance for people from marginalized backgrounds."

The senator shot her a funny look. "It does, because you

made that request the last time we met. You were the one who recommended I reach out to Senator Gupta as a collaborator."

Beatrice's stomach plummeted. Why had she felt the need to elaborate, instead of leaving it at a simple *Thank you, let's get some time on the calendar?*

"Let's discuss in more detail soon," Beatrice said quickly. "Have a lovely evening."

Hearing the gentle dismissal in her words, Francesca murmured her goodbyes and retreated. Beatrice let out a defeated breath and glanced back around the ballroom.

Teddy was here, though he and Beatrice had kept an unspoken distance between them all night, like planets caught in opposite orbits. She'd barely seen him since their walk in the gardens. Beatrice was trying not to think about that—the way she'd snapped at him, *I don't remember!*—but the memory kept cutting at something inside her, sharp like teeth.

Jefferson and Daphne still stood near the exit, bidding farewell to the few remaining guests. The band was still playing up on the stage; it would keep going until every last person had departed, because there was never an official "last song" at a royal event. The high-top tables were scattered with crumpled napkins, crystal wineglasses marked with lipstick smudges, even a stray necktie.

"Your Majesty! May I have a moment alone?" Anju asked, walking toward her. When Beatrice nodded, the chamberlain lowered her voice. "I found the former Guard you wanted me to track down."

Beatrice's breath caught. "Yes?"

"He's now employed by the Duchess of Texas. I'm sorry I didn't think to check there sooner," Anju said quickly; "you know the duchies' internal human resources servers aren't accessible to us, to protect regional governments from federal oversight. . . ." She kept tripping over herself to apologize for the delay, but Beatrice had stopped listening.

161

Connor was in Texas. She could summon him here, and—

And then what? When she first woke up in the hospital, all Beatrice had wanted was to see him, to hold him. Now she didn't know *what* she wanted.

She was so dazed that she almost didn't notice her brother coming to join them. "Beatrice! I need to talk to you about something. It's important," he added.

There was an urgency to his tone that dispelled her exhaustion. "Of course. Let's go to my office."

It was still a bit jarring to think of this room as *her* office rather than her father's. Beatrice flicked on the lights, illuminating the upholstered armchairs by the fire, the desk looming beneath the far window. Roses spilled out of a vase on the central coffee table, their scent lingering on the air.

Jeff headed to the antique cabinet on one wall, which held a gloriously mismatched set of crystal decanters, all inherited from various past kings. He reached for the whiskey, then glanced back to Beatrice for permission. When she nodded, he poured two tumblers of amber liquid.

"I don't need one," she protested when he came over with her drink.

"You might change your mind once you hear this."

Prickling with anticipation, Beatrice took one of the armchairs, and her brother followed suit.

He squirmed, visibly uncomfortable. "Something weird happened earlier. The Duke of Virginia asked me to share a cigar out on the terrace."

"Okay," Beatrice prompted slowly.

"I could tell he wanted to ask me for something; I thought it might be another ambassadorial appointment. Instead . . ." Jeff paused. "He asked if I would be open to testifying against you in Congress."

"He *what?*"

"He wanted to know if I was interested in, um . . . a coup?"

Her first instinct was to laugh. This couldn't be real; it was something that used to happen centuries ago, but not now, not when the power of government was firm and stable and established.

Except it *was* real. Ambrose would invoke the unfit-to-rule clause against her, claim that Beatrice was mentally damaged from her accident and couldn't carry out her duties as queen.

"He obviously doesn't know me at all, if he thought I wanted to overthrow you or . . . depose you?" Jeff fumbled for the right word. "He kept saying what a good job I had done as Acting King, and didn't I think I deserved to be king for real?"

Beatrice felt like she was seeing spots. She closed her hands around the crystal tumbler so tight that its ridges imprinted in the flesh of her palm.

"*Do* you want that?" she whispered.

"Hell, no. It's a miserable job."

She let out a strangled laugh, and Jeff winced. "Sorry, no offense."

"None taken."

"It's just . . . it's nonstop work. And no matter how hard you try, you inevitably offend *someone,* and no matter how much you accomplish, there's always a mountain of other problems waiting to be addressed. How do you *do* it, Bee?"

"I don't know." Because she had no other choice. Because she had trained for it her whole life.

It was nice, though, knowing that another family member finally understood the burden she carried. She had to grapple with the weight of so many things: America's past, its present, its future.

A future that might not include her.

"I have a whole new appreciation for you after being your Regent." Jeff lifted his glass in her direction. "You make the toughest job in the world look easy."

Beatrice gave a wry smile. "There's nothing easy about it, is there? But you did a fantastic job covering for me. Thank you," she added.

"I should say, it wasn't *all* bad. I loved getting to meet so many people." Jeff hesitated before saying, "It was nice, feeling like I actually made a difference for a change."

"You've always made a difference!"

Jeff shot her a glance, and she fell silent, well aware what he'd meant. As the third in line to rule, Jeff had occupied a uniquely relaxed and uncontroversial position—until now.

"I'm sorry," she said quietly. "You're right, we didn't give you the opportunity to make much of a difference before."

"To be fair, that was Mom and Dad's decision, not yours. Also, the jobs I had were really fun ones. I don't want to give those away."

"Like when you parachuted into the Super Bowl halftime show?"

"That was for charity!" Jeff protested. "But, yes, I like doing those things—raising awareness for causes, building connections where we need goodwill. I just don't want them to be the *only* things I do."

"What are you thinking, then?"

Jeff seemed nervous as he replied, "Once I'm done with school, I want to serve in the military."

He kept talking, explaining how he felt called to give back in some way—how he dreamed of flying the attack helicopters used in specialized operations—but Beatrice cut him off.

"You realize it would require a full press blackout, if we wanted to keep you safe."

"We could negotiate that," Jeff insisted.

"What does Daphne think?" Something about the look on her brother's face made Beatrice pause. "Jeff. Do you still want to get married?"

He stared down into his whiskey. "I can't imagine losing

Daphne. She's always been there for me when I needed her, especially over the past few months."

It wasn't a direct answer, but Beatrice didn't press him. She knew that feeling well—the need to cling to something, or someone, constant, when the world was changing all around you.

"So, what are you going to do about Madison?" Jeff asked, after a beat. "I got the sense that he's going to move forward with or without my help."

"You think he's already gathering votes against me?"

"He'll request a vote for your removal in the new year. I think he knows about your memory loss, or at least he suspects."

And if Madison found proof that she had *hidden* her memory loss, he could argue that she was deceiving her subjects.

"The only good thing in all of this is that he talked to me first. He revealed his hand too early. Now you know what he's planning," Jeff pointed out.

"But what should I do?"

"Go on the attack, right? If Madison is gathering senators to support his bill, then you have to find senators who will vote against it."

Beatrice nodded slowly. As the monarch, she wasn't traditionally meant to engage in campaigning or politicking; that was for Congress or elected officials.

Maybe it was time she stopped worrying about what she was meant to do, and focused on what she *needed* to do.

Beatrice reached for her phone, newly galvanized to action, and pulled up the list of senators—she used to think she knew it by heart, but there'd been some changes over the past year, and she could use a visual aid. Jeff came to stand behind her, bracing his hands on the back of her chair as he studied it with her.

"Madison will get most of the Old Guard," Beatrice mused aloud.

165

"That's only thirteen duchies," Jeff pointed out, in an attempt at optimism. "You just need to recruit some other heavy hitters."

"Heavy hitters?"

"You know, people who come with entourages. Key votes that swing an entire region in their direction."

Beatrice nodded, slightly amused by his terminology. Trust Jeff to frame everything in sports terms. "The Duke of Ohio tends to set the tone for the Midwest. . . ."

"What about Anna Ramirez? I mean, Texas is a pretty big deal, isn't it?"

The Duchess of Texas. She was formidable, a force of nature in the Senate—and Connor was currently working for her.

"You're right, Texas is a pretty big deal," Beatrice agreed, repeating her brother's words. "I should probably talk to her."

"Do you want me to come with you?"

She was touched by the offer, but shook her head. "You should focus on school now that you're back." Normally a student who'd missed so many weeks would have to drop out for the rest of the semester, and start over in the spring, but not Jeff. His professors had quietly excused his absence and were letting him take his exams alongside his classmates, which meant that Jeff was still on track to graduate with his class.

"Jeff . . ." This next part was hard to say, but Beatrice forced herself to get it out. "If Congress does vote on this, and it passes, then promise me you'll do it. You'll be king."

He shook his head adamantly. "I'll refuse!"

"And what, leave Uncle Richard to pick up the pieces?"

"Maybe they'll let Sam do it?" Jeff asked hopefully.

Beatrice barked out a humorless laugh. "If Congress is opposed to me, they'll certainly be opposed to Sam. No, it has to be you." She looked over at his profile, dim in the light of the sconces. "Thank you, though, for warning me. And for taking my side."

He seemed startled by that. "Of course I took your side. You're my sister."

They both fell silent, achingly aware of Samantha's absence. Beatrice wondered what she was doing now. At least she was staying with Nina; Beatrice trusted Nina to get Sam through anything.

Her eyes drifted to the portrait of their father hanging above the fireplace. "I miss him so much," she murmured.

"Me too. All the time."

It felt like their grief was a physical thing, like they were holding it between them, knees buckling beneath its weight.

Beatrice stood. "We should get some sleep."

Jeff nodded and drained the rest of his whiskey. Before they stepped back out into the hallway, he surprised her by pulling her into a hug. Beatrice was stiff for a moment, then relaxed into the embrace.

"If Dad was here, he would tell you that you can do this," Jeff told her.

"Thank you." Beatrice attempted a lighthearted tone as she added, "Wish me luck in Texas. I think I'll need it."

19

SAMANTHA

"I love Washington in the winter," Sam declared as she and Liam walked the few blocks home. Their other friends were still at Enclave, singing karaoke into the microphone, but Sam had begged off. She felt tired, in a satisfied way that reminded her of the boat in Hawaii—the sense of having accomplished something, even if it was only pouring beers.

Liam shot her a skeptical glance. "No one likes Washington in the winter."

"Well, I do. I've never gotten to walk outside like this before." It felt liberating, strolling past apartment doors and the canvas awnings of bodegas, their steps lit by the golden glow of streetlamps. In her old life Sam had gone everywhere in a chauffeured car, or at best walked with a protection officer on her tail.

"It'll get old fast," Liam warned. "Especially once we're shoveling snow off the driveway."

"I don't mind shoveling snow!"

He laughed. "Then you can be the first one out there once we get a heavy snowfall. It can be your chore," he added, teasing.

Her first morning at the house, Sam had kept asking what "chores" everyone did—she'd seen enough sitcoms to know the term, and was proud of herself for asking. But the other housemates had just looked at her with amusement. "We all do things when they need doing," Jessica had explained, which made zero sense to Sam.

She had watched them all day, mystified at their silent choreography. How did they each know when to unload the dishwasher, or take out the trash? How did they keep track of each other's groceries, or buy toilet paper? By now, though, she'd settled into more of a rhythm, and could even help contribute to the house expenses with her earnings from Enclave.

Her phone buzzed, and Sam yanked off a glove to fumble in her bag. She expected a text from Nina, who kept reminding Sam that she was welcome back in the dorm room anytime, no matter how often Sam kept assuring her that she was happy here.

When she saw the name on the screen, her heart skipped. It was Marshall: *Heading back from the beach, call you in twenty?*

Sam liked the message, only to pause when she noticed the news alerts on her home screen. Most of them were coverage of Daphne and Jeff's engagement party.

"You okay?" Liam asked, watching her.

Sam had slowed to a stop. A gossiping group of friends passed them, and then a couple holding hands, but none of them paid her any notice; they were too absorbed in each other or in navigating through the cold.

"My brother and Daphne had a big engagement party tonight. I wasn't included, obviously," Sam explained.

Liam huffed sympathetically. "Have you tried talking to him since that day at the palace?"

"I've called Jeff and Beatrice a few times, but they never pick up. And when I text they send awkward responses." Sam laughed hollowly. "When I asked Jeff if I could come over, he replied, 'Things are a little hectic right now, sorry I haven't replied sooner.' It's like I was a bad date and he's trying to ghost me!" she exclaimed. "Then he told me again to go to Grandma Billie's."

"Okay, I have to ask," Liam chimed in. "Why do you call her Grandma Billie?"

"Her name is Wilhelmina. Billie is a logical nickname."

"Right," he agreed, in a tone that made Sam want to smile.

She couldn't go to her grandmother's house, no matter how much easier it would make things for her family. Now more than ever, she needed to prove that she could stand on her own two feet. She wasn't just some spoiled princess who'd run away to Hawaii when things got tough. She would stick around, even if her family didn't want her, even if it felt difficult. Because that was what you did for people you loved: you stayed with them through the good and the bad.

She expected Liam to change the subject, but his next question surprised her.

"What's it like having a twin?"

Sam thought about it for a long moment, considering. "It used to be simple."

When she and Jeff were children, they had done everything as a unit, had shared the same tutors and the same friends and played in the same coed soccer league. They ate the same snacks, buying peanut butter crackers and passing the bag back and forth wordlessly between them. When they were very little, even their clothes had matched, everything color-coordinated or monogrammed.

"I once met identical twins who told me that having a twin was like looking in a mirror all the time," Sam said slowly. "For years I felt like that with Jeff. Not physically, of course, but Jeff and I . . . we lived the same experience. And now that's changed."

At some point their paths had parted ways. Jeff was getting married and Sam was cut out of the family, and she didn't know what to do without the easy camaraderie she had once taken for granted.

"Don't you think it's a good thing that you're becoming your own people?" Liam asked. "That's the whole point of growing up, isn't it?"

"Maybe. But a good thing can still hurt."

Samantha had always assumed she would have Jeff to lean on, to prop her up. He was the person she had marched into this life with, the two of them tangled together from the very beginning. She had never imagined circumstances that might break her bond with her twin—yet those circumstances had arisen anyway. And it was her fault.

Sam cleared her throat. "What about you and your brother? Are you alike?"

"Not at all. Parker is so detail-oriented and serious; he's nothing like me. Like my parents, he's a *tax accountant*," Liam added ruefully. "You'll see when you meet him."

The promise implicit in that statement brought an unexpected smile to her face.

They headed through the back door and paused in the kitchen. "Are you hungry? I could make us something," Liam offered, leaning against the counter.

Before Sam could reply, her phone buzzed with an incoming call. *Marshall.*

"Sorry," she called out, already kicking off her heels and running into the hall. "It's my boyfriend!"

"Okay, um, see you later," Liam replied, a little awkwardly.

Sam flung herself into her room, lifting the phone to her ear. "Marshall! I'm so glad you called!"

"Hey, Sam. How are you?"

The mere sound of his voice curled around her like a quilt, soothing and steadying. She sat back onto the air mattress and closed her eyes, wishing he'd gotten a smartphone so that they could chat on video. More than anything, she longed to see the emotions darting over his face.

"I'm okay." Suddenly the force of it all crashed over her, and she let out a breath. "Jeff and Daphne had a big engagement party tonight, and I couldn't go."

She heard a rustling sound on the other end of the line and wondered if Marshall was getting undressed. Or maybe he'd already showered and was pulling a clean shirt on, then falling backward onto the bed . . .

"Sam, you wouldn't have liked that party anyway," he said gently.

"It's my brother's engagement party!"

"It's a stuffy state occasion," Marshall insisted. "Jeff and Daphne probably didn't get to invite many of their real friends. That ballroom was packed with people they *had* to include, judges and nobility and whoever else is on the palace's list. As for you . . ." She could almost see him shrug. "America has never had a former princess before. There's no precedent for this."

"I hate when you're reasonable," Sam joked, but he had cheered her up, at least a little.

"I'm guessing your night was more fun than if you'd been at that party. What did you do, anyway?"

Sam bit her lip; she hadn't yet told Marshall about her job at Enclave, or about living at Liam's. She hadn't *meant* to be deceitful. It was just so hard to get him on the phone—they'd only talked a couple of times in the past week—and whenever she did get to hear his voice, she'd found an excuse not to bring it up.

But now that it looked like she was crashing here indefinitely, she needed to tell him everything.

"I actually tended bar tonight," she admitted. "At a club on the east side."

Marshall chuckled. "Good one, Sam."

He thought she was joking. She started to explain, but Marshall's next question struck her silent.

"How much longer do you think you'll stay in Washington?" he asked. When she didn't answer right away, he added, "You're coming back soon, aren't you?"

Sam's heart lurched. "I haven't given it much thought."

"Look, you tried your best with your family. And Beatrice is better, right? So you can leave, give everyone time to cool off."

She *had* promised that she would return to Hawaii once Beatrice was recovered. Yet everything in her recoiled at the thought of getting back on a plane and leaving her family behind—running away from it all, a second time.

"I'm sorry." Her voice cracked over the words; she swallowed and tried again. "I'm not coming back yet. I can't leave now—not like this." She had to find a way to make things right with Jeff, and with Beatrice.

"I understand," Marshall said heavily. "I just . . . I miss you, Sam."

She rolled onto her side, pressing the phone tighter to her ear. "I miss you, too!"

"It's not the same here without you."

Sam could hear the pain in his voice. He had asked her to come back to him and she'd said no; of course he was hurt. She may have had good reasons, but she had still rejected him.

"You feel so far away right now," she whispered.

"Yeah. Long distance really sucks."

Things had been so simple in Hawaii, where their lives were completely intertwined. Sam hadn't realized how much those day-to-day interactions had mattered: wandering out to the beach and collecting stray shells; cooking stir-fry together and eating it on the back deck; recounting stories from their childhood that they hadn't yet shared with each other, until they felt like they knew every last one of each other's anecdotes.

Those small moments were the mortar holding a relationship aloft, and without them, its structure began to wobble.

"How's Nina?" Marshall asked, clearly trying to change the subject. "Are you being a good houseguest?"

She swallowed. "Actually, I'm not at Nina's."

"You went to Loughlin House after all?"

"Um, I'm crashing at a house in Tribedo." Briefly, Sam explained how she'd met Liam: that she was living in a house with his bandmates and friends, and working at Enclave.

When she'd finished, Marshall's voice was oddly tense. "You're staying with some random guy, and you didn't think to tell me?"

"I'm sorry I didn't mention it. But it's not as bad as you're making it sound," she hurried to clarify. "It's a house full of people—boys and girls! And Liam is just a friend. Trust me on this."

Marshall sighed. "I do trust you, Sam. But I don't trust this Liam guy, or all the other people in this house. What if they sell you out to the press?"

"Then I'll leave," Sam said simply. "But I don't think they'll do that."

"And you're really working as a bartender? Don't you think that's risky?"

"I need to keep myself busy, Marshall. And no one has recognized me so far. It's all about context. They don't expect to see me, so they *don't* see me, even when I'm right in front of them."

Sam could feel Marshall's frustration from thousands of miles away. She stared out the window and remarked, if only to change the subject, "It's snowing here." A few small flakes drifted lightly downward, melting the moment they hid the windowsill.

There was another beat of silence, as if Marshall was

deciding whether or not to keep being angry. Then he said, "It's snowing here, too."

"Wait—what?"

He laughed. "I'm kidding. That would be some pretty bizarre weather."

"Utterly terrifying," Sam agreed.

"But it would be fun, in a way. If we were both looking out the window and seeing snow, it would almost feel like we were in the same place."

Her heart ached at that. "I know what you mean."

In refusing to come back, Sam had cut away at some fundamental ease between her and Marshall. Of course, their relationship was complicated in plenty of ways—the media attention, the racism he faced, their families' hesitation— but not this. Not the two of them, together. When they were alone, everything had always been effortless.

And now it took effort.

"I love you." Sam felt a little like her sister during a press conference; like she was pretending things were fine even as they deteriorated around her.

"I love you, too, Sam," Marshall told her.

It wasn't until much later that Sam realized he'd used her real name—that he hadn't called her by a silly nickname since she left Hawaii.

20

NINA

Nina found, to her surprise, that she liked being in the play.

The first few rehearsals, she'd thought of the performance as an obligation: she had auditioned, after all, and the right thing to do was to follow through on her commitments. But far from gritting her teeth and enduring it, Nina was *enjoying* herself. It felt exhilarating, standing onstage and reading lines someone else had written. She could be the center of attention and at the same time disappear, as if she'd folded her real self away and hidden inside the persona of Helena.

Jamie hadn't kissed her in any of the rehearsals again. Not that she was waiting for him to.

The two of them had fallen into the habit of walking back together after rehearsals, chatting about the play or their mutual friends until they arrived at Nina's dorm. Tonight, as Nina slung her tote bag over one shoulder, Jamie pushed open the auditorium door for her.

"Have you finished *Henry IV* yet?" he asked, referring to their reading for Dr. Larsen's Shakespeare class.

"I'm about halfway through." Nina looked over at Jamie. "Have *you* finished?"

"I've read it before. And seen it performed."

"It must be a little disconcerting, watching all your ancestors murder each other," she replied, fighting back a smile.

"If there's one thing the historic royals excelled at, it's murder," Jamie agreed.

She started on the path that led toward her dorm, but he paused. "I was actually going out to watch the game. Want to come?"

Nina hesitated, uncertain whether he'd just asked her on a date. "What game?"

"The only game worth watching, of course. Calgary versus Vancouver. *Hockey*, Nina," he added, when she was still staring at him in confusion.

"Okay." She smiled. "But for the record, I know nothing about hockey."

"Don't worry, I know enough for both of us," Jamie said easily, and started toward the student lot on the edge of campus.

Nina trotted to keep up. "You didn't want to get one of those permits that let you park anywhere?" Jeff's protection officer had one; his car sometimes idled right outside the classrooms, on the narrow driveways that were supposed to be for university service vehicles only.

"I get enough special treatment as it is."

"Right, being a prince must be so hard," Nina deadpanned.

"Being a prince? Nah, I get special treatment because of my devastating good looks," Jamie replied without missing a beat. He led her to a sedan that was surprisingly un-flashy, and opened the passenger door with a flourish.

Nina couldn't remember Jeff driving her anywhere himself, then was angry with herself for thinking about Jeff at all. He certainly hadn't spent any time lately thinking about *her*.

When they pulled up to a bar, Nina took one look at the red-and-white painted sign and laughed. "The Maple Leaf? Isn't that on the nose?"

"Since we can't go to Canada tonight, this is the next best

thing," Jamie informed her. "And don't worry, no one here will post anything. There won't be any media coverage of our date," he added clumsily.

So it *was* a date.

"That's good, because I hate being photographed."

"I know." Jamie grinned. "If you didn't mind being famous, you wouldn't make it so hard for me to ask you out."

Nina choked on a laugh. She couldn't help it; there was something about Jamie, an irrepressible sense of mischief that reminded her of how things had once been between her and Jeff, back when they were just friends—before the night of graduation when they first kissed, and everything got so complicated.

Except that he was different from Jeff. Beneath the riotous laughter and cavalier charm, Jamie carried a streak of loneliness. Someone had hurt him. It made Nina wonder how many people he truly trusted.

They stepped through the front doors, and Nina noted with surprise that the Maple Leaf was pretty empty. There were just a few guys in sports jerseys gathered around the flat-screen TV on the far wall, none of whom paid her and Jamie any mind.

Jamie gestured to the bar, and Nina perched on a stool. A bartender with a high ponytail came toward them. "What can I get for you?"

"A pitcher of Labatt, thanks."

When the bartender returned with their beer and two mugs, Jamie insisted on paying. Nina's eyes widened.

"Twenty-five dollars for a pitcher of beer? That's extortion!"

He handed over his credit card, clearly amused. "This beer is the national drink of Canada. It's imported; of course it's more expensive."

"Did someone literally walk down from Canada carrying the keg on their back? Otherwise you were ripped off!"

"Just try it," Jamie insisted. Nina sighed and did as he asked. "Well?" he prompted.

"It *is* good beer," she admitted.

His eyes twinkled with delight. "Better than American draft beer. Right?"

"Okay, fine, it's delicious. Are you happy?"

"Inordinately happy. Beer is one of the many things that Canada does better than America."

Nina leaned an elbow onto the surface of the bar and took another long sip of beer. "What else is on this list?"

"Poutine, first and foremost. It's such an upgrade from French fries. Or cheese tots," he added, with a sidelong look at Nina. "And our slang is better. Did you know we say *cheers* when we leave people, instead of *goodbye*? It's so much more uplifting."

"Because *cheers* makes you think of clinking glasses," Nina pointed out.

"And Canada trumps America where princes are concerned," Jamie added cheekily. "The Prince of Canada is higher ranking and, we can all admit, vastly better-looking than the Prince of America."

Nina made a noise that was somewhere between a cough and a strangled cry of outrage. "I can't believe you just said that!"

"You were thinking it. I'm just the one who said it aloud."

"You're terrible," Nina protested, but her insult didn't land because of the laugh that was bubbling out of her chest.

"Of course I am. I've been told it's a large part of my appeal."

Nina's laughter faded, and she shifted on her barstool to look Jamie full in the face. "Jeff is in class again, now that Beatrice is better. You might run into him on campus."

"So?"

"So, I thought you'd want to know, since you and Jeff are

apparently in some kind of silent competition! Are you ever going to tell me what that's all about?"

Jamie's blue eyes fixed on hers. "I will if you tell me who hurt you."

Nina must have flinched, because his expression instantly softened. "Sorry. I didn't mean to intrude." He grabbed his beer mug, then set it down again. "I get this feeling sometimes, in rehearsal, that you're thinking of someone who caused you pain."

Jamie probably thought Jeff was the one who'd hurt her, and he had. But so had Daphne.

"It's a long story," Nina warned.

He nodded. "It goes without saying that I won't tell anyone, if you want to share it."

And the thing was, Nina did trust him.

She explained how she and Daphne had teamed up against Gabriella, how Nina had thought they were becoming unlikely friends, only to learn that Daphne had been playing her the whole time: trying to keep her far from Jeff.

When she finished her story, Jamie frowned. "Didn't Daphne's family lose their baronetcy anyway? How did that fit into her plan?"

"I . . ." Nina hesitated. Why had she never considered this crucial detail? An uneasy regret spiked through her, and she almost reached for her phone, but now wasn't the time.

"What happened between you and Jeff?" she asked, flipping the focus back to Jamie.

He stared down into his half-full beer. "Jeff broke up my parents' marriage."

Nina stared at him, dumbfounded. Whatever she'd expected, it wasn't this.

"It was the summer of that last visit to Washington, when Jeff and I were twelve. We caught my mom and her tennis instructor together. Yes, Henri came on tour with us," he added, in response to Nina's questioning look. "I guess that should have been the first clue, right? She told my dad that she wanted to keep working out while traveling, and he never questioned it."

Nina made a sympathetic noise but didn't interrupt.

"Jeff and I went to get our rackets for water-balloon tennis—you may remember that game; he and Sam had invented it that summer and were all obsessed. It had been raining that morning, and we didn't expect to find anyone on the courts. But then we got to the equipment shed and heard voices." Jamie swallowed, tightened his grip on his beer mug. "I would give anything to unsee it . . . my mom and Henri, in there, together."

Nina reached for Jamie's hand; she couldn't help it. There was nothing in this moment of the bold, confident prince who sauntered through life with such fearlessness. He looked like a lost little boy.

"That's terrible," she said softly.

"I'm okay, really. I've had years of therapy to work through it." Jamie spoke flippantly, but there was something raw and wounded beneath his words, as if he'd tried to put on his armor but couldn't quite make it fit.

"We both panicked and ran back to the palace in silence," Jamie went on, picking up the thread of the story. "When we got back, I asked Jeff not to tell anyone what he'd seen. Maybe not the most mature reaction, but . . ." He sighed. "I kept hoping that if no one else knew, it wouldn't be real.

"The next day, though, my parents were fighting about Henri. Jeff must have told someone—probably his parents, who'd felt obligated to tell my dad," Jamie explained. "My dad wasn't even angry. He kept begging my mom to stay, saying that they could move on as if this whole thing had never happened, but it was too late. She'd already chosen to leave him."

Nina's hand was still resting on top of Jamie's; she forced his palm over and laced her fingers in his. He gave her a grateful squeeze.

"Jamie. I'm sorry that happened, and that you were put in the middle of it, but you can't blame Jeff for your parents splitting up," she said gently.

"I know. I blame him for failing to keep a secret," Jamie insisted. "As a friend, I asked him not to tell anyone, and he did it anyway."

"You were both so young. I'm sure Jeff did what he thought was best." Nina wasn't sure why she was defending him, except that this whole situation sounded far too complicated for a pair of twelve-year-olds to navigate.

"And then Jeff utterly dropped me," he went on, voice heavy. "We left in a rush that same day, without saying goodbye. I kept thinking Jeff would check in, but . . . nothing. He never even texted." Jamie shook his head wearily. "He abandoned my family when scandal hit us, just like everyone else did."

"What do you mean, everyone abandoned you?"

"The other royal families all dropped us. Why do you think my dad is so reclusive up in Canada? He's never invited to anything. The Windsors didn't like us to begin with, because they think Canada should be part of their *commonwealth*"— Jamie said this last with a touch of derision—"and once Dad was divorced, they had a perfect excuse to cut his invitation from all their weddings. It's why he hates the League of Kings conference so much, because he feels like everyone is judging him."

"There have been other royal divorces," Nina pointed out.

"Not many. My parents' was one of the first high-profile divorce cases. Except, of course, for the Grimaldis'."

Nina attempted to lighten the mood. "Monaco, the country where princesses marry circus clowns and race-car drivers."

A smile tugged at Jamie's lips. "This is why I like you, Nina."

"Because of my witty one-liners?"

"Because you don't treat my title like it's the only relevant part of me," Jamie said bluntly. "No matter how hard I try to meet people on my own terms, I feel like the girls I've dated in the past all went out with me because I'm a future king. They were interested in *what* I am, not *who* I am."

"That's a terrible way to think about people."

Jamie shrugged. "I can't really blame them; that's all they know about me. You're different, though. You've grown up around royalty. Case in point: you make jokes about Monaco." He grinned. "I like that I have to work hard to impress you, instead of falling back on my usual tricks."

"What's your usual trick? You flash your signet ring and a girl jumps into bed with you?" Nina asked sarcastically.

Jamie shrugged as if to say, *More or less.* "It's just nice to be with someone who doesn't like me for the royal trappings."

"If I liked you at all, it would be in *spite* of the royal trappings."

"My point exactly. I've never met anyone like you, Nina." The irreverence had fallen from his tone; he was as serious as she'd ever seen him. "You're so brave, and smart, and un-apologetically you. You take people at face value, which is a pretty rare thing."

Nina liked the version of herself that Jamie apparently saw, the one reflected back to her in his eyes.

Without pausing to think, she grabbed his face and pulled it to hers, right there in the middle of the Canadian-themed Midtown bar.

Jamie kissed her back eagerly, skimming his hands around her back to play with the hem of her shirt. She felt cool air kiss the skin above the waistband of her jeans, and leaned further into him, deepening the kiss.

When she pulled away, Nina should have felt self-conscious, yet she didn't. She was buoyant, electrified.

Whatever this was between her and Jamie, she wanted more of it.

"Should we get out of here?" she heard herself ask.

Jamie was off his barstool before she'd even finished the question. "Absolutely. We can teach you the fundamentals of hockey another time."

21

DAPHNE

Ethan stared at Daphne's phone, eyes wide. "You seriously sent this? What were you thinking?"

She sat back onto her bed, crossing her arms stubbornly over her chest. "I was *thinking* that I wanted to draw Gabriella out into the open, force her to confront us face to face. Then maybe we could talk her into backing down."

With less than a month to go before her wedding, Daphne had decided she couldn't keep waiting for Rei to come through. She needed to take action.

So she'd pulled up the most recent threatening email and composed a reply: *I am in possession of some valuable information about the queen. I'll tell you Beatrice's dark secret if you'll agree not to act on mine. Let's meet to discuss.*

She hadn't been certain the anonymous email address could even receive an inbound email, but apparently it could.

Fine. I'll meet you and Ethan at 4 PM, came the reply, with a link to an address outside the city.

Daphne had bit her lip as she typed, *Ethan won't be there, just me.*

I know you're working together, the anonymous emailer had scoffed. *Bring him or the deal is off.*

Which was why Daphne had called him and insisted that he come over *now,* because they had an urgent situation on their hands.

Ethan shook his head, his eyes still fixed on her message. "I'm guessing you didn't run this by Rei."

Daphne slid off the bed and paced toward the windows. "Rei isn't moving fast enough! I need to get Gabriella off my back before she destroys our lives."

"And you thought poking the bear was your best option? Do you even *have* a secret of Beatrice's to give in exchange?"

Daphne did, actually. Samantha had once let slip that Beatrice was in love with someone else—someone who was *not* Teddy. Whoever it was, Daphne assumed that person must be very unsuitable, otherwise why hadn't Beatrice just dated them?

She had then warned Beatrice that she knew about the secret relationship (though Daphne hadn't a clue who it was with), effectively strong-arming the queen into sending Himari to Japan.

Not her finest moment, but she and Himari had made up afterward. As for Beatrice, she had never mentioned the interaction again.

"I don't have anything on Beatrice," Daphne fibbed, because she had no intention of actually using what she knew. She'd done enough damage the first time. "I just assumed Gabriella would only be tempted by the highest-ranking person in the country. So?" she demanded. "Will you please just come, like Gabriella wants?"

Ethan groaned. "I'll come, but only because I don't trust you to go alone."

♛

As they pulled off the freeway toward the address in Ethan's GPS, and colorful castle turrets rose up before them, Daphne blinked in surprise. How had she not realized where Gabriella was sending them?

Ethan choked out a laugh. "Say what you will about Gabriella, she's got a sense of humor, sending you here."

"To a kitschy Disney-knockoff theme park?"

Ethan shrugged as he pulled toward a sign marked ENCHANTED FIEFDOM. They had borrowed his mom's car for the afternoon; Daphne was too spooked to get back on the motorcycle after that car had chased them the last time.

She hung back while Ethan bought their admission tickets, though she probably needn't have worried. No one here was on the lookout for stray royals, or almost-royals. Forty minutes outside downtown, Enchanted Fiefdom was mainly visited by bored teens, or parents desperate to distract their young children.

When they passed through the turnstile and into the main park, a cobblestone street unfurled before them, vaguely evoking a European hamlet. Afternoon crowds surged in and out of the various storefronts.

Daphne's eyes cut to a merchandise store, and she elbowed Ethan. "Should we get disguises?" There were plenty of costume pieces in the windows: pointed medieval princess hats, baseball caps with elf ears sticking out the sides.

He rolled his eyes but ducked into the shop. While she waited, Daphne drew further to one side, pretending to check her phone. A massive Christmas tree stood at the center of the town square, a kid-sized train chugging in a loop around its base. The sight filled Daphne with an odd sense of nostalgia for a childhood she'd never had, one where she would have assembled toy trains with her parents or hung up strings of golden lights.

"There you are!" Ethan came to join her. "You need to stay close by, Daph! You were too short for me to see in all these people."

She sniffed. "I am not too short. Most people would say I'm the *perfect* height."

"Yes, the perfect height for getting lost in crowds." Ethan tossed her the shopping bag. Daphne opened it to find a black cat-shaped mask with feathery whiskers, as well as a Santa beard and red felt hat.

"You're going to be Santa?" she asked as she fixed the cat mask to her face.

"Nope. You're the only one being paranoid," he reminded her. "I just wanted to give you options."

"As if I would walk around dressed as Santa," she muttered.

"Why not? You'd make a pretty cute Santa."

There was a beat of silence after that declaration, a bit too meaningful for Daphne's liking. She nodded back toward the park entrance.

"We need to figure out where Gabriella is waiting. Should we retrace our steps?"

When they were back at the turnstiles, there was no sign of Gabriella, or of anyone waiting for them. Daphne sighed and pulled her phone from her bag. She saw at once that she had a new email from the anonymous address: *You couldn't leave well enough alone, could you, Daphne? You really thought you could convince me to meet in person? Ha. Enjoy your afternoon at Enchanted Fiefdom.*

Daphne had stopped in her tracks. Ethan stared at her quizzically, and she held out her phone.

"She's not coming," she said simply.

Ethan read the email, brow furrowed. "I don't get it. If she wasn't ever going to meet us, then why did she pretend to agree, and drag us here?"

"She's hazing us. She probably loved the thought of us traipsing around this theme park trying to find her."

Ethan gestured to the turnstiles. "Should we get going, then?"

Daphne hesitated. Her eyes cut back toward the park: the colored ribbons of the roller coasters looping above the horizon, the music emanating from a nearby show. Something smelled tantalizingly like sugar and cinnamon, and it made her stomach growl.

"We could stay," she heard herself suggest. "We did come all the way here."

Ethan seemed startled. "You want to stay?"

"I might as well take advantage of this rare chance to be out in public in sneakers."

Daphne had to wear heels at all her official appearances. Last year, when she and Jeff showed up at a youth softball game, she'd ended up running a lap in her heeled boots, because what other choice did she have? There was something breathtakingly liberating about being in public, surrounded by people, in sneakers.

Ethan smiled, his cheek dimpling in a way she rarely saw. "Okay. What do you want to do first?"

"The Dragonfire coaster," Daphne said automatically. She had a secret love of roller coasters, the ones so fast that they made your stomach drop.

Ethan coughed self-consciously. "I forgot you're such a thrill seeker. Can we start on something smaller?"

"Like what?"

Daphne followed his gaze and laughed as comprehension struck. "The *carousel*? Ethan," she asked, "are you afraid of heights, and I never knew?"

"First of all, it's rude to make fun of people's phobias," he said stiffly. "And if you must know, I'm afraid of roller coasters. They're really high and fast, okay?"

"Says the guy who blasts around town on his motorcycle," she noted, amused.

"I always follow the speed limit!"

"The last time you drove me, we crossed an intersection so fast I nearly flew out of my seat!"

"I did that for *you*!"

She fell silent, chastened. "Sorry. Let's go do the carousel. It looks fun."

"Okay, you don't have to lie to me," Ethan mumbled, but a smile curled at the edges of his lips. "I know you don't think it's *fun*."

They passed a line of children clutching their parents' hands. Daphne glanced over, wondering what had caused so long a queue; the sandwich-board sign read PHOTOS WITH THE SNOW QUEEN! Beyond a makeshift blue curtain, Daphne saw the character: a girl around her age dressed in a white dress reminiscent of ice crystals. A smile was pasted to her face, her blond hair spilling down her back. No, she realized, that probably wasn't the girl's real hair.

Daphne felt a sudden moment of kinship with the Snow Queen. The people in this line didn't care about her as a person; to them she was a living doll, a shop-window mannequin they could dress in a wig and glittery gown and pose for photos with.

It was exactly what people did to Daphne at her various meet-and-greets or walkabouts. Except, unlike Daphne, this girl got to take off the wig, walk through the front gates and back out into real life. While Daphne was trapped in the princess realm forever.

Trapped? She shook her head, confused by her own thoughts. She had *chosen* this life, and would choose it again.

There was no line for the carousel; most of the park's small children were already being loaded into strollers or fed an early dinner. Daphne and Ethan had their pick of animals to perch on. She selected a bright pink elephant. Ethan shrugged and took the unicorn next to her.

As the music started up and the carousel began its slow revolution, she glanced over at him. "You're not going back to Malaysia, are you? You'll be at King's College in the new year?"

"Yeah. I need to get on track with my premed requirements."

"I didn't realize you still wanted to do premed. I mean, I remember you used to say that in high school. . . ."

The unicorn and elephant were bobbing up and down in apposition, so that Daphne was low while Ethan was high. It made their conversation feel slightly ridiculous. But his tone was serious as he replied, "My mom was in college, finishing her premed requirements, when she got pregnant with me. It's why she never went to medical school."

"I didn't know that."

"I don't really talk about it," Ethan said quietly. "I feel too guilty that she didn't get to be a doctor because of me."

Daphne felt a hollow ache in her chest. "You can't carry the blame for the fact that your mom isn't a doctor."

"Her entire life got derailed because of an unplanned pregnancy," he pointed out.

"Your mom *loves* you." That much Daphne would stake her life on. She had only met Ethan's mom—a high school biology teacher, which made more sense now that Daphne knew her backstory—a handful of times, but Daphne could always tell that Ms. Beckett was the nurturing type. She packed lunches with neatly trimmed carrot sticks; she helped with homework; she carved out time for her son despite being a single mom.

Daphne fumbled for the right phrasing. "What I'm trying to say is that your mom wouldn't want you to follow her dream; she'd want you to follow *yours.*"

"Maybe you should take your own advice," Ethan shot back.

Daphne recoiled, and he sucked in a breath. "I'm sorry, that was over the line. I just . . . I want to make sure that you're going through all of this for the right reasons. That you want to marry Jeff for you, and not for your parents."

It was dizzying and acutely unnerving, having someone see into her motives like that.

"I wasn't actually one of those little girls who twirled around in tulle princess dresses," Daphne admitted. "Believe it or not, I used to want to be a doctor, too."

"Wait—what?"

"I had one of those plastic stethoscope sets." Daphne wasn't sure who had given it to her; it didn't seem like the sort of thing her parents would have bought. "I wore it all the time, checking my teddy bear's heartbeat. When I decided he was sick, I would feed him Goldfish and sips of water to recover."

Ethan's brow furrowed in concern. "It's not too late. You could be a doctor, if you wanted."

"Oh, definitely not! I would be a terrible doctor," Daphne said quickly. "I just mean, dreams change. If you need to let go of yours, you should feel like you can."

Still, Daphne couldn't help wondering if a shred of her childhood dream still lived inside her. She had been drawn to the idea of healing people because it felt *important*. Doctors dealt in life and death—what stakes could possibly be higher?

Perhaps that explained the appeal of becoming a princess: she wanted to feel like the decisions she made had real impact.

"When I was a little kid, I wanted to be a pirate," Ethan said into the silence.

Daphne recognized the statement for what it was—a peace offering.

"It's not too late for you, either! I bet Enchanted Fiefdom is hiring," Daphne teased.

"You just want to see me in a pirate costume, don't you?" Ethan replied, shaking his head. "You've got to cool it with the dirty talk; this is a family-friendly place."

Daphne burst out laughing. It felt nice, seeing Ethan like

this—not scheming or sneaking around but simply talking. She was glad to know that they could do more than bicker with each other. They could share things; could be earnest, and playful, and *fun*. The way friends would be.

When the carousel drew to a stop, Daphne slid off her elephant and gave its plastic side an affectionate pat. "Want to get a pretzel? I'm starving."

"Should we try that café down the street?" Ethan suggested.

Daphne adjusted her cat mask, then glanced back over her shoulder with a provocative wink. "Race you there."

She took off running before he could react. Moments later she heard his laughter behind her, but it only made her sprint even faster.

Daphne knew how this particular fairy tale would end: at midnight the spell would lift and she would face reality again. But she was determined to enjoy this magical interlude as long as it lasted.

22

BEATRICE

The iron gates—which were simple and devoid of decoration, offering no clue as to the owner of this ranch—swung open, and Beatrice's car began climbing uphill. She was at the Ramirez family property in the Texas hill country.

If Connor was the head of security, he had to know she was coming. What was he thinking? Did he want to see her, or was he hoping to avoid her?

These were not the types of questions one should be asking on the way to an important political meeting.

As Beatrice approached the main house, the front door swung open, and the Duchess of Texas hurried out. She was nearing sixty but looked much younger, with wisps of dark hair falling loose from her ponytail.

"Your Majesty!" she exclaimed as Beatrice stepped out of the car. She sank into a curtsy, which looked especially ridiculous given her ratty old fleece and dirt-streaked jeans. "I'm sorry to be so casual; I've been at the stables all morning," the duchess went on, reading the queen's mind. "One of our mares is foaling!"

"That's exciting." Beatrice felt an answering smile on her own face. There was something unpretentious about the duchess that had always set her at ease, though she knew that beneath her warm exterior, Anna had a backbone of steel. It was notoriously difficult to change her mind once she'd set out on a course of action.

"Roger is still in Houston with José and Christina," the duchess went on, naming her husband and children. "I thought it might be best if it was just the two of us. I hope you don't mind."

So she knew Beatrice wasn't here on a social call.

"Of course, though I'm disappointed to miss them," Beatrice replied. José was only a year younger than she was, and had been on her parents' list of "approved" royal consorts for Beatrice—the same list that had led her to Teddy.

"I'm sure you want to rest. I'll show you to your room," the duchess began, but Beatrice shook her head.

"I'd love to join you with the horses, actually."

She had changed before the plane landed, and was wearing what she thought of as her royal ranch outfit: dark jeans, a long-sleeved shirt stitched with embroidery along the cuffs, and her cowboy boots. They were simple brown ones, as soft as butter, despite the fact that Beatrice only wore them twice a year to agricultural fairs or rodeos.

Anna smiled and led Beatrice to the stables out back. The skies overhead were a brilliant blue, and Beatrice shrugged out of her jacket in surprise. It was so much warmer here than in the freezing capital.

She kept glancing around, her nerves on a low hum of alertness, but she didn't see Connor anywhere.

When they reached one of the stalls, Beatrice let out a little cry of delight. The newborn horse inside was already trying to stand on shaky legs. The duchess smiled and opened the stall door to slip inside. "Isn't it miraculous? She's not even an hour old." Her hands ran along the mother's withers. "This is Peppie's third, and they've all been strong."

"Peppie?" Beatrice repeated. The mare huffed out a breath, as if irritated so many humans had come to bother her.

"Her real name is Dr Pepper, but we've always called her Peppie."

"As in the soda?"

The duchess seemed amused by the question. "Yes, as in the soda."

Peppie wandered over to Beatrice, ears twitching with idle curiosity. Beatrice grabbed a handful of oats and let Peppie nip them off her palm. The duchess watched her, seeming to reach some decision.

"Would you like a tour of the ranch? It's best seen by horseback. If you ride, that is."

"I'd love that." It had been a few years since Beatrice was in the saddle, but surely it would come back to her.

"Excellent. Connor!" Anna called out.

The smile slipped from Beatrice's face, and a roar of white noise filled her ears. She should have been prepared for this—she had *known* he was here—yet nothing could have readied her for the sight of Connor again.

He turned a corner and drew to a halt, his blue-gray eyes meeting hers.

Her first thought was that he'd changed. He looked so unlike the Connor she knew, in his faded jeans and cowboy hat. A line of stubble grazed his jaw, something he could never have gotten away with at the palace, but standards seemed to be looser here.

Connor bent forward into a bow. "Your Majesty."

Somehow Beatrice managed to find her voice. "It's good to see you again, Connor. You look well."

"Oh yes, I keep forgetting, you two know each other!" Anna exclaimed, oblivious to the tension. "Connor, weren't you the queen's personal security detail?"

"Her Majesty was still a princess then." His expression

was impassively polite, as if Beatrice were nothing but a former employer, not someone he'd once said *I love you* to.

Beatrice watched as the grooms began saddling a bay gelding for her. Connor disappeared into a neighboring tack room, then emerged with a black velvet helmet. "Your Majesty," he said gruffly.

Beatrice would rather have worn a cowboy hat, like he and the duchess were doing, but she clipped on the helmet without complaint.

She sucked in a breath, surprised, when Connor knelt down next to her horse, lacing his fingers into a makeshift stirrup. He was standing so close that she could smell him, the familiar scents of spicy soap and deodorant but also new ones, horse and hay and sunshine. It was disorienting.

Connor's gaze moved over her face, watching her. "Are you ready?"

Beatrice had no choice but to place her boot in his hands, letting him vault her into the saddle.

They set out down a rock-strewn trail: Anna and Beatrice together, with Connor riding ahead and one of the grooms following several horses' length behind them.

The duchess launched into an explanation of the ranch's history, pointing out landmarks as they passed. Beatrice nodded distractedly. She knew she should pay attention; the whole reason she'd come was to win Anna over. Yet she couldn't stop sneaking discreet glances at Connor.

It wasn't just his clothes that had changed. He looked older, somehow; and his face was tanned, even sunburned in places. He seemed completely at ease in the saddle, which surprised Beatrice; she didn't remember him being able to ride.

She forced herself to look away before the duchess caught her staring.

"It's been a long time since you visited Texas, hasn't it?" Anna asked.

"Too long." Sensing that the duchess would appreciate honesty, Beatrice added, "I'm sorry to have descended on you like this. I know a royal visit is always an imposition."

"Not at all. I'm just sorry again for not greeting you in proper form," the duchess replied. "My children think I spend too much time with the horses myself. They're always reminding me that I have a whole staff to do these things for me, but there's no substitute for putting in the time. The horses decide when you've earned their trust."

"That's why I'm here, in a sense," Beatrice heard herself say. "Because senators are rather like horses. You have to engage with them yourself, earn the right to ask a favor of them."

To Beatrice's relief, the duchess burst into appreciative laughter. "Good, you're direct. I like that," she declared. "Your father was a great king, and it was an honor to know him, but he was always beating around the bush. Here in Texas we'd rather you be frank. We don't have the patience for oblique messages and dropped hints."

They turned onto a trail that led uphill, their horses scattering small stones behind them with each step. Cedar trees cast their faces in mottled shadow, the impossibly blue sky visible between their branches. Down below, Beatrice saw the sedate blue-green ribbon of the Guadalupe River.

There was something therapeutic about riding again. Her memory loss was of no consequence here; her body knew how to do this on an instinctive, cellular level.

"Then you may have already guessed, I came here to discuss the bill for my removal," Beatrice said quietly.

She'd half expected Anna to accuse her of interfering in legislative affairs, or perhaps to feign ignorance, but the duchess nodded impassively. "Go on."

"I'd like to persuade you to vote against it. I'm not mentally damaged."

Anna's hands looped through the knot in her reins, twisting it through her fingers and then letting it fall again. "I don't see how anyone could be *un*damaged after the year you've had. You lost your father, you inherited the throne far too young, and then you were in a terrible car accident! Don't you want a break? God knows I want one, all the time," Anna added, with something like a sigh.

"With all due respect," Beatrice countered, trying to smooth the impatience from her voice, "this isn't about me. It's about America."

"Aren't those one and the same thing?"

Beatrice answered the question with one of her own. "Do you think the country would be better off in my brother's hands?"

"Who said it has to be your brother? I always hoped your uncle might step in. Or your mother." The duchess leveled a stare at Beatrice. "You know she and I are old friends, though we haven't kept up in recent years."

Except that a Queen Mother could never ascend the throne. Adelaide hadn't been born into the royal family; she had married into it. A crucial distinction.

"Your Majesty, you must know that the Washingtons have seemed erratic lately," the duchess went on. "Trust me when I say that I understand how difficult it is, navigating family issues when the entire world is watching. Especially when your family dramas have national repercussions: on the economy, the jobs market, inflation. When things at the top are constantly changing, it means whiplash for those below."

"Of course it's been a bumpy year—we lost our king." *My father*, Beatrice wanted to cry out. "And we hosted the League of Kings conference."

"*And* you canceled a wedding, *and* your sister got herself kicked out of the family," the duchess pointed out. "The accident wasn't your fault, of course, but it meant more upheaval.

You should know that Texans' faith in the monarchy is at an all-time low."

No one could accuse Anna Ramirez of sugarcoating the truth.

"There's no question that you should vote according to the needs of Texas," Beatrice agreed. "Which is why I'm asking you to help strike down Madison's bill. *More* upheaval is obviously not the answer."

"The needs of Texas," Anna repeated, an eyebrow raised. "How much do you really know about those, Your Majesty? Have you seen the price of gas lately? Do you know how little money I have to pay our public-school teachers? Are you aware that a terrible heat wave this summer strained our electric grid to the breaking point, and we need an overhaul of the entire system?"

"This is exactly the problem with politics. It's too individualistic, too—*narrow-minded!*"

Beatrice hadn't meant to snap. But for so long she had kept her emotions neatly bottled up, far below the surface, and now they were bubbling up out of her like molten lava. She had to say this before she lost her nerve.

"There is a reason our country banded together as one nation, under God, indivisible," she went on. "We are better together than we are on our own."

Their horses had slowed, as if sensing the magnitude of this conversation. Beatrice swallowed. "For most of my life I've tried to go it alone. I wanted America to think I was strong, just as strong as any king, so I assumed that I couldn't show weakness or ask for help. I never leaned on anyone. But going into battle alone doesn't make you strong; it makes you vulnerable. Asking for help when you need it is the true strength."

Something flickered behind the duchess's impassive facade as Beatrice spoke. "So here I am: asking you to join forces with me and offering, in exchange, to be your partner in as much as I can. Let's find a way to collaborate on the issues you've brought up. We could start a new focus group, draft new legislation? I don't know exactly what the solution is," Beatrice admitted, "but I feel confident that we can find it if we work together."

A bird called somewhere in the distance, underscoring her words. Beatrice sat ramrod straight in her saddle, waiting.

"All right, Your Majesty. I'll support you against Madison, and will try to rally others to vote against him as well."

"You will?"

"You expected more of a negotiation?"

Frankly, yes. Beatrice had assumed Anna would come at her with a list of demands.

"I've been in this role too long to enjoy negotiating any-more. What's that saying—the sign of a good compromise is that neither party is happy with the outcome?" Anna shook her head. "You asked if we could *collaborate*. A word I hear far less often than I should."

Her eyes seemed to twinkle as she added, "I like that you weren't afraid to come to me, hat in hand, to ask for my help. You've proven that you're humble and unafraid of criticism. You'll need those qualities to face the challenges ahead."

"Thank you," Beatrice said softly.

"I faced the same kind of opposition in my day, you know. I was one of the only acting duchesses of my generation. I know what it's like to face down men who tell you that you aren't good enough." The duchess seemed suddenly galva-nized, as if the prospect of taking on Madison had infused new purpose into her. "I look forward to working together, Your Majesty."

"As do I."

Beatrice stood in her stirrups, leaned across the distance between their two horses, and shook the duchess's hand right there on the dusty trail. Exactly how she expected things to be done in Texas.

✦

When they returned to the barn, the duchess informed Beatrice that dinner would be in a few hours. "Very casual, we're having barbecue outside. You haven't seen a sunset until you've seen one in the Texas hill country."

Then she headed back into the main house, leaving Beatrice and Connor together. Alone.

"Hey, Bee," Connor said softly. It was only two syllables, but hearing them made it seem like no time had passed at all.

Beatrice swallowed against a sudden tightness in her throat. "How are things in Texas?"

"I'm happy here." At the bleak expression on her face, Connor hesitated. "What is it?"

"I don't know. I've actually . . . I've wanted to talk to you since the accident."

He looked at the grooms still untacking their horses and lowered his voice. "Why don't we take a walk."

They started along a grassy field, past paddocks of glossy-looking horses and a single donkey that, from the way it kept nudging the horses out of the way, thought it was one of them. Beatrice caught a glimpse of the river through a veil of cypress trees.

She drew in a breath, then explained about her retrograde amnesia, how she'd forgotten most of the events of the past year.

Connor shook his head in surprise. "You could have fooled me. You seem as calm and collected as ever."

"If I seem that way, it's all an act."

It was strange, being so near him and feeling distant. Once upon a time Connor's body had been as familiar to Beatrice as her own, yet now she didn't reach for his hand. Because she didn't feel like she was allowed—or because she no longer felt a compulsion to?

"Bee. You didn't come here for me, did you?" His eyes burned with intensity. "Because—well, I—"

He broke off abruptly, leaving Beatrice staring at him in confusion.

"I came here to meet with the duchess, though seeing you was an important bonus. I was hoping you could give me some answers."

"I'll do my best," he said hesitantly.

"What happened to us?"

Connor didn't answer right away. Beatrice knew from the set of his jaw that he was deliberating his response.

"We grew apart," he said at last.

"How?"

"It just . . . happened."

"You don't love me anymore," Beatrice summarized, because it had to be spoken aloud.

"I don't love you," Connor agreed, "and you don't love me. I think you know that already."

Beatrice knew that he was right; she *felt* the truth of his words, with an instinctive, almost primal certainty.

"Things changed for us when your father died, Bee. You pulled away from me, and you fell for Teddy," Connor told her.

"I didn't marry him, though."

"I don't think you called it off because you were having second thoughts about Teddy." Connor seemed to be forcing out the words. "You told me that very afternoon that you loved him. You had other reasons, whatever they were." He sighed. "I hope this helps give you closure, if that's what you came for."

Closure. What a strange concept. Was it possible to close

your heart to someone you had loved that fiercely for that long?

Beatrice reached for Connor's hand.

He hesitated for an instant, then laced his fingers in hers. At the feel of his familiar calluses, the old electric current seemed to hiss between them. It made Beatrice think back to the night she'd first acknowledged her feelings for Connor: the night of the twins' graduation, when she and Connor had driven from the Madisons' house back to the capital. She had seen his hand on the central console of the car and daydreamed about taking it in her own.

"Do you remember when we got stuck on the highway, and I knighted the cashier at that rest stop?"

The hint of a smile tugged at Connor's mouth. "How could I forget? Sir Stan Stevens."

"I wonder what happened to him," Beatrice mused.

"Want me to find out?"

"Nah. I'm okay not knowing," she decided. "It's better this way."

They stayed like that for a moment longer, their hands clasped, and Beatrice knew it would be the last time they ever touched.

When they let go, Connor wordlessly turned back toward the stables.

"I meant what I told you when we last said goodbye. I'll always be here if you need me."

Beatrice had no memory of that statement, yet hearing it made the world feel a little brighter.

"Thank you. I'm always here, too. Whatever you need."

It felt like the tectonic plates of her life were shifting: as if the old Beatrice had cracked and a new Beatrice, fierce and resilient and unafraid, had stepped out of the wreckage.

"You know, you look good in a cowboy hat." Beatrice

immediately flushed; she hadn't meant to sound flirtatious. "What I'm trying to say is that you seem very at ease here."

Connor's smile was as warm as she remembered. "Turns out I like being a cowboy. We could get you a hat, if you want one," he added. "It would go with your boots."

"That's okay. I'll leave the real cowboy attire to you and the duchess."

"So things between you and Her Grace went well? I saw you shaking hands. It looked like you got what you came for?" Connor asked.

"Yes." Beatrice let out a breath as she stared up at the blue expanse of sky. "I got everything that I came for."

23

SAMANTHA

Samantha reached for her phone the moment she woke up, hoping that Marshall had texted while she was asleep. She would take any text right now, even a string of incomprehensible emojis—anything to convince her things between them were okay, when she knew deep down that they weren't.

They hadn't spoken much since their phone call the other night, which didn't make sense, because Sam wanted to call Marshall more than ever. But she didn't know how to explain her situation to him when she didn't quite understand it herself. What was she even *doing* here, sleeping on an air mattress in a house full of people she'd just met, instead of going back to the man she loved? It made no sense, yet she couldn't bring herself to leave.

The few times they had talked, she and Marshall had stuck to frothy, superficial topics like the surfing conditions or Sam's bartending anecdotes. It felt like they were both pretending not to notice the tension between them, which only made the tension more acute.

Sam tossed her phone into her bag, then pulled on black leggings and a lime-green hoodie.

Liam sat on the sisal carpet in the living room, his back against the couch and legs sprawled out before him as he scribbled in a notebook.

"Why do you always sit on the floor instead of the couch?" Sam asked.

Liam's pen was still scratching over the page. "When I'm too comfortable, I write bad lyrics."

"Can I see?"

"Not yet." He abruptly shut the notebook, blinking as if emerging from a creative haze. It reminded Sam of how Nina looked when someone interrupted her reading.

"Are you off today?" Sam asked. "Want to go out?"

Liam nodded slowly. They hadn't explicitly discussed that things between her and Marshall were strained, but he knew; the entire *house* knew. That was the thing about living so closely with other people; your lives became intertwined whether you wanted them to or not.

"There's an eighties cover band at Vibrant tonight," Liam offered. "Jessica is always begging us to go dancing there."

Sam shifted her weight. "I didn't mean I want to go out dancing; I just need a change of scene."

"Oh." Liam seemed confused. "I have to run some errands, but we could go on a walk later?"

"I'll come with you on your errands!" That sounded like the perfect distraction.

Liam hesitated. "I'm going to Costco. It's not a ton of fun, unless bargain shopping is your thing, which I doubt."

"Costco? Is that . . . grocery shopping?" Sam guessed, and Liam choked out a laugh.

"More or less. It's definitely an experience," he added, which was enough to make up Sam's mind.

"Sounds perfect."

He grabbed his keys and they headed out back, to the twenty-year-old sedan that the roommates shared. Liam paused, glancing at Sam. "Don't you want to put on a hat? Or one of those scarves that cover half your face?"

Oh, right. When it was just the two of them, Sam almost forgot that she was incognito. She pulled on a hot-pink beanie and a pair of oversized sunglasses. "Better?"

"Maybe ditch the glasses? You look like one of those reality stars who secretly wants to get her photo taken. Sorry," Liam said, at her outraged expression. "It's all the neon."

"Neon is my signature color," Sam muttered, but she removed the sunglasses and traded her green hoodie for one of his spare gray sweatshirts.

When they walked into Costco, Sam's eyes widened. She'd been in American grocery stores a few times on royal tours: the management would cordon off various aisles so that her family could pretend to shop while photographers eagerly snapped photos.

Costco was nothing like the grocery stores of her memory. Its massive aisles held everything from electronics to garden hoses to area rugs. She stared around in awe, but Liam was walking with single-minded purpose to the grocery section, where he began throwing items into the cart—gallons of milk, a two-pack of rotisserie chickens, several bags of frozen berries.

"Tomato soup?" called out a woman in a red Costco shirt. She stood before a wheeled cart, which was covered in tiny paper cups of tomato soup.

Sam felt tears pricking at her eyes. Back at home, whenever she'd felt sick, her mom had always brought her tomato soup in bed. She would sit with Sam, feeding her one spoonful at a time with infinite patience.

"I'd love a soup." Sam approached the cart. "How much?"

The salesperson gave her a funny look. "These are free samples. Take one."

"Really?" The urge to cry dissolved in her chest into something verging on laughter. Sam grabbed a couple of paper cups and brought them back to Liam, handing him one.

"Look, these are free samples!" she told him in a stage whisper.

"You'd think this was the first time you'd ever gotten something without paying," he teased, and clinked their paper cups as if they were flutes of champagne. "Cheers."

Sam tipped the cup back; the soup was warm and creamy and tasted like childhood. She looked around the store and realized that this wasn't the only cart offering free samples: there was a man scooping hummus and crackers onto disposable plates, and was that a dumpling stand in the corner? *Marshall would love this*, she thought—and sucked in a breath, because of course she couldn't bring Marshall here to show him; Marshall was thousands of miles away. Living his own, separate life.

A shopping cart veered in their direction, packed with diapers and industrial-sized boxes of cereal. A toddler in a red reindeer sweater perched in the front of the cart, trying determinedly to unpeel the Velcro tab on his sneaker.

"Look, Mommy." A little girl, maybe six years old, tugged at the curly-haired woman who pushed the cart. "It's Princess Samantha!"

Sam's heart plummeted. Liam reached for her arm and gave it a sharp squeeze, but she couldn't parse what he was doing—warning her? Telling her to run?

"No, it's not, sweetheart," the mom said distractedly.

Sam shuffled guiltily away, but this part of the store had wide-open aisles and there was nowhere to hide except behind a cardboard display of ramen noodles.

"Mom! The princess is *right there!*"

The woman looked up to meet Sam's gaze. "Sorry, my daughter has an overactive imagination," she started to say— and then her eyes widened comically. "Oh my god," she murmured. "It's you. Isn't it?"

Sam had wondered if this might happen eventually. She

just hadn't anticipated a child would be the one to recognize her: that after all her nights tending bar, a little girl at Costco would see right through her disguise.

She felt the weight of Liam's gaze on her, but ignored it as she knelt down to the little girl's level. "I'm actually not a princess anymore. I'm an ordinary girl, just like you."

The girl shook her head solemnly. "Being a princess isn't about wearing a crown. It's about who you are in here." She reached out to place her palm on Sam's sweatshirt, square in the middle of her chest, and Sam's heart wrenched.

"You're very wise." She managed a wobbly smile before rising to her feet.

The little girl ran off, but her mom hardly noticed; she was staring at Sam in complete shock.

"What are you doing here? I thought you'd fled the country." The woman's cheeks colored. "Sorry, Your Royal Highness, I didn't mean to— It's just so surprising—"

"It's okay. I didn't flee the country. I took an extended sabbatical." Sam liked the sound of that. "And I'm here to shop, same as you. Actually, where did you find the Cheerios?" she added, pointing to the woman's cart. "I was devastated this morning when I realized we'd run out."

Sensing his mother's distraction, the toddler leaned out and stretched his hand toward the tower of ramen boxes. He knocked them over with a spectacular crash, then clapped in delight.

"*George!*" The woman knelt and began gathering the boxes into her arms. Sam crouched down to help, Liam following suit, which seemed to make the woman even more flustered.

"I'm sorry, Your Royal Highness, you really don't have to do that," she exclaimed.

Sam began stacking the boxes back in order. "It's no trouble. And please—just call me Sam."

"Mommy! Can I buy this puh-*lease!*" The little girl had returned, holding a plastic inflatable beach ball.

"Hang on, Sam," the mom replied. It took a moment for Samantha to realize that the words weren't addressed to her.

"Your children are George and Samantha?"

"I— Yes. I'm Mallory," the woman said haltingly. "It's just that your family have such beautiful names. I never thought, when I named her Samantha, that I would ever *meet* you."

An unexpected warmth blossomed in Sam's chest. She knew that the Washingtons' names were popular, but Beatrice had always topped the lists of girls' names, followed by Adelaide; there had been three Addies in Sam's high school class alone.

She didn't meet a lot of Samanthas, though. No one was particularly eager to name their newborn after the royal family's rebellious wild child, the one so problematic that she wasn't even royal anymore.

"I'm honored," she breathed.

The younger Samantha tossed the beach ball in Sam's direction. "Samantha! Catch!"

This was why elementary school appearances had always been her favorites. Children didn't treat you any differently if you were a princess, or an ex-princess; they didn't care about the color of your skin or how much money your family had. They didn't gasp in shock if you dated someone who wasn't the same race. They treated everyone with the same cheerful indifference—unless, of course, you had cookies, and then you were their favorite person.

If only adults were as wonderfully blind to prejudice, the world would be a much better place.

Sam caught the beach ball with a grin. "This is a pretty great ball."

"It's from over there." The little girl waved to a sign marked

CLEARANCE: SUMMER ITEMS 60% OFF, which made Sam want to laugh. Summer felt like a million years ago, back when she'd been on a royal tour with Nina. When her relationship with Marshall had still been easy and uncomplicated.

She tossed the ball back toward the little girl, who clasped her hands together and tapped it up in a volleyball move. "Think fast!"

"Samantha, come on, we need to leave the princess alone," Mallory protested, but Sam was delighted. She bumped the ball back in her new friend's direction.

"We can't let it hit the ground!" young Sam squealed.

"Definitely not," Sam agreed. Liam was watching her with unmistakable amusement, but he didn't say anything.

She and Samantha kept bumping the ball back and forth, moving steadily down the aisle as they did, toward the display of on-sale summer gear. Sam's eyes were drawn to a floating tennis net, meant to be set up across a swimming pool, complete with buoyant racks and squishy neon tennis balls. She fought off a sudden wave of nostalgia, because it was exactly the sort of toy that she and Jeff would have obsessed over when they were little. They used to constantly make up games with water balloons or pool noodles, challenging each other to endless matches that neither of them won because they kept changing the rules.

"Heads up!" Samantha giggled, and Sam quickly tapped the beach ball back toward her.

Their volley had drawn a few curious onlookers. Sam could tell that word of her presence was spreading; several people had begun recording with their phones, but she didn't care as long as Mallory was fine with it. Besides, even if Sam had tried to take their phones away, the news was already out.

She knew from experience that this was one genie she couldn't put back in the bottle. Her anonymity in the capital was gone for good.

The palace would have a heart attack when they saw this video. They didn't even want people to know she was in *town*, let alone see her at a wholesale shopping store, criminally underdressed in her sneakers and hoodie. When members of the royal family interacted with ordinary people, it was always scripted—a choreographed interaction on a royal tour, or at one of those stuffy garden parties. Even the moments that seemed fun to outsiders, like the time Jeff had played darts at a dive bar on tour, were all staged.

Sam couldn't help it; she began to laugh. The sheer *fun* of what she was doing seemed to stretch out space within her chest, making her feel light as air, the way she used to feel when she was a child and anything seemed possible.

♛

Later, after she'd said goodbye to Mallory and helped Liam find the rest of the items on his list, he turned toward the home decor section. "Did you want to get anything for your room? I mean—they sell mattresses here," he added a little clumsily. "And bed frames."

Sam edged closer to an enormous display of toilet paper, trying to stay out of earshot of an employee who was restocking nearby. "You want me to stay long-term?"

"Sam, you know I love having you at the house. But do *you* want to stay? What's your plan?"

"I don't have much of a plan. I've been taking it one day at a time."

Liam was quiet, so she exhaled and went on. "I came back to see my family, but they don't want anything to do with me. And I'm not sure what the path forward looks like now that I'm . . . ordinary."

Liam nudged her hip with the shopping cart. "Hey, watch it. I'm ordinary too, remember?"

"But you have a plan!"

"I have a *goal*. And I know you have one, if you can just clarify what it is."

"That sounds easier said than done."

"Welcome to being in your twenties. We're all trying to figure out this whole adulting thing," Liam told her. "Would you rather have known your destiny from birth, like your sister?"

"No," Sam said automatically.

Liam tilted his head, studying her. "What do you miss about being a princess?"

The personal chef, Sam wanted to joke, but she sensed that this wasn't a moment for levity. And the truth was, there were many things about her former life that she *didn't* miss. The hovering security, the formal state dinners, the endless rules, which she was always breaking.

"I miss the feeling of knowing exactly who I was. I feel so adrift now," she admitted.

"But you *do* know who you are," Liam said simply. "You're a surprisingly clean housemate, you make a killer margarita, you sing woefully off-key—"

"Okay, we can't all be the front man in a band—"

"You're Samantha," he kept going, which effectively silenced her. "My friend."

Sam looked at him: the handsome line of his jaw, the green flecks in his amber eyes, his hair loose and tousled around his ears. Attraction flared between them like heat, and she knew from Liam's expression that he felt it too.

She stepped away, because Liam was right. They were friends. And they needed to keep it that way.

"Let me work a few more bartending shifts, and when I've saved enough, I'll come get a mattress. You'll bring me back, right?" Sam asked.

"Of course I'll bring you back. Or you can borrow my

Costco card and come without me," he added, with a hint of a smile. "I know this is your new favorite place."

"Ooh, can we get here on the metro? That's another thing I've been wanting to do."

At that, Liam laughed outright. "You're excited about the *metro?*"

"I've never been on it! It's too hard to manage with security," Sam explained. "Beatrice always said it was creepy, disappearing down those long escalators underground like mole people. I thought it looked fun, though."

"The metro is zero fun, but I'm happy to help you navigate it." Liam's eyes sparkled. "Anything else on your ordinary-people bucket list? Changing the oil in your car? Paying your insurance?"

"Seeing a movie in a theater," Sam declared.

"Done." Liam turned to wheel their cart toward the checkout aisle. "Okay, lesson number one in being a nobody: you always stop at the Costco food court on the way out. Soft serve in the summer, churros in the winter."

A lesson in being a nobody. Sam thought of the little girl she'd just played volleyball with, and decided it wasn't such a bad thing after all, being a nobody.

24

BEATRICE

Beatrice glanced across the car at Teddy, a little nervous. She hadn't felt like herself since she got back from Texas.

Perhaps she should say that she hadn't felt like her *old* self, the one she'd thought she was after the accident. Seeing Connor had answered plenty of her questions, but it also raised new ones. Beatrice had tried to ignore the sensation; she had enough on her plate without a post-amnesia identity crisis, including the whole mess with Samantha, whose cover had finally been blown at, of all places, a wholesale discount store.

But she couldn't adequately face the rest of it until she knew where things stood with Teddy.

When she'd started composing a new text to him, her phone had filled the screen with their message history, and Beatrice's thumbs paused.

The most recent text was from Teddy, the night before her accident: *I can't wait to see you.*

Beatrice had scrolled upward and realized that he'd been in Nantucket for most of the League of Kings conference, sending the occasional picture of a sunset or *Nantucket's not the same without you* note.

Beatrice had kept going. It was hard to follow the thread of their conversation, because there *was* no coherent thread. Most of their dialogue was composed of out-of-context declarations (*so much for Russians never changing their minds—what* did that mean?) or emojis that Beatrice couldn't make sense of. It was the sort of text exchange that spoke of inside jokes and shorthand, of people who knew each other so well that they could communicate with easy intimacy.

She'd written and deleted a few different versions of her text to Teddy before finally settling on *Are you free for dinner?*

Which was how she ended up in the car with him, on her way to a Chinese restaurant that had opened just last month.

As if reading her mind, Teddy said, "When you told me you wanted to get dinner, I thought we were eating at the palace."

"I want to go somewhere new." Beatrice couldn't take another interaction at the palace, where she'd done so many things she couldn't remember. She wanted to see Teddy on neutral ground, somewhere neither of them had any memories.

Teddy glanced over. "Would you mind if we took a quick detour? There's somewhere I want to take you. As a friend," he added quickly.

She thought of that text thread, of all the months they had clearly spent being much *more* than friends, and wondered what Teddy was thinking.

Truthfully, she could use a friend right now.

"Let's do it," she told him, and Teddy broke into an eager smile. He leaned forward to whisper with the Guard in the front seat.

They passed through the financial district and over the Armistead Bridge, then crawled up a hill on the far side of the Potomac. The tires crunched on fallen leaves as their driver backed into a spot.

Beatrice zipped her thin jacket up her torso, then walked hesitantly around the side of the car. They were at a lookout point above the river, the setting sun turning its waters a burnished gold. Past the river, the buildings of the capital were so crowded together that it seemed you could cross the entire city like a hero in an action movie, jumping from rooftop to rooftop.

She glanced at the other parking spots, all empty. A protection officer had obviously radioed ahead to clear them out when Teddy requested this stop, but Beatrice couldn't shake the sense that this was serendipitous, as if they'd just happened to stumble across this empty lookout point.

The current of restless energy that normally spun through her seemed to fall still.

"Have you been here before?" Teddy asked.

"No," she admitted, a bit chagrined to have lived in Washington her whole life and never seen this. "Have you?"

He shook his head. "I've been wanting to come for a while, but didn't want to go without you."

Behind them, the protection officer had thrown open the rear of the SUV and flattened the middle seats, so that the entire trunk was exposed to the view. "Want to sit?" Teddy offered, as the driver discreetly retreated to wait by the hood of the car.

Beatrice hoisted herself up, then scooted back so that the edge of her booties tipped out over the edge. Teddy looked to her for permission, and when she nodded, came to sit next to her.

"Washington looks the prettiest like this," she mused aloud.

"What, from a distance?"

"At sunset." She held out a hand, indicating the city in the distance. People moved on the streets like tiny ants. So many millions of them, and every last one of them wanted something different from her, from America.

"In daylight it feels so sharp, all the historic buildings squeezed up next to modern glass ones. And at night when the streetlights click on, it's too harsh. It feels more approachable at twilight, more gentle. It's the only time this city has ever really felt like home to me," she admitted.

"Walthorpe was never quite home, either. I was happy growing up there, and I will always love it, but . . . I never felt about it the way home is supposed to feel."

"Which is?"

"Home should make you feel secure and safe and utterly at ease. When you're home you should feel like you *belong*. Like you fit perfectly."

Beatrice knew what he meant. No matter how fiercely she loved her family, her role as future monarch had always held her at a slight distance from them. Her life was dictated by the Crown, and the Crown didn't love her at all.

"I'm sorry you never got to feel that," she murmured, and Teddy shook his head.

"Oh, I did—just not at Walthorpe."

"Really?" Beatrice asked, her curiosity piqued. "Where?"

Teddy looked away, seeming reluctant to have brought it up. "A person can be home, you know, just as much as a place."

The only sound was the soft rise and fall of their breath. Beatrice had thought of this car as an SUV, but she was becoming aware that it wasn't as big as she'd imagined. She and Teddy were very nearly touching in a dozen places.

She wrapped her arms around herself, and Teddy noticed the movement. "Are you cold?"

"I'm fine. Just . . . thinking," Beatrice replied, but he was already shrugging out of his coat and handing it over.

The polite thing to do was to put it on, so Beatrice did. The coat was still warm from the heat of his body, and it *smelled* like Teddy, a scent that was soft and clean and hit her with an unexpected wave of longing, or maybe nostalgia.

"What are you thinking about?" When she didn't answer,

he added, "Want to think out loud?" *Think with me*, his eyes pleaded.

She settled on the simplest thing to explain. "I wasn't in Texas on a social call. I was there to ask for help, because the Duke of Virginia wants to depose me."

"He *what?*"

The whole story came spilling out in a confused jumble, which wasn't at all like Beatrice, who usually had her thoughts—and emotions—tucked in tidy folders in her mind.

When she'd finished, Teddy leaned forward. "Let me help, please. I can lobby more senators, strategize with you, whatever you need. We won't let Madison take the crown from you."

"But what if he does? Or worse, what if I do something wrong and clear the way for him? Everyone is already watching, just waiting for me to slip up, and if I fail in this monumental way . . ." She drew in a breath. "I know you understand what I mean when I say that my position has always defined me."

"It shouldn't. Your position doesn't define you; *you* define your *position.*"

"The Crown doesn't work that way," she said heavily.

"Why not? Without you the Crown is a bunch of robes and jewels and titles. *You* are the one who brings it all to life. I know you don't remember what a great queen you are, but I'm here to remind you. You can do this," Teddy said fervently. "You've done it already."

Beatrice's mind snagged on those words. *I'm here to remind you.*

"That's it!" she cried out. "You can help me remember!"

Teddy frowned in confusion, so she jumped to explain. "You were with me the entire time I was queen, weren't you? You know what I did better than anyone; you saw my victories and my mistakes. You can help me navigate the political landscape until I get my feet under me."

"What do you mean?" Teddy asked, seeming confused. "Should we re-create a timeline of the past year?"

"Just help me avoid all the errors I keep making. Like in my press conference, or all the excruciating conversations I had at Jeff and Daphne's engagement party—I could have avoided so many missteps if I'd known more context. Can't you coach me through everything, remind me what I've forgotten?"

Teddy still seemed hesitant. Beatrice couldn't imagine why until he asked, "Does this mean you won't ever admit the truth?"

"What, announce to the world that I have amnesia?"

"Yes, exactly."

"Why would I do that when Madison is gearing up to take me down? Then everyone would know he's right!"

"Just because he's right about your amnesia doesn't mean that he's right in saying you can't be queen," Teddy said gently. "If it's going to come out, it's better the country hear it from you than from some reporter who goes digging into the hospital records. People will forgive you for your amnesia—of course they will, it's not your fault—but they won't forgive you for lying about it."

There was truth in Teddy's warning. It felt eerily like what her father would have said if he were here right now.

But—publicly confessing that she had retrograde amnesia and had forgotten the past year? It would be tantamount to handing her enemies a round of ammunition and saying, *Here I am; please take aim.*

Beatrice reached for Teddy's hand. She felt him startle at the contact, but he didn't pull away.

"You said we were friends. Right?"

Something flickered across his expression, but he nodded. "Of course."

"The best way to be my friend right now is to help me hide my memory loss." She saw him hesitate and pressed her advantage. "Prompt me when I've forgotten an important detail, make it seem like I'm back to full health. Steer me away from conversational pitfalls. Keep me from making a fool of myself again, like I did at the press conference. Please," she begged, her voice nearly breaking.

Teddy flipped his hand beneath her palm, his fingers warm as they laced through hers. Beatrice's head was suddenly full of a dizzying tangle of thoughts. Her entire awareness seemed to center there, where their hands touched.

"For the record, I think this is a terrible idea and will only come back to hurt you," Teddy stated. "But, yes, I'll help."

"Thank you," she breathed.

They sat there together, hands clasped, as the last rays of the sun disappeared behind the city's skyline.

25

NINA

Nina laced her hands above her head and stretched, soaking in the quiet of the library. She'd been working on her application to the Oxford program all morning, and couldn't shake the sense that it was missing something.

She looked back at the second question on the application: **Describe the coursework you have done at King's College which will prepare you for the rigorous academics at Oxford.** Nina had answered, *My coursework in British literature is extensive. Most recently, I wrote a final paper for ENG531: Gothic Literature on the paradox of multiple narrators, and how untrustworthy narrators could articulate the unspeakable. . . .*

Forget it. There was no way she could revise on her computer screen; she needed to work the old-fashioned way, by writing in the margins with red pen. Nina sent her application to the nearest printer bank, then began scrolling through her phone while she waited.

Jamie had texted: *Are you finished with your application yet, because I found an arcade in the bottom of Samuelson Hall. Come race me in the go-cart game?*

Nina replied, amused: *You just now discovered the arcade? That was a rite of passage for freshmen.*

Last night in rehearsal, she and Jamie had kissed for so long that they'd gotten wolf whistles from the rest of the cast. A part of Nina worried about the attention—she, of all people, knew the downsides of dating a prince—but something about Jamie kept pulling her in. When she was with him, the world seemed brighter somehow, dense with adventure and with possibility.

And she knew where she stood with him. Jamie was direct about his feelings, which hadn't always been the case with Jeff.

So far, no one at school had sold them out, and Jamie had been right when he'd promised that no one at the Maple Leaf would alert the tabloids. Perhaps the type of people who frequented Canadian-themed bars in Midtown simply had no interest in photographing the Canadian prince. More likely they'd been too invested in the hockey game to even notice.

Nina started toward the printer bank, walking past long tables of students finishing up their final papers. When she turned toward the room that housed the two printers on the B level, Nina almost didn't believe who she saw inside.

"Nina. Hey." Somehow, Jeff didn't seem surprised to see her—but the library was her home turf, after all.

"What are you doing here?"

"I go to school here too, remember?"

Was he *teasing* her? Nina blinked, disoriented, and Jeff's expression grew almost sheepish.

"I know I wasn't at school for a while, but I'm back now," he said, as if his return to campus hadn't been national news. A document spat out of the printer, and Jeff grabbed it. "My econ final," he explained. "Can you believe the professor is making us submit a hard copy to his faculty mailbox, instead of letting us email it in?"

"How old-school," Nina managed, still dazed.

Silence stretched out between them. Jeff reached for a stack of papers on the counter, flushed, and held it toward Nina. "This one is yours. Sorry, I wasn't trying to—I just got to the printer and it was right there."

"Thanks." Nina took the papers from him.

Jeff paused awkwardly. "So you're applying to the Oxford program? I'm glad. You'll love it there."

It was the same thing Jamie had told her, and for some reason that bothered her. "I'm just applying, Jeff. There's no guarantee I'll get in."

"Of course you will. You're the smartest person I know."

It felt surreal, talking to Jeff as if they were old friends—but that was what they were, weren't they? Nina tried to focus on the present, yet a highlight reel of their history had begun playing in her mind.

She saw them as children, scooping the goldfish from Sam's room and hiding it from her. They told her it had evaporated, when the entire time the goldfish was swimming blissfully in a gold-rimmed porcelain bowl they'd stolen from the butler's pantry.

She saw the carefree teenage version of him: the Jeff who once showed up to a black-tie gala with a hundred helium balloons. He proceeded to tie a balloon to everyone in attendance—to Nina's bracelet, to the back of his tails, to his grandmother's tiara. (Nina would never forget the way it had lifted that tiara just half an inch above the pouf of Grandma Billie's hairstyle.)

She saw her and Jeff in his bedroom at the Telluride house, their kisses soft and lingering and infinitely sweet.

And she saw the Jeff who had gotten engaged to Daphne before the whole world—even though he and Daphne were so fundamentally wrong for each other.

"Jeff, can I ask you something?"

He seemed startled but nodded. "Sure."

A million questions burned on her lips. *What changed your mind about us? Were you always going to choose Daphne, or was there ever a moment when we had a shot? Why* me?

Instead she asked, "Have you talked to Sam?"

"I . . . it's complicated."

"I think she deserves another chance," Nina said quietly.

Instead of answering, Jeff looked up at her with an unreadable expression. "I heard you've been hanging out with Jamie."

"We're doing *A Midsummer Night's Dream* together. The school's winter play," Nina explained, since he obviously had no clue what she meant. "It's this weekend, actually."

"So you're just costars in the show? You're not dating?"

"Okay, stop right there," Nina said hotly. "*You* don't get to be angry with *me*."

Jeff's eyes widened. Quite possibly no one had ever spoken to him this way in his life.

"You kissed me, and then you went off and got engaged to Daphne the next day? What was I supposed to do—wait for you to change your mind and bounce back from Daphne to me *again*, except this time you've given her a ring?"

Jeff's face flushed. "You don't know all the details."

"Explain it, then!"

He opened his mouth as if to say something—then let out a breath, defeated. "Of course I'm not angry with you, Nina. If anything, I'm angry with myself for the way I handled things. You deserved better."

I did, Nina thought, but she felt almost sorry for Jeff in that moment. Perhaps that was why she said, "Things between you and me were never going to work out."

"Why? Because I'm a prince?" Jeff shook his head. "I used to think that was the problem, that my titles were getting in the way. Until you started dating a *crown prince*, Nina. You do realize that he's the heir, right? He's even more a prince than I am!"

Some part of Nina wanted to laugh at the sheer absurdity of this conversation. Were she and her royal ex-boyfriend seriously debating levels of *princeliness*?

She leaned against the wall, clutching her application to

her chest. "We were never going to work because *Daphne* was always in the way. Not your titles." She looked Jeff in the eye as she added, "You were always going to have to choose between us."

And in the end, he'd chosen Daphne.

Jeff winced. "I'm sorry. For a while there, I had hoped there was a way we could all get along."

Hadn't she hoped the very same thing, back when she'd believed in Daphne's friendship? Nina had told herself that she would find a way to keep them both—Jeff and Daphne.

Jeff stared at her as if he knew precisely what she was thinking. "It seemed like you and Daphne were becoming friends. What happened?" When Nina said nothing, he added clumsily, "Whatever it was, I hope it wasn't because of me."

"Oh, Jeff" was all Nina could say.

Of course it was because of him. Didn't he understand by now? It was *always* because of him.

His eyes met hers, and she wished he would just stop looking at her like that. "I miss you, Nina. I mean—I miss having you in my life."

"I miss you, too." The words came out of her unwillingly, like a breath stolen from her chest.

"Do you think we could ever be friends again?"

Typical Jeff. He had always asked for too much, tried to make everyone happy, tried to have it all.

How many times had she and Jeff tried to go back, retrace their steps, and be "just friends"?

Nina blinked to hide the tears in her eyes. "I'll always care about you, but I'm not sure I can be friends."

Sadness flickered over his expression, but he nodded. "I understand."

"Congratulations, by the way. On the wedding."

Nina started to turn aside, but Jeff stepped into her path. For a wild instant she thought he would kiss her.

She hated that a part of her wanted him to.

"About your essay," Jeff said awkwardly. "I know you probably don't want my opinion, but it should be a little more personal."

"You read my essay?"

"Sorry. It was there in the printer tray, and I just . . ." He held his hands out in apology. "It's so academic, Nina."

"This is an academic program," she said tersely.

"Sure, but there's so much more to you than your thoughts on Gothic narrators. You should talk about your love of books! Like that time you stole a library book and racked up five hundred dollars in fines."

"I didn't steal it; I just forgot to return it!"

"Or that time we were kids and decided to build a fort. Sam and I went off looking for pillows, and by the time we came back you had already built a fort out of books."

"Books are clearly better! They're so much more protection against the elements."

A flicker of amusement shone in Jeff's eyes. "What elements, Nina? We were inside."

"The *imaginary* elements!"

"That's exactly my point," he insisted. "This application makes you sound brilliant, which you obviously are. But the departmental committee should also know that you're passionate, and creative, and . . ." He fumbled for the right word before finally saying, "And whimsical."

Nina was struck silent. She couldn't believe that Jeff remembered all those moments. He spoke as if it was no big deal, as if he wasn't breaking her heart little by little with each sentence.

That was the thing about people who had known you since childhood: they understood you in ways that you didn't even understand yourself.

They could hurt you better than anyone, even when they didn't mean to.

♛

Two days later, Nina was onstage for the final performance of the weekend, curling up amid the painted greenery and stretching her arms overhead with a yawn. "O weary night, O long and tedious night, / Abate thy hours!"

In reality she wasn't weary at all; she was thrumming with energy, feeding off the excitement that pulsed through the theater.

She had actually done it. She, shy and bookish Nina Gonzalez, had done something she'd never expected and starred in a play. She almost didn't recognize herself.

After the curtain call, her parents found her backstage and handed her a bouquet of sunflowers. "Nina! You were spectacular," her mom exclaimed, pulling her into a hug. "And your cute costar! I can't believe he's the Prince of Canada."

"He seems very normal," her mamá chimed in, eyes fixed on Nina. "There weren't any tabloid reporters here tonight."

Nina heard the criticism of the Washingtons folded into that comment. Her mamá had always been wary of her friendship with Samantha, afraid that Nina would get sucked into a toxic whirlpool of feeling less-than. And in many ways she'd been right.

"Jamie isn't on home turf. The rules are different here," she mumbled. Mercifully, her mamá let it go.

"Nina!" Rachel came to join them, holding an enormous arrangement of two dozen red roses. "One of the royal security guards just dropped this off for you."

"How sweet of Samantha!" Nina's mom exclaimed, craning to look over her shoulder. "Is she here?"

Nina smiled and reached for the roses, touched. Sam had come to last night's performance, and had sent cupcakes to the entire cast backstage. Nina certainly hadn't expected her to do anything tonight.

Rachel drew Nina aside, lowering her voice cryptically. "I'm not sure it was Sam."

Nina tore open the envelope attached to the flowers.

You were fantastic tonight, Nina. Congratulations.

It wasn't signed, but that didn't matter, because Nina would have known that handwriting anywhere.

She looked at Rachel, stunned. "Jeff was here?"

Her friend let out a breath. "He came late and sat in the back row. He was really discreet about the whole thing; none of the audience had any idea he was here." She hesitated. "I think he just wanted to see you."

Though she knew he was long gone, Nina glanced out at the auditorium, heart hammering.

"Nina!"

Jamie came bounding toward her. He saw her parents and grinned eagerly. "Hi, you must be the Gonzalezes. It's so nice to meet you. I'm Jamie." He spoke easily, without any pretention or artifice, and Nina saw even her mamá's eyes soften. He was winning them over.

She handed the roses wordlessly to Rachel, who nodded and promised to take them to the dorm.

Then Nina turned toward her parents and Jamie, smiling as if everything were completely fine. As if her royal ex-boyfriend hadn't just barreled back into her life and upset the delicate balance that she'd fought so very hard to build.

26

DAPHNE

Daphne shifted, the better to catch the light streaming through the palace's floor-to-ceiling windows, and studied her reflection in the trifold mirror.

Her wedding gown was spectacular. Its intricate lace scooped over her arms and neck in an illusion cut before meeting the fitted bodice, and then the skirts: frothy layers of tulle that fell to the ground like enchanted snowdrifts. She should have felt like a fairy-tale princess.

Instead, her mind kept circling back to this morning's ominous email: *Time's running out, Daphne. If you don't tell Jeff it's over, then I will. Don't settle for living a lie because you're afraid to live the truth. P.S. Sorry I missed out on Enchanted Fiefdom!*

The tone of the email had lingered with her all morning. Somehow it didn't sound like Gabriella, especially the part about living a lie. If Daphne hadn't known better, she almost would have thought the author of the email *cared* about her. Which was really a ridiculous notion.

Of course it was Gabriella—who else could it be?

Queen Adelaide gestured to Daphne's shoulder, where the gorgeous illusion netting stretched over her skin. "Should we add another segment of lace here?" she suggested.

Daphne's phone trilled in her purse, but she ignored it. "That sounds lovely."

They had been doing this for the better part of an hour, directing the seamstress as she painstakingly fixed small rosettes and snippets of lace to the sheer fabric. Even Daphne, who loved being made a fuss of, was losing her patience.

"What do you think, Rebecca?" the queen added.

"Absolutely." Daphne's mother reclined on a nearby couch, a half-empty champagne flute in her hand. If the queen had suggested that Daphne shave off all her hair, her mother would have nodded in fanatic agreement. She would never express an opinion to contradict royalty.

When Daphne's phone buzzed a second time, the queen lifted an eyebrow. "Do you need to get that, Daphne?"

"I—yes. Please excuse me." Daphne's dress suddenly felt too tight, the silk scratching against her back.

She stepped down from the seamstress's platform, her spiky heels clicking on the floor as she walked over to her purse. As she'd expected, the screen read UNKNOWN CALLER.

"Hello?" she answered coolly, heart pounding.

"Daphne." It wasn't Gabriella, Daphne noted with a mixture of relief and anger—it was Rei. "I need to talk to you. I found something important."

"Thank you for your interest. I am always open to sponsoring more charities." It was the only thing Daphne could think of to say.

Rei let out an exasperated sigh. "I get it, you can't talk. Just meet me at Ethan's house now, okay?"

"I'm afraid that's not possible," Daphne began, but the line was already dead.

She looked up to see everyone staring at her, and forced a smile. "Can we take a break? I just remembered that I'm supposed to meet a friend for lunch."

Rebecca Deighton glanced up sharply, recognizing the lie.

She knew perfectly well that her daughter didn't have any friends—no real ones, anyway.

"Of course! You must be exhausted," Queen Adelaide apologized. "We'll do your final fitting next week, anyway!"

Daphne stepped behind the folded screen that they'd brought into the sitting room, where she changed into a blouson top and skinny jeans. She tapped out a rapid text to Ethan—*Rei says she wants to meet at your house?? Pick me up at the back of the Monmouth Hotel asap.*

"Daphne?" her mother called out, in a tone that should have sounded sweet, though Daphne heard the suspicious edge beneath. "Who are you meeting?"

"Gabriella Madison." It was the best lie Daphne could come up with on short notice. At least her mother would understand this was part of a scheme.

Rebecca pursed her lips but didn't argue.

The palace valet was happy to drop Daphne at the Monmouth, where she slipped discreetly through the lobby, past the massive Christmas tree and sprawling gingerbread house. She caught a few sidelong glances but kept moving, toward the staff entrance that fed into a narrow alley behind the hotel. She'd done this enough times with Jefferson that it was second nature by now.

By the time she got there, Ethan's motorcycle was already purring in the alley. "Let's go," Daphne said, looping one leg over the back.

"I thought you didn't want to ride my bike anymore." Ethan sounded far too amused for her liking.

"Desperate times," she snapped, and he dropped it.

They wound through the streets toward Ethan's neighborhood—which was only fifteen minutes from the palace but more understated than Herald Oaks, full of single-story homes with tire swings or trampolines out front.

Christmas trees winked cheerfully from living room windows; in one yard, an inflatable snowman fought for space next to an oversized cartoonish Santa. Inflatables weren't even *allowed* in Herald Oaks, per the homeowners association guidelines.

"I've never been to your house before," Daphne pointed out as Ethan pulled into a circular driveway.

"Yeah, well." He shrugged, then killed the engine. "I wasn't exactly jumping to host parties in high school."

"Of course not. We were always at the palace."

They both knew the real reason neither of them invited anyone over: they were embarrassed. Daphne because her parents were trying to be something they were not—filling their narrow townhouse with fake antiques and anonymous portraits, as if they could fool anyone into thinking their low-ranking title actually mattered—Ethan because his family was so painfully ordinary.

It wasn't easy trying to fit in when all your friends were titled, or obnoxiously wealthy, or both.

"My mom is at work. It's just us," Ethan explained, opening the side door into a cozy kitchen.

Daphne's eyes darted from the tin of peppermint bark on the island to the crayon sketch on the refrigerator (had his mom kept it there since Ethan was in preschool?) to the blue tile backsplash. The space had such a cheerful, lived-in feeling, unlike the Deightons' kitchen, which was all cold white marble and stainless steel.

Rei was already seated at the island, sipping a mug of tea. "Thanks for letting us meet here, Ethan. It's better if my parents don't know about my . . . activities."

Ethan braced his palms on the countertop. "Did you find out who's harassing us?"

"No, I still haven't been able to break through that firewall. It's a really intense one." Rei's gaze flicked to Daphne. "My news is that I hacked the Madisons, as you asked."

Daphne made a strangled noise of relief, but Ethan rounded on her. "Seriously? I thought we decided against that!"

"*You* decided against it. I had to do something, okay? Gabriella was closing in on us."

"It's not safe to go poking at her. What if she fights back?"

"Look," Rei cut in, "as much as I love being part of your lovers' quarrels, I need to go. Do you want my intel or not?"

"*Yes*," Daphne breathed. Ethan crossed his arms.

Rei pulled a manila folder from her tote bag and slid it across the counter. Somehow Daphne hadn't expected an actual stack of documents.

As if guessing her thoughts, Rei added, "I never do this kind of thing digitally. Hard copies are much safer. Can't be hacked."

"Makes sense," Daphne said, and turned to the first page.

It only took thirty seconds of scanning the column of numbers for Daphne to realize what was going on.

"The duke is embezzling?"

Rei nodded. "Siphoning off money from various government accounts, including his own charity initiative."

"And this information was just . . ."

"Saved on his hard drive. Once I got into their home network, it was all there for the taking." Rei sounded unmistakably smug.

The relief that flooded through Daphne was so acute, she felt almost dizzy. She didn't have to call off the wedding after all. She would destroy Gabriella before Gabriella could return the favor.

When she'd asked Rei to hack the Madisons' home network, she had hoped to find something on Gabriella, maybe embarrassing photos or incriminating emails—but it would be just as satisfying taking down the duke himself. Better, in some ways, because he was the one who'd started the feud between their families.

And any blow to their family's social standing would be devastating to Gabriella, who lived on their status as if it were oxygen.

"Thank you. This is exactly what I needed," Daphne said quietly.

"I know." Rei went to rinse her mug in the sink with an ease that suggested she'd been there many times before. "See you two later," she added, then let the door clatter shut behind her.

Daphne stared down at the papers. For weeks she had felt like she was navigating a tightrope, that any sudden or wrong move would send her tumbling to her downfall. And now, thanks to Rei, she'd found safe ground again. She could *breathe* again.

She tugged her phone from her bag. Ethan watched as she pulled up this morning's anonymous email and typed out a response: *I know who you are, and I have some information about your family that you won't want to go public. Let's meet in person to discuss. Don't no-show again.*

"You sure about this?" Ethan murmured, but Daphne had already clicked Send.

"I can't have her telling anyone about us! I need to put a stop to this blackmail now. I'm getting married in *ten days*."

Her last sentence echoed with ringing finality.

"Look, Daphne, I just want to make sure you're okay," Ethan persisted. "That you're not having second thoughts . . ."

He waited for a long moment before adding, "About this plan."

That pause had been purposeful, hadn't it? What Ethan meant to ask was whether she had second thoughts about the wedding.

"That isn't fair." Daphne's voice came out dangerously quiet. "You can't do this to me, Ethan."

"Do what?"

"I was just fine until you came back from Malaysia and upended everything—"

"Now you're the one being unfair," he protested. "The mess with Gabriella isn't my fault."

"I'm not talking about Gabriella; I'm talking about *us*! You said you didn't want me, remember?" Part of her couldn't believe she was speaking this out loud. "At Beatrice's wedding, you said that you wanted nothing to do with me."

Ethan had gone very still. Daphne noticed again how close they were, noticed that she'd turned her body to face his, that his gaze had dropped to her lips.

They were going to kiss again, like they had at the engagement party, except this time it would be purposeful. This time it would mean something.

"I guess letting go of you was harder than I expected." Ethan shifted closer, looping an arm tentatively around her waist.

Daphne leaned in to him—and something glittered in the corner of her vision.

Her diamond engagement ring was sparkling like a warning flare, like a blowtorch.

She forced herself to take a step back. "I was never yours to let go of."

There was an uncharacteristic flash of hurt in Ethan's eyes, and Daphne forced herself to ignore the stabbing feeling of regret.

She couldn't afford to be near Ethan. When they were together, the world seemed to melt away, as if there was nothing but the two of them.

But it wasn't just the two of them. It never had been.

"Do you need a ride back to the palace?" Ethan asked stiffly.

Daphne swept the file of incriminating papers into her

tote bag. Of course he couldn't give her a ride back to the palace. What would she say if anyone saw them together?

"My house is fine. Thank you," she replied, her voice as coolly distant as his.

It was better this way, for both of them.

27

BEATRICE

Beatrice had never really liked the merry-go-round of events leading up to the holidays: embassy parties, charity galas, end-of-year celebrations for volunteers and bureaucrats and clerics and staff. But this year she was grateful for the social whirl, because it meant almost all the senators were in the capital. She needed as much time with them as possible, to lobby them for support against Madison.

And every last senator was here tonight, which made sense, since this was the congressional holiday party.

There was no space inside Columbia House that could fit this many people, so Congress had rented an enormous tent that sprawled over the back lawn: the expensive, semipermanent kind of tent with space heaters in the corners and chandeliers twinkling overhead.

So far, things had gone much better than they had at Jeff and Daphne's engagement party, when Beatrice had kept saying the wrong thing. It was all thanks to Teddy.

From the moment she'd walked in, he'd been at her side, rapidly feeding her information about the members of Congress. *Richard Tomlinson is in contentious disagreement with the rest of the Committee on Infrastructure. Don't mention Andrea Donnelly's son; he's in rehab and she hates talking about it. Do mention the new tax bill to Dominic Rauch; he likes taking credit for it, even though he joined the deliberations at the last minute.*

Armed with Teddy's information, Beatrice was starting to feel almost like herself again.

It was time for her to leave soon; this party was intended for the members of Congress and their hundreds of staff members, not for the monarch. But since everyone here was a part of Her Majesty's government, Beatrice was expected to stay for the first hour.

As with so many of her appearances, there was a formal script—greet the Speaker of the House, offer to host the party (she suspected that was why Congress had erected the flashy tent, since they knew full well the Crown would pick up the tab), dance a single dance, then leave.

When the Speaker of the House started toward her with a microphone, Beatrice knew that was her cue. She felt the voices in the tent die down, heads turning expectantly toward her.

"Representative MacDougal," Beatrice said, using the same phrases that countless monarchs had spoken before her. "Thank you for spearheading my government for another year. Please, let this event be a gift from the Crown, though it in no way repays all your service."

The congressman inclined his head. "It is an honor to serve," he said formally. "Will Your Majesty please have the first dance?"

Beatrice felt a little pang. She thought of all the times she'd seen pictures of her parents doing this same end-of-year dance: whispering to each other, eyes twinkling. And now, somehow, it was her turn.

Teddy was already waiting at the edge of the dance floor. Nearby, a videographer in black trousers panned her camera toward them expectantly.

Beatrice placed her palm in Teddy's, and something seemed to spark where they touched.

As the music started up, he led her into a waltz. Beatrice felt herself relaxing a little with the familiar steps.

"Thank you for helping tonight," she murmured. "I can't believe you remembered all those details."

She must have leaned on Teddy more than she'd realized, and he must have paid close attention, if he was so familiar with the inner workings of her job.

He shook his head, smiling. "Trust me, Bee, you keep track of far more details than I do. I only know the pieces that you share with me, that we think through together."

Thinking through things together. Beatrice was struck by a sudden image of being curled up with Teddy on the bed, her head tucked into his shoulder, his other hand toying with her hair as she recounted something that was troubling her.

She couldn't tell if this was a memory or just something she was imagining. It should have unnerved her, but instead, a not-unpleasant shiver traced over her skin, as if Teddy really *was* brushing his fingertips against the nape of her neck.

The musicians had reached the first chorus of the song, and other couples began spilling onto the dance floor. Beatrice instinctively tipped her face closer to Teddy's.

"Oh, I meant to tell you!" Teddy whispered. "I may have just gotten you the Duke of Montana."

"*What?*" Beatrice was so excited that she almost tripped, but Teddy was a smooth enough dancer to cover for her. "He's impossible to talk to! He's so . . ."

"Enigmatic?"

"I was going to say grumpy," Beatrice admitted.

"We found common ground. Turns out the duke is a sailor."

"In Montana," Beatrice said slowly.

"He keeps a boat in the Caribbean and another in Seattle."

She shook her head, impressed. "So you offered him a weekend at Nantucket in exchange for his vote?"

"Beatrice! Resorting to bribery already? I'm shocked," Teddy teased.

"I suppose it depends on the type of bribery, doesn't it?"

The words came out flirty; she hadn't meant them to be. Or . . . had she?

"What about you?" Teddy asked softly. "I saw you talking to the Duke of Roanoke."

"I figured he was my best shot at the Old Guard," Beatrice replied. The duke, Gerald Randolph, had suffered at the hands of men like Madison when he and his husband, Michael, got married almost a decade ago. No one ever denounced him outright; their cruelty was far more subtle and insidious.

"Maybe you can explain what he meant," Beatrice added, glancing up at Teddy. "He told me that he didn't want to get involved, but then sighed and said he had to, because Michael was insisting on it."

Teddy smiled. "That was *you*, Bee. Michael is probably grateful that you stood up for him at our wedding."

"I did what?"

"Robert Standish had seated Michael in some obscure pew, away from his husband. He said that protocol demanded it and refused to let Michael come in by the main door. You found out and quietly moved Michael where he belonged." Teddy reddened a little as he added, "I guess it wasn't that big a deal, since the wedding never happened, but it must have meant something to Michael."

"Oh. I'm really glad I did that." At the thought of their almost-wedding, Beatrice decided to voice a question that had been troubling her for a while. "Teddy . . . what happened with our wedding? Why didn't we go through with it?"

Teddy swept her farther into the empty space at the center of the dance floor. It took a moment for Beatrice to realize that the empty space was there for *them*, that people had drawn back from the royal couple, the way they always used to do for her parents.

"You were worried about the message it sent, getting married before your coronation," he told her.

Beatrice nodded slowly. She still hadn't been formally crowned; a monarch's coronation typically took place a year after the death of the previous monarch, during the summer. There was a powerful symbolism in Beatrice beginning her reign as an unmarried woman rather than a wife. If she got married before her coronation, people might say that Teddy was the one actually doing her job. It would weaken her.

"But we were in love," she clarified. *I loved you* was what she meant to say. *I was ready to spend a lifetime with you.*

"We had said I love you." Teddy's words were so soft that she almost didn't hear them, not that it mattered. She already knew the answer.

She knew that he'd loved her then, and loved her still.

They turned slow circles until the colors of the evening began to blur together—the greenhouse flowers on the tables and bar, the deep jewel tones of women's gowns, and the sleek black of men's tuxedos.

"I need to tell you something." Beatrice wasn't sure why she was doing this, except that it suddenly felt urgent she clear up all secrets between them. "I saw Connor recently. He's, um . . ." She started to explain, then halted at the look on Teddy's face. "You know who Connor is," she said, realizing.

"I do," he admitted, eyes glowing an impossibly bright blue. "Is Connor here?"

"I saw him in Texas. He's working as the Ramirezes' head of security now."

"So are you back together?" Teddy's shoulders were coiled with tension.

"It was good to talk to him." Immediately Beatrice regretted those words. "I mean, I'm glad I saw him, because it answered some questions for me, but no. We are not together."

She waited for Teddy to ask what mysterious things her

conversation with Connor had helped resolve, but he was silent.

Beatrice was unnervingly aware of everything: her heart beating against her ribs, the tulle gown drifting around her legs, the weight of Teddy's gaze on hers.

Fine, then. She would be the one to say it. "What I mean is, I've changed my mind."

His brows drew slightly together. "Changed your mind?"

"Remember when I first woke up after my accident, when I said that I just wanted to be friends?" Beatrice was fairly certain that her exact words were *Can you keep pretending to be my fiancé,* but that sounded so harsh.

"I remember," Teddy said cautiously.

"That's not true anymore. I mean, I'm not remembering anything yet," she added hastily, "but I want to see you. More than I see you right now. Not just at formal events, as my memory-loss coach."

What was wrong with her? Why couldn't she just say it clearly?

Because you hate being vulnerable and talking about your feelings, a voice inside her replied. It sounded eerily like Samantha.

Thankfully, Teddy seemed to understand what she meant, because he smiled.

"Bee. Are you saying that I'm allowed to ask you out?"

"Yes," she breathed.

Her face was already tipped so close to his. When they kissed, it was featherlight, almost a part of the dance. Beatrice felt herself melting instinctively into it, because this was a kiss they had done before. One that her body knew, even if her mind didn't remember.

When they pulled apart, a new confidence coursed through her. She could do it, all of it—could explore these new possibilities between her and Teddy, could round up enough votes to defeat Madison and convince America that she should be their queen. She would survive this threat to her position. Not just survive: she would *rebuild*, would stitch back together the life and memories that had been lost to her in the accident.

Or maybe there were too many pieces lost to rebuild—maybe she wouldn't get her memories back at all. Suddenly that seemed less important than it used to.

28

SAMANTHA

"Are you sure your family doesn't mind that I'm crashing Christmas?" Sam asked as Liam loaded their overnight bags into the trunk. His parents lived a few hours away, in Delaware, and when Liam realized she was going to be alone for the holidays, he'd insisted that she come.

"My parents are excited. As you can imagine, they've never hosted royalty before." Liam grinned. "I told them you're shockingly low-maintenance, but I don't think they'll believe it until they see you wad up your napkin and throw it into the trash."

"Hey, I'm getting better at my three-pointers!"

Sam had tucked a few presents into her small duffel: a new notebook and fountain pen for Liam, a scented candle for his parents. Her gifts for her own family were already at the palace; she'd left them with a startled-looking security guard the previous afternoon.

"Thanks again for taking me shopping this week," she added. Sam had never done her own holiday shopping before. Usually she wrote out her gift ideas and one of the palace assistants handled the actual purchasing. Browsing the various stores at the mall, looking for things that might inspire her, was a lot more fun.

The Washingtons always gave each other gag gifts, because there was no point in buying expensive presents for people who had everything. Sam was especially proud of what she'd gotten Jeff—she'd returned to Costco for the inflatable tennis net—and Beatrice: a coffee mug that read I'M A ROYAL PAIN WITHOUT CAFFEINE.

Not that she expected to hear from her family. They'd all been silent since her cover was blown, probably livid that she'd been spotted in such an undignified and unroyal setting. Some of the tabloids had reported Sam's return with predictably cruel headlines, like HOT MESS EXPRESS! SAMANTHA BACK IN TOWN SPORTING A REGRETTABLE HAIRCUT! and PRINCESS NO MORE, AND WOW DOES SHE LOOK IT!

But Sam had been surprised by how much positive press she'd received, too. As she kept on living her ordinary life, more videos surfaced of her doing normal-person things: taking the metro, ordering coffee at a chain restaurant where she waited in line like everyone else, counting out bills at the register. Even if the tabloids mocked her, there were plenty of bloggers who praised her for "shopping with the people."

When the news broke, Sam had worried that the group of roommates might ask her to leave; but they'd mainly just been bewildered or amused. When Sam had asked if they had any questions, Jessica had immediately jumped in to say, "Are you going to dye your hair now? Because you really can't pull off blond." At which Sam had laughed and asked if Jessica would help her change it back.

The only disappointment was that she couldn't keep tending bar anymore: it was too big a security risk, for her and for everyone at Enclave. When Sam had begged for work anyway, the manager had agreed to let her help Amber backstage, so at least she kept busy.

As their car pulled out of the driveway, Sam's phone rang, and she immediately bent down for her purse. What if it was Marshall, calling from Hawaii?

To her shock, the caller ID said BEATRICE.

"Sam?" Her sister sounded relieved that she'd answered. "I saw that you brought over presents. Thank you for doing that."

"Of course." Sam covered the phone with her hand and mouthed *Beatrice,* and Liam put the car back in park.

"You're coming for dinner tonight, right? It's Christmas Eve," Beatrice reminded her.

"I don't . . ." Sam blinked, uncertain what to say.

Reading her confusion as agreement, Beatrice said, "Great. I'll see you soon," and hung up.

"Everything okay?" Liam asked, once Sam had lowered the phone.

"Beatrice just invited me to Christmas Eve dinner."

"And this is . . . a bad thing?"

"I was kind of excited to meet your family," Sam said, dodging the question.

Liam didn't let her get away with it. "You can meet my family anytime. This is exactly what you wanted: the chance to make up with your siblings and fight to get your titles back. Why are you hesitating?"

Because things weren't clear-cut anymore. Sam loved her family, but she was also building a life outside their orbit— a real life, not a fantasy existence like the one in Hawaii. She was learning to stand on her own right here in Washington, not as Martha but as herself. It had forced her to stretch and grow beyond the person she'd been into a new person that she was still discovering.

"It'll be awkward" was what she told Liam.

"Isn't that what family holidays are all about? Enforced quality time and awkwardness?" Liam shrugged. "I haven't felt at home at my parents' house in years. My room is like a time capsule from high school and I have to share a bathroom with my brother and his wife and the walls are way too thin. But it's not about that; it's about the people."

Sam knew he was right. "If I go, promise me one thing. You'll take me to see your high school time capsule another time?"

Liam grinned. "I'll send you a photo with my angsty teen posters in the background. Deal?"

When Sam showed up at the palace in the nicest dress she had thought to grab from her old closet—a black velvet one with an asymmetrical bow on the shoulder—a security guard was there to welcome her. The palace operated with a skeleton staff at the holidays, no footmen or maids, but there was always someone at the door, at least.

"It's good to see you, Miss Samantha," he said gruffly.

So she was *Miss Samantha* now. Sam wondered who had decided that.

It was strange how much had changed in the past weeks. The palace looked the same as it always did at Christmas— the enormous tree in the ballroom, sourced from somewhere in the forests of Maryland or Virginia, and then the smaller tree in the family's private living room that was decorated with personal touches, including papier-mâché or clay ornaments that the siblings had made in elementary school. The same garland wound up the main front staircase, the same mistletoe hung from the crystal chandelier in the entry hall. Yet it felt curiously unfamiliar to Sam, as if she no longer belonged here.

Had she ever *really* belonged here?

Her family was all gathered in the living room, clutching tumblers of whiskey sour, which dug a bittersweet pang into

Sam's heart because that was her dad's signature drink. She glanced around the room and saw that Aunt Margaret was here from Orange, along with her husband, Nate, and Sam's uncle Richard and aunt Evelyn with their two children.

Daphne, who looked as perfect as always in a cranberry-red cocktail dress, was the first to look up and notice Sam. She must have made a small noise, because Jeff followed her gaze and went still.

"Sam?"

It was only one word, but it hurt. He sounded shocked, almost confused, to see her.

"Hi, everyone." Sam lifted a hand in an awkward wave, then remembered she didn't have a title, and they did. Slowly, she curtsied—first to Beatrice, then to Jeff and her mother, then to her grandmother.

It was one of the more excruciatingly quiet moments of her entire life.

"I didn't know you were coming," Jeff said haltingly.

"I invited her." Beatrice swept forward. "Congress may have stripped Samantha's titles, but last I checked, they haven't stripped her from our family. We aren't the British, who exile their relatives to Paris and never speak to them again. We need to stick together."

"Thanks, Bee." Sam ran a thumb nervously along the strap of her purse, as if it were a life jacket keeping her afloat.

Slowly, everyone's conversations started back up. Sam felt Aunt Margaret's eyes boring into her, questioning and sharp. Of course Aunt Margaret was curious; she was the one who'd helped Sam escape to Hawaii in the first place. Sam made a mental note to thank her for not telling everyone where Sam had been.

"I'm so glad you could make it." Beatrice looped an arm through Sam's and began tugging her in the direction of Daphne and Jeff.

"Merry Christmas," Sam said feebly, unnerved by Jeff's silence.

He must have sensed Sam staring at him, because he finally looked up from his drink, seemingly at a loss. "Um, yeah."

Um, yeah? That was all she got from her twin brother at the holidays?

The realization of just how much distance yawned between them hit Sam like a physical blow.

"Excuse me," she muttered, then whirled on one heel and started blindly down the hall. When she saw the double doors to the library on her left, she pushed them open.

She almost never came in here; the library was one of the rooms open to the public, a favorite of tourists with its black lacquered panels and inlaid wood floor. Slowly, Sam began wandering the bookshelves along the wall, trailing her fingers over the spines as she blinked back tears. When she found the nineteenth-century history section, she grabbed a volume and plopped into an armchair.

There was a creak of doors being pushed open, and Sam glanced over. "Beatrice?" Part of her had hoped it was Jeff.

"Hey," her sister said cautiously, coming to sit in the neighboring armchair.

Sam leaned her head back and closed her eyes. "I'm sorry I ruined Christmas. Do you want me to go?"

"Sam, you didn't ruin Christmas."

"No one really wants me here," Sam started to say, but Beatrice talked over Sam's protests.

"If Christmas is ruined, it's because Dad isn't here. Not because of you."

Sam nodded, unable to speak.

"Remember how much fun Christmases were before Dad became king? Like that time we went to the mall and rode tricycles around the empty toy store?"

"I remember that," Sam said slowly. "The photographer asked you to talk to the elves, but you kept insisting that you had to speak to Santa himself. Pulling rank, even at a young age," she added, slightly teasing.

Beatrice reddened. "I just wanted to make sure Santa got my Christmas list. The elves looked kind of . . . untrustworthy."

"What about the year we sent all the staff home and tried to cook our own dinner?" Sam recalled.

"Everything was so burned! It's a miracle we didn't set the palace on fire."

"The only thing that wasn't destroyed was the mashed potatoes, and they were . . ."

"Lumpy."

"Inedible." Sam grinned. "Didn't Dad try to order pizza to the palace, and the delivery guy refused to come because he thought it was a prank call?"

Silence fell between them again, but it felt softer than before, its edges sanded down to something smooth.

"Sam, you're not the only one who feels lost. It feels like every time I start to get my footing, there's another twist or setback," Beatrice said quietly. "What if my memories never return?"

Sam stood, struck by a sudden idea. She headed to the bookshelves with new purpose and scanned the spines.

"Sam?" Beatrice asked, but Sam knew exactly what she was looking for.

"Here it is!" She reached for a volume labeled *King Benjamin: A Royal Life* and handed it triumphantly to Beatrice. "Promise me you'll read this."

"The whole thing?"

Sam rolled her eyes. "If you must, you can skip to the second half, after Benjamin has his riding accident."

"Riding accident?"

"He fell from his horse at age forty-five, trying to jump a fence, and suffered a serious head wound. Queen Tatiana effectively ruled America for months, though Congress never actually named her as Regent. She told everyone she was just acting as her husband's 'secretary,' dictating responses from his sickbed, but she was totally pulling the strings," Sam explained. "You could say that she was America's first ruling queen during that time."

Beatrice blinked. "Why have I never heard this story?"

"Even back then, the palace PR team was a well-oiled machine. They kept it all very hidden," Sam told her. "And of course, most people didn't believe Tatiana was doing anything, because it was inconceivable to them that a woman could rule." *Plenty of people still think that*, Sam almost added, but Beatrice knew that better than anyone.

"What happened to Benjamin?" her sister asked.

Sam tapped the book's cover. "You'll see when you read."

"I hate when you give me homework. You're as relentless as Dad," Beatrice replied, but she was smiling.

Then her smile faded as she asked, "Sam, what's going on with you and Marshall?" She added hastily, "You don't have to talk about it, of course. I'm just worried about you."

Sam let out a shaky breath. "Marshall is still in . . . he's far away."

Haltingly, she tried to explain—that she missed him so much, and worried she was being selfish by staying in the capital, yet she couldn't leave.

"It's not selfish of you to stay," Beatrice assured her.

"I know." You had to pour some of yourself into a relationship, but you couldn't give away *all* of you. And Marshall hadn't asked her to.

"Maybe you just need time and space to figure out what you want, and how Marshall fits into it."

"That was very wise. Right now *you're* the one acting like Dad," Sam declared, and stood. It was time to go face everyone again. "Should we head back?"

The Washingtons were all still gathered in the living room. Per family tradition, each person would open a single Christmas present before dinner—and from the look of things, Sam's cousins Annabel and Percy had lost patience. Wrapping paper and ribbons were scattered around them like the carnage of war.

Sam's heart leapt when she saw that Jeff was sitting on the couch, her present in his lap.

He tore back the wrapping paper, which was printed with tiny cartoon reindeer. "A floating tennis set," he realized aloud.

Daphne was sitting next to him; she reached for the box quizzically. "What fun. And is this a bag of . . . balloons?"

She looked utterly lost, but Sam saw the understanding on Jeff's face. He looked up and met Sam's gaze with the hint of a smile. "For water-balloon tennis?"

"I figured you're a little rusty."

Sam held her breath, and was relieved when Jeff teased her right back.

"Not as rusty as you. Could be a good game for Telluride, as long as we keep the pool warm."

"A punishment for whoever is the last to make it to the Prospect lift?"

Jeff grinned. And there it was again, a flicker of their old twin connection. Turned out it wasn't broken after all.

Everyone stood to head into the dining room, and Jeff fell into step alongside her. "So, I saw the video of you bargain shopping. You were awesome."

"Sorry the news broke like that," she said quickly. "It was an accident."

He didn't seem all that bothered. "Are you really not living with Nina? Because I'm not sure where we should send your invitation."

When his words sank in, excitement flooded her chest. "To your wedding?"

"You'll come, won't you? I'll understand if you don't want to. But it would mean a lot to me if you were there."

Sam smiled so broadly that it almost hurt. "Of course I'll be at your wedding, Jeff. I wouldn't miss it."

29

DAPHNE

Daphne and her mother stepped out of the car, and a man in a navy suit bustled forward to usher them into the department store. Velvet ropes cordoned off a path to the escalators. The scattered shoppers looked up and gasped, then quickly got out their phones and surged against the barriers.

"Mrs. Deighton, Miss Deighton," the store's manager exclaimed, flashing his whitened smile. "We are so honored to welcome you this morning."

"Thank you," Daphne murmured, though this whole outing had been her mother's idea. When Daphne had protested that she didn't want to go out shopping—it was such a hassle, especially now that they could get clothing messengered to them straight from the designer—Rebecca had just snapped that she'd already called ahead to the store, and it wouldn't be fair to disappoint them.

Daphne's eyes drifted to the royal-wedding-themed display near the makeup counters. It took up two enormous tables, which groaned beneath the weight of flags and coffee mugs, commemorative china and aprons and calendars. There was even a photo booth where shoppers could pose for pictures and transpose their own faces onto Jefferson's and Daphne's bodies.

"Our wedding-themed merchandise has been this quarter's top performer," the manager said, following Daphne's

256

gaze. "People can't get enough! I've never seen anything like it, not even—"

He broke off awkwardly, but Daphne had a feeling she could finish the sentence. *Not even when Her Majesty was planning a wedding.*

Jefferson had been America's favorite sibling since he was born—because he was a boy, or perhaps because of his easygoing charm, or because he was so unbearably handsome.

She glanced again at the wedding-themed table, where a pair of young women were holding up what looked like a newborn onesie. She didn't remember licensing for baby clothes, but she supposed that had been covered in their general contract. According to the most recent reports, Americans had spent over fifty million dollars on souvenirs for her wedding.

It was as if everyone in the nation had forgotten their various complaints—their grief over the late king's death, their anger at rising home prices, the resentment and alienation they felt every time their government disappointed them—and had turned into a nation of sappy romantics. This was the whole point of a royal wedding, after all. It gave people a rallying point, one that had nothing to do with party lines. One that wasn't about an issue, but simply about *love*.

Daphne used to be flattered by all this. There had been a time, not long ago, when she would lie awake during sleepless nights and scroll through the various Daphne-related items on the internet. Every time she searched her own name and found more merchandise—action figures, CGI avatars meant to look like her, an oven mitt printed with her *wedding ring*— it felt as satisfying as drinking from a cool bottle of water, slaking her bottomless thirst for attention.

Now, when she looked at the table of commemorative gear, Daphne just felt ill. What was the point of all that stuff? What was it *for*, really?

At this rate, she didn't know if the wedding would happen anyway.

After her last email, when she'd asked Gabriella again to meet up, the anonymous emailer had sent a simple reply: *No deal. Keep your blackmail.*

Daphne had stared at it in shock, then called Ethan. Gabriella really wasn't going to cooperate? Fine, she and Ethan had agreed. They had no choice but to go public with what they knew. So they'd wrapped up Rei's files and deposited them on the front steps of the *Times.*

Hopefully the newspaper would make a move on Madison before Gabriella decided to leak what she knew about Daphne and Ethan. And even if she told, afterward, no one would take her seriously—would they?

Daphne managed a wobbly smile as the manager led them to a fitting room on the top floor, where a small army of sales assistants waited next to racks of couture. A side table held a bottle of wine, chilling in a silver bucket, and a tray of pastel macarons that would certainly go untouched. Along the back wall were stacked boxes of shoes in Daphne's size—because, apparently, her shoe size was public knowledge now.

"Thank you, but we need a moment alone," Rebecca told the sales associates, who obediently scattered.

Daphne reached for a dusky-purple high-low dress, but her mother swatted her hand away.

"You're not trying anything on until you tell me what you're up to."

Panic spiked in Daphne's stomach, sour and fizzy, like when she drank too much champagne. She swallowed back the feeling. "I have no idea what you're talking about."

"Where were you the other day when you claimed you were going to lunch with the Madison girl?"

Rebecca didn't know anything, Daphne noted with relief.

She suspected, but she didn't know for certain. Daphne could play that to her advantage.

"I was dealing with something. Don't worry, it's handled."

Her mother's bottle-green eyes, the same green as Daphne's own, narrowed. "I don't trust you to handle things anymore. Not after you interfered with the Duke of Virginia and lost us our titles."

"You mean, when *Father* lost our titles?"

The slap was so unexpected that at first Daphne didn't process what had happened: that her mother had pulled back her hand and struck her across the face.

Her cheek burned. Tears sprang to her eyes, not so much from the pain, but from shock. Her mother certainly was a believer in tough love, but she had never *hit* Daphne before.

Rebecca sucked in a breath, seeming almost remorseful. "I didn't mean to—it's just—Daphne, you can't speak about your father like that. He has sacrificed so much to get you where you are. Didn't you see those displays downstairs? Do you not understand what's at stake?" Her voice was quiet but fierce. "This family has given up everything to get you that ring. Don't you dare ruin things now. You have come too far to slip up at the finish line."

"You're right, I am at the finish line." Anger pulsed through Daphne. "Which is why I don't need a *bruise* on my wedding day."

Her mother's eyes darted to the mark on Daphne's cheek. "That will heal. Whatever is going on, promise me you'll put a stop to it. *Now.*"

There was a dead silence in the room.

Daphne turned toward the door. "I'm going to clean this up."

The ladies' room was at the other end of a hallway. Inside, Daphne ran a few paper towels under cool water, then held them to her cheek. The mark on her face already looked normal, and Daphne felt irrationally angered by this, as if her body was betraying her by healing so quickly. She swiped some concealer over it and started back with a sigh. It hadn't escaped her notice that her mother wasn't able to say *I'm sorry*.

As she passed a row of empty fitting rooms, Daphne drew to a halt. An all-too-familiar figure stood behind an open door, studying her one-shouldered sequined dress.

Their eyes met in the mirror, and before Daphne could think twice, she took a step forward. "Nina. I'm glad I ran into you."

Jeff had told her that Nina was with Prince James now. *It's weird, right?* he'd demanded, and Daphne had nodded in fervent agreement, uneasy that Jeff was still keeping tabs on Nina.

Whatever game Nina thought she was playing, she was playing it too well for Daphne's comfort.

"Daphne. Um, it's been a while," Nina said awkwardly.

Daphne felt suddenly desperate to bring things to a head. "You can tell your friend Gabriella to stop threatening me."

"What?" Nina asked, bewildered. "Gabriella is definitely not my friend."

"Quit with the act, okay? I know you sold me out to Gabriella so that you could get your financial aid reinstated and have Jefferson to yourself!"

The shock on Nina's face was so immediate and intense that Daphne felt a prickle of surprise.

"First of all, my financial aid had nothing to do with Gabriella. As for Jeff"—Nina looked pointedly at Daphne—"seems like *you're* the one who has him to yourself."

"But you've been trying to break us up!"

Nina sighed wearily. "Do you accuse everyone of that, or just me?"

"Just you. Who else has the motive or the ability? Not that you could pull it off," Daphne added quickly. "But you could do some damage trying."

"If I did any damage, it would be because I've learned from your example."

Oddly, that made Daphne want to laugh.

What had Ethan said all those weeks ago, when she first told him that Nina had betrayed her? *It just doesn't sound like Nina.*

Daphne thought back to that night at the League of Kings banquet, trying to remember why she'd been so convinced that Nina had double-crossed her. Nina's financial aid had been reinstated, and then Nina had kissed Jefferson in the gardens. . . . What if it hadn't been part of a devious master plan at all?

Maybe the kiss was nothing more than that: a kiss.

Maybe Daphne had seen antagonism where there wasn't any, because she had grown up with knives in her hands, in a family that was constantly at war with everyone else, and especially with itself.

Daphne was suddenly exhausted from fighting. The thought of laying down her weapons didn't seem so unreasonable anymore.

She nodded at Nina's dress. "I hope you're not planning on wearing that to the wedding. I know it's New Year's Eve, but surely someone told you, sequins are *not* appropriate at a state function."

A wary mistrust flickered over Nina's face. "Daphne, you and I both know I'm not coming to your wedding."

"But isn't Prince James bringing you?" Actually, that was a great idea. It couldn't hurt for Jefferson to see Nina with James—to remind him that his ex was off the table now.

Nina hesitated. "He did ask, but I figured it wasn't a good idea."

"Why not?" Daphne pressed. "Don't you think it's time we put all the drama behind us?"

"Um . . . yes, but . . ."

Daphne peered further into Nina's fitting room and let out a little cry of triumph. "Don't even pretend you weren't planning on coming, because this room is full of black-tie gowns!"

Nina's neck reddened. "That was a misunderstanding. I told the salesperson I wanted a party dress for New Year's. My friends and I are going out to a hotel bar downtown."

"You have the rest of your life to do the all-you-can-drink thing at a hotel bar," Daphne said firmly, and began sorting through the dresses. There was nothing like evaluating other people's fashion choices to help you escape your own problems.

"This one would look great on you, except it's tea-length. . . . This neckline is too high; you should show off your shoulders. . . . This is from last year's winter collection; they shouldn't have even brought it out. And oh my god, what is this color? Puke?" she asked, at the same time Nina quipped, "Vomit-colored?"

They made eye contact again, and for a brief moment Daphne felt the bright, buoyant sense of connection from earlier this year, when she and Nina had been friends.

She looked back at the rack of dresses, dismissing one after another until she paused on a plum-colored gown. It was classic, with a fitted bodice and fluted skirt, but there was something edgy about the shimmer of gold threads that shot through the purple. "You should try this," she said, holding it up against Nina's torso.

Daphne stepped behind the fitting room door and heard the rustle of Nina unzipping the sequined dress and stepping into the gown. When she reemerged, she fiddled with the torso, yanking it higher on her chest.

"It looks fantastic," Daphne breathed.

"You don't think it's too revealing?"

Nina's shoulders and neck were bare, the fabric skimming over her upper arms to fasten in a knot at her back.

"It's revealing, but in an elegant rather than inappropriate way."

"I don't know whether to believe you," Nina said baldly. "This feels like a trap. Like you want me to show up in the wrong thing and embarrass myself in front of all the world's royalty."

Daphne was unexpectedly saddened by this, though Nina had a point. It wouldn't have been the first time Daphne tried to sabotage her.

"It's not a trap. Don't you know by now, I lie about many things, but *never* about fashion."

She was pleased when that got a laugh from Nina.

"You really do look good. I hope you'll come," she added.

Perhaps Nina heard the sincerity in her voice, because she shook her head in defeat. "I can't believe I'm saying this, but fine. I'll come."

30

NINA

Nina sat on the bed in Jamie's dorm room, wearing a red cocktail dress and heels, holding their two invitations to the royal wedding. Each piece of ecru stationery had been hand-calligraphed, as the royal family had done for centuries, so that each invitation was personalized for its corresponding guest. She wasn't sure whether they did that to keep out interlopers, or simply to show off.

The Lady Chamberlain is commanded
by Her Majesty to invite

Miss Nina Perez Gonzalez

to the Celebration and Blessing of the Marriage of
His Royal Highness

Jefferson George Alexander Augustus

Prince of America

&

Miss Daphne Madeleine Deighton

Thursday, the thirty-first of December,
at two in the afternoon

This was certainly an invitation she had never expected to get.

"Look at how different ours look," she mused. The calligrapher had been forced to tighten the rows of text on Jamie's, since it was addressed to *His Royal Highness James Charles Alexander Douglas, Prince of Canada*. And there were subtle differences in the shape of the letters—the loop of the *y*, the curlicue at the end of *Highness*.

"It just feels excessive," she went on. "Why can't they print the invitations and just hand-address the envelopes like normal people?"

Jamie looped his tie into a knot with fluid ease, not even looking in the mirror. "Haven't you learned by now that royals spend money on completely useless and archaic things?"

"I still can't believe Daphne sent me my own invitation." Nina had already recounted the story of their department store run-in to Jamie, who'd been as surprised as she was.

"Maybe it's a peace offering?" Jamie guessed.

She met his gaze in the mirror and couldn't help observing, "You look different without your glasses. Have you been wearing them at school so that people don't recognize you?" *Like Sam and her drastic haircut,* Nina thought.

"I wear my glasses at school because I hate contacts, especially when I'm staring at a projector screen. They make my eyes feel itchy and dry."

"I like you better in glasses," Nina decided. "They make you look . . ."

"Devastatingly brilliant? Artistic? Thoughtful?"

"I was going to say they make you look like *you*."

He grinned. "Maybe that's why I wear them at school, Nina. Because I knew you had a thing for nerds."

Nina wasn't sure how things between her and Jamie had escalated so quickly. It was all the hours they had spent in rehearsals together, and the flashes of vulnerability she saw beneath his cheerful exterior, and the fact that he'd come out for pasta with Nina's parents after the final performance and won them over. Nina could tell her mamá didn't like the thought of her daughter dating another prince, but by the end of the meal, even she had caved.

As they'd said goodbye, her mamá had pulled Nina in for a hug and whispered into her ear, "I get it, Nina. He's . . . well, he's easy to like."

"Should we head out?" Jamie asked, and Nina groaned.

"Isn't it enough that we're going to the wedding tomorrow? Do we really have to be at the rehearsal dinner, too?" She'd been shocked when she realized that their invitations both included cards for tonight's event as well.

"Sure, we don't have to go." Jamie flopped back onto his bed and laced his arms behind his head, the pose utterly incongruous with his expensive navy suit. "I would much rather stay in with you."

Nina's phone vibrated on the bedspread next to her. Her eyes drifted to the screen, and she let out a gasp as she saw the subject line of her new email. "Oh my god!"

Congratulations on your admission to the King's College Oxford Exchange Program

"I got in!" she squealed, showing him the phone. "I got in!"

Jamie grabbed her around the waist and yanked her down next to him, making her dissolve into laughter. "Jamie!" she exclaimed, knowing she was wrinkling her dress but not really caring.

She shifted so that her back was pressed to his torso. The expensive wool of his red-and-gray blanket felt warm and a little scratchy beneath her cheek. It surprised her, how instinctively their bodies melded together these days. Nina wasn't ready to go all that far, but Jamie didn't seem to mind, and she was growing more and more at ease here, in the safe circle of his arms.

She'd spent a lot of time in princes' beds for a girl who hadn't actually slept with either prince.

"Congratulations, Nina. You deserve this."

"Thank you." She forced herself to sit up and glanced in the mirror, making a halfhearted effort to fix her hair. "We should get going."

"Your ex-boyfriend's rehearsal dinner, the perfect way to celebrate your success," he agreed, which made Nina laugh. But at least Sam would be there, and she could share the news in person.

It took three times as long as normal to drive the mile and a half to the palace. The city had devolved into a giant street party; behind the ropes blocking off the parade route, people sat by the thousands, some with tents or sleeping bags. They huddled into parkas to stay warm, passing around flasks of hot chocolate or liquor. Nina saw picnic baskets, bottles of champagne, silly hats, and countless American flags. Earlier this evening, the guns of the Royal Horse Artillery had fired a salute into the sunset, though the real show—the parade, the wedding, the evening fireworks—was tomorrow.

After three separate security checks, their car finally crawled into the circle drive. Nina sucked in a breath, then stepped onto the marble steps with a smile. Jamie reached for her hand, and she let him—knowing people would see, knowing she had taken the plunge.

Tonight's event wasn't in the ballroom upstairs, but the Grand Gallery on the first floor. "The ballroom is for state occasions only," Nina explained, when Jamie asked. "This is an intimate party among close family and friends." *Intimate* by Washington standards meant anything under a hundred and fifty people.

They paused at the threshold to the Grand Gallery, both a

little awestruck. The room had been transformed into a fairy-land, the round tables covered in cascading centerpieces of white roses and soaring white tapers. A display in the corner held their table assignments, which were stamped on pink macarons nestled in crystal boxes. But the real pièce de résistance was the flower ceiling. Standing in the room, you looked up at a rich carpet of ombré roses, which started at deep red and cascaded through all the shades of pink and blush until they finally became ivory.

"This feels so totally Jeff, doesn't it?" Jamie deadpanned, which made Nina choke back another laugh. It was clear to everyone in this room that the décor was Daphne's princess fantasy come to life.

Nina and Jamie headed to the bar, a vast antique mirror behind it reflecting the room back to itself. She made eye contact with one of the servers. "Hey, Rick, got any beers?"

He smiled in recognition. "Hi, Nina. Sorry, but no beer tonight. You know how it is."

Nina had hoped there might be a secret stash of beer bottles back there. Sam used to request that the bar stock a few for her; but, Nina had to keep reminding herself, Sam wasn't a princess anymore. "Sorry," she told Jamie. "We'll have to stick with champagne—"

"You know, I could use a beer too," came an achingly familiar voice.

Nina turned around, startled, to see Jeff.

He glanced dismissively at Jamie, then jerked his head toward one of the exits. "Want to come grab one from the stash in the Weapons Room?"

"Um . . . I can bring you one," Nina offered, because surely the groom shouldn't leave his own cocktail hour, but Jeff started forward. Bewildered, she followed, Jamie close behind her.

The only sound as they walked down the hallway was their

footsteps on the ornate scrolling carpets. When they reached one of the sitting rooms, Jeff pushed open the door.

It looked the same as always, its walls hung with the ceremonial épées that gave the room its name. Not long ago, Nina and Jeff had come in here and started fencing, slashing at each other with the swords like children.

Maybe that was the problem with her and Jeff: they had never been able to outgrow their childish patterns of behavior. Maybe things felt different with Jamie because they had met as adults.

Jeff headed to a chest of drawers along one wall, its surface painted in French figurines of shepherdesses and sheep, and pulled on the handle. The drawer opened, revealing that the inside was actually refrigerated.

That was the type of thing the Washingtons did: took a seventeenth-century chest out of storage and hired an engineer to line the interior with appliance-grade insulation and electric wiring, so that there was an entire refrigerated drawer nested within the old French wood. They couldn't just buy a mini-fridge like ordinary people.

The refrigerated drawer was mostly full of beers, though a few bottles of wine clinked around in there, too. Jeff grabbed three beer bottles and handed one to each of them.

"Okay, I need to get one of these refrigerators for my office," Jamie said. "Thank you."

Jeff still seemed unwilling to make eye contact with Jamie. He kept looking at Nina, or over Jamie's shoulder as if he wasn't really there. "No big deal," he mumbled.

The awkward, stifling silence descended again, and suddenly Nina couldn't take it anymore.

"Can you two please stop being weird? You don't need to be best friends; I'm just asking that you be civil!"

"This *was* civil," Jeff protested at the same moment Jamie said, "I don't think Jeff has any interest in being friends."

Jeff rounded on him. "You're the one who disappeared one year and never came back!"

"You never called me! You went completely silent!"

"Because I thought you were coming again the next summer!"

The intractable expression on Jamie's face softened just a little. "Jeff, that was a really tough year, and I never heard from you. Not once."

Jeff was struck momentarily silent, then swallowed. "I didn't really know what to say. I mean, what happened in the pool house . . . that was serious stuff, and we were just kids." He stared down at his beer bottle as if it might hold all the answers. "I guess I just assumed you would come back the next year and we could pick up like nothing had happened. I figured I could tell you then how sorry I was."

"Sorry that you shared a secret I *specifically* asked you not to tell anyone, and broke up my parents' marriage?"

Jeff blinked. "What?"

"You were the only person who knew about—about Henri," Jamie stammered. "You really expect me to believe you didn't tell your parents?"

"I didn't! The only person I told was Sam. I know I promised not to," Jeff said quickly. "But she figured out something was wrong and got it out of me."

"Sam told, then," Jamie said, exasperated.

"Or one of the footmen overheard me telling her?" Jeff sighed. "Look, Jamie, I don't know exactly what happened. Maybe your dad realized something was going on, and it had nothing to do with us."

Jamie looked so young in that moment, so heartbroken and sad, that Nina wanted to wrap her arms around him and hold him close—but she couldn't. She needed to let him face this on his own.

"I know it's not your fault that my parents split up," Jamie said at last. "Their issues had nothing to do with you. But I *trusted* you, Jeff. When I asked you not to tell anyone what you saw, I was counting on you to keep that promise."

"I get it," Jeff told him. "And I swear to you, I didn't share it with anyone but Sam. Certainly not my parents."

Jamie sighed. "I guess I foolishly thought that if no one spoke it aloud, it wouldn't be real. And then my parents might find their way back to each other."

Nina couldn't help reaching for his hand. "Oh, Jamie. That isn't foolish at all; it's hopeful."

Jeff stared at her fingers interlaced with Jamie's, and said nothing.

Jamie swallowed. "I'm sorry I didn't come back the next year. I just assumed, when you never said anything, that you wanted to stay far away from my family and all our scandal. You certainly weren't the only royal family to drop us."

"I'm sorry, too," Jeff said hoarsely.

Nina let go of Jamie as he stepped forward. She watched as they did one of those guy hugs, giving each other a rough thump on the back as if it might hide the sentimentality of the gesture.

When they stepped away, both blinking rapidly, she pretended not to notice.

"Hey, guys. What's going on?" Samantha's voice sounded from the doorway.

"Sam!" Nina took an involuntary step forward. Sam looked good, more rested and bright-eyed than you would guess for someone living on an air mattress.

"Sorry to interrupt," Sam went on. "I saw you all leaving, and you looked like you might . . . well, I didn't want you getting married with a black eye," she explained, nodding to her brother.

Nina flushed at the realization that it might have looked that way—like Jamie and Jeff were leaving so that they could fight. Presumably over her.

"We should get back to the party," she said quickly, and turned to Jeff. "Thanks for the beer."

"Wait, I want one before we go!" Sam took a few steps toward the antique chest.

Jamie grabbed Nina's hand and tugged her through the doorway, leaving the Washington twins alone.

In the hallway, he drew to a halt and pulled Nina close, wrapping his arms around her and tucking her head beneath his chin. "Thanks for doing that," he told her. Nina felt the rumble of his voice echoing through her own chest.

"You mean, forcing you and Jeff to finally talk?"

"Yes, exactly." He smiled into her hair. "Have you ever considered a career in international crisis mediation?"

"No way. This is all the international drama I can handle," she teased.

Jamie stepped back. "Nina—I wanted to wait before bringing this up, but we need to talk."

"Oh. Okay," she replied, over the sickening feeling in her stomach.

Jamie was about to say goodbye. They were going to break up after tonight, because really, what kind of future could they possibly have?

"Can I visit you in Oxford?"

She stared at him uncertainly.

"I know we haven't talked about this . . . about us," he went on, seeming nervous. "But I don't want to stop seeing you once you leave for England. I really like you, Nina. You're brilliant and you're snarky and you're thoughtful and you're *real*."

At first she didn't process his words. "We'll be on opposite sides of the Atlantic."

272

"I have a private plane. It's a six-hour flight. Worth it," he added softly, "to see my girlfriend."

Girlfriend. In all the time they had dated, Jeff had never used that word. The tabloids had, when they called her a tacky nobody, but Jeff had never put a label on things.

Hope fluttered in Nina's chest, but it warred with anxiety and self-doubt.

"Jamie . . . I'm not the type of person you're supposed to date."

"And what type of person am I supposed to date? I would think, for starters, someone who makes me happy."

"If you're going to date a commoner, it should at least be a commoner from your own country!"

Jamie waved his hand at her objections. "What are all these rules you seem so worried about? Who wrote them, and why should we follow them?"

"I—" Nina broke off, dumbfounded, because he was right. When had she started letting her fears dictate her actions?

That was the thing about listening to the media. If they kept telling you, over and over, that you weren't good enough, classy enough, perfect enough, then eventually you started to believe it.

"You want to hear the great thing about dating a future king? We can make our own rules. We can rewrite the entire *rule book* together." Jamie's playful tone faded as he added, "Unless you don't want to."

Unless you still have feelings for Jeff lay unspoken between them.

But she didn't still have feelings for Jeff. She couldn't. He was walking down the aisle tomorrow, and Nina needed to carve out her own life, far away from him.

She had worried that dating Jamie would be just as constricting as dating Jeff had been, but maybe it didn't trap her at all. Maybe it was liberating.

"No, I do," she decided. "I mean, I want to keep seeing you."

She thought of the things she looked forward to about Oxford: curling up to read in the Bodleian Library, taking weekend trips to Vienna and Prague and to Jane Austen's cottage in Hampshire. It would be nice, going on those adventures with Jamie.

"Is that a yes? We're doing this?" he asked, and she nodded.

"Yes. We're doing this."

31

SAMANTHA

As Nina and Jamie disappeared into the hallway, Sam cast an uncertain glance at her brother. She felt like things between them had taken a step in the right direction at Christmas, but it was hard to know for sure. There was still so much they needed to talk about.

"Is everything okay with you and Jamie?" she asked hesitantly.

"Yes, but it's a long story. I'll tell you another time."

Sam shifted her weight, wondering if they should re-join the party, but Jeff surprised her by heading to the refrigerated drawer in the Louis XIV dresser and grabbing another beer. He started to hand it to Sam, but she took a second beer from the fridge and flipped it over, using the bottle cap of the upside-down one to loosen the other's cap.

"You know there's a bottle opener right here," Jeff pointed out, amused.

"I like doing it this way. Marshall taught me." Her voice caught a little on Marshall's name. Jeff clearly heard, because he sank back onto the sofa, eyes softening.

"I'm sorry. Are you . . . did you break up?"

"No, or at least, not yet." She sighed and sank into the cushion next to Jeff. "We haven't been talking much lately, though."

She hesitated for a beat, but if she couldn't trust her twin brother with this, then who could she trust?

"He's in Hawaii," she admitted.

Surprise flashed in Jeff's eyes, and she knew he saw the confession as the olive branch it was. "So that tip we got, that you were on Molokai . . ."

"I worked on a fishing boat until I heard that Beatrice was hurt. Marshall offered to come back with me, but he's really finding himself. I told him to wait for me until I came back," Sam added softly.

"What do you mean, he's finding himself?" Jeff wasn't sarcastic, just curious.

Two months ago, Sam wouldn't have been able to answer this question. But she'd found herself lately too, and understood now what it meant—what Marshall would be forced to give up, if he came back to America.

"He's testing the boundaries of what he wants, letting go of his insecurities, finding new strengths. And Jeff," she added, "you know how much pressure Marshall's family puts him under."

Jeff nodded slowly. "Look, I'm hardly a relationship expert . . ."

"Says the first one of us to get married," Sam teased.

He didn't laugh at that, the way he should have. Instead a cloud darted over his expression and he replied, "No one saw it coming, did they?"

Before Sam could ask about that in more detail, he went on: "I've always thought that you and Marshall seemed like the real deal. You have some issues to resolve, but I have a feeling you will. You're obviously crazy about each other."

Sam hoped he was right. She missed Marshall, with a dull ache that seeped into every waking moment. She kept pushing it to the back of her mind, because once she let herself wallow in it, she wouldn't ever get out of bed. But if she and Marshall were happy in different places—if they were building very different lives—then what future could they possibly have together?

She stood and wandered to the heavy wooden sideboard, where pictures in silver frames were arranged at neat angles. The twins' baptism, the pair of them in matching white gowns covered in ribbons and lace. A family portrait of all five Washingtons at Christmas, Sam and Jeff matching in red plaid—hers a dress, his a pants-and-shirt combination. Finally, a portrait of the twins celebrating their joint eighteenth birthday, both of them in jeans and white Oxford shirts. Lord Colin Marchworth, the photographer, had cried out in protest when Jeff tried to roll up the sleeves of his shirt and reveal his forearms: "You cannot show *skin* in a royal portrait!" As if their bare wrists were the scandal that would break the monarchy.

"Remember when we used to dress in matching outfits?" she mused aloud.

Jeff came to join her by the photos. "It would look a little weird if we tried to do that now. Though I have to say, I could probably still rock a shortall."

Perhaps it was odd to admit, but a part of Sam missed those matching outfits, with the coordinated piping, the white knee socks and monograms. There had been a comfort in presenting a united twin front to the world, of being one instead of two. The force of their personalities doubled. The pair of them together, indivisible.

But they *weren't* the same anymore. At some point they had set out on different paths, and now they were so far down those paths that Sam didn't know how to find her way back to her brother anymore.

"I'm sorry I abandoned you like that. It wasn't fair," she told him.

"No, I'm the one who needs to apologize. I was too hard on you when you came home." Jeff met her gaze and ventured an almost-smile. "Though I have to say, I'm a little glad I was such a jerk, only because it prompted you to show everyone how awesome you are."

She stared at him. "What?"

"Sam, you're proven yourself in a way that none of us ever have. You went out into the world and lived without titles or palaces, and you landed on your feet. You reminded us all how talented and resilient and smart you are." He spoke with an emotion that Sam used to hear in her father's voice all the time. It took a moment for her to recognize it as pride.

"I'm really sorry for how I reacted when you came back," Jeff went on. "I was just . . . hurt. I just couldn't believe that you would run away without talking it through with me. Or at the very least, warning me." Jeff drummed his fingers on the side of his beer bottle. "We used to tell each other everything."

"I know," she said softly.

"What happened to us, Sam?"

"Nothing happened *to* us, exactly. It's more that things stopped happening *between* us. You started spending more and more time with Daphne, and then Dad died. . . ."

"And then *you* started spending all your time with Beatrice, training as her heir, and I was left behind."

Sam blinked. For most of their lives, Jeff had been blithely content to be one of the spares, shirking any real responsibility in favor of the easy royal tasks. *All the perks and none of the problems,* he and Sam used to joke. But then their dad had died and Sam became the heir . . . and now she was out of the picture entirely, and the burden had fallen entirely on Jeff.

"You're not left behind anymore," she reminded him. "You're the heir now."

"Sam, I never cared about my place in the order of succession, whether it was the heir or the spare or the second cousin everyone forgets about. I just cared about being a part of whatever *you* were doing."

Guilt twisted in Sam's chest at that, and she swallowed.

Jeff sighed and went on. "I get it now, at least a little. After all this circus with the wedding . . . I understand why you and Marshall felt like you had to run off to Hawaii to escape it all. It's not the same for me and Daphne, obviously," Jeff hurried to add, "but it still sucks."

"I know what you mean," Sam assured him.

Things were different for them, because Daphne was a woman, and white, and even if her family had lost their baronetcy, she had spent her entire life following the rules—whereas Marshall, a future duke, had always delighted in breaking them. Jeff and Daphne weren't facing the same hurtful racial commentary that had plagued Marshall and Sam.

But the wedding had escalated things, turned his relationship into a commodity, an object of mass consumption for the entire world.

"Jeff . . . is everything okay?" Sam asked tentatively.

There was so much loaded into that question. *Are you sure you should be getting married? Can I help?*

"I'm okay. I love Daphne, it's just . . ." He sighed. "I never told you this, but when we first got engaged, we had our reasons."

Sam nodded. "Because Beatrice was in a coma, and no one knew if she would ever wake up."

"And Daphne thought she was pregnant."

Sam nearly choked on her beer. "Wait, *what?*"

"She wasn't pregnant," Jeff said. "It was just a false alarm. But by the time we figured it out, we had already made the announcement, and . . ."

Sam flashed back to what Anju had said when she met Sam at the airport, that she couldn't deal with another pregnancy right now. If only Sam had been perceptive enough to recognize it as a remark about Daphne and Jeff. Except—what could she have done to help, anyway?

Her heart ached for her brother. No wonder he'd lashed out at her when she came back from Hawaii; he was dealing with some very adult issues, at a much younger age than he should.

"Jeff." She spoke in a stern tone, forcing him to meet her gaze. "Do you not want to get married tomorrow?"

Jeff shook his head. "I love Daphne."

That wasn't an answer to her question, though, was it?

"We should be getting back." Jeff started toward the door, and Sam knew this topic of discussion was closed. She wasn't sure how worried she should be.

"By the way," he added, "do you want to be in the wedding tomorrow? We had a bridesmaid dress made for you."

"You did?"

"Yeah, apparently they had your measurements already?" Jeff posed it like a question. "I don't really know how that stuff works."

Sam grinned. "Of course. I'd love to."

She knew it would never be the same as when they were children, back when she and Jeff used to know each other's minds without speaking, when it felt like they were two halves of the same person. Back when they had worn matching outfits, had shared the same goals and likes and dislikes and fears. Had *dreamed* the same things.

Now their differences far outweighed their similarities. Jeff was about to be married and Sam's relationship was in turmoil; Jeff was royal and Sam had been cast out; Jeff was stable and Sam was . . . no longer adrift, but still searching for the right landing spot.

But as long as they could still find common ground, they would be fine.

32

BEATRICE

Beatrice hadn't expected Ambrose Madison to be at the rehearsal dinner, but here he was, casting snide smiles at her from across the room. His wife and children had come, too: Gabriella was in Daphne's year at school, but Beatrice couldn't understand why her brother, James, had been included. Beatrice had never liked either of them, especially James, who always stared at her in a way that was both condescending and objectifying at once.

When she'd asked her mother why the Madisons were here, Adelaide had just looked at her oddly and said, "The Duke of Virginia is a member of the Old Guard and your Queen's Champion. Of course we included his family."

Some Queen's Champion, eager to kick her off the throne.

From his pleased smirk, Beatrice had the sickening realization that Madison had gotten the votes. His bill to remove her would pass. She wished she could *do* something, go make a speech or lobby more supporters or, better yet, slap the duke across his selfish face, but of course she couldn't. She had to just keep on smiling and exchanging pleasantries as if her life weren't about to be wrenched apart, her future decided by a Congress that had shown no love for her family lately.

A chime echoed through the room, and everyone began to take their seats for dinner. Beatrice started toward the head of the table—even at someone else's wedding, the monarch presided over the meal—but paused when she saw Anna Ramirez.

"Your Majesty!" The Duchess of Texas came forward eagerly, lowering her voice. "I have news."

"Yes?"

"I've done a little straw poll leading up to next month's vote, and you're in the clear. Apparently you've done quite a bit of campaigning lately," the duchess added approvingly.

Beatrice's heart picked up speed. "Are you sure?"

"As sure as I can be. The Dukes of Roanoke and Montana have both been advocating for you, and did you know the Duke of Orange has quietly lobbied on your behalf, too?"

Marshall's grandfather? Beatrice never would have guessed. Perhaps he regretted coauthoring the bill that had stripped Sam of her HRH.

"I don't think Madison knows," Beatrice murmured.

Both women stared across the room at the duke, who was taking a large swig of red wine.

"I doubt he's figured it out yet," Anna said faintly. She smiled at Beatrice. "Congratulations, Your Majesty."

Beatrice looked down the table at Teddy, who was seated, per protocol, nearly as far from her as possible. Feeling her gaze on him, he glanced up.

I won, she mouthed. His eyes widened in excitement, and he grinned.

Suddenly, Beatrice felt knocked off-center by a longing that was new and familiar all at once.

Heart beating with relief and something else—adrenaline, or maybe nervousness—she took her seat. White-gloved

282

footmen sailed forward with the first course, a butternut squash soup with toasted almonds.

Was it possible to fall in love with someone a second time? Well, why not? It wasn't any more impossible than any other impossible thing in this wild, unpredictable world.

How strange to think that when she'd woken up from her accident, she'd been baffled by Teddy's presence in her life. They had spent so much time together these past weeks that his habits all felt familiar to her: The way he ended every text message with a period, which made him sound angry, though he so rarely was. That faded college T-shirt he wore, insisting it was lucky. The smile he sometimes cast her way, which made her insides go unexpectedly warm.

As the dinner progressed, people began rising from their seats to say a few words about Daphne and Jeff. Beatrice wasn't able to make any remarks herself—it was frowned upon for the reigning monarch to participate—but she loved listening to Jeff's high school friends, and especially Sam. They took a quick break before dessert, and she looked across the table to Teddy. When they made eye contact, she pushed back from the table and headed out into the hall.

He followed her out a moment later and wrapped his arms around her from behind, pulling her into a hug. Beatrice let out a very unqueenlike sound that was a squeal and a yelp of laughter all at once.

"Bee! I'm so proud of you! Tell me everything," he exclaimed, once he'd stepped around to face her. "The Duchess of Texas figured it out?"

Beatrice nodded. "She's been asking around, and realized I have enough votes."

"Congratulations," Teddy said warmly.

She had done it. Even without getting her memories back, she'd defended her throne. Her position was safe.

So why did she still feel a lingering sense that something was out of place?

Teddy watched her expression, his own smile faltering. "What is it?"

In answer, she reached for his hand. She didn't even register at first that her fingers had laced instinctively in his. "Come with me. I want to show you something."

At the end of the hallway, Beatrice tugged him into one of the smaller, less utilized staterooms. She flicked on the lights and started toward an enormous painting of a turkey flying through the sky.

"We're looking at this turkey?" Teddy asked, puzzled.

The turkey's wings were stretched out proudly, its feathers a brilliant array of reds, oranges, and golds. And even though the painting made no sense, there was something unexpectedly charming about the determined expression on the bird's face.

"King Benjamin painted this." She pointed to the signature in the bottom corner of the canvas. Two letters, *BR* for Benjamin Rex. The same monogram as hers.

Teddy's brow furrowed. "Is it a Thanksgiving painting?"

"It's meant as commentary on political symbolism. Because Ben Franklin wanted the turkey to be our national bird, and he got outvoted by the other Founding Fathers—but that's not the point. The point is that King Benjamin painted it at all." Beatrice had learned all of this from the book Samantha had insisted she read. "Benjamin became obsessed with painting after his riding accident."

"What riding accident?"

"He fell off his horse in 1885 and was in a coma for weeks. When he woke, he'd forgotten the past few *years*."

"What?" Now Teddy was starting to understand. "Oh my god, Bee, that's . . ."

"Just like my accident," she agreed. "When he recovered, Benjamin was different. He was missing memories, just like I am, but he also wanted to be an artist."

Teddy stared at her, waiting for her to continue.

"I asked Dr. Jacobs about it. Apparently the brain is a very resilient organ. If you injure part of it, the brain will try to rebuild its pathways in the undamaged tissue, which means your neurological wiring fundamentally changes. For instance, you might suddenly consider yourself an artist when you've never cared about art in your entire life."

"This happened in 1885?" Teddy asked, and Beatrice saw him doing the math in his head. "Benjamin ruled another twenty years."

"And he painted the whole time. He did over a hundred works. The rest of them are all stored in the archives." Beatrice fought to keep a straight face. "This was the only one they could hang in the palace, because the others are . . . not suitable for public consumption."

"They're terrible?"

"They're nudes." She pursed her lips but failed to hide her smile. "Queen Tatiana posed for all of them."

Teddy barked out a laugh. "For the record, if you start to feel the urge to paint, I'm happy to model—but only if you burn every last painting."

"Deal," Beatrice managed. Then she glanced back at the turkey painting, and her laughter died.

"What I was trying to say is that King Benjamin's accident *changed* him. I'm worried that mine changed me, too," she confessed.

Teddy studied her for a moment, his eyes so impossibly blue, full of concern and sorrow. "Bee, of course it changed you. How could it not?"

"But I don't *want* it to have changed me!"

"Why not? Change isn't something to be afraid of." He hesitated, then added, "I, for one, think that the accident made you braver."

"But I'm afraid of so many things," Beatrice protested.

"Being brave doesn't mean you aren't afraid. It means you refuse to let your fears guide your actions."

Beatrice wondered if he was right. In her old life she'd followed the dictates of protocol to a T, and now she was seeking votes on a congressional bill, chasing down senators on their ranches.

"I love you." She hadn't consciously decided to say it; the words seemed to float from somewhere deep in her chest.

Teddy pulled her close. "Oh, Bee. You must know that I love you, too."

Their kiss began soft, tender, and sweet. Beatrice laced her hands behind Teddy's head, playing with the threads of his wheat-gold hair, her entire body melting into the kiss without a thought. She made a sound deep in her throat and tightened her grip on him, until after a moment, Teddy broke away.

He closed his eyes and tipped his forehead against hers. "I love you so much, Bee," he said roughly. "When I heard about the accident, it was one of the scariest moments of my life."

At first his words didn't sink in. When they did, Beatrice went very still. "What do you mean, when you heard about the accident?"

Her security team had done an extensive, and very discreet, investigation into the car crash. They had wanted to make certain it wasn't an assassination attempt. When Beatrice saw the folder on her desk, she'd skimmed the first few paragraphs: . . . *poor road conditions, variable lighting . . . Driver worked an overnight shift the night before and was likely exhausted; he should have clocked out. . . . no evidence of foul play . . .*

Somehow, Beatrice had never considered the implications of the fact that Teddy wasn't in the car with her.

"Teddy. Where were you when the accident happened?"

He must have heard the distress in her voice, because his expression clouded. "At the airport. You were headed there, too," he added softly.

"Why weren't we in the same car?" she asked, and frowned. "And where were we going? I wouldn't have left the League of Kings before the farewell breakfast."

Teddy hesitated. Beatrice found herself holding her breath, her pulse beating too fast. The air felt heavy with her sudden premonition that they were on the cusp of something big, something that might break them.

"I was on my way to Nantucket. We had argued that night," he admitted reluctantly.

"About what?"

"It's not important. All that matters is that you're okay—"

"Tell me," she commanded.

He winced. "We were struggling to figure out what my role would be in our marriage. I . . . the thing is, I didn't have much to do while you were at the League of Kings conference."

"How did our fight end?" she whispered.

"We were going to work it out! We had just decided to take a little bit of space."

"A little bit of space," Beatrice said hollowly. Teddy started to reach for her, but she pulled back.

"Bee—I almost lost you once. I can't bear to lose you again," he pleaded. "I love you. I would give up everything for you."

But she didn't *want* him to have to give up everything.

A loud, screaming confusion roared in her ears. Teddy had been so stable, so constant, that without even realizing it, she had come to lean on him, trusting that he could handle it. Learning that their relationship wasn't as solid as she'd assumed—it felt like the rug had been pulled out from under her.

"I have to go," she mumbled, and fled back to the Grand Gallery before Teddy could see the tears in her eyes.

33

DAPHNE

The rehearsal dinner was winding to a close. Footmen circulated through the room, pouring coffee and serving cherry tarts with dollops of whipped cream, a traditional Washington family dessert.

Daphne's face hurt from smiling. All night well-wishers had given toasts to the happy couple: mostly Jefferson's high school buddies and family members, though a few of Daphne's old classmates had gone up to the microphone to gush about how *fantastic* she was. Daphne wasn't actually close with any of those girls—they just wanted to be able to brag that they had participated in the royal wedding— but it was almost nice, feeling like a normal bride who had friends to toast her. Even her father had mustered up a father-of-the-bride toast, full of such trite and generic platitudes that Daphne could only assume he'd pulled it from the internet.

The evening was nearing its conclusion when Daphne's skin prickled with sudden awareness. Gossip had begun hissing through the room like a winter wind; many of the guests were staring at their phones in shock, whispering to their neighbors. A momentary panic stabbed through Daphne— had Gabriella leaked the truth about her and Ethan after all?—but then she realized that her mother was smiling a narrow, catlike smile.

"Was this you?" Rebecca asked, holding her phone toward Daphne.

The headline on the landing page of the *Times* read DUKE OF VIRGINIA ENGAGED IN MULTIMILLION-DOLLAR FRAUD SCHEME.

Daphne sucked in a breath and kept reading.

The FBI has opened a formal investigation into His Grace the Duke of Virginia, who stands accused of stealing millions of dollars from various government accounts under his care. A federal judge has frozen the duke's assets and placed him on a no-fly list. . . .

"It looks like I underestimated you," Rebecca went on softly. "Well done, Daphne."

For years Daphne had been striving for that note of pride in her mother's voice, and now that she had finally earned it, she just felt hollow. She didn't especially care what Rebecca thought anymore. Perhaps when her mother had slapped her, it had knocked Daphne's compulsion to please her right out of her brain, the way you might shake the last candy from a box.

The entire room seemed to be staring at Ambrose Madison. He stood, his voice thunderous as he shouted, "You did this. How dare you?"

For a wild moment Daphne thought he was yelling at her. After all, this had been *her* doing. But then she realized his invective had been directed at the queen.

Beatrice met his gaze coolly. "Your Grace?"

"You crazy—" He used a word that was not typically spoken in polite company, certainly not to Her Majesty. "You're mentally damaged, and everyone knows it!"

Before he could say more, a burly Revere Guard approached to escort him out of the room. "Get your hands off me," the duke exclaimed. He prodded his family, who quickly turned toward the exit, all of them sneering haughtily.

Everyone was watching the Madisons' retreat amid a low roar of speculation, so they didn't notice Daphne leaving the Grand Gallery through the opposite door.

She ducked through a service corridor, ignoring the footmen's shock as she wove around their carts full of empty wineglasses or dirty dinner plates. "Excuse me!" she chirped, and reemerged into the main hallway near the front entrance.

"Gabriella!"

The duke and duchess looked over their shoulders. When they saw that it was Daphne, they turned aside, pulling James in their wake—but Gabriella's steps slowed.

"I need to talk to you," Daphne said quietly. She jerked her head toward an alcove, and Gabriella warily followed, standing near a suit of armor.

"I know you're here to gloat, but nothing will come of this," Gabriella insisted. "Daddy isn't going to prison."

As she tugged her expensive mink coat tighter around her shoulders, vulnerability—and fear—flashed across her features. For a moment, Daphne almost felt sorry for her.

"Gabriella, your father is guilty," she said gently.

"Who said anything about guilt or innocence? He won't go to jail because no one would ever send him there." Gabriella laughed, a caustic, cynical sound, and Daphne's momentary sympathy for her evaporated. "He skimmed a little money from some accounts. So what? That's how the world works."

"It doesn't have to work that way." How did Gabriella possibly think it was okay for her family, who had so much of everything, to steal from people who had *less*?

Daphne decided to get straight to the point. Her plan was almost complete, as long as she could play this last card.

"I want to call a truce."

Even backed into a corner, Gabriella held her ground; you

had to give her that. She put a hand on one hip as she asked, "Why on earth would I be interested in a truce?"

"Because I could *help* you!" Daphne lowered her tone. "I want to be done with this war between us. If I help, will you stop with the threats?"

"How would you help?" Gabriella asked warily.

"I'm marrying the heir to the throne tomorrow. I'm about to have a direct line to the royal family. The Washingtons can either make an off-the-record phone call to the Justice Department in your father's favor, or . . ." She made the sort of airy, delicate gesture that Gabriella normally made. "Or we can do nothing. You'll find that I'm a far better ally than enemy, Gabriella. Just promise not to tell anyone that—" She broke off before saying *that Ethan and I hooked up.* "Not to tell anyone my secret," she finished.

Gabriella was staring at her with resentment, and something else that might have been surprise, or curiosity. Finally she gave a single nod. "You have a deal."

Daphne held out her hand. "The war is over?"

Gabriella shook her hand with visible reluctance. "Your war with *me* is over. But, Daphne . . . this is hardly the only war you're going to fight." She laughed, almost sadly. "If you think your wars will be over tomorrow, you're more naïve than I expected. It won't end with marriage. Even once you reach the peak, you will have to fight to remain there. You will always be at war with someone."

Daphne wanted to protest, but she sensed that Gabriella's awful, ominous words were true.

On her way back to the Grand Gallery, she typed out a quick text to Ethan. *Come find me? We need to talk about Gabriella!* She slipped back into her seat, ignoring her mother's sharp stare, and lifted a glass of champagne to her lips.

When the gossip about the Madisons had finally died down, Jefferson caught Daphne's eye, then made his way to the microphone. It was common for the groom to give the closing remarks at a royal rehearsal dinner, since this was his only real chance to speak throughout the weekend. Royals could never do anything as nontraditional as compose their own vows.

"Thank you all for joining us tonight, and sorry for that disturbance. There never seems to be a lack of drama at my family's weddings." Somehow Jefferson managed to turn the Madisons' scandal, and the atrocious way he'd spoken to Beatrice, into something that people laughed over. That had always been his gift: the ability to set people at ease.

"Daphne and I are lucky to be surrounded by so many wonderful family and friends, who have showered us with love and support throughout our lives," he went on. "Of course, the biggest thank-you goes to my beautiful bride."

All eyes in the room turned to Daphne, and she smiled, never tearing her gaze from the prince.

"Daphne. I have loved you ever since that fateful day I saw you on the St. Ursula's campus. You were sitting on a bench, reading *Candide*, and I will never forget the look on your face—how totally absorbed you were in the book," he recalled. "You are so beautiful, but that has never been the most attractive thing about you; it's the sheer force of your passion. You are intoxicatingly brilliant and stubborn and defiant and strong. Seeing you walk down the aisle tomorrow will be the happiest moment of my life. . . ."

As he spoke, Daphne felt a spark of surprise—and, unexpectedly, relief. She had always worked so hard to *hide* her ruthless ambition that she hadn't imagined Jefferson had ever seen it. But maybe he knew her better than she'd realized. Maybe their marriage wouldn't be the endless performance she thought she'd signed on for.

A tiny voice within her whispered that something about the toast didn't fit, but she ignored it.

"To Daphne," Jefferson was saying.

Everyone obediently stood and lifted their glasses, the chorus of their voices echoing his words. "To Daphne."

She stepped forward and kissed him, as they all expected her to. "That was a beautiful toast," she murmured.

"It actually . . ." Jefferson paused, then shook his head. "Never mind. I'm glad you liked it."

As they posed for the photographer, Daphne couldn't help noticing that something wasn't quite right about her fiancé's expression, as if he was smiling a little too hard.

That was when she felt the touch of Ethan's gaze on her.

It had always been like that: no matter how many people surrounded them, she would sense Ethan looking at her, and their eyes would meet. And for a moment Daphne would forget where she was—a high school campus, a crowded royal gala, her own rehearsal dinner—because the way Ethan was looking at her seemed to draw her into a separate place, a temporary room of his own creation.

As their eyes met, Daphne realized with sudden, bitter clarity what was wrong about Jefferson's speech.

St. Ursula's wasn't where she and Jefferson had first spoken; it was where she and *Ethan* had.

Later, a knock sounded at her suite at the Monmouth Hotel. Daphne went to the door, expecting another delivery of flowers or perhaps a last-minute message from the event planners—and her heart skipped a beat.

"Ethan!" she hissed, tugging him quickly inside. "What are you doing here?"

He was still wearing his tuxedo from the rehearsal dinner, though he'd untied his bow tie the way Jefferson always did, letting it hang jauntily from beneath the corners of his collar. It made Daphne self-conscious about the fact that she was already in her pajamas, her hair falling in loose waves down her back.

"You sent a text that said, 'Come find me,'" Ethan reminded her. "I tried calling, but you didn't pick up."

Daphne glanced at her phone. She'd forgotten it was on silent.

He glanced around the suite: at the sleek grand piano in the living room, the kitchenette full of unopened gift baskets, the flower arrangements on nearly every surface. In one corner hung an enormous calendar, which was really just a poster of the entire week with Daphne's schedule broken into ten-minute increments.

"Remind me why you're staying here instead of at your house?"

"Jefferson's mother offered to host me and my parents at the hotel for the week, and I figured, why not? It's so much more convenient than being at home. So much closer to all the events," she said tersely.

"Right."

From the way Ethan looked at her, Daphne knew he understood the real reason she was here. She couldn't stand to be in her high school bedroom anymore, filled with stale and painful memories. If she was about to become a princess, she wanted a fresh start.

He cleared his throat. "Anyway, I just thought you'd want to know that Gabriella's dad was taken in for questioning."

"That's why I texted!" she cried out, remembering the reason she'd messaged Ethan in the first place. She quickly recounted how she'd confronted Gabriella and negotiated a truce.

A shadow passed over Ethan's face. "Sounds like you're in the clear. Your epic royal wedding can happen, exactly as you've always dreamed."

"Exactly," Daphne replied, though the word didn't come out as definitive as it should.

Ethan started toward the door. She knew it was best that he leave: walk away from her for the very last time, all their plots and schemes and sexual tension firmly in the past. Where it all belonged.

His hand was on the doorknob when she blurted out, "Ethan—did you write the toast that Jefferson gave tonight?"

Ethan's hand fell to his side, and his eyes flicked back toward hers. "It's not that big a deal," he muttered.

"It is to me."

"Jeff asked for my help, the same way he asked me to edit his English papers in high school. He was struggling to articulate his feelings for you," Ethan said gruffly. "So I helped him put it all into words."

Except that speech wasn't what Jefferson felt at all; it was what *Ethan* felt.

These thoughts were dangerous, combustible, and Daphne knew she shouldn't engage with them.

Instead she said, "It was a beautiful toast. You know me so well."

A charge sizzled in the air between them. Daphne felt longing and fear battling inside her. She thought of everything she and Ethan had shared—and everything they would never get the chance to. The only time they had held hands in public was at that theme park, when Daphne's face was hidden behind a mask. God, they had never even been on a *date*.

When she next spoke, Daphne chose her words very carefully.

"You know me," she said again, "better than Jefferson ever will."

Unexpected hurt flashed over Ethan's face. "That isn't fair, Daphne."

"What?" She realized, dimly, that she'd told him the same

thing not long ago—that he wasn't being fair, coming back from Malaysia and ruining everything.

"I'm not a *prince*! I will never have Jeff's titles or wealth or position. I will never be as famous or as well liked as he is. I will never be able to give you all of this." Ethan threw out a hand to indicate the suite, the wedding gifts, the clothes. His face was angry and anguished at once. "I'm not the hero of this story, and I never have been. I'm just a secondary character who failed to get the girl."

They were poised on the precipice of something dangerous and wild. Daphne knew that she could still send Ethan home, pretend none of this had ever happened.

Her eyes closed as she let her desire for Ethan flood through her. She'd been holding it in for months, for *years*, letting it gather inside her slowly, like smoke in a burning building.

Jefferson and the wedding felt distant and unimportant, a future that belonged to someone else.

She felt Ethan startle when she stepped forward and kissed him. Some part of her was glad to know she was still capable of surprising him.

Then Ethan's hands were in her hair and he was kissing her back, and it was *nothing* like kissing Jefferson. It was the type of kiss that would keep her lying awake at night for weeks afterward, replaying it; the type of kiss that sent currents of hunger swirling through her body. Dimly, Daphne wondered why they hadn't been doing this from the beginning, instead of wasting months—years—antagonizing each other.

She broke away impatiently and tugged Ethan toward the bedroom. Still, he hesitated.

"Daphne . . . are you—"

"Yes." She cut him off with another kiss.

Daphne knew she was risking everything she had worked so hard for. But none of that seemed to weigh anything right now.

Without breaking the kiss, Ethan scooped her into his arms and carried her into the bedroom, then deposited her onto the crisp white duvet. Daphne pulled him down on top of her, hooking her legs around his waist. Her hands slid beneath his waistband, over the dip at his waist, and up the planes of his back.

Her body seemed to have reverted to pure muscle memory, as if they'd slipped back in time to the night of Himari's birthday party, the night they were first together. Before all of her manipulations and plots and fake pregnancies and utter desperation.

"I love you," Ethan whispered. His breath was hot in her ear.

In answer, Daphne kissed him harder, more hungrily. Because even if she wanted to say it back, she didn't dare to.

How many times had Jefferson told her he loved her? But none of them had felt like this, because he didn't know her— didn't see every last flawed part of her, the way Ethan did.

There must have been a small, undefended corner of Daphne's heart that still hoped, in spite of everything she'd done, that she was worthy of truly being loved.

34

NINA

"I can't believe you're going to Oxford!" Sam exclaimed, leaning back on the velvet pillows. "I'm really going to miss you, you know." They had retreated to the far side of the Grand Gallery, where couches upholstered in rose-colored silk were arranged next to delicate side tables. After the drama around the Madisons' departure and Jeff's subsequent toast, the rehearsal dinner had drawn to a close, but Nina hadn't been ready to leave—not when she and Sam could finally catch up. Nina hadn't seen nearly enough of her best friend lately.

The two of them had spent the last hour filling each other in on everything: Sam's reconciliation with her family, Nina's excitement at having done the play, and her news about Oxford.

"I won't be gone long. Just a semester," Nina said in answer to Sam's complaint.

Her best friend laughed. "You say that now, but I have a feeling you'll never leave. A city full of history and libraries, where all you have to do is read?"

"Read *and* write massive weekly papers."

"You can write papers in your sleep." Sam waved away the objection. "Should I come visit for your spring break?"

"I would love that. Maybe another time, though? Jamie might be coming at spring break. . . ." Nina trailed off at the look on Sam's face.

"I see. Things are serious, then." Sam seemed pleased, and a little surprised. A teasing note entered her voice as she added, "I should have known you were serious, if you were willing to face this dinner for him."

"It wasn't that bad, actually." Nina hadn't minded hearing all those toasts about Jeff and Daphne; she'd hardly listened, too busy daydreaming about Oxford. And it hadn't hurt that she had a handsome prince of her own on her arm.

She glanced back at Sam. "Speaking of wedding dates, have you talked to Marshall lately? I assume he's not coming tomorrow?"

Sam shook her head and sighed. "He can't come, for the same reasons I asked him to stay behind in the first place. The second he shows his face in America, it's all over for him."

It was obvious to Nina that Samantha wanted Marshall here. Of course she did; this was her twin brother's wedding, and she didn't want to face it without her boyfriend. But Sam was trying to do the best thing for Marshall by not needing him—even if it might not be the best thing for their relationship.

Sam stood, and the skirts of her tulle cocktail dress drifted around her legs. "I should go check in with my mom. Congrats again on Oxford, Nina."

"You got into the Oxford program?"

They both looked up to see Jeff standing there. He ran a hand through his hair, making it stick up in a slightly boyish way. "Sorry, I didn't mean to eavesdrop."

Nina felt Sam staring at her, clearly wondering why she'd told Jeff about her study-abroad application when they supposedly weren't friends anymore.

"Okay . . . see you both later." Sam hesitated, then walked off, casting one last glance over her shoulder.

"Thanks for coming tonight, Nina. And—for earlier, with Jamie . . . ," he fumbled to say. "It meant a lot."

"I'm just glad you two made up."

Nina suddenly realized how late it had gotten. The staff were already cleaning up: quietly dismantling the tables from the evening's event, moving the flower arrangements to the ballroom, where a team of florists would probably work all night, rearranging them into new vases for tomorrow.

"I should get going." Nina reached for her clutch, then frowned at how light it was.

"You okay?"

"I just remembered that I left my phone on the terrace." She and Jamie had been out there for a few minutes during the cocktail hour.

To her surprise, Jeff fell into step alongside her. "It's dark out there; I'll come with you."

It *was* dark; even with the ambient light from the city, Nina was grateful for Jeff, who put his own phone in flashlight mode and shone it before them like a lantern. They found Nina's phone, with its lime-green case, on an iron table.

She started to head back inside, but Jeff lowered himself into a chair and said, "Sit for a minute?"

He looked so unbearably handsome in his tuxedo, the crisp lines of it emphasizing the angle of his jaw, the soft curve of his lower lip. Nina looked away.

"Hey," Jeff said, "do you remember Up Chickens?"

He was holding a quarter; he must have grabbed it from the table, because Nina doubted that he carried loose change around. What would he possibly use it for, the dryer in the dorm laundry room?

She took a seat against her better judgment, fighting back a smile. "The game is called Up *Jenkins*."

"My name for it is better," Jeff declared, unperturbed. "We aren't British; we shouldn't be shouting for someone named Jenkins."

"This is what you get for eavesdropping on adults when

you're a kid—you keep mispronouncing things. Like when you walked up to the bartender at one of your parents' events and asked for a Roman Coke."

"A Roman Coke sounds good. A lot better than a rum and Coke."

He set down the quarter and for some reason, Nina picked it up. In the semidarkness she could just barely see King George I's profile stamped on one side.

"Up chickens," Jeff told her.

"What? No! You can't play this game with just two people!" Despite her protest, Nina clasped her palms, holding the quarter tight between them.

"Down chickens!" Jeff proclaimed.

She slammed her hands against the wrought-iron table. Jeff flashed her a mischievous smile, and suddenly they were both laughing, the sort of infectious laughter that dissolves into a heady afterglow.

It was always like this with Jeff, wasn't it? The old magic kept pulling her in, the way it always did.

When Jeff had stopped laughing, he stared at Nina's hands, her palms flat against the surface of the table. He looked like a contestant on one of those shopping-network shows, choosing between two doors that contained prizes.

Finally he tapped Nina's left hand. "This one."

She flipped them both over. The quarter was beneath her right hand.

Jeff exhaled, no longer smiling. "I never can read you, Nina Gonzalez."

Nina was hyperaware of the distance between them, the way that the space was suddenly shrinking.

"You and Jamie . . . ," Jeff asked hesitantly. "Are you serious about him?"

She sucked in a breath. "You can't ask me that."

"Why not? I'm your friend—"

"Just *stop!*" She slammed her hands against the table again, much harder than she had during their game. Jeff's eyes widened.

"*Sam* is my friend," she went on. "You and I are too complicated, okay? There's too much history."

He looked stricken. "I don't want to lose you."

"But you are losing me." Some of the fight drained from her. "Don't you get it? You're marrying Daphne tomorrow."

He did reach for her hand then, and Nina let him.

The night was heavy and soft, headlights tracing down the city streets like fireflies. Nina heard the low rumble of traffic, the voices of all the thousands of people gathered to watch tomorrow's parade. She had space to drink in all these details because the world had gone utterly still. The only thing that moved was her blood, pulsing beneath her skin where her hand held Jeff's.

Jeff shifted, his eyes gleaming in the darkness. "Do you ever wonder what would have happened if the paparazzi hadn't gotten those photos of you, back when we dated?"

Of course she'd wondered.

What might have happened if she'd told Jeff how she felt about him earlier? If she hadn't been so worried about the tabloids' negativity? If the media hadn't sunk its teeth into their relationship when they had just barely started dating, would she and Jeff have stood a real chance?

If, if, if. Nina was sick of imagining the countless ways their relationship could have played out. This was the way it *had* played out, and she had to live with that, for better or worse.

She snatched her hand away and tucked it safely in her lap. "You didn't mean to do that," she declared, thinking of his question and the way he'd held her hand. "You're drunk."

"I'm not drunk," Jeff insisted.

"Yes, you are. Because otherwise you're being unbearably cruel: to me, and especially to Daphne. We both deserve better."

Jeff ran a hand over his face. He looked like he was on the verge of crying, or shouting. "I'm sorry. It's just . . . so much has changed over the past couple of years, and I'm struggling to keep up with it all, and I feel like I can't *breathe*." He shook his head. "I know it's ridiculous and you shouldn't feel sorry for me, but I just wanted to explain why I'm doing this. Why I keep coming back to you. I still—"

"Don't," she cut in angrily. "Don't say it." If he said *I still love you*, she might burst into tears.

Because no matter how hard she tried to scrub it away, a part of her still loved him, too. He had been her first love, and perhaps Nina was old-fashioned or just plain foolish, but she didn't find it that easy to swing from love to antipathy.

"I hope you and Daphne are happy together. I really do." Nina tried to mean it. "But I can't be friends with you, Jeff."

Oxford would be good for her. Maybe she could forget Jeff, not having to constantly see his face on the cover of every tabloid. In England, they were far too preoccupied with their own royal family to care all that much about America's.

She would always be friends with Sam, but it was time she put some space between her and Jeff. She wasn't strong enough to go on any more Washington family trips where she would be forced to watch him and Daphne together. It would cut her to the quick, being around them and knowing he had once been hers. Maybe that was cowardice, but Nina liked to think of it as self-preservation.

All she knew was that she couldn't keep doing this: being pulled close to him, then losing him again.

"I understand," Jeff said quietly.

He didn't look very princely in that moment. He looked like a bewildered young man who had lost his father and sought comfort in the wrong people; who had been thrust into a role that no one had trained him for and had squared his shoulders and carried the burden anyway. He looked pained and confused, and Nina had to force herself to mumble goodbye before she messed everything up by hugging him. Or worse.

She made it all the way downstairs and into a car before the tears escaped her eyes. Something caught in her chest and she turned her face toward the window, not caring if the driver heard her sobs. Surely he'd driven a crying girl home before.

There was a sharp pain in her chest that reminded her of the time Rachel had dared her to drink straight vodka—a sharp burning sensation that trailed all the way down to her core.

Nina told herself it was the feeling of letting go of Jeff. This time, for good.

35

BEATRICE

Beatrice had inherited many things from her father: his analytical brain, his deep brown eyes, his tendency to escape into work during times of emotional stress. Which was why, after Jeff's rehearsal dinner, she retreated into her office and shut the door.

On her desk sat the Royal Dispatch Box, a wooden box lined in leather and embossed with *BR*. She opened it and began to read the first few papers in her stack, a congressional report on natural gas pipelines. It was nowhere near interesting enough to keep her mind from wandering: replaying that conversation with Teddy on a vicious loop.

"Béatrice!"

The voice that sounded outside her office was somehow imperious and giddy at once. Beatrice heard a footman reply, "I'm sorry, Your Royal Highness, but Her Majesty has retired for the evening—"

"There is light from inside the office!" Louise pronounced it as *ze off-isse*, her French accent getting thicker as she grew agitated. "I know she will see me!"

Beatrice stood, intrigued by the interruption. Teddy had told her all about her new friendship with Princess Louise, how close they'd gotten during the League of Kings conference. She went to open the door and smiled tentatively.

"Hi, Louise."

Before she could say anything more, the French princess threw her arms around Beatrice in a hug.

Beatrice stiffened in momentary surprise, then hugged her back. She felt memories fighting to rise to the surface, but she couldn't quite grab hold of them, as if they were fragments of plaster dissolving in water.

"Can we talk in private?" Louise asked when they stepped apart.

Beatrice nodded. "Take a seat," she offered, but the princess shook her head.

"Not in your office! This isn't a *work meeting*." Louise grabbed her tote bag from the floor, and Beatrice heard the telltale clatter of a wine bottle. "I brought Sauternes," Louise explained, with a wink. "Should we go outside?"

"It's freezing!"

"So?" Louise replied, undaunted. "Or don't you have an indoor pool?"

Which was how they ended up driving a golf cart, its sides zipped up in insulated plastic, past the orchard to the Washington family's pool house. The twins used to bring groups of friends here, sneaking liquor in stainless-steel water bottles that didn't fool the guards, though Beatrice had never been so daring.

Louise marched straight to the blue-tiled hot tub, yanking a sweatshirt over her head to reveal a ruffled bikini. "Do you have a bottle opener?" she asked, brandishing the bottle of wine.

Beatrice found a bottle opener in the wet bar, then grabbed a pair of wineglasses. "I can't believe you packed a swimsuit," she observed. "It's the middle of winter."

"I always pack a swimsuit; you never know when you're going to need one." A mischievous look entered Louise's eyes as she added, "Alexei and I broke into a hotel's hot tub, once, in Ibiza. Our rental house didn't have one, and . . . well, it seemed necessary at the time."

Alexei, the tsarevich of Russia. As Beatrice slipped into the hot tub, a memory rose in her mind, more like a conviction than a recollection of any specific moment. He and Louise were together.

"Tell me everything," Louise commanded. "I have been so worried ever since the accident! And you hardly answered any of my texts! You're an even worse correspondent than Bharat," she added, visibly piqued.

"It's a long story," Beatrice said evasively, but Louise wasn't deterred.

"Why do you think I brought wine? I want to hear the story in all its detail." Louise began expertly uncorking the bottle, beads of condensation already forming along its side. She poured the honey-colored wine into the glasses and handed one to Beatrice.

Beatrice took a sip, and her eyes widened. "Is this wine or dessert?"

"I told you, it's Sauternes. It's wine *and* dessert." Louise lifted an eyebrow. "You like it?"

"I think so." It tasted rich and sweet, like apricot and butterscotch. Beatrice took another sip, letting the warmth of the wine settle somewhere below her collarbone.

Louise drained half her glass in a sip, then set it aside with a clink. "Is this about Teddy?"

Beatrice sensed that she could trust Louise. She wasn't sure why she felt so convinced of this; she just seemed to *know* it, in the blind instinctive way you know when you are hungry, or that sunlight is good.

"Things have been a mess since my car accident." Beatrice looked across the hot tub at Louise and took a breath. "I lost a year of memory."

Her friend gasped in shock but didn't interrupt. Beatrice explained everything: her amnesia, Ambrose Madison and his plot against her, and the ugly things he'd shouted at the rehearsal dinner tonight. She explained how she'd fallen in love with Teddy all over again, only to learn that they had been on the verge of a breakup the night of her accident.

When she finished talking, Louise's blond hair was curling from the humidity, and she'd had to refill both of their wineglasses.

"No wonder you wrote such bland answers to my texts," Louise said slowly. "I worried you didn't want to be friends anymore, but now I understand, you didn't remember that we *are* friends. Thank you for sharing all of that," she added, seeming touched.

Beatrice fumbled to explain. "I know that you're trustworthy. Even if I don't remember the reasons why I came to believe that, the knowledge is still there. If that makes any kind of sense."

"How very French of you." A smile played around Louise's lips, and she ran her hand through the bubbles that churned in the hot tub. "As for Madison, I always knew there was something off about him. The entire time he was your ambassador in my court, he was so . . . slimy."

"Everyone heard him call me mentally damaged! Gossip like that always gets out, and if reporters find a way to dig into the hospital records, they'll learn about my amnesia."

Louise reached up to retie her hair, which was falling loose from its knot. "What if you try to get ahead of it? Tell America the truth: you suffered a head injury, but it hasn't impacted your ability to rule."

"You sound like Teddy."

"I didn't realize he wants you to go public, too," Louise said meaningfully. "Was that why you fought earlier?"

Beatrice sank lower into the water, until it was nearly up to her neck. "It was about a much bigger issue," she admitted. "The night of my accident, we weren't in the same car because we had argued earlier that night—about the fact that

Teddy doesn't have a real job, that there's nothing for him to do except support me."

"And all those issues are still unresolved," Louise finished for her.

"Exactly! How do I know that history won't repeat itself? That he won't get upset by the constraints of being king consort and run off when things get tough?"

"Oh, Béatrice. You cannot know that. You can never be certain of anything except your own decisions."

"Well, that's comforting," Beatrice said drily.

Louise stared at her. "Sometimes you have to believe in things you can't get proof of. It's called faith. Like the way you knew you could trust me tonight," she added. "That was faith, wasn't it?"

"More like a memory I couldn't grasp hold of," Beatrice replied, but Louise's words had given her pause.

Despite the Pledge of Allegiance she had recited thousands of times in her life, despite all the people who got on one knee before her and swore to serve her "in faith and loyalty," Beatrice had never been good with the concept of faith. It felt too much like blind hope. She was her father's daughter, and felt far more comfortable in the realm of facts and hard evidence.

She wanted to ask how Louise and Alexei were dealing with this, but didn't quite know how to phrase it. "When did you realize that Alexei was the one?" she asked instead.

Louise frowned. "I don't like that expression, *the one*. It implies that there's only one person who fits with you, and love doesn't work that way. It's not like romance novels and ballads make it sound—some kind of lightning-bolt moment that happens *to* you, through no choice or agency on your part, and suddenly you're hot and bothered about someone you barely know. That is infatuation, and physical attraction." Louise shrugged. "When you feel that way about someone, act on it, if you'd like. But that doesn't mean you should build your life or your future around that person."

"So you think love is a choice?"

Louise twirled her empty wineglass. "Love is a conscious decision that you have to make over and over: committing to someone, choosing not to be with anyone else. Some days you will make each other happy, and some days you will disappoint or hurt each other. But even when Alexei breaks my heart, I choose to love him, and that is better than never getting to love at all."

"And you think it's worth it, despite the obstacles."

Louise looked almost amused at that. "*Obstacles* is putting it mildly. Neither of us wants to give up our throne." She paused for a moment before adding, "That's part of why I wanted to talk to you tonight. I have some news."

"Yes?" Beatrice prompted.

"Alexei proposed to me."

Beatrice let out a sound that was vaguely like a squeak. "Louise! That's exciting," she exclaimed, recovering.

"You're the only person I've told. It's not like we're about to make a big announcement." Louise caught Beatrice stealing a glance at her hand and smiled sadly. "He gave me a ring, but I can't exactly wear it."

As future rulers, Louise and Alexei were expected to marry—but to marry someone who would serve as a supportive spouse. If they wanted a real future together, either Louise would have to renounce her rights and move to Russia as his tsarina, or Alexei would have to go to France as her king consort. There was no way for them to be together and rule their respective nations.

"Congratulations," Beatrice said, striving for optimism. "I'm sorry, I shouldn't have talked about myself for so long when you had big news!"

"It's okay. Your news is more pressing, and mine . . ." Louise trailed off. "It's not as if we have a plan."

Beatrice knew what her friend meant by that. She and Alexei hadn't yet agreed which one of them would give everything up for the other.

"Are you really considering walking away from it all?" she whispered.

"I don't know. All I know is that I cannot imagine my life without him." Louise hesitated, then added, "Béatrice—you are the one who inspired me to try to make things work with Alexei."

"I did?"

"When you told me that you looked up to me. You said that you'd always thought I was so tough, that I made decisions for myself and not for other people." Louise smiled softly. "It made me want to become the person that you thought I was. Being brave or true to ourselves . . . it's not exactly something that princesses are trained in."

"No, it's not," Beatrice agreed.

Despite the wine, despite the warmth of the hot tub, she felt light and buoyant instead of drowsy.

She had always carried her burdens in quiet isolation. It was nice to have a friend she could talk things over with, to let someone else share her half-formed thoughts.

Beatrice knew that she loved Teddy. And what was love if not a form of faith? When you fell in love, you took your whole heart and gave it into someone else's keeping.

If Louise was really putting her entire position on the line for Alexei, then maybe Beatrice should have a little more trust, too. In Teddy, and in herself.

36

DAPHNE

Daphne yawned and burrowed deeper into the duvet. Her entire body felt sated and deliciously heavy, as if she'd turned to human taffy.

When her eyes opened, she blinked up at the crystal light fixture overhead, and then she remembered—she was at the Monmouth Hotel, and it was her wedding day.

The sound of steady breathing came from the other side of the bed.

She shifted to stare at Ethan. He slept on his side, one arm tucked beneath the pillow, a lock of dark hair falling across his forehead. Even now, his brow was slightly furrowed, as if he was trying to solve some complicated problem in his dreams.

The memories crashed over her in relentless detail: stumbling in here and falling back onto the bed; Ethan meticulously unbuttoning her pajama shirt, kissing the bare skin of her collarbone as he undid each button; Daphne pulling him back so that his weight settled on top of her . . .

She remembered falling asleep with her back tucked into the curve of his body. She had tried to move away, but Ethan slipped an arm around her and pulled her close, as if he couldn't bear not to have her tucked right there against him. As if she was something wondrous and infinitely valuable.

Daphne's eyes cut to the clock on her bedside table, and

she sucked in a breath. A team of people would be here in one hour to start her hair and makeup.

She lifted a hand to shake Ethan awake, but instead she found herself tracing a finger over him—down the line of his jaw, the slope of his neck, to his shoulders and biceps. She felt suddenly ravenous for this, the sheer joy of touching him.

Ethan's dark eyes opened and fixed on her. He was silent as she kept up her tactile inventory, sketching him as an artist would a drawing. When she reached his chest, Ethan tugged the duvet lower, letting her fingers brush over his abs, and Daphne felt herself nestling closer in response. He really was so handsome, not in the classical, picture-perfect way that Jefferson was, but in a way that felt more real and somehow more alive.

"Good morning," he murmured, reaching a hand behind her head. But Daphne pulled away before he could kiss her.

It shattered the spell that had fallen over the room.

"Ethan, this has been—" She hesitated, because what could she say? "You have to leave."

He sat up. The duvet fell down around his waist, and Daphne made herself look away. It was hard to focus with Ethan sitting there, shirtless. A sickening sense of déjà vu coiled in her stomach; she couldn't believe she was once again shuffling Ethan out of her bed.

"We should talk about this," he said carefully.

"What is there to talk about? We made a mistake—"

"Don't do that!" His voice was so sharp that she looked up at him, startled. "It's not a mistake," he went on, more gently. "Not when you love someone."

She froze, unable to speak.

"You know how I feel about you," Ethan added.

And she did know. His feelings were there in every line of the toast she'd heard last night—the toast that Jeff had spoken but Ethan had written. For her.

"Please don't do this," she whispered.

"Daphne, *we* already did this! Both of us!" Ethan flung out a hand to indicate the clothes scattered on the floor, his white shirt glaring in the predawn light.

She swallowed. "You don't understand."

"Then *help* me understand! Talk to me. Just don't run away again."

"Are you serious?" She dug her hands into the fluffy duvet and twisted them into angry fists. "You're the one who ran away, Ethan! You're the one who gave up on us, that day I poured my heart out to you!"

He flinched. "I'm sorry about that, but I'm here now."

Daphne wasn't finished. "I begged you to love me, and you said you were choosing Nina!"

"I'm sorry!" Ethan repeated, his voice low but thrumming with intensity. "Look, I could make sense of Nina. The way I felt about her was manageable, straightforward, simple. She is . . . easy to love."

"You love her?"

"No, I said that she's easy to love!" Ethan cried out. "But I *didn't* love her, because my heart belongs to you! It always has, since the very first day we met."

To her horror, Daphne felt tears pricking at her eyes. Ethan reached for her hand and held it in both of his.

"The way I love you feels impossible, Daphne. I love you so much that I've dated other people to make you jealous, that I've committed *crimes* for you. I love you so much that when you chose Jeff, I retaliated by putting as much distance between us as I possibly could. But I can't keep running from this anymore."

"Jefferson . . . ," she protested.

His eyes softened. "Jeff is my best friend, and clearly I'm the worst best man in the history of weddings. But, Daphne—you and I keep coming back to each other. Time after time, year after year. Even on the night before your wedding."

He squeezed her hands tight, the weight of her massive engagement ring pressing against his skin.

"Please don't marry him," Ethan finished softly.

Daphne flinched. "You know I can't do that—"

"Why, because you're going to disappoint the tabloids? Stop worrying about what other people think of you, and worry about your own happiness!" Ethan exclaimed. "You don't love Jeff."

"I do love him!"

"Don't lie to yourself! You may love him like a friend, but we both know it's nothing like this."

This. This electric, kinetic pull between her and Ethan, this thing that had spanned the last four years of her life; that had made them hate each other and confide in each other and trust each other with their worst secrets. This thing that was so massive, it had a gravitational pull all its own.

"Jeff doesn't love you the way I do. He can't, because he doesn't *know* you like I do," Ethan went on. "I love everything about you—your determination and your inner fire and your fierce loyalty. I love that you go out there and wrestle the world into giving you what you want. You're a fighter, and a bit of a narcissist, and I know it and see it and love all of it. Please, don't do this," he said, and kissed her.

This was nothing like their turbulent, fevered kisses from last night. This kiss was slow and soft and heartbreakingly tender. Ethan's lips parted hers gently, his hand cradling the back of her head and lacing in her hair.

For a selfish moment, Daphne lingered in the kiss, letting reality waver and dance around her. It felt as though two distinct versions of her life were floating before her like soap bubbles, each of them close enough to reach out and grab.

The sound of her ringtone sliced through the haze of her thoughts, and she pulled away.

What had she been thinking? Of course she couldn't choose Ethan. She was marrying Jefferson.

"You need to go," she told him.

Ethan's expression went hard. "If you're really choosing him, then I'm leaving."

"That's what I said!" She pointed toward the door.

Ethan was already out of bed, tugging his tuxedo pants over his boxers. "No, I'm leaving the country. You won't see me again after the wedding."

That made her pause. "You're going back to Malaysia?"

"Maybe." He shrugged. "Or South America, or India. All I know is that I can't stick around in the capital, watching you and Jeff pretend that your life together is perfect. I can't sit around constantly waiting for you to decide you want a random night with me when you're bored."

Daphne's mouth snapped shut. Some part of her had been thinking exactly that, hadn't it? That she could marry Jefferson, but this relationship or affair—whatever it was—with Ethan didn't have to end.

"I can't live some kind of half life with you, Daphne," he told her. "I'm not sneaking around anymore, betraying my best friend. I want all of you, and I always have. I won't settle for less."

With that, Ethan grabbed his tuxedo jacket and walked out.

Daphne waited until the front door to her suite clattered shut. Her entire body was trembling, but she forced herself to slide her legs over the side of the bed and stand. The ambient light streaming in from the windows caught the diamond on her left hand, which seemed to shine with a wicked, almost taunting glitter.

She went to the closet, where all her dresses for the week

hung in garment bags, each labeled with a laminated tag. Impatiently she tugged on a hotel robe and tied it around her waist, then reached for her phone.

Daphne had assumed the call was from the wedding planner, or perhaps from Jefferson, but her phone said UNKNOWN CALLER. Whoever it was had left a voice mail. Daphne immediately clicked to listen.

"Hey, Daphne? It's Rei. Call me when you get this." She left a 1-800 number, which Daphne dialed at once.

Rei picked up on the second ring.

"Daphne! I've been trying to reach Ethan, but he's not picking up."

Because he was with me. "What's happening?" Daphne asked impatiently.

"I finally hacked the firewall!" Rei exclaimed. "It belongs to the government, just like I suspected. Really tricky to get through without being detected, but I managed it."

Daphne nodded. "I know. The email came from the Madison family."

"The Madisons?" Rei repeated, puzzled. "No, those emails came from a personal computer registered to the royal family."

What? No, that didn't make sense—

"The computer that sent them belongs to Samantha Washington."

37

SAMANTHA

Samantha snapped her tote bag shut, then glanced up as footsteps sounded on the staircase. Liam clattered down into the living room, his hair still tousled from sleep.

"I'm glad you're up," Sam said eagerly. "I need to ask you something."

Liam eyed her pink sweatpants and messy bun with amusement. "Shouldn't you be in a dress?"

"Not yet. I'm getting hair and makeup done at the palace."

He nodded. "And you want a ride? I don't mind; I'm not on duty until noon."

"I actually have a car waiting. But you don't have to work today—I mean—I called your supervisor and asked if you could have the day off." She drew in a breath, bracing herself. "Will you come with me to the wedding?"

Liam took a step closer, seeming confused. "You want me to be your date to your brother's wedding?"

"Yes."

His gaze traced over her face, from her eyes down to linger on her lips. A beat too late, Sam realized what was happening.

When Liam lowered his mouth to hers, Sam tipped her face up. She didn't consciously think about it; it just *happened*, almost reflexively, because he was tall and warm and solid, and it felt so good to be held.

It should have been a perfect kiss. Liam's mouth was

infinitely soft; his arms curled gently around Sam's torso, settling low on her back. But it wasn't perfect, because it wasn't Marshall.

Oh god. What was she *doing*?

Sam broke away and took a quick step back. "Look, I didn't mean to—"

"I'm sorry," Liam cut in. "I mean, I'm not sorry that we kissed, because I've wanted to for ages, but I misread that invitation, didn't I?"

"I should have clarified," Sam said gently. "Will you come with me to Jeff's wedding, as my friend?"

"Your friend," Liam repeated, not trying to hide his disappointment. "So you and Marshall are still together? You haven't really talked about him lately," he fumbled to explain. "I thought maybe you'd broken up."

Sam shook her head. "I don't know what's going on with Marshall, but . . ."

But whatever it was, her heart still belonged to him.

She shouldn't have let Liam kiss her, should have pulled away more quickly. Still, Sam couldn't quite bring herself to regret it, if only because it had reminded her of how acutely she longed for Marshall. Of how desperately she would fight to save their relationship—even if it meant going back to Hawaii, walking away from everything she had started to build here.

Sometimes you had to be on the brink of losing something before you realized precisely how much it meant to you.

Sam tucked her hands into the pockets of her hoodie, fiddling with the stacked rings on her finger. "Liam, this wedding will be my first formal appearance since I lost my titles. I was hoping you'd come with me, to keep me company through all the etiquette and protocol, and . . . to help me escape, in case I'm ruining everything and need to leave."

He frowned at that. "How could you ruin everything?"

"What if people boo me in the streets?" Sam asked. "You know, a British king lost his titles and he could never appear in England again without the crowds hissing at him! I've always been the least favorite Washington, and that was *before* I fell from grace. Now I'm just Samcelled."

"I think things have changed for you lately," Liam argued.

Maybe, but Sam didn't want to take any chances. "Please?"

He let out a breath. "Of course I'm happy to come. I will hold your purse during photos and bring you drinks and whatever else etiquette says royal dates are supposed to do. And if you need an escape route, I'll be ready with the garbage truck," he added, with a hint of the old teasing tone.

Sam smiled in relief. "So you and me . . . we're okay?"

"We're okay." He reached for her bag and hoisted it over his shoulder. "Can I walk you out?"

As they headed past Sam's room, she realized she'd left the door wide open. Liam sucked in a breath when he saw the deflated air mattress, everything folded as neatly as when she'd first arrived here, all those weeks ago.

"Looks like you're moving out."

"Jeff texted last night and asked if I wanted to stay at the palace for a while. Now that we've made up, it makes sense. At least until I figure out my next move." Her eyes met Liam's and she added, "Thank you for taking me in when I was . . . when I needed a friend."

Liam nodded. "Sam, as much as I would've liked to date you, I love having you as a friend."

She stepped forward and hugged him then, burying her face in his T-shirt to hide her tears. Liam had changed her in ways that she had never expected. He'd helped her put the pieces of her life back together—or, more accurately, he'd helped her find her way to a *new* life, one where she felt stronger and more capable. The Samantha who'd stormed into Beatrice's hospital room and fought with Jeff about her titles felt like a distant and far-off person, someone who didn't have a clue how to calculate sales tax or cook an omelet or switch lines on the metro.

Her whole life, Sam had been trained in being a princess. But no one until Liam had taught her, simply, how to be a person.

Later that morning, Sam was in one of the downstairs sitting rooms with Beatrice and their mom, fastening her strappy heels. They could have gotten ready with Daphne in the Brides' Room, but it was such a cramped space, and Beatrice said Daphne would want to be alone with her own mother right now. *Let them have this special time together,* Beatrice insisted, though Sam suspected that Daphne's mom wasn't all that sentimental.

As promised, Sam's bridesmaid dress—a gorgeous color somewhere between slate gray and smoke—fit perfectly. A few strands of her pixie cut had been pinned back, white flowers fastened to the bobby pins. It was excruciatingly girly and so very Daphne, but Sam had to admit, she liked the contrast of the ivory petals against her dark hair.

"You okay, Bee?" she asked, realizing that Beatrice had been very quiet this morning.

Beatrice shrugged, but Queen Adelaide looked over in surprise. "What do you mean, Sam?"

"You seem worried." Sam directed her reply at Beatrice, ignoring their mom. "Is something wrong?"

Beatrice ran her hands over the skirts of her own bridesmaid dress. Since she was the reigning monarch, she wouldn't stand at the altar, to keep from detracting attention from Daphne, but she'd still worn the dress out of solidarity.

"Oh. Well . . . I saw Louise last night. She gave me a lot to think about. . . ."

"About Madison?" Sam guessed.

Queen Adelaide's expression soured. "I still can't believe the things he shouted before he was arrested! We'll have to strip him of his position as Queen's Champion, obviously, and name someone else in his place. Maybe Teddy's father?" she added hopefully. "That way it could be Teddy himself someday?"

At the look on Beatrice's face, Sam realized that Beatrice's inner turmoil involved Teddy, far more than the Duke of Virginia.

A footman knocked at the door. "Miss Samantha? Miss Daphne has asked to see you."

Sam hesitated, but Beatrice nudged her forward. "We'll talk later, I promise," she said under her breath.

Sam started down the hall, wondering what Daphne wanted. Maybe she was hoping Sam could deliver a note to Jeff?

When she knocked at the Brides' Room, she heard Daphne call out, "Come in," and pushed open the door.

A swirl of people orbited Daphne, makeup artists and designers' assistants and hairstylists all brandishing mascara wands or fabric tape or hot curlers, decorating her as if she were a human Christmas tree. Every inch of her was contoured or pinned or covered in lace or hairspray. And atop it all glittered a tiara: not the Winslow tiara, which Beatrice usually wore, but one that Sam didn't recognize. Daphne must have pulled it from the depths of the Crown Jewels vault.

"Please, I need a moment with Samantha alone." There was something eerily calm in Daphne's voice. The various assistants all curtsied—a little ahead of schedule, since Daphne wasn't actually a princess yet—and retreated.

When they were alone, Sam took a hesitant step forward. "Can I help with something?"

"You could explain why you hate me so much."

Sam blinked. "What?"

"Why don't you want me to marry your brother? You think I'm not good enough to be a Washington?" Hurt flashed in Daphne's bright green eyes as she added, "I might have expected that from other members of your family, but not from you. I thought we grew close over the past year."

"We did," Sam replied, bewildered. She and Daphne would never be best friends, but they had spent a lot of time together after Sam's father passed, working on etiquette, since Sam had become the heir. She'd grown quite fond of Daphne's unique blend of wit and tough love.

"If you don't hate me, why did you send all those emails?" Daphne demanded.

"*What* emails?"

"The ones where you threatened me to break up with Jefferson or you'd tell everyone about me and Ethan!"

Daphne's self-control had finally snapped, and those last words came out a bit too loud. Silence echoed through the room.

"You hooked up with Ethan?" Sam asked. "Before you and Jeff started dating?" Surely that was what Daphne meant, because if not . . .

Daphne's face fell. For the first time she seemed uncertain. "I tracked the emails to your laptop."

"I haven't used my laptop in months. I do everything on my phone," Sam protested, flustered.

Daphne braced her palms on the seat next to her. "Well, then, your laptop must have been stolen. Because whoever has it is harassing me."

Sam paused, thinking back. "I last saw it in my car before

the League of Kings conference, and my car has been here in Washington the whole time. I lent it—"

She realized that she should stop, but somehow her mouth was working faster than her brain, and the next two words came out before she could swallow them back.

"—to Nina."

38

NINA

Nina had come to the palace early, just in case everything she'd set in motion finally imploded.

She'd told Jamie that Samantha had asked her to keep her company, and he hadn't questioned it, just dropped a quick kiss on Nina's mouth and said he would see her later. She was on a permanent preapproved list with palace security, so even though she showed up two hours before her invitation commanded, they just waved her through.

Only a few minutes after her arrival, one of the footmen came over with a request that Daphne would like to see her.

Nina walked down the endless hallway to the Brides' Room, her heels seeming to echo a soft chant in time with her thoughts: *It's here, it's here, it's here.* The epic confrontation that the angry, wounded part of her had craved for months.

When Nina pushed open the door, she saw that Sam was in the Brides' Room with Daphne. They both whipped their heads toward her, Daphne's features sharpening with anticipation, Sam's with disbelief.

"Nina I'm so glad you're here Daphne is under this awful impression that you've been threatening her." The words came out in a single breath, running together incoherently.

"You can go, Sam." With that statement, Nina spoke volumes.

She tried to ignore the horrified shock on Sam's face. She

would explain everything to Sam later, but right now the person Nina owed an explanation to was Daphne.

"Okay," Sam replied, her voice small. "I'll just, um . . . I'll be down the hall, if you need me."

And then she was gone, and Daphne and Nina were in the Brides' Room alone.

Daphne clearly noticed Nina's dress—the plum-colored one she'd selected at the department store—but she said nothing.

"You look beautiful, Daphne," Nina murmured, because it simply had to be said. Daphne looked like a bride from a magazine, which of course, she was: her hair was pinned half up, with perfect red-gold curls falling to frame her face, and the cascading volume of her white tulle skirts seemed to go on and on.

Maybe the emails hadn't done all that much, because she certainly looked like a girl who was getting married today.

"I know you sent those emails, so don't bother denying it," Daphne snapped.

"I don't deny it. I sent them," Nina said evenly.

Her placating tone made Daphne stumble. Clearly, the other girl had been geared up for a fight. "You're jealous, obviously. You're mad that Jefferson chose me, and you're still in love with him—"

"You're wrong about that part," Nina cut in. "I sent those emails because *you* aren't in love with *him*."

Daphne's hands balled into fists at her sides. "I could have you arrested for this. You blackmailed me and manipulated me!"

"Wonder where I learned skills like that," Nina said drily.

Something flashed in Daphne's eyes. "If you think he's going to break up with me for you, you're delusional."

Nina thought of last night, when Jeff had reached for her hand and almost, *almost* said he still loved her. Maybe the idea of Jeff choosing her wasn't as delusional as Daphne thought.

She shook her head. "I didn't do any of this because I want him back. I did it because Jeff deserves better—"

"How dare you!"

"—and so do you."

Daphne sucked in a breath, obviously stunned by Nina's audacity, but Nina kept going.

"You don't love Jeff. You love Ethan."

It was so rare, in modern life, that you got to speak like this to people: with the brutal, unvarnished truth. Even with friends, so many conversations splashed playfully at the surface, stuck to safe topics like academics and mutual acquaintances. With closer friends, you might venture to share your problems or fears. But there was no one Nina could talk to the way she did to Daphne, plunging all the way down to the darkest, ugliest part of the iceberg, to say the truly difficult things.

She and Daphne were able to do this, not because they had been friends, but because they had started as enemies.

She walked slowly around the room, picking up various items—an eyelash curler, a spray of peonies in a bud vase— before setting them down again. Daphne held her breath, as tense as if Nina were prowling the room with a weapon, though the only weapon she had right now was her words.

Of course, Nina knew from experience that words could be sharper than any knife.

"Did Ethan tell you that we chatted a few times while he was in Malaysia?"

"He mentioned it," Daphne said tersely.

The first time she and Ethan had talked, Nina had deliberately tossed out Daphne's name as a sort of conversational barometer, curious to see his reaction. Ethan's eyes had flicked nervously to the side. And when Nina added that Daphne and Jeff were getting serious, he'd flinched.

"I realized that he was still in love with you, and I suspected that you still loved him, too. As for Jeff . . ." Nina sighed. "I know he was about to break up with you the night of the League of Kings banquet. But the next day, you were back together as if nothing had happened!"

Daphne pressed her mouth into a thin line and said nothing.

"I told myself your relationship was none of my business. Until I found out you were engaged." Nina swallowed. "That night I lay awake for hours, thinking what a mistake you were making."

As she sat there with Samantha, reading the press release, Nina had been hit by a wave of outrage. Someone had to stop this wedding. Not because Nina wanted Jeff for herself; even then, before she'd gotten involved with Jamie, she had been weary of the endless back-and-forth between her and Jeff. But Jeff and Daphne didn't belong together. They weren't *in love*—not the way you were supposed to be before you swore to spend the rest of your life with someone.

If anyone was going to make Daphne reconsider this wedding, it had to be Nina. Everyone else in Daphne's life was too invested in the happily-ever-after of it all. *What would Daphne do?* Nina had thought, and the answer came to her at once.

Daphne would take matters into her own hands. So Nina would do the same.

The next morning, Nina had grabbed the laptop out of Samantha's car, well aware that every palace computer was protected by a high level of security and data encryption. She'd taken it straight back to her dorm room, where she'd created a dummy email address and composed the first email.

Nina cleared her throat self-consciously. "I thought that if I sent you some helpful nudges, you might remember how you feel about Ethan."

"*Helpful nudges?*" Daphne repeated, incredulous. "You blackmailed me!"

"What other choice did I have? You weren't exactly going to sit around getting mani-pedis with me, asking my advice about your wedding. I tried to keep the emails from being too scary," she added, knowing it was a flimsy excuse. "I never said anything violent!"

Daphne's anger seemed to have melted away, letting other emotions—sadness, and something that might have been a begrudging respect—float to the surface. "I get why you wanted to blackmail me, but why did you go after Ethan, too?"

Wasn't it obvious? "I hoped that if I targeted you both, you might work together to figure out what was going on. The more time you spent together, the better your chances of realizing that you're in love." She hesitated, then added, "Didn't you have fun at Enchanted Fiefdom?"

Nina had been especially proud of that one. She'd wanted to send them somewhere far enough from downtown that it would take them a while to get home, even once they realized she wasn't coming—somewhere they might have fun together, on the chance they decided to stay.

She saw Daphne reach the same realization. "Wait a second. You sent me and Ethan to that theme park on a *date?*"

"Was it a good date?" Nina asked hopefully. "I love that place. My parents used to take me all the time when I was little. My favorite was the magic-carpet ride."

Daphne let out a strangled sound that was somewhere between a laugh and a sob. When she lifted her face, her eyes were bright with unshed tears.

"You know, I once thought you were my friend," Daphne said softly.

"I *was* your friend." Nina found that she wanted to cry, too. "When I saw you with Jeff in the hospital that day—the hateful way you stared at me—I thought you'd been playing me the whole time. It wrecked me, Daphne."

"I didn't play you." Daphne's voice was small.

"I know that now."

Nina had realized as much at the department store, when Daphne had accused her of working with Gabriella. She and Daphne had both imagined betrayal where there wasn't any.

It saddened her that they'd been so ready to think the worst of each other.

Nina forced herself to apologize. "I'm sorry if I went too far, sending those emails. Clearly I was wrong, since I bullied you and threatened you and you're *still* here, ready to marry Jeff. I just wanted to make sure you really knew what you were signing on for." *What you were giving up,* she almost added.

Daphne stared at Nina in disbelief. "How can I possibly call off the wedding now?"

"I think the better question is, how can you marry someone you don't love?"

A knock at the door interrupted them. Daphne and Nina exchanged a glance, and then Daphne called out, a little hoarse, "Come in."

A young woman with a perky smile, probably one of the PR team, ducked inside. "Excuse me, Miss Daphne, but it's time for your bridal photos in the orchard."

Nina stared at Daphne in disbelief. "The orchard? Really?"

"It's beautiful this time of year, and I need a branch from the bridal tree, anyway." Daphne stood and slipped her arms into a luxurious white coat. Then she looked at Nina as if reaching some decision. "Are you coming?"

39

SAMANTHA

Samantha hoped she'd done the right thing, leaving Daphne and Nina alone together. The looks on both their faces had frightened her a little. But there had been a steely determination in Nina's voice when she told Sam to go, and that, at least, made her hope that Nina had a plan.

"Sam?"

Slowly, heart racing, Sam turned around.

There he was, standing a few yards down the hallway—the boy she'd given her heart to, who had it still.

"Marshall?"

If this was a movie, she would run headlong into his arms, and they would kiss as the soundtrack—probably violins or something else romantic—swelled in volume. *I'm sorry, and I love you,* they would both say, as if their time apart had never happened.

But this wasn't a movie; it was real life, and Sam found that she couldn't run. She just stood rooted to the spot as Marshall started toward her. He looked like he'd come straight from the plane, in an old college sweatshirt and sneakers.

The world spun around Sam. She blinked, fighting off the disorienting, dizzying feeling, and tried to speak.

"What are you *doing* here?"

"I came back for you," he said simply.

"So you're staying?" Sam's heart leapt.

Marshall's smile faltered at her words. "I thought . . . don't you want to come back to Hawaii after the wedding? You've accomplished everything you came here to do. You must have resolved things with Jeff, if you're in the wedding," he added, nodding at her bridesmaid dress. "I was thinking we could go to the wedding together, then leave straight from the reception. I called your aunt Margaret for help, and we have a plane ready."

She blinked; this was all happening too fast. "Your family will be at the wedding. They'll see you."

"What are they going to do, arrest me and drag me away? I'll tell them we're going back to Hawaii and there's nothing they can do to stop us. I'm not afraid to take on my grandfather, Sam," he said fervently. "I would do anything to protect us."

Marshall took another step toward her; they were only a few feet apart.

He was going to kiss her. The thought of it was so tempting: melting into Marshall's arms, pulling him close and breathing him in. Running away again, far from everything that was hurtling toward them.

No. Sam refused to bury their issues beneath a kiss, and she was done running away.

"I'm sorry, but I can't go back," she breathed.

Marshall went still. Hurt flickered over his eyes as he asked, "Is there someone else?"

Liam popped into her mind—Liam, who would show up at the palace in a couple of hours, ready to help however Sam needed.

Liam, whom she couldn't even kiss without thinking of Marshall.

"There has only ever been you, Marshall," she said truthfully. "But I don't know where we go from here."

The fabric of her bridesmaid dress felt itchy and hot. Sam

wished they were somewhere else—anywhere but the stifling confines of the palace, a place that felt less like home than it ever had.

"I have no idea what to say." Marshall's voice was raw. "I missed you so much while you were gone. Every night I would lie awake in bed, thinking about you, wondering if you were okay."

Sam lifted her chin stubbornly. "Then why didn't you call more? I missed you, too, Marshall. As glad as I was that you were happy in Hawaii, I felt isolated and lonely here. I worry that we've been living separate lives, drifting apart."

"I wanted to give you space! All I do is cause problems for you: with your family, with the media . . ."

"Those problems were caused by both of us, and I thought we were facing them together." A tear streaked down her cheek, ruining her camera-ready makeup.

"What do we do now?" Marshall asked.

"If I liked you less, I would say we should just keep trying, see how it goes. But, Marshall . . . I love you too much for that." She swallowed. "I love you so much that I think we owe it to ourselves to figure out what makes sense."

Marshall looked stricken. "That sounds a lot like a breakup, Sam."

The distance between them hurt like a physical thing. They used to lie intertwined together, skin to skin, and now Sam had thrown up an invisible wall between them and they couldn't even touch. He was standing right before her, yet he might as well still be five thousand miles away in Hawaii.

"I don't want to break up, but I can't go back to Hawaii as if nothing has happened. My time here has changed me. Losing my titles, living as a nonroyal person . . . It's all made me rethink things. I'm not the same girl you fell in love with."

His hands clenched into fists at his sides, as if he was

forcibly restraining himself from reaching for her, but he nod-ded. "Maybe you've changed, but I haven't. I still want the same thing I thought we both wanted. A life together, far from all of this."

"I'm sorry," she told him, because what else was there to say?

Marshall looked utterly destroyed as he turned and walked away, his footfalls echoing down the hall.

Sam stood there for several long minutes, watching him. She wanted to scream and cry at once; her heart was thump-ing erratically in her chest, yet she stood there like a statue, saying nothing.

"Sam, thank god! I've been looking for you. I asked Beatrice where you were, and she said you'd gone to see Daphne—"

Jeff ran up to join her, then fell silent at the look on her face. "Oh my god, did something happen? Are you okay?"

"I'm fine," she lied, dabbing at her eyes.

Her brother clearly didn't believe her, but let it go. "Can we talk?" he asked hoarsely. "I need your help with something."

She sniffed. "Of course. What is it?"

"I need to call off the wedding."

At first Sam thought she hadn't heard him correctly. She just stared at him, wondering if this was some kind of prank, but the bleak truth of it was written there on his face.

"Okay, you obviously need to talk to Daphne."

"Right," Jeff said, though he looked a little queasy at the thought.

Sam glanced at the enormous grandfather clock near the en-trance to the Weapons Room. Unbelievably, its spindly metal hands still told the time. "I was supposed to meet Daphne and Beatrice in the orchard soon for bridesmaid photos, which means that Daphne is probably on her way there. I think she was doing solo portraits first."

She grabbed her brother by the sleeve and began to drag

him through the warren of downstairs hallways, past the utter chaos reigning in the kitchens, until they threw open the back door.

A brace of cold air greeted them, but Sam just marched them forward. Several golf carts were parked near the garage, their sides zipped up in insulated plastic against the cold. Plaid blankets were folded neatly on the seats. Clearly they were here to shuttle Washington family members back and forth from the orchards.

One of the valets leapt forward when he saw them. "Miss Samantha—Your Royal Highness—"

"We need a golf cart." Sam peeled back the plastic cover from the nearest one. Perfect, the keys were already in the ignition.

"Please, I can drive!" The valet looked slightly terrified at the prospect of letting Sam behind the wheel, but no way was she letting a valet overhear whatever Jeff was about to say, staff NDAs or no.

"Sorry," she mumbled.

Jeff slid into the seat next to her, and Sam tore across the lawn, leaving mud tracks in the grass behind her. She swerved onto the gravel path that led to the orchards and nearly collided with one of the florist's vans, but cut the wheel at the last minute, forcing the van abruptly to the left.

"We should not have let you drive!" Jeff was grabbing the cushioned seat with both hands.

"Stop being dramatic. I drove all the time in Hawaii."

"Pull over and switch spots with me," Jeff said.

Sam let out a breath, lifting a few strands of hair that had fallen out of her bobby pins, and took the speed down a few notches. "Better? Now tell me what's going on."

Jeff swallowed, seeming torn. "I've been having second thoughts about the wedding for a while now. I agreed to it when we thought Daphne was pregnant, but once we learned that she wasn't . . . I don't know," Jeff said feebly. "Suddenly we were swept along in the wedding planning, focusing on this whole day—on the *party*—more than on the fact that we were getting married. There have been plenty of times lately when I wanted to slow down, but everyone kept telling me how amazing we were together: the press, our family. And I kept thinking about this one time that Dad told me Daphne would be a great princess. . . ."

"Oh, Jeff." Sam knew what he meant by bringing up their dad; anything the king had once said took on a new significance now that he was gone.

"I don't want to hurt Daphne," her brother said, clearly tormented. "Do I owe it to her to honor the promise I made?"

"I think, more than anything, you owe it to her to be honest about your feelings," Sam said gently.

Her brother had always been more sensitive than he let on. He surrounded himself with a constant whirl of people but trusted only a handful of them. And Daphne was one of those people. He would never willingly cause her pain.

Jeff let out a breath. "I know. It was just . . . overnight, Daphne's and my relationship became some kind of *symbol*."

"You're the Prince of America. You'll always be a symbol," Sam murmured. Marshall had told her that once, when they were wrestling with the media spotlight. *You're a symbol because you were born to be. We both were.*

A pang shot through her at the thought of Marshall; she did her best to ignore it. "Hey, if you're sick of being a symbol, you can join me on the dark side. It's kind of fun out here."

Her brother shot her a glance, surprised and a little bit amused.

"Jeff . . ." Maybe she was overstepping, but she had to ask. "Are you calling off the wedding because of Nina?"

At that, suddenly, he looked so lost. Sam thought back

to last night, to the charged feeling that had hung in the air between Nina and Jeff.

"Nina wants nothing to do with me, and I can't blame her," Jeff said at last.

Sam didn't point out that it wasn't an answer to her question.

She slowed the golf cart to a crawl as they pulled up to the Cottage, a quaint structure in the middle of the orchard that normally sold tourists apples by the pound, or homemade jams and pies. All the retail goods had been cleared out so that the Cottage could serve as the home base for Daphne's bridal portraits. Sam saw the photographer already stationed in the clearing, arranging his camera on its massive tripod while an assistant fiddled with a glaring light.

At the center of it all was Daphne, surrounded by the voluminous lace skirts of her gown. And was that *Nina* with her?

Sam looked back at Jeff. "I mean it, I'm here for whatever you need. I can cause a diversion, break the news to Mom, plan your escape route. It wouldn't be my first time fleeing the country on a private jet," she added, in a teasing tone that masked just how serious she was. "We could be in Mexico in three hours, drinking margaritas poolside."

"I may take you up on that." Jeff sighed and pushed open the insulated plastic to step out into the cold.

Sam pulled the blanket tighter around her. "I'll wait for you here. What are you going to tell Daphne?"

"The only thing I can tell her. The truth."

"Good luck."

She watched as her brother headed toward one of the toughest conversations of his life. It was so much easier thinking about Jeff's problems than her own—easier if she could keep herself from thinking of Marshall at all.

40

DAPHNE

Daphne held on to her smile with all her might as the photographer knelt before her, his camera's shutter clicking rapidly.

She was oddly grateful that Nina was here, hunched in a puffy coat over her gown. "I still can't believe you're taking photos *outside* in the middle of winter," Nina muttered.

The photographer shot Nina a sideways look, but Daphne replied, "I have to get a sprig from the cherry tree anyway." When Nina stared at her in confusion, Daphne added, "Every Washington bride for the last century has carried a blossom from this orchard in her wedding bouquet. Since it's winter, I'm carrying a twig."

"A twig," Nina repeated, her voice flat.

"Yes, Nina, a royal twig! Like the sprig of myrtle the Windsors all carry in their wedding bouquets. At least ours is grown here on the grounds. They ship theirs in from a myrtle tree that Queen Victoria planted on the Isle of Wight."

"The Brits, always high-maintenance," Nina replied, in a way that made Daphne want to laugh.

Truthfully, she loved how the orchards looked during winter. There was a light dusting of snow on the branches, making them seem frosted against the slate-gray arc of the sky. The ambient light would photograph beautifully, its layers so much more nuanced than the bright light of spring.

"If you please," the photographer muttered. He directed

339

the comment at Nina, but Daphne obediently sucked in her stomach and smiled.

Underneath, her mind was in turmoil.

For years she had dreamed of marrying Jefferson. They were perfect together. Everyone thought so: just look at the cheering crowds outside the palace, and the newspaper articles full of praise, and the gushing fans who wrote those weird romance scenes about the two of them. Daphne would do a better job as princess than Samantha ever had, not that Samantha set an especially high bar. Daphne would organize charity events and always be perfectly dressed and charm everyone she met. . . .

And then what?

At some point, the events would end and the tiaras would come off, leaving Daphne alone with a husband who didn't actually know her at all.

Ethan's words echoed in her mind. *I love everything about you—your determination and your inner fire and your fierce loyalty.*

Ethan, who had seen into every last dark corner of her heart and chosen to love her anyway. Who loved *all* of her, not just the parts of her that were convenient or easy to understand. Ethan, who'd been her co-conspirator, her partner, her friend.

"You're shivering." The photographer stood up, waving at an assistant. "Can we get a space heater? A mug of tea?"

"Actually, I'd like to take five. I need to go warm up inside. Nina?" Daphne gestured to the veil that trailed behind her like a fragment of cloud, and Nina obediently grabbed it. Funny how after everything they'd been through, Nina was acting like her maid of honor.

As they started toward the Cottage, Daphne whispered, "You're right."

Nina seemed as surprised as Daphne by the admission. "You're changing your mind?"

"Yes. I need to call it off. But . . ."

She fell silent, noticing the golf cart that had just driven up to the Cottage. Samantha was behind the wheel—and Jefferson was stepping out of the passenger seat.

He looked utterly resplendent in his ceremonial dress: his navy blazer with shining gold epaulets, his white gloves, the sash of the Edwardian Order over his chest. But there was a worried gleam in his eyes that didn't belong there on his wedding day.

"Hey, Daphne?" He sounded a bit nervous. "Can we talk?"

"It's bad luck for him to see you before the wedding!" the photographer exclaimed, and Daphne almost burst out laughing, because how could anyone possibly be worried about luck at a time like this?

"Let's go inside," she told Jefferson.

Nina looped the veil around Daphne's arm, then retreated a step. "I'll sit with Sam," she murmured.

Jefferson held the door open so that Daphne could shuffle inside, the weight of her outfit making it hard to move. The interior of the Cottage had been repurposed as a prep station for wedding photos. Near a small love seat was a buffet table with water bottles, coffee, slices of wedding cake, and an enormous full-length mirror. Daphne's eyes darted toward it reflexively; she always looked at every mirror she passed.

The young woman reflected there didn't feel like her at all, but some twin who had walked into her life and taken her place. She reached up to touch one of the curls that fell from the tiara to frame her face, then ran her hands over the intricate lace of her skirts. Was this really her wedding gown? It felt like it belonged to a stranger.

She needed to say it now, the single sentence that would act as the pebble that starts down a mountainside and causes the earth-shattering avalanche.

Daphne knew it was a betrayal of everything she'd spent

her life working toward: her childhood fantasies, her parents' ambitions, the hopes and dreams of the entire nation. And still she spoke.

"I'm worried we're rushing things," she told him at the same moment that Jefferson said, "I don't think we should get married."

When she realized what he'd said, Daphne was struck by the sheer absurdity of it all: the bride and groom in the wedding of the year, both independently calling it off mere hours before the ceremony. Of all the contingency plans the palace PR team had made, she doubted they had one for this.

A voice sounded from the doorway. "Oh my god, *seriously?*"

Daphne turned to see Gabriella Madison standing in the open door, her mouth curled into a vicious red smile. As they stared at her in stunned shock, Gabriella crowed, "It's a good thing you're calling it off, Jeff, because Daphne is *cheating* on you!"

Nina and Samantha stumbled up behind Gabriella, each of them grabbing one of her arms as if they were bouncers at a club, trying to drag out an unruly guest. But they couldn't stop Gabriella's next words.

"She slept with Ethan last night!"

The silence that followed was the sort of ringing, profound silence that comes in the wake of an explosion. Nina and Samantha were both startled into letting go, and Gabriella wedged herself further into the doorway, glaring at Daphne like a cat toying with its prey.

"You brought this on yourself, Daphne. If you hadn't confronted me yesterday, I wouldn't have even realized you were hiding something. From the way you kept begging me not to tell anyone, it made me wonder what secret you thought I knew. So I followed you back to the hotel."

No one interrupted Gabriella. No one even seemed to

move. It was as if they'd all fallen under an enchantment and were paralyzed where they stood.

"I saw Ethan go into your room late last night, then leave this morning around dawn." Gabriella made a *tsk-tsk* noise. "The girlfriend and the best friend? Could you *be* any more painfully clichéd?"

Jefferson's hands clenched into fists at his sides. Daphne tensed, expecting him to lash out at her—

"Gabriella, you need to leave."

He spoke with a sharp, unmistakable authority, something he'd picked up in his days as Acting King.

Gabriella put a hand on one hip, all pretense of civility gone. "Are you serious? Your fiancée cheated on you and you're angry at *me*?"

"This is between me and Daphne."

Gabriella barked out a humorless laugh. "Until I tell the tabloids, and then it's between Daphne and the world—"

Jefferson took a few steps forward, until his face was close to Gabriella's.

"Let me make one thing very clear. You are not going to repeat what you just said, not ever, not to anyone. In fact, I suggest you leave town," he added. "You've done enough damage lately, don't you think?"

Gabriella took a step back, eyes narrowing. "This isn't the Middle Ages, Jeff. You can't *exile* me because my father embezzled some money."

"Of course I can't exile you," he agreed. "All I can do is personally ensure that you are never invited to a single party in this town ever again. And this has nothing to do with your father," he added. "I would never punish someone for the actions of their parents. This is because you are selfish and vicious, and a terrible friend."

Daphne fell a little bit in love with Jefferson right then,

for being such a consummate gentleman. For extending the umbrella of his protection over her, even when she so clearly didn't deserve it.

Gabriella stamped her foot like a petulant child, then whirled around and stormed outside.

Samantha shot them a worried glance, mumbling about how Gabriella had tricked the guards into letting her back here. Then she and Nina left, quietly shutting the door behind them.

Daphne looked up at Jefferson, and her resolve momentarily wavered. He was so achingly handsome, like the fairy-tale prince of her childish daydreams.

"Thank you," she breathed.

Jefferson nodded stiffly. "I would never let someone slander our relationship like that. But . . . is it true?" he asked, in a softer voice. "You and Ethan?"

"Yes." There was no point in denying it.

She had always prided herself on her ability to read Jefferson, so she saw the emotions that flickered over his face in rapid succession: shock and anger and pain and, underneath it all, unmistakable relief.

He didn't want to get married today, and she was making that decision easier for him.

"Was it a one-time thing, or did it happen more than once?" he asked hoarsely.

Daphne closed her eyes, wincing. "More than once. I'm so sorry, Jefferson—I never meant to hurt you," she added. The words felt paper-thin against the crushing weight of her betrayal.

Jefferson circled the room once, then sank back onto the love seat and rested his head in his hands. "I'd be lying if I said I wasn't upset. I trusted you, and Ethan." He sighed. "But I guess we've both made mistakes."

"You and Nina?" she said softly, knowing the answer.

Jeff reddened. "Nothing happened last night, I swear."

She hadn't realized that he and Nina were even together last night.

There was something almost funny in the knowledge she and Jefferson had both been with other people the night before their wedding—amusing in a dark, twisted way. What a piece of work they were.

Ignoring her strict instructions not to sit once she was in her gown, Daphne collapsed onto the love seat next to him. Her lace skirts frothed up around her like an enchanted cloud.

"Do you love Ethan?"

Whatever Daphne had expected Jefferson to ask, it wasn't that.

"Ethan and I . . . We understand each other," she said carefully.

He nodded slowly. "I've always known he had a thing for you. I saw the way he looked at you when he thought no one was watching. I figured it was just attraction, because how could anyone *not* be attracted to you?" Jefferson sighed. "Until he wrote that rehearsal-dinner toast, which was far better than what I would've come up with."

Somehow, Daphne couldn't bear for this to be the note they ended on. "I do love you, Jefferson. It's just not the type of love that you deserve."

"Did you ever love me that way? For myself, I mean," he explained. "Or were you always in love with the *idea* of me?"

To Daphne's surprise, she couldn't bring herself to tell him how much of their relationship had been a lie—an ingenious and flawless lie, because lying was an art and she was its greatest performer. She had never loved Jefferson in the passionate, tumultuous way he'd assumed she did. The way Nina had once loved him.

Yet there *was* love between them, wasn't there? The sort of love that comes from knowing someone's whole heart, from years of history. Daphne looked at Jefferson and felt their shared youth shimmering between them like a fragment of sunlight. Like a ghost.

"You were my first love," she told him, and for once, she wasn't lying.

There were many kinds of love. Jefferson would always be her first, even if he wasn't meant to be her last.

"And you were mine." He looked at her with a half smile. "By the way, Daph, you look beautiful today. I hope you know that."

She ran a hand over the exquisite lace of her gown. "I'm keeping this, in case I ever *do* get married," she said, testing a joke.

"I figured that was a given. The clothes come with the wedding, even if it's canceled."

With some regret, she reached for the ring on her left hand and twisted it off. "This, though, I think I have to give back. It came from the Crown Jewels vault."

It was beautiful, yet it already felt like a ring that had been chosen for someone else: a misguided and mistrustful girl who wore pantyhose and wrote thank-you notes in perfect cursive and tried to please everyone.

If she did get engaged again someday, it wouldn't be with a traditional diamond solitaire. Her next ring would be something wild and unexpected—something that fit the person she was becoming, a person she was still figuring out.

She and Jefferson sat there for a moment, adjusting to the strange new honesty between them. Then he walked over to the buffet table, to the silver platter arranged with wedding cake—the pastry chef always made a few sheet cakes of the same recipe, along with the enormous decorative one that was on display in the ballroom. The extras would be given to the staff to take home for their families.

"We might as well try this, right?"

Jefferson speared a piece of cake and held out the fork for

Daphne, as if they were actually at the reception and posing for the photos. She wasn't sure whether it made her want to laugh or cry.

She leaned forward to eat the cake from the outstretched fork. It was light and fluffy, with a faint hint of almond and vanilla. When she took the fork from Jefferson and offered him a bite, he got a smear of buttercream icing on his lip. Daphne had half a mind to call the photographer in here: *Look, the most celebrated couple in the world, eating their wedding cake picnic-style before they cancel the whole thing!*

"I know it wasn't always easy, dating me," Jefferson said ruefully. "For the record, you would have been a fantastic princess."

"Of course I would." Daphne gave a wistful half smile. "Jefferson, dating you—becoming a princess—*is* a job, no matter how much you probably wish otherwise. But the fact that I'm a great candidate for the job was never a good reason for us to get married."

She thought of Nina, who probably still loved Jefferson on some level, but hated the demands that came with dating him. "You deserve someone who can handle the princess side of things *and* who belongs with you. You deserve to love someone so much that you propose for real—someplace romantic and quiet, just the two of you, instead of being pressured into it. I'm sorry about that," she added, knowing her apology was wholly inadequate.

It felt like Daphne had been swept along on an invisible wave since that night she saw Nina and Jefferson kissing in the gardens—a wave of ambition, or vindictiveness, or rage—and now the wave had crashed over her, leaving her gasping and drenched in regret.

Jefferson set aside the cake. "Can I ask you something?"

If he asked her about the pregnancy, Daphne resolved to tell him the truth.

"Was I a bad boyfriend?"

Relief coursed through her. Of course Jefferson hadn't considered whether the pregnancy was faked; his mind was too honest to even imagine such a thing.

She wondered why he thought he was a bad boyfriend. Perhaps Nina had said something last night? Maybe Jefferson had made a play for Nina, and Nina had rejected him, and whatever words she'd used had landed in his heart like arrows. Daphne doubted Nina had even *meant* to cause such harm; it wasn't in her to use words cruelly, like weapons. The way Daphne did.

But when the people you loved told you hard truths, it could hurt worse than insults ever could.

She reached for Jefferson's hand. "Listen to me. You are a good person. You put people at ease; you are earnest and thoughtful and kindhearted. If there's anything wrong with you, it's that you love too much."

Really, his flaw was that he loved too easily—that he'd fallen for her and Nina and hadn't been able to choose between them. But Daphne couldn't exactly throw stones in that regard, given how long she'd walked a tightrope between Jefferson and Ethan.

"Thank you for saying that." He gave her hand a squeeze, then released it.

They were both silent for a moment. Then Daphne said, "What now?"

What she really meant was, what would *she* do now? Jefferson would survive this scandal unscathed, but not Daphne.

She'd spent the last four years living in the fishbowl of tabloid attention, and knew how readily it could turn into a shark pond. At a scandal like this, the media would sharpen their teeth, out for blood.

Oh, how they would punish her for this canceled wedding. When Beatrice had broken off her engagement, a bill had cropped up in Congress attempting to remove her from the *throne*. And she was a royal by birth!

It would be much, much worse for Daphne. She couldn't hide behind a title and wait out the scandal, because she had no position to hide behind anymore.

"It's going to be ugly, especially for me," she admitted. "I'll need to lie low for a while. Leave the country, maybe."

Ethan would run away with her in a heartbeat. Daphne thought fleetingly of escaping with him to Malaysia—hiding together in a small beach town, riding his motorbike and soaking up sunshine and living a drowsy, carefree existence. Far away from court, from the epic mess she'd made thanks to her own loveless, limitless ambition.

But Daphne knew she couldn't just trade Jefferson's arms for Ethan's. She was stronger than that.

If—and it was still an *if*—she and Ethan were going to have any kind of shot, then he couldn't be her safety net. She would need to find her own way out of this.

♛

They headed back to the palace in search of Beatrice, who was in the ballroom, talking in a low, earnest voice with Princess Louise.

Part of Daphne's heart broke, seeing the room ready for her wedding reception—vases spilling with flowers, the stage set for a full eighteen-piece band, the glow of the champagne arranged behind the white-tableclothed bar.

It was all so beautiful, and all for nothing.

"Bee? Can we talk?" Jefferson reached for Daphne's hand in a show of solidarity, and Daphne gave him a grateful squeeze. The only small blessing in this moment was that Jefferson's mother was still downstairs, and Daphne would only have to face *one* disapproving Washington woman.

"What are you two doing together? You weren't supposed to see each other until the ceremony," Beatrice began, then fell silent at the look on Jefferson's face.

Louise took a step back. "Perhaps I should leave you *en famille.*"

Beatrice cast a plaintive glance at her friend, clearly unwilling to abandon whatever they'd been discussing, and Jefferson shrugged. "You can stay, Louise. Everyone is going to find this out eventually."

There were a few staff members bustling through the room: plucking a flower from an arrangement if it looked the slightest bit tired, checking the place cards on the dinner tables. Beatrice called out, "We need a moment, please," and they scattered like leaves blown by the wind.

When they were alone in the ballroom, Jefferson looked at his sister and said, "Daphne and I want to call off the wedding."

Louise gasped, her manicured hands flying to her mouth, but Beatrice didn't flinch. She was as perfectly composed as if he'd remarked upon the weather.

He kept talking, explaining that they'd both had reservations for a while but that the wedding preparations had steamrolled over their concerns, how they had both decided this morning—independently—that they couldn't go through with it.

Daphne held her breath, knowing that this was better coming from Jefferson than from her.

When he'd finished, Beatrice glanced around the ballroom with a nearly imperceptible sigh. "I wish you'd figured this out a bit earlier than the day of your wedding. It would have saved us a lot of headache."

"Two canceled weddings in the span of a year," Louise chimed in. "No one will come to your next one."

"I'm happy to do a press conference, if it helps," Daphne offered.

Beatrice shuddered. "I'm sure that won't be necessary." A typical Washington family response, to want to avoid the press at all costs.

Daphne had nothing left to lose anymore, which must have been the reason she argued with the queen. "I know it's not typical, but the circumstances aren't typical. If we say nothing, people will interpret our silence in unflattering ways, but if we say something—even just a few remarks—then we've set the tone. It'll be hard for people to accuse us of being unfaithful if we go out there holding hands, as a team, and say that we mutually reached this decision."

Beatrice's eyes flashed at Daphne's hint that one of them, at least, had cheated. "What reason are you going to give for the decision?"

"We don't need to give them any reason at all. Just keep the announcement short and to the point. 'The wedding between Prince Jefferson and Daphne Deighton will not take place today. The Washingtons and the Deightons ask for privacy during this difficult time.' Jefferson will go back to King's College and take on some more responsibilities for the Crown, maybe some new charity initiatives? And in a few months, he'll go on some high-profile dates with potential girlfriends. I'll compile a list," Daphne added, her mind working at top speed.

Jefferson stiffened next to her. "Wait, what? Did you just say you want to set me up?"

She ignored him. "The tabloids will salivate over the fact that he's single, debating which of these girls might replace me. They'll be so focused on Jefferson's dating life that they won't even care anymore why our relationship ended. And if they do ask, he and I will only ever speak of each other in the most glowing terms. We'll say that we were carried away by our youthful passion and moved too fast."

She felt Louise staring at her. "An interesting plan. It could work," the French princess remarked.

All eyes turned to Beatrice, who nodded slowly. "We might as well try it. What do you need from us? A plane?"

Daphne nearly sagged in relief. No way did she want to face a commercial airport right now, and get mobbed with photographs. "I'd love to leave the country for a while. A plane would be fantastic."

"I'll call Anju." Beatrice pressed one of her speed-dial buttons and started toward the hallway, Jefferson trailing along after her.

Louise waited a moment before clearing her throat. "Daphne. You and I don't know each other well."

It was a funny thing to say, but royals could be odd ducks. "No, Your Royal Highness," Daphne agreed.

As usual, the French princess looked impossibly chic in a dusky-blue gown that plunged daringly low in the back. But it was her expression that caught Daphne's interest—an excited, almost mischievous expression. One that Daphne had seen before, when she looked in the mirror.

Louise nodded. "Since we don't know each other well, this may seem a presumptuous question, but I have to ask. Did you engineer your whole relationship with Prince Jefferson?"

"Excuse me?"

"You have managed your entire life like it's a business operation, haven't you? You cultivated favor with the press, made the American people fall in love with you. Your father's behavior would have ruined most girls' chances at a royal marriage," Louise mused. "But not you. You didn't let his scandal drag you down."

Were the French always this blunt?

"I've gotten very good at handling the media. I had to,"

Daphne said carefully. "I understand the tabloids, how they operate, who the major players are." If anyone could make America believe something, it was Daphne.

Louise smiled, satisfied by this reply. "I need someone like you to help me manage my image. I'm about to do something so shocking, it will make your broken engagement to Jeff look like child's play."

Daphne was intrigued in spite of herself. "What?"

"I'm engaged to Alexei. The Prince of Russia," Louise added, as if Daphne wasn't perfectly aware which Alexei she meant.

"Oh my god," Daphne whispered, stunned.

"Come work for me," Louise urged. "After seeing you in action just now, I realize that you might be just the person I need. Someone who can see all the pieces on the chessboard and how to play them. Someone cunning and insightful and manipulative."

"You say that like it's a good thing." It felt surprising, hearing Louise acknowledge the parts of her that Daphne had always, painstakingly, kept hidden.

The princess waved a hand dismissively. "I am the very first woman to ever rule France, and I'm still only doing it as my father's Regent. You think I haven't had to be manipulative? It can be an asset, you know. It all depends on whose mind you're attempting to sway, and toward what. Come on," Louise pressed. "Quit wasting your talents trying to become a princess, and come work in *real* politics."

For years, Daphne had tried to prove she was special by attaching herself to a special man. But maybe she didn't need to prove anything at all.

Maybe she was special all on her own.

She smiled at Louise, and it was the most genuine smile Daphne had given in a long time. "How soon can we start?"

41

BEATRICE

Beatrice sat in her office with Anju, who was conducting three conversations at once: talking to Beatrice, occasionally murmuring orders to a note-taking assistant next to her, and typing furiously on her tablet.

They were trying to make a frantic plan for damage control, since the first round of guests would arrive in ten minutes. Should they tell them anything, or just let them take their seats in the throne room as if the wedding was still on? What about Daphne's suggestion that she and Jeff handle their own press conference?

Beatrice's mind had felt fuzzy and slow all day; memories of another, very different wedding kept rising to the surface of her consciousness. She saw herself in an enormous ivory wedding gown; she saw Samantha pulling her into a hug; but the memories kept cutting off before she could get to anything meaningful, like a film clip that ended too soon.

Somehow, Beatrice was unsurprised when Teddy's blond head appeared in the doorway. He always did have a sense for when she needed him.

"Hey, Bee. I thought we were supposed to be meeting for photos soon, but the PR team said there was a delay?" At the expression on her face, he hesitated. "Is everything all right?"

Anju looked to Beatrice as if asking for permission, and Beatrice sighed. "It's complicated."

"Can I help?" he offered.

Yes, Beatrice thought desperately. Not with the wedding, but by helping to clear up her own emotional confusion.

"Let's take a walk," she suggested, because the palace felt suddenly stifling, filled with too many expectations and opinions.

Teddy followed her out to the back lawn, the skies a bleak gray overhead. Beatrice stuffed her hands deeper into the pockets of her jacket, an old one of her mom's that she'd found in the coat closet and thrown on without really noticing. Her breath frosted in the air, but she didn't actually mind the cold. It felt invigorating.

She was still wearing her bridesmaid dress beneath, its wispy skirts skimming around her heels with each step. Franklin ran an eager circle around them, tail wagging furiously, before sprinting off toward the empty fountains. In the distance she saw the trees of the orchard, where they would have just finished taking bridesmaid photos with Daphne if things were still on schedule.

"Thanks for coming out here. I needed to get my bearings somewhere I could breathe." Beatrice sighed. "Daphne and Jeff have decided to call off the wedding."

Teddy glanced over sharply. "Oh my god. Is Daphne okay?"

Something about his phrasing gave Beatrice pause. "They decided this together, you know. It wasn't like Jeff dumped Daphne at the altar."

"Sorry, I shouldn't have jumped to conclusions," Teddy said clumsily. "I just always thought that Jeff was dating Daphne out of . . . inertia, maybe. He trusts her, and he really cares about her, but I never got the sense that he loves her. Or at least, he's not *in* love with her."

"Oh," Beatrice managed, startled by his bluntness. She hadn't noticed Jeff having any reservations about Daphne, but Teddy was always so perceptive.

He tugged his wool hat lower over his ears. "Daphne, though, was really invested in the relationship. I hope she's doing okay." Teddy hesitated, then went on: "I know how much it hurts, to think you're marrying one of the Washingtons, only for the whole thing to be called off at the last minute."

At the mention of their canceled wedding, tiny flames of something—regret, or a poignant sort of heartache—kindled to life in Beatrice's chest.

"Teddy, about last night . . ." She hesitated, suddenly desperate to explain. "Things have been terrifying ever since I woke up in the hospital. I couldn't have navigated any of it without you." Her eyes flicked up to meet his. "But I'd be lying if I said I wasn't afraid."

"Of what, Bee?" he prompted.

"I don't know how to *do* this! I've only ever loved one person aside from you." And she and Connor had never been in a real relationship, or at least, not a public one.

Beatrice was used to practicing for everything she did. She liked to study, to anticipate problems before they arose. She had been trained in negotiation and contracts, in people management and public relations.

But no part of her education had trained her to be a good partner.

"I'm worried that my job will always get in the way of things," she said softly. "That it has made me . . . selfish."

"You're the least selfish person I know!"

"Not selfish on my own behalf, but on behalf of the Crown. My entire life I was told, over and over, that the Crown came first. That everyone's needs must be subjugated to it, even—or especially—my own. It hasn't exactly left a lot of room for romance."

She attempted a weak smile, and failed. "I did love Connor, and there's a part of me that will probably always love him." He was a living link to the girl she'd been before she became queen: the version of herself she'd left behind when her father died. "But I'm *in* love with you, Teddy," she added, repeating the words he'd just used about Daphne and Jeff. "That is something much bigger." And exhilarating, and far more frightening.

Teddy's blue eyes deepened in the sunlight. "You just said you love me, but you're looking at me like you're about to say goodbye."

"Because I love you so much that it terrifies me. Teddy— I don't know how to bring you into this life without hurting you! I'm always going to be torn between our relationship and the Crown. I'm like the mermaid from the Hans Christian Andersen story, only half-human. The part of me that belongs to the Crown . . . it's not mine to pledge to anyone. Even to you."

Tears rose to her eyes as she added, "The reasons we fought, the night of my accident, are all still here. I hate that you had to give up your legacy for me."

"I would do it again in a heartbeat."

"But you shouldn't have to! You deserve a real, full life, with someone who can spend lazy mornings in bed with you, and attend Little League soccer games without it being an issue of national security. I can't even travel like a normal person! I will never be able to stroll around the Duomo eating gelato."

"Oh, Bee." Teddy sighed. "I don't want any of that, if I can't have it with you."

Her protests faltered as he took her hands in his. Despite the cold, his grip was warm and certain. A gentle breeze picked up, lifting the hairsprayed curls on her neck.

"I'm guessing you don't remember that mug you found at Walthorpe, the one with Penelope's picture on it?" Teddy asked.

For some reason, the name made Beatrice's hackles rise. "Is Penelope your ex-girlfriend?"

Teddy nodded. "If I'd wanted an easy, uncomplicated relationship, I would've kept dating someone like her. But we broke up for a reason."

"Teddy, everyone wants easy and uncomplicated," Beatrice protested. "No one deliberately signs up for problems and—and—*friction*."

"I do. I like the friction." Somehow Teddy made that sound a little bit flirtatious. "I want the kind of love I have with you: extraordinary, breathtaking, wondrous love. It might be difficult at times, but the best things in life always are. Nothing worth having comes without a bit of effort."

"What are you saying?" she whispered.

"I'm saying that you're worth it. I'm not letting this mermaid swim back to the sea. I love you, all of you—including the Crown and everything that comes with it." Teddy's voice grew husky as he added, "I know better than to try to pick and choose the pieces of you to love."

Franklin was barking cheerfully in the distance, collecting stray sticks from the orchard and then dropping them again. Beatrice was still holding tight to Teddy's hands.

"How do you know we won't fight about those things again?"

"I'm sure we *will* fight about them," Teddy admitted. "We're only human. We have to just trust that we'll find a way through it."

Beatrice thought of what Louise had told her last night: that love, in its own way, was a form of faith.

She thought of what she'd said to the Duchess of Texas, about learning to trust—and lean on—other people. She'd been talking about politics, but didn't the same thing apply to love? When you were in the right relationship, you were stronger together than you were on your own.

Beatrice pulled Teddy close and kissed him.

It was the kind of kiss that reverberated through her body like church bells, as if the fundamental *rightness* of it was clanging somewhere in her heart. Beatrice let herself savor every detail of the moment: the delicious sensation of Teddy's lips on hers, the way his arms wrapped around her, steadying her from behind.

When they finally pulled apart, they were both smiling.

And then Teddy shocked her by falling to one knee.

"Marry me, Beatrice."

She couldn't speak as Teddy unbuttoned his coat and reached into his jacket pocket for a velvet box. He opened it, revealing a beautiful sapphire engagement ring.

At the sight of it, a memory stirred loose. "This isn't the first time you've given me this ring, is it?"

Teddy smiled in cautious hope. "It was my grandmother's, and, yes, you've seen it before. The night of your accident."

"You've been carrying it around this whole time?"

"I've wanted to marry you this whole time. I guess I was just waiting for the right moment. Please, Bee, let's get married," he said again. "I can't wait any longer."

It took a moment for Beatrice to realize what he was suggesting. "You want to get married *today*?"

He smiled again, a bit shyly. "Why not? Everyone is already here; the palace is decorated. We can still give the guests a royal wedding, even if it's not the one they came for."

"That's—" Beatrice fumbled for the right word. *Outrageous, impulsive.* "Unprecedented," she said at last.

"So is having a Queen of America. I thought you and I were throwing precedent to the winds, remember?"

Beatrice tugged Teddy gently to his feet, and he stood, still holding the velvet box.

"Please don't do this just because you think it'll help avoid a public relations scandal," she told him.

Teddy's gaze was intent, his hands steady as they went to rest on her shoulders.

"I'm doing this because I want to be married to you. I've never cared about the wedding part; I care about the part where I'm your husband. In my mind, this is actually a bonus," Teddy added, his blue eyes dancing. "I have no desire to plan a wedding all over again. This way Daphne and Jeff did all the heavy lifting, and we can just take over their wedding without any effort."

Beatrice hesitated. "It's not such a terrible idea."

If she and Teddy got married today, the guests would still get a royal wedding—and not just of the prince, but of the queen. Some of them might consider that an upgrade. And it would certainly deflect attention from the Jefferson-Daphne scandal. Anju would be thrilled.

"This isn't our guest list," she reminded him.

Teddy shrugged. "My family is here. That's all that matters to me."

"We didn't pick the food, or the band, or the flowers."

"I don't really care. Does it bother you?"

No, Beatrice had to admit, it didn't. Still, she kept going. "There's no chance I'll fit into Daphne's wedding gown."

"Good thing *your* wedding gown is still in the palace," Teddy reminded her.

At that, a wild, eager laugh bubbled out of Beatrice, the sort of giddy laugh that was normally Sam's territory. Teddy was right. They could step into the wedding that Daphne and Jeff had planned as easily as understudies filling the places of actors who'd gotten called offstage.

But that wasn't the reason she wanted to agree. She thought of walking down the aisle, seeing Teddy waiting for her at the end of it, and a deep satisfaction thrummed through her body.

She didn't know what the future held. No one could. But

Beatrice was determined to stop worrying about the past, fretting over memories that might never come back. She needed to lean on the things she did feel certain of. The job she had been trained for, and the people she loved.

"Okay," she said slowly. If loving someone was a leap of faith, then she was ready to jump.

Teddy sucked in a breath. "That's a yes?"

"It's a yes."

He startled her by reaching under her armpits to lift her, spinning her around in the air so that her hair whipped out in the wind.

"Teddy!" Beatrice laughed so hard it brought tears to her eyes. "What are you doing?"

"Celebrating," he said simply.

When he lowered her back to earth, he brushed another quick kiss on her lips. Beatrice whistled for Franklin, then looked back toward the palace.

"Let's go get married," she declared.

42

SAMANTHA

Samantha was used to being her family's decoy, the one they could count upon to reliably deflect attention, so she wasn't surprised when Beatrice asked her to do a walkabout.

Beatrice made the request as she and Sam hurried down the hallway toward the Brides' Room. The wedding, which the world still thought was Jeff and Daphne's, was scheduled to start in one hour—and Beatrice needed to get into bride mode.

"Can you just distract everyone for a little while?" Beatrice pleaded. "Give social media something to buzz about, so they don't realize how behind schedule we are. You can take Mom, if you want?"

Sam smiled. "I think Mom would rather be here with you. How did she react when she heard about Jeff and Daphne?"

"She's worried for them, but it's all happening so fast that I doubt she's had time to fully process it." Amusement glittered in Beatrice's eyes as she added, "Anju literally *squealed*. She's downstairs getting my gown out of storage right now."

"I'm so happy for you, Bee." Sam's voice snagged on the words.

Hearing it, her sister halted in her tracks and pulled Sam in for a hug. "I love you, Sam," she whispered.

Sam closed her eyes, willing back the tears. Beatrice had been so many things to her over the years: her opposition when they were children, her fiercest advocate when they were older, and always her role model. Quiet and selfless and brilliant and strong.

Beatrice deserved every ounce of joy that was headed her way today.

"I can't believe you're going to use *Daphne's* wedding," she couldn't resist adding. "It's just going to be so . . ." So full of white flowers and frilly lace linens and pink champagne, everything that Daphne thought of as happily ever after. "So princess-y," Sam concluded.

Her sister snorted out a laugh. "That's okay. I don't mind a little bit of princess-y."

"In that case, I'll go buy you as much time as I can," Sam promised. "See you in the throne room, Bee."

When she stepped out into the cold winter afternoon, a sea of noise greeted her, and an unwitting smile rose to Sam's face.

There were thousands of people out here, holding bottles of wine or confetti cannons, wearing plastic tiaras and veils and shrieking with excitement. They reached toward Sam, shouting questions about the wedding and who had designed her dress and was she single or not, and, to her shock, they were *smiling*.

The same crowds that had always been indifferent toward her at best, and actively disapproving at worst, now seemed delighted that she'd shown up. They waved American flags and set off noisemakers and threw shiny silver confetti. Most of the posters were about Jeff and Daphne—Sam saw one that read JEFF WILL ALWAYS BE PRINCE OF MY HEART!—but a few of them were actually about her: I'M ON #TEAMSAM and JUST TRY TO SAMCEL ME!

Her eyes were drawn to a little girl holding tight to her father's hand, wearing a pink peacoat over a T-shirt printed with Jeff's face and cartoon hearts.

The girl tilted her head, curious. "What are you doing out here? Aren't you supposed to be taking wedding photos right now?"

"We got a little behind schedule this morning, so I came out to say hi." Sam knelt down to the girl's level and winked. "I like your shirt. I need to get one of those for my brother."

"Oh, my dad designed it!"

Sam glanced up at the girl's father, who visibly reddened. "I have an online merchandise shop."

"We make some amazing gear about you, too!" the girl told Sam eagerly. "My favorite is our SPARE ME THE DRAMA shirt. We've sold thousands since you came back to town!"

"Michaela," the dad said warningly, but Sam chuckled.

"Spare Me the Drama? I like it." Because she'd been born the spare—and, she had to admit, she did have a flair for drama.

The crowds erupted in another roar of noise. When Sam heard the direction of the cheers, and saw everyone's eyes darting behind her, she realized that someone else had walked out of the palace.

She turned around slowly, a part of her already knowing who she would see.

Marshall looked achingly handsome in his tails and waistcoat; even his white gloves were clasped with a gold button at the wrist. Then Sam saw the telltale gleam on his lapel—the grizzly bear pin that was the symbol of the Dukes of Orange.

He started walking toward her, and Sam was hit by a crippling mixture of fear and longing.

"Marshall—what are you doing?" she whispered. Now a showdown with his family would be inevitable. Now everyone in the entire *world* would know he was here.

With that very first step outside the palace doors, he had thrown away his chance at going back to Hawaii.

"I'm coming to the wedding. If you'll let me, I mean."

Marshall looked at her with a tentative smile. "I believe they call this a grand gesture? A way to show someone you love them, when telling them isn't enough."

Vaguely, Sam was aware of the thousands of people staring at them, the lights of flashbulbs exploding over her skin. It all felt inconsequential compared to Marshall.

"I love you, too," she told him. "But nothing has changed. We still want different things."

"I want *you*, Sam. None of the rest matters."

The roar of the crowds seemed to retreat behind a curtain as Marshall went on: "Hawaii wasn't the same after you left. I loved the people I met there, and the things I learned about myself. But paradise doesn't really feel like paradise if you're not there to share it, Sam. I kept hoping you would come back soon, but the longer you stayed away, the lonelier I got."

"Marshall, I was lonely too. I needed you just as much as you needed me."

His lips pressed together in regret. "I'm sorry, Sam. I realize now that even though Hawaii was great, it wasn't real life. It was a form of avoidance—hiding out and hoping the world would have magically changed when I came back. But the world doesn't fix itself," he added softly. "A very smart girl once told me that if we want things to change, we need to change them ourselves."

She took a step toward him, her body acting of its own volition, and Marshall's breathing caught.

"I love you, Sam. I have loved you from the moment I saw you on that museum balcony, kicking the iron railing like you were going to destroy it through sheer force of will. I fall more in love with you every day, if that's even possible."

Sam took one last step forward, and then her head was on his chest and she was breathing in the scent of him, letting his arms close tight around her. The sheer joy of touching him after all these weeks apart sent a jolt of electricity through her body, as if she'd been sleepwalking and now every inch of her was suddenly and brutally awake.

With her face still muffled in his tuxedo, she asked, "What does this mean for us?"

"I don't know what the future holds," Marshall said gruffly. "All I know is that I don't want to face it without you. It's no use building a life in Hawaii if we aren't building it together. Wherever you are, that's where I want to be."

Sam felt her fears evaporating in the face of this—their history, and, more importantly, their future.

She tipped her face up to kiss him. Her body flooded with heat despite the freezing temperatures, her hands reaching up to grab the lapels of his jacket and clutch them tight.

When they pulled away, Sam became aware of thunderous applause, plus a few scattered whoops of approval. She smiled against Marshall's chest, laughing. She'd forgotten they had an audience.

"I can't believe you went full-on grand gesture."

"I took a page out of your playbook," Marshall teased. "Remember when you pulled me into the imperial state carriage and informed me that we were dating?"

"That's not how I remember it!" She stared at him, suddenly realizing that his tuxedo looked a little snug around the shoulders. "Is that your tux?"

"Oh, um, I borrowed it from your family. I didn't pack mine," Marshall admitted. "Anju helped me track one down."

"What about your pin?"

"I got it from my grandfather. He's been carrying it around ever since I left it in Bellevue, that day we ran away."

"You saw your grandfather?" Sam nearly screeched, but Marshall didn't seem worried. "Why didn't you say that sooner? How did it go?"

"As well as could be expected. I'll tell you everything later," he promised. "Should we head back?"

Sam laced her fingers in his, then turned to wave one last time at the wedding crowds, who cheered in approval. Camera flashes went off around them like the blinking lights of fireflies.

"By the way, why were you out here doing a walkabout alone?" Marshall asked under his breath.

"There were some complications with the wedding. Beatrice sent me out here to distract everyone," Sam explained.

Marshall barked out a laugh, and had to cover it with a cough.

"Your job was to distract everyone?" he repeated. "I think it's safe to say you succeeded."

43

NINA

"I forgot how absurd the protocol is for royal weddings," Nina muttered as she and Jamie stared around the throne room. "Am I really only allotted eighteen inches of this bench?"

"Here, scoot closer. I don't mind if you cross into my space," Jamie teased.

The embossed card that had arrived with their invitations had warned that seating was limited, so women should avoid "full-skirted gowns or long trains." Daphne and Jeff were apparently trying to fit nearly six thousand people into the throne room—the most it had ever held. But then, the wedding of a ruling monarch was state business, while the wedding of a younger sibling was really just an excuse for a nationwide party.

Nina's oh-so-helpful protocol card had also instructed her about cell-phone use (phones were allowed but flash photos prohibited), gifts (donations to one of three charities were gently suggested), and, most importantly, her scheduled check-in time (staggering the arrival of the guests in an attempt to control traffic).

As one of the highest-ranking people in attendance, Jamie had been granted a prime arrival time just thirty minutes before the ceremony. Nina, an ordinary nobody, was asked to show up nearly two hours prior. Though of course, she'd been here even longer.

She still couldn't believe everything that had had happened this morning. When she'd started emailing Daphne and Ethan—she hated to think of it as blackmail—she'd hoped to knock some sense into them both. She'd certainly never imagined that Gabriella might intervene, and make a turbulent situation even uglier. Gabriella had lobbed the secret about Daphne and Ethan into the room like a live grenade.

So far, the ushers and staff were all acting as if the wedding was still taking place, but it felt to Nina like a very big *if*. She wondered what the Washingtons would say when forced to confront the aftermath of not one but two canceled weddings.

Jamie reached for her hand, which had clenched into a stiff claw. "You okay?"

Nina realized that he thought she was upset to be at her ex-boyfriend's wedding. Of course he did; it was the logical assumption, because who would ever dream she felt guilty about sending ominous emails to the bride?

She unclenched her fingers to lace them in Jamie's, trying not to think about what Jeff had said last night: *I don't want to lose you* and *I keep coming back to you*. About the way he'd held her gaze, his eyes so bright and disarming, his voice so serious.

It was unfair to her—and to Daphne. And that, if nothing else, had reinforced Nina's conviction that she'd been right to interfere. No one who was desperately in love with his bride would talk to another woman that way, the very night before his wedding.

And, as irrational as it was, there was still a stubborn part of her that missed Jeff. A part of her that wished things had gone differently, that they could be friends again.

Maybe Nina was being unfair to Jamie, too.

"So I was thinking. *Hamlet* is opening on the West End in a couple of weeks," Jamie said, interrupting her thoughts. "I know it's not your favorite Shakespeare, but the Duke of Cambridge invited me to the premiere. Want to come? You could take the train down from Oxford, and my family has a house in town—"

"Jamie."

Something in the tone of her voice made him break off. He shifted, letting go of her hand. It took every ounce of Nina's willpower not to reach for it again.

"You are so amazing," she went on, her voice wobbly. "I've had the best time with you."

"But . . . ," he supplied, watching her.

"But I think I need to take this next step, in Oxford, on my own."

Jamie drew in a swift breath. "Are you saying you want to break up?"

"No!" It burst out of her, and she winced, ignoring the few startled glances from various royals or aristocrats seated around them. "I'll understand if *you* want to break up, if you don't want to wait for me. But I need to slow down, Jamie. I'm falling for you, and it scares me."

"Falling for someone should be a good thing. Why does it scare you?" he asked, which was a very reasonable question.

Nina looked up at him, willing back the tears that were tight in her throat. He looked so unbearably handsome in his uniform, his blond hair curling against the gray of his fur-trimmed vest, the traditional attire of the kings of Canada.

"I'm so glad I met you, Jamie. Our time together . . . it's changed me. You made me confident enough to go *onstage*, and to apply to the Oxford program."

"You would have done those things with or without me."

"I doubt it." Nina ventured a smile. "The only reason I went to that first rehearsal, instead of quitting on the spot, was so that I could slap you for that kiss at auditions."

Something flickered behind his blue eyes. "But you didn't slap me."

"I'm holding the slap in reserve," she joked, then shook her head. "Last night, you called me your girlfriend."

"And you didn't want me to," Jamie said slowly.

"I thought I did, but . . ."

He ran a hand through his hair, seeming perplexed. "Nina, I'm falling for you, too. And aside from that, I respect you. I don't like the idea of hooking up with you without making things official."

"You did *try* to make things official. I'm the one who asked to slow down. I promise that you're not a bad guy if you want to keep hooking up with me," she said, and then her smile faded. "Jamie, I'm not ready for everything that comes with being your official girlfriend. The media attention, the invitations to events, the style bloggers coming after me . . ."

"We could get you a stylist! And a PR person to reply to event invitations!" Jamie hurried to say, then saw the expression on her face. "Sorry. Not helping, is it?"

Nina shook her head. "Oxford is something I need to do on my own: not as your girlfriend, but simply as myself. I've never carved out my own space before. I came to college close to home; I've always hovered at the edge of the royal orbit because of Sam. . . . It's time I went somewhere just for me, somewhere no one judges me on anything except my own merit."

Jamie's gaze locked on hers, intent and yearning. "That makes sense, Nina. But what does it mean for us?"

"Nothing has to change! I want to keep seeing you—I just want to take it slow. I want to stay . . . unofficial." She tried to smile. "So, I'd love to see *Hamlet* with you, but can we sit in a private box and maybe not walk into the theater through the main entrance?"

Yes, they were in public together right now, but for all anyone knew they were just guests who happened to be seated in the same pew. Nina had worried that someone might publish photos of them arriving at the rehearsal dinner together, but the tourists around the gates must have been waiting for someone more famous, or maybe they'd been too far away to get a good picture.

Her relationship with Jamie was still safe, and Nina hoped desperately that she could protect it for a little while longer.

Jamie slid closer on the bench, so that the entire left side of his body was pressed against hers. Nina resisted the urge to tip her head against his shoulder.

"Does this mean I get to woo you?"

"Woo me?"

Nina's phone vibrated in her clutch, but she ignored it, eyes fixed on Jamie.

"The way I see it, I need to take a page from a Jane Austen novel and court you. I need to convince you that being with me is worth all the irritating complications and media attention. So I'm going to court you," he told her. "I'm going to write you handwritten letters and send you flowers for no reason except that it's a Monday, and I'm going to constantly tell you how much I value you. I'm going to woo you so well that you'll decide our relationship is more than a secret affair, and you'll agree to the whole nine yards—the Canadian police protection, the events, all of it."

Nina blinked, a little dazed. There were a million things she wanted to say, but what came out of her mouth was "A secret affair sounds so . . . scandalous."

"You decide how scandalous it is," Jamie said evenly. "You set the pace, Nina. But as long as you're okay with it, I'll be here, wooing you the whole time."

She couldn't help but smile at that declaration. "I look forward to it."

"Oh, you should." Jamie grinned. "Just you wait. I'm *excellent* at wooing. As I am, really, at everything."

Her phone vibrated a second time, and Nina tore her attention from Jamie long enough to open her bag. When she saw the text from Samantha, her eyes widened.

SOS. Marshall is here! Are you still in the palace? Can you come meet me?

She blinked, the words swimming before her eyes. Marshall had come back from Hawaii? Was this some kind of big romantic gesture, or was he here to break up with Sam?

She kissed Jamie once, then stood. "Sorry, Sam texted me an SOS. I need to go find her. I'll be back before the ceremony," she added, as if she believed the wedding was still on track.

As if she hadn't been the one to completely derail it.

44

DAPHNE

It was only a matter of time, Daphne knew, before the hail-storm of her mother's anger descended on her. So she wasn't all that surprised to hear a shrill "What have you done?" from the doorway of the Brides' Room.

Daphne looked up from the tote bag she'd been packing; she needed to clear out of the room so that Beatrice could come get dressed, and besides, she wanted a quick exit after the wedding. She sighed and turned around. "Hello, Mother."

Rebecca Deighton swept into the room like an avenging goddess. Her eyes seemed to glow an even fiercer green than usual thanks to her emerald trumpet gown, which had been custom designed for what she'd thought would be her crowning social success.

"What's *wrong* with you?" her mother exclaimed, glaring at Daphne's slate-colored bridesmaid dress. The palace had bought two extras, in case Samantha or Beatrice damaged theirs, and it turned out the extras had been put to good use, since a seamstress had just frantically hemmed one to fit Daphne. The bodice was a tiny bit snug over Daphne's cleav-age, though no one would dare say so.

There was something deeply ironic about being forced to wear the bridesmaid dress that she had picked out, but Daphne wasn't ready to laugh about it yet.

"This is between me and Jefferson," she began, but her mother cut her off.

"When that chamberlain woman told me the wedding was off, I said she was mistaken. My daughter would never allow that to happen. She wouldn't be so foolish as to throw away everything that she's spent years working toward." Rebecca took a step forward, almost menacing. "You need to go to Jefferson and *beg* him to take you back!"

"Mother, it's over," Daphne said wearily.

"It's *never* over! You have years of history together; remind him of that! Do it now, before it's too late." When Daphne shook her head, Rebecca pressed her mouth into a thin line. "Do it, or I'll . . ."

"You'll slap me again?" Daphne asked, with an unmistakable—and uncharacteristic—bite of defiance.

Color rose to her mother's cheeks, but she held her ground. "I won't stand by and let you throw away this family's entire future."

"What about *my* future?"

"Exactly! What *about* your future? You could have been a princess!" Rebecca crowed.

Daphne zipped her tote bag fiercely shut. Her anger felt like something primal, pulled from the very depths of her. "I'd rather be happy."

"Happy?" her mother repeated incredulously. "What does that even mean? You could have titles and tiaras and a life of unimaginable privilege; you could be famous throughout the world. Your children could be raised in a palace! You're trading that away for so-called *happiness?*" She spoke the word with skeptical uncertainty, as if it was in a foreign language and she wasn't sure she'd gotten the pronunciation right.

"I'm sorry," Daphne said heavily.

Rebecca stared at her. In that moment Daphne saw past

her mother's flinty beauty, as if the glamorous mirage she presented to the world had evaporated like smoke, and her real self—tired, brittle, defeated—was revealed to the naked eye.

Daphne knew her mother hadn't married for happiness, or for love. Rebecca had been a runway model, living on cigarettes and free clothes, when she met Peter Deighton, the future Baronet Margrave. He had a title, lowly as it was, and she'd thrown her lot in with him at once. How disappointed she must have been when she realized just how unimportant his baronetcy was in the vast tangle of the aristocracy, and how little money he actually had.

She had traded her life away, and for what? Their titles were gone. She was a plain Mrs. Deighton now, and all her hopes were pinned on Daphne.

But just because Rebecca had made a hard bargain, Daphne didn't have to.

"If you won't fix this, and salvage your marriage, then you're dead to me," her mother said coldly. "No daughter of mine would accept such a spectacular failure. Don't bother setting foot in our home ever again. You're not welcome there."

Daphne had thought she was numb to Rebecca's insults by now, but that one still stung.

"Don't worry. I won't be back," she assured her mother. It had never been much of a home to her, anyway. All she'd learned from her mother was pettiness, and cruelty, and a toxic, all-consuming ambition.

Rebecca stared at her daughter for a long moment in disbelief, the way you might stare at a painting or a piece of jewelry, wondering why on earth you had paid so dearly for it.

Then she sighed and walked away without a backward glance.

Daphne sank onto the love seat and closed her eyes before

her legs could give out beneath her. It felt like she'd run a marathon in the last five minutes.

When she heard footsteps, Daphne looked up sharply— but it wasn't her mother, coming back to apologize. It was Nina.

Nina took a hesitant step forward. "I wasn't sure you'd still be here."

"When I set my life on fire, I like to stick around and watch it go up in flames," Daphne said laconically.

Nina almost smiled at that, but her eyes still seemed troubled. "Are you okay? That conversation was, um . . ."

"You heard that?" Daphne couldn't even muster up a shred of embarrassment. So what if Nina, with her two loving parents and happy home life, had finally seen what a vicious wolf pack Daphne's family was?

"Your mom was pretty harsh. I'm sure she didn't mean it," Nina rushed to add, in an attempt at magnanimity. "She's just in shock."

"She meant it, I can assure you."

Nina glanced at Daphne's wedding gown, which still hung from a hook on the wall, its fabric cascading down in gorgeous satin layers. She looked at Daphne, who nodded permission, then stepped forward to trace the delicate lace overlay. "Daphne, this is beautiful."

"I know," Daphne agreed. "It's too bad no one will ever see it."

"Can't it hang in a museum, at least?"

"A relic from a wedding that didn't happen? Are you kidding?" Daphne sighed. "Maybe I'll give it to the Dickens Museum in London; they could use it for the Miss Havisham exhibit."

One corner of Nina's mouth curled upward. "It's a good sign that you can joke about it."

"Joking seems to be all I can do at the moment." Daphne

kicked her feet out from beneath the hem of the bridesmaid dress. Her toenails in her peep-toe shoes were painted the softest shade of pink. "Speaking of dresses, I'm glad you wore the one I recommended."

"I did learn not to question you on fashion."

When Nina glanced at the chair opposite her, Daphne sighed. "You might as well sit down."

It was a reluctant invitation, but Nina sat. "I can't believe Teddy and Beatrice are taking over your wedding."

"I hope Beatrice knows how lucky she is." Daphne sniffed. "I have *exquisite* taste. All she has to do is show up! I've already planned and thought of everything."

"No one has ever denied that you have exquisite taste," Nina agreed. "Maybe you have a future as an event planner?"

"Maybe," Daphne said vaguely. Nina wasn't all that far off the mark.

Nina bit her lip, still clearly anxious. "About what happened earlier. I wanted to apologize—"

Daphne cut her off. "You were right. Not that I enjoyed being blackmailed, but Jefferson and I should never have gotten engaged."

A part of her wondered whether it changed things for Nina and Jamie, that Jefferson was newly single again, but she didn't want to ask.

Nina hesitated. "Are you and Ethan . . ."

"I broke up with Jefferson for myself, not for Ethan. Not everything is about a man," Daphne said tersely.

"Of course not. Sorry," Nina agreed, chastened.

Daphne heaved a breath. "It's okay. I just . . . I've made a lot of mistakes. I need to get away from it all, you know? I'm leaving the country for a while."

"So am I, actually," Nina told her.

"Really? Where?"

"Oxford."

"Oh, that program through the English department? Congratulations, Nina." Daphne tried not to sound jealous. She had always wanted to apply to something like that—if she'd gotten to be a student.

"Where are you headed?" Nina asked.

"France. I could use a fresh start."

"I know the feeling."

They were silent for a moment, both caught off guard by the sincerity of this conversation, sifting through the strange constellation of their thoughts. Daphne drummed her fingers over the armrest of the love seat.

"Nina, I owe you an apology, too. The night of the League of Kings banquet, when I saw you and Jefferson together—"

"I shouldn't have kissed him!" Nina interrupted. "I knew you were together, and I let it happen anyway. I never meant to hurt you, I swear. It just sort of . . . happened."

Daphne should have been angry, but she knew better than anyone how easily a kiss could *just happen.*

"Trust me," she heard herself say, "if you knew what I did that night, you wouldn't be apologizing for a little kiss."

Nina's expression grew solemn. "This is about Jeff, isn't it?"

"I told him . . ." Daphne couldn't bear to say it aloud. Even now, knowing that Nina was the one who'd blackmailed her— was equally capable of hurting people for what she thought was a good reason—Daphne still didn't want to admit this.

"I told him a very cruel lie," she finished softly

Nina didn't seem all that surprised. She'd probably already realized that Daphne had done something drastic to keep her hold on Jeff, when he'd been about to leave her for Nina.

Daphne hated, suddenly, that the two of them had been at each other's throats like this for so long. Was Jefferson really worth it? Was *any* man worth it?

"I'm sorry," Daphne said again, her voice breaking.

Nina's reply was unexpectedly gentle. "Daphne, whatever you said that night, it's between you and Jeff. The forgiveness you want isn't mine to give."

"You're very wise, you know." Daphne strove to ignore the tears stinging her eyes. "As angry as I am about those emails, I'm also glad you weren't working with Gabriella against me. This time or last time."

"I can't believe you thought I would do that! I *barely* agreed to work with you, and Gabriella is a million times worse."

"That's one of the nicer things anyone has ever said to me." Daphne's mouth lifted at the corner. "By the way, can you believe what happened with Gabriella? The way Jefferson exiled her?" Not that it was legally binding or anything. But Daphne had loved the way Jefferson told her to get out of town, that she wasn't welcome at a party in Washington ever again.

Nina snorted. "I will never forget the look on her face in that moment."

"Honestly, we should have just involved him from the very beginning, instead of trying to scheme our way through the whole mess."

"I don't know, our scheming was kind of fun. I don't regret it," Nina said wryly.

Daphne shot her a look. "I clearly rubbed off on you, if you were able to scheme against me so well that you had me fooled."

"The student becomes the master," Nina agreed.

"A master, really? You do think highly of yourself."

"What can I say, I learned from the best. And I didn't really know how else to get through to you. After all, schemes and subterfuge are sort of your love language."

Daphne choked out a laugh, and the air in the room seemed to soften.

It was strange, that she and Nina had shared so much. They had been rivals and friends, had both loved the same man, and now here they were, at the end of the road, cautious allies once more.

No, Daphne silently amended, this wasn't the end of the road.

It was the beginning of one.

45

BEATRICE

Beatrice stood before the double doors that led into the throne room, her heart pounding a staccato rhythm in her chest. Inside, the trumpets crescendoed to a final dramatic finale, then fell silent.

That was her cue.

"Your Majesty?" Anju closed her eyes, as if she regretted what she was about to say. "Are you really sure about this?"

"Yes," Beatrice promised.

There were many things she felt uncertain of. She didn't know what had happened for most of the past *year*, for starters. But this decision—her faith in Teddy, in the solidity of their relationship—was something she knew, with the sort of bone-deep certainty that transcended logic or facts. Perhaps Louise was right and she should think of it as faith.

Beatrice nodded to the footmen standing at attention, and they flung open the doors. She took a single step forward.

The room seemed to draw in a single, collective gasp as everyone realized the bride wasn't Daphne, but their queen.

Sam and Daphne slipped from a side entrance to stand near the altar in their bridesmaid dresses. They hadn't wanted to reveal themselves earlier and spoil the surprise.

Beatrice had to hand it to her: Daphne was a genius when it came to public relations. Once she'd learned that Beatrice and Teddy were planning to take over her wedding, some strategic part of Daphne had clicked into action, and she'd lit up like a fuse, incandescent with ideas.

"We should pretend this was always the plan," Daphne had suggested. "That Jefferson and I were just decoys, protecting you and Teddy!"

It made an odd, convoluted kind of sense. The palace would insist that the whole thing had been a PR masterstroke: that, embarrassed they had postponed one big state wedding, Beatrice and Teddy felt loath to go through the whole thing again, with all the requisite engagement parties and appearances and media attention. So they had sent out Daphne and Jeff as their decoys, readying the nation for *a* royal wedding while the *real* royal wedding was planned behind the scenes.

You really thought Daphne and Jeff were engaged? Beatrice imagined Anju teasing the gobsmacked reporters. *They're so young! Of course they weren't getting married!* The reporters would then trip over one another claiming to have seen through the ruse the entire time. Every tabloid would scramble to pull recent photos of Beatrice, with captions about how she was "smiling secretively" or had a "bridal glow."

Daphne had explained that she and Jeff would wait a few weeks, letting the furor of public opinion calm down, before they leaked the news that they had broken up. Of course, Beatrice could see why Daphne preferred this plan. It offered her a graceful exit. Now she could claim that while she had been a "fake bride" as a favor to Beatrice, she'd come to realize what her own royal wedding might be like, and decided that she and Jeff didn't belong together. The optics would be much better than if she'd admitted to what really happened—that she'd called it off the day of her multimillion-dollar wedding.

Beatrice couldn't worry about any of this right now, because Teddy had stepped out from behind the altar and taken his place at the steps. All she could think about was reaching him.

The heavy hem of her skirts kept dragging, forcing Beatrice to kick them out in front of her so that she didn't trip. She could have asked her mother to walk her down the aisle, or Jeff. But as Samantha had pointed out, there was no one in the country who outranked her, and it felt right that Beatrice should be the one to give herself away.

She was halfway now. Her eyes were still locked on Teddy's intent blue gaze, and the way he was looking at her sent shivers down her bare arms. This gown wasn't meant for winter, with its delicate lace-capped sleeves, but that was the sort of inconsequential detail that didn't really matter.

When she finally reached Teddy, a smile illuminated his features. "I love you so much," he whispered. "You look beautiful."

Beatrice reached for his gloved hands and squeezed them in reply.

The Archbishop of Georgetown, an elderly man with kind eyes who had known Beatrice since she was little, bowed to her—the only acknowledgment of her sovereignty that Beatrice would allow. During their brief, somewhat frantic meeting before the ceremony, he had asked to call her *Your Majesty* throughout the service, which she had apparently agreed to let him do in their first, canceled wedding. As in, *Does Your Majesty take this man to be your husband . . .*

This time, Beatrice had refused. It no longer sounded quite right.

"Dearly beloved," the archbishop began. A microphone was pinned to his robes, but even without it his voice would have carried through the throne room, the soaring baroque arches funneling sound throughout the space.

"We are gathered here in the sight of God, and in the face of this congregation, to join together this man and this woman in holy matrimony. . . ."

The service seemed to wash over Beatrice in a quiet hum, her entire focus centered on Teddy.

When it came time for her vows, the archbishop turned to her. "Do you, Beatrice, take Theodore to be your husband? Do you promise to be faithful to him in good times and in bad, in sickness and in health, to love him and to honor him, for all the days of your life?"

In good times and in bad, in sickness and in health: she and Teddy had already been through those highs and lows. She had lost her memory and still they had found their way back to each other.

For all the days of her life. It was a monumental promise, yet it was one that Beatrice, of all people, felt comfortable making. After all, she had sworn her life before this—to her country and to the Crown.

She was grateful that the archbishop had agreed to use her first name. As she spoke her vows, Beatrice didn't want to be Her Majesty Beatrice Regina, the very first Queen of America.

Their wedding might be offered up for public consumption, photographed and broadcast throughout the world, replayed over and over for years to come, but Beatrice wasn't thinking of any of that as she looked into Teddy's eyes. It felt like it was just the two of them, like this moment belonged to her and Teddy alone.

Right now she was just Beatrice, and right now, that was enough.

"I do," she promised.

♛

"We're married!" Teddy exclaimed, once they had processed back up the aisle and reemerged into the hallway.

Beatrice flung her arms around him and pulled him close, relishing one last moment of privacy, and calm. "We're married," she repeated.

Laughter bubbled up around them as their families came forward, their faces bright with joy and a healthy dose of shock. Beatrice's mom was crying; Teddy's mom wrapped her arms around her; Teddy's younger sister, Charlotte, was recording everything on her phone; and Beatrice saw Sam whispering something to Teddy's two younger brothers—probably some stunt she wanted to pull at the reception, Beatrice thought fondly. She realized that this was how it would be from now on, their two families blending into a rowdy and chaotic whole, and felt so happy she almost hurt from it.

Anju edged forward, a bit hesitantly. "I'm sorry, Your Majesty, but it's almost time for you to leave."

Beatrice and Teddy were supposed to depart on a parade, more technically known as the Carriage Procession of Her Majesty and Her Bridegroom with a Sovereign's Escort of the Household Cavalry. They would wind through the cordoned-off streets, past all the crowds who had been waiting for hours in the freezing cold, before finally returning to the palace, where they would appear on the balcony for a photo op and kiss.

Instead Beatrice asked, "Should I speak to the press first?"

Anju began to stammer excuses. "You don't need to—you just got married, Your Majesty! No one expects you to hold a press conference!"

Except that the world had erupted into feverish speculation about today's events. This was the sort of personal news that should come directly from the royal family, and for better or worse, Beatrice was now the head of that family.

She hesitated on the threshold of the Media Briefing Hall. The last time she'd been in here was for that awful press conference, the one she wished she could forget.

But Beatrice was stronger now. As she looked at the people around her, she knew that she would never feel alone in this role again. She had her family, and Teddy, and the new family that she and Teddy would build together.

As Beatrice walked inside, a sea of flashbulbs immediately lit up. She was still wearing her bridal gown—the optics of her addressing the press as a newly married woman were too irresistible, because who would dare argue with a bride?—but the great length of the train had been bustled and fastened with tiny silk buttons.

She stepped up to the podium as a roar of questions erupted around her: *Why did you decide to hide the wedding news, Your Majesty? How many people were in on the secret? Will Daphne and Jeff get married soon, for real this time?*

Beatrice lifted a hand, the way she'd seen her father do on countless occasions, and the noise died out.

"First of all, I want to thank everyone for the support and love that you have shown my family, throughout my life and especially over the past year. I am so grateful, and touched." She leaned closer to the viper's nest of microphones before her. "Of course, I owe a massive thank-you to my brother and Daphne Deighton, for allowing me and my husband"—the word felt thrillingly unfamiliar on her tongue—"the freedom to plan this wedding in privacy and in secret. After the up-heavals of the past year, it was a real gift to have something that belonged just to us.

"I will now take questions one at a time," she concluded, and every hand in the room flew into the air.

"Mr. Kellerman." Beatrice nodded to one of the reporters, who stood.

"Why the secrecy, Your Majesty?"

"If you had known it was me getting married, would you have given me any breathing room in the past months?" She tried to smile conspiratorially, the way Daphne would, and waited for the reporter to shake his head. "Exactly," she agreed. "You would have suffocated the wedding in questions and speculation. While my subterfuge might seem excessive, it was also effective. I was able to plan this wedding in peace."

For once, Beatrice didn't feel any compunction about telling a public fib. She was doing this to protect Daphne and Jeff, especially Daphne, from the outraged criticisms the press would have piled on them if they knew the truth.

That was what you did for family—you protected them.

Beatrice nodded at another reporter, who cleared her throat. "Now that you and His Lordship are married, what title will he use?"

It was a fair question. There had never been a king consort before, at least not in America. In England, the man married to a queen was styled as a Royal Highness—like Prince Albert had been—but Beatrice and Teddy were carving out new territory. And the question still remained of what he would actually *do*.

"These are all questions that Teddy and I will decide together," she said calmly. "As a married unit, and as a team."

Everyone in the room kept trying to catch her gaze, but Beatrice's eyes had drifted to Helen Crosby, the reporter who'd asked her that question about the League of Kings months ago—the question she'd flubbed.

"Miss Crosby," she said, and the reporter nodded.

"Your Majesty, you may be aware that there is a bill in Congress that calls for your removal. Among other things, it claims that you suffered severe psychological and neurological damage from your accident and aren't capable of reigning. Do you have a response to those who would say you're unfit to rule?"

Well, Helen certainly didn't mince words.

Beatrice could dodge the question, say that she was only here to talk about her wedding; or that she wouldn't dare comment on a congressional bill before it became law. But she suddenly felt so weary of all the evasions and falsities.

Who said that being queen meant she had to hide all her flaws? She was human; she was allowed to show weakness. Men didn't pretend they were perfect. Why should she?

Dimly she was aware of Anju standing in the wings, wincing, but she would face Anju's consternation later.

"As you all know, I was in a car accident," Beatrice began. "I suffered extensive head injuries. Since the accident, I have been under the care of Dr. Malcolm Jacobs, who is treating me for retrograde amnesia. I have lost some of my memories of the past year."

Everyone stared at her with wide eyes. Beatrice tried not to think of all the people watching the live coverage of this, gasping in shock or calling her nasty names or telling one another, *I knew she was a liar!*

She forged ahead.

"I may not remember all the specifics of the past year, but there are many things I could never forget. The sense of duty my father taught me as a child. My love of this country. My desire to help create a better America, to the best of my ability. To anyone who has concerns about my abilities, I assure you that I am up to the task."

Her voice rose as she added, "History matters, but the future is far more important. And I promise you that I will be with you for the future, whatever comes."

EPILOGUE

DAPHNE

Six months later

There was a rap at her door and the sound of a voice calling out, "Daphne!" With the French accent it came out more like Dahff-*nay*.

"*Dix minutes, s'il vous plaît, Marie, merci!*" Daphne replied in a single breath, then glanced back at her phone. "Ethan, I have to go."

He leaned forward, causing his dark hair to flop into his eyes. Afternoon sunlight illuminated his face, the Gothic buildings of King's College behind him. He was currently enrolled in a rigorous course of summer classes, hoping to get back on track with his premed requirements after his time in Malaysia.

"Have I mentioned how hot it is when you speak French?" Ethan asked.

Daphne rolled her eyes affectionately, leaning her elbows onto the heavy wooden desk. She was in the small room adjacent to Louise's office that had become, lately, her home—or at least the place she spent the majority of her time. "Have fun later. And take some photos for me? I want to see the city!" The coronation wasn't until Friday, but from what Daphne could tell, America seemed to be taking the entire *week* off to celebrate. Tonight Ethan and some of his friends were headed to the bars on Embassy Row, which were all offering "Coronation Specials" and which were certain to be filled with hyped-up tourists wearing red, blue, and gold.

"Washington is chaos right now, Daph. Worse even than it was for your canceled wedding." The fact that he could say this without an ounce of awkwardness—as if he'd had nothing to do with that canceled wedding—was so very Ethan. "Some of my classmates in the summer program are actually renting out their dorm rooms. If you live in Randolph Hall, third floor or above, you can see the parade route. The kids with balconies are charging extra."

Daphne smiled at the thought of tourists coming to town and renting college dorm rooms just so they might catch a glimpse of the queen. "You could go to the coronation if you wanted to, you know."

"You could, too. He did invite both of us."

By *he*, of course, Ethan meant Prince Jefferson.

Ethan was slowly, tentatively, trying to rebuild his relationship with his best friend, though it would take time. As for Daphne, she'd texted with Jefferson once or twice, but that was it. Someday, when she saw him in person again, she would apologize properly for everything she had done. She knew she owed him that.

For now, she was content to focus on this—whatever it was—between her and Ethan.

After the wedding debacle, she hadn't dared reach out to Ethan. It felt unfair to Jefferson, and fundamentally wrong. She had no desire to slide one man out of her life and slide another into his place, as if they were interchangeable paper dolls.

Misguided as it had been, she and the prince had been about to get *married*. Daphne was determined to do things differently this time around. She and Ethan hadn't even discussed whether they were dating; they hadn't seen each other in person yet, just begun these video chats that had become increasingly frequent.

It had started a few weeks into her time here, when Daphne

was newly settling into her life as Louise's employee. She saw Ethan's name on the incoming video call and scrambled to answer, heart pounding in her chest. Just looking at him had sent static dancing over her skin, a low-frequency hum of nostalgia and want.

"It's better that I'm not there," Daphne said now, replying to Ethan's remark about the coronation. "Besides, I'm pretty busy *ruling France.*"

"And how is the reign of Queen Daphne so far?"

"France should be so lucky," she teased. "Really, though, I can't believe Louise gave me her power of attorney while she's gone."

Princess Louise was currently in Washington. It wasn't typical for foreign royals to attend each other's coronations— being crowned was nothing like a wedding, after all. A wedding was a social event and a celebration of love, whereas a coronation was a sacrament of duty between rulers and their countries. The guests invited to Beatrice's coronation were almost exclusively American: aristocrats, bureaucrats, judges, and hundreds of ordinary citizens who'd been chosen out of a lottery.

Louise had gone anyway, in a personal capacity rather than an official one. "Of course I'll be there to support my friend. Women in charge need to stick together," she'd insisted, her eyes lighting on Daphne's as she said this last: "You can take care of France while I'm away."

And Daphne was doing exactly that. Technically her title was Director of Media Relations, but over the past six months her role had grown into something much bigger. By now she was Louise's right-hand woman.

A nice perk of the job was living at Versailles rent-free. Louise paid her a generous salary, so Daphne could have afforded her own place, but she was saving that money for tuition. She would start taking part-time classes at the Sorbonne in September.

Besides, why would anyone *voluntarily* move out of a palace? She had her own suite of rooms on the second floor. Everything was elegant and classically French, from the blue wallpaper in a delicate floral motif to the antique desk, its drawer pulls shaped like miniature fleurs-de-lis, to the breathtaking white marble countertops and enormous Jacuzzi tub in the bathroom. A massive antique mirror reflected all the opulence back to her, the patina on its golden frame suggesting that countless women had admired themselves here over the years.

Actually, a maidservant had told her, these rooms had once belonged to Madame de Pompadour, the commoner whose relationship with Louis XV nearly brought down the French monarchy.

Daphne had to hand it to Louise; she had a sense of humor.

"In other news," Ethan said, more tentatively, "the Duke of Virginia's trial begins next week. I wonder how Gabriella feels about it all."

Daphne gave a derisive snort. "Who knows? Last I heard, she was in Mallorca with Juan Carlos."

Daphne had seen the whole thing unfold, the day after Beatrice and Teddy's wedding, when she went to the private airport with Louise. The VIP reception area had been crowded with foreign royals, all of them gossiping with fascinated annoyance about the Washingtons' wedding switch. Daphne had been tying her printed scarf around her head, trying to go unrecognized, when she'd heard Gabriella's imperious voice.

"What do you mean, my family's plane has been *seized?*"

"I'm sorry, ma'am," the woman at the private airport's front desk had said, flushing. "But your plane has been confiscated by the government, under orders from the FBI."

Daphne had watched as Prince Juan Carlos of Spain—the carefree playboy prince, the one with the eponymous tequila company—had approached Gabriella. "I'm going to Mallorca. Can I give you a ride somewhere along the way?" As if dropping her off by private jet was as easy as pulling to the side of the highway.

"I still can't believe it," Ethan mused. "Gabriella and Juan Carlos, I mean."

"I can. That girl was dead set on marrying a prince." Daphne said it disdainfully, ignoring Ethan's raised eyebrow.

"You're not jealous of all her millions of followers?" he teased. Ever since she'd hooked up with Juan Carlos, Gabriella's social-media army had skyrocketed to the millions. Her feed was a study in hedonism, all sparklers and beach raves in Ibiza and Spanish aristocrats chugging the infamous royal tequila.

"I have a country to run. I can't be bothered with some socialite's online presence," Daphne sniffed. "Honestly, Gabriella and Juan Carlos seem perfect for each other."

Ethan chuckled, then changed the subject. "So I was looking at the calendar, and I was thinking—what if I come to Paris next month? I'd get my own hotel room," he said quickly, reddening. "I mean—it's probably best if we, um, don't rush into anything—"

"I'd love that." Daphne's breath hitched at the thought of Ethan, here. Of having him entirely to herself. No subterfuge, no secrets. Holding hands as they walked together through Paris, wandering in and out of museums, sharing a gelato from her favorite place on Île Saint-Louis. "And don't be ridiculous. My room is plenty big, and the French have no qualms about overnight guests."

"Well . . . if you're sure."

His eyes deepened at that, and Daphne forced herself to look away, grabbing her calendar. "Any weekend but the seventeenth."

"Going somewhere with Louise?"

"Not exactly," Daphne said vaguely. She wasn't ready to talk about these plans yet, in case they went horribly wrong.

"I really should go," she added, and Ethan nodded.

"I'll text you later. Daphne—I'm proud of you."

After they hung up, she glanced down at the pile of paperwork on her desk. Managing things during Louise's absence was a job on top of her already full-time job. She needed to review the notes on the Assemblée Nationale's upcoming legislation, and then she had a call with Alexei's Imperial Secretary, Gus: a gruff, grouchy Swedish man who hadn't been easily won over by Daphne's charm or charisma. Between the two of them, she and Gus were building a new system of diplomatic firewalls and information protocols that might—hopefully—allow Alexei and Louise to *both* rule.

It would mean a lot of staff, and private lines, and top-secret documents that neither monarch could share with the other. But the biggest obstacle was that each country needed to approve the marriage in a national referendum. Which meant that Daphne was managing the biggest royal PR campaign of all time, selling Louise and Alexei's romance to the world as an epic, impossible, sweeping love story.

So far the French were polling in support of their princess, which wasn't all that surprising; the French had always been sentimental. Daphne was having a harder time winning over the Russians. But she knew she could get there, in the end—and told everyone so.

Perhaps that was the best thing about this job: she no longer had to hide just how smart she was.

At home she had always downplayed her intelligence. All her life she'd been told she was beautiful; small wonder that she'd thought the pinnacle of her achievement was trading on those looks to climb higher in the world.

Trying to become a princess, Daphne realized now, had

been too small a dream. It was a role that hinged entirely on her relationship to someone *else*.

For the first time in her life Daphne was free: of her mother's ambition, of the constraining persona she had built, of the demands of being a princess. She was free to be anything she wanted.

Who knew where her path would lead. Maybe she and Ethan would end up together, or maybe not. She might become an ambassadress or a congresswoman or the CEO of a company. Whatever she did, she was going to do it on her own merit, without manipulation or scheming.

Well . . . maybe with a *little* bit of scheming.

NINA

"The only work we haven't discussed in detail is *Lady Susan*." Dr. Lytton leaned back in her overstuffed chair. "What do you make of Blalock's assertion that Susan is just another figure in the British villainess tradition, à la Lady Macbeth?"

"I actually think that *Lady Susan* was more inspired by non-English works. Like *Les liaisons dangereuses*," Nina argued, stumbling over the French pronunciation.

Dr. Lytton lifted her eyebrows. They were in her office, which was a study in cozy chaos, with books on every single surface, stacked so perilously high that Nina always feared they might topple. Sunlight streamed through the windows that overlooked the quadrangle, dappling shadows over Nina's spiral notebook.

Nina loved Oxford. She loved the creak of the staircase that led to this office, the treads warped from centuries of scholarly footsteps. She loved the city, with its winding cobblestone paths and quaint bakeries, a place that had remained seemingly untouched by the passing of time. It had been freezing when she arrived, and as she'd wandered the snowy, fairy-tale campus, she'd wrapped Jamie's scarf tighter around her neck and thought how lucky she was to be here.

That was months ago. Now it was summer, and she'd traded her snow boots and scarf for sundresses that became damp with sweat in the June heat. The semester had ended weeks ago, but Dr. Lytton—Nina's tutorial professor—had offered her a job as a research assistant, and Nina had jumped at the chance to stay.

"An interesting suggestion," Dr. Lytton replied. "But as we know, Jane didn't speak French, and the English translation of *Les liaisons dangereuses* wasn't in wide circulation yet."

Nina nodded. She loved how the professor always referred to the novelist as *Jane,* in a warm, casual tone that seemed to suggest they were old friends, all three of them.

"Still, it's worth checking on. I don't know if anyone has made the connection to Laclos before." She nodded, reaching a decision. "Nina, why don't you pop down to London tomorrow and visit the British Museum archives? They have the records of all the nineteenth-century publishers. You can let me know if Jane might've had access to the translation."

"Of course. I'll check circulation in Hampshire, and I'll do some reading of Jane's friends' diaries as well. Maybe one of them references it somewhere?"

The clock in the tower struck twelve, its chimes long and mournful-sounding. "I think that's enough for today," Dr. Lytton declared, shutting her notebook with a smile. "Why don't you go enjoy the afternoon."

As Nina clattered down the staircase, she accidentally hit the Play button on her phone, and it resumed the song she'd been listening to before her meeting. It was something Sam had sent her: a new single released by Liam's band, which Sam insisted was about her, though the lyrics never mentioned her by name. Already it had skyrocketed to become the most downloaded new song of the week.

Nina paused the song and typed out a quick text: *You might appreciate this: I'm building an argument comparing Les liaisons dangereuses to Lady Susan.*

Daphne's answer was immediate. *GENIUS. I totally get it.*

Nina couldn't help chuckling. Two characters who were both manipulative and devious? Of course Daphne saw the connection.

Her phone buzzed with Daphne's next message. *So, in Provence, should we do a day of biking or go to Van Gogh's house?*

Can we bike TO Van Gogh's house? Nina typed back.

Hang on, I'll check. Then, a few moments later: *Louise's people will set it up with a private guide.*

We don't need a private guide, Nina started to reply, though she knew it was no use. Daphne never could resist a royal perk. At least now she came by them honestly.

Part of her still couldn't believe that she and Daphne were spending a whole *weekend* together. She hadn't told anyone back home, not Rachel or Sam or her parents; they wouldn't understand. After everything that had happened between her and Daphne, Nina should hate her, or at least want to avoid her. And yet . . . she didn't.

It had started a few months ago. Out of the blue, Daphne had sent Nina a text saying that she was heading to London on some diplomatic business, and was there any chance Nina could make time for her?

They had met at a small, unassuming pizza place with checkered tablecloths, not the type of trendy restaurant that Nina had expected Daphne to suggest. To Nina's surprise, they talked for hours: about Daphne's new job and Nina's semester abroad. Nina had laughed so hard at the news of Gabriella Madison and Prince Juan Carlos, she'd gotten a stitch in her side.

And inevitably, once the red wine had loosened them both, they had talked about Jeff.

When Daphne returned to her side of the English Channel, the conversation had continued. Now she and Nina were . . . friends, as unbelievable as it seemed.

And really, why shouldn't they be friends? Jeff had always been the wedge between them. He was out of the picture now; Nina was still spending time with Jamie, avoiding the limelight, but that was no obstacle to her hanging out with Daphne.

She stepped out into the sunshine and blinked in surprise.

She must be daydreaming. Her thoughts of Prince Jefferson had caused her mind to hallucinate him, because surely he wasn't here, in Oxford, standing there in the quadrangle and waiting for Nina.

He looked as handsome as ever in a button-down with the sleeves rolled up, revealing his tanned forearms. At the sight of Nina, his eyes brightened hopefully.

"Nina—hi."

"Jeff?" How could he say *hi* as if this wasn't a complete and utter shock? She hugged her notebook tighter to her chest. "What are you doing here? Shouldn't you be in Washington for the coronation?"

"The official events all start tomorrow. I'm about to fly back; I was in London and figured I'd swing by," he explained. "I just . . . I needed to see you."

"Okay," she said slowly, still dazed.

"Can we, um, take a walk? Are you busy?"

She nodded toward a courtyard framed by pointed arches, stone gargoyles carved into the pillars. "Sure."

Jeff started walking quickly, then seemed to notice he was outpacing Nina and slowed his steps. He was distinctly nervous.

"I've been thinking a lot since I last saw you," Jeff began.

The last time we saw each other was six months ago, at your re-hearsal dinner, when you almost said "I love you." Nina knew better than to voice those thoughts aloud, but Jeff was obviously thinking of the same thing, because he cleared his throat.

"Nina . . . I want to tell you that I'm sorry. The way I've treated you the past few years has been selfish. You were right when you said that it wasn't fair to you, or to Daphne."

Nina traced a hand along one of the stone columns, trying to ground herself in the present, because this still felt like a dream. How many times had she longed for Jeff to say he was sorry? And now the moment had arrived, and instead of feeling a stab of pleasure, she was simply hollow with regret.

"It was hard on me, seeing you with Daphne," she admitted. "Especially when you got engaged just weeks after we had kissed."

"I hate that I put you through that. I'm sure it's too little too late, but I need you to know—I loved you the whole time, even when I did a terrible job of showing it."

"If you loved me the whole time, why did you get engaged to her?"

Jeff looked at the flagstones beneath their shoes. When he glanced up again, his eyes gleamed with remorse. "It was . . . complicated."

Nina thought of what Daphne had confessed in the throne room, *I lied to him,* and a sliver of compassion wormed its way into her heart.

"Nina, what I'm trying to say is that you're right. I shouldn't have committed to Daphne, no matter the circumstances, not feeling the way I did about you."

"Jeff . . ." Nina fell silent, unsure whether she was inviting him to continue, or begging him to stop.

"Please, just let me say this, and if you still hate me at the end of it, then I'll leave you alone forever, I swear." The words tumbled rapidly from his mouth, as if he needed to say them quickly, before he lost his nerve.

"I love you, Nina. I've loved you since we were kids chasing each other around the palace. I love you so much that when we did actually date, I kept waiting for the other shoe to drop, because I was afraid that all of it—everything that comes along with dating me—would scare you away. And it did scare you away," he added mournfully.

Nina nodded, fighting back tears.

"When we became friends again last fall, I started to hope that maybe your opinions about my position had changed. That maybe you would give us another chance. Then Beatrice got in her accident, and I was under so much pressure, and Daphne—" He broke off, sighed. "I thought that getting engaged to Daphne was the right thing, the noble thing, but of course it wasn't. It's never the right thing to pledge your heart and not mean it."

Jeff stopped in their walk and took both her hands in his. "Do you think we could try again? Start over?"

After everything that had happened, Nina wasn't sure they were *capable* of starting over—if she were even free to.

She felt guilty that she'd let him make his grand declarations without saying this sooner. "I'm still seeing Jamie."

Jeff's hopeful expression crumpled. "Oh," he breathed. "I didn't read anything about it in the tabloids. Not that I've been stalking you in the press, I mean . . ."

"We're keeping it very quiet." She hesitated, then added, "And we're taking things slow."

She knew that by saying that, she was opening a door, ever so slightly.

The whole point of Nina's coming to Oxford was to learn and grow. To explore what *she* was capable of—not as a prince's girlfriend, but simply as Nina. She and Jamie still talked on the phone, and he'd come to Oxford several times, but she had put the brakes on things—commitment-wise, and physically. When Jamie visited, he stayed at the Canadian embassy in London, not in Nina's room with her.

True to his word, he was wooing her, with a quiet, steady courtship that would have surprised the media, given his cheeky image. He sent Nina flowers and signed first-edition novels and the early screener copies of the new season of *Kingmaker* (which they had watched at the same time, on opposite sides of the Atlantic, staying on the phone throughout each episode). Another bonus of their low-key behavior was that their relationship had still, for now, escaped public notice.

"Would it be okay if we got a coffee, at least?" Jeff asked.

I've loved you since we were kids, he'd told her—and Nina knew that a part of her still loved him, too. Perhaps that corner of her heart would always love him, throughout all the years, no matter what mistakes either of them made, no matter where life took them.

Could she and Jeff possibly start again? As friends . . . or as something more?

There was only one way to find out.

"All right," Nina told him, smiling. "Let's get a coffee. I know just the place."

She turned and started down the cobblestone path, letting His Royal Highness Prince Jefferson hurry to catch up with her—because they weren't in America, where she had to let him walk ahead; they were on foreign soil, in *her* city.

Finally, it felt like they were equally ranked.

SAMANTHA

It was disorienting, being back at the palace. As expected, nothing had really changed: it was the same heavy drapes and echoing halls, the same crimson carpet being hand-brushed by a series of maids because it was supposedly too delicate for a vacuum, the same heavy oil portraits glaring down at her from the walls.

Perhaps *she* had changed, Sam thought, tugging at her gown: a pale peach one with a skirt that fanned out in a wide swan tail behind her. She hadn't worn black-tie in months. These days she was exclusively in biker shorts or leggings—clothes that would never have been allowed in her former life, as a princess.

"You'll be great today, Sam," Marshall assured her, reading her mood. He reached for her hand and she laced her fingers gratefully in his.

"Thank you, but I won't be doing anything except sitting there," she pointed out.

"They'll all still be staring at you."

They'll be staring at *us*, Sam thought. The famous ex-princess and her boyfriend, the prodigal son. And they both looked the part: Sam conspicuously not wearing a tiara, Marshall as excruciatingly handsome as ever in his ceremonial attire. The golden bear pin that had started it all gleamed on his lapel, echoing the glint of his deep brown eyes.

"I love you," Sam told him, and Marshall grinned.

"Love you too, shortcake."

Sam rolled her eyes, but it was nice hearing the old absurd nicknames again. At least that hadn't changed.

"I should go find Beatrice. I'll see you in the throne room, okay?"

When Samantha reached the Brides' Room—where Beatrice was getting ready for today's events, though of course she wasn't a bride—a footman opened the door for her. Sam's hands flew to her mouth in a very un-Samantha-like gasp.

"Oh, Bee. You look spectacular."

Beatrice was surrounded by several fluttering assistants

who fastened her bracelets and touched up her lipstick. The ivory satin of her coronation gown was embroidered with heavy gold thread. Sam realized the stitches made up a series of American motifs—a rose, a cascade of stars, and was that an ear of corn? The shapes were so soft and abstract that she wasn't quite sure. Seed pearls and shimmering crystals were sewn into the overlay, and the ermine-trimmed robe of state hung behind her, ready to be pinned at her neck.

The Imperial State Crown, of course, wouldn't be added until the ceremony itself.

It was such a monumental moment, the coronation of the very first queen in America's history. Which explained why Beatrice didn't look like Sam's sister anymore. She didn't look like a mortal woman at all, but like a goddess, or a painting come to life.

"Sam!" Beatrice flashed her a broad smile, and the illusion was broken. "I have something for you."

"Really?" Sam perked up a little, the way she always did at the mention of presents. "But it's *your* coronation; you shouldn't have gotten me anything."

"You got this for yourself," Beatrice said cryptically. "What I mean is, everyone is so proud of you. Stanford!" She shook her head admiringly, then waved the attendants out of the room so they had some privacy. "You deserve it."

"Thanks, Bee."

When Sam had applied to Stanford, she hadn't had much of a plan beyond joining Marshall in the place he clearly needed to be. But after she was accepted, a new life had started to form. One of Marshall's friends in San Francisco needed a roommate for the summer; Sam had moved into her extra bedroom. She could even pay her fair share of the rent, now that her family had reinstated her access to her personal bank accounts. Lately, she hadn't spent much time there, anyway; she was too busy helping Marshall readjust to his role within his family, and preparing for the start of classes in the fall. She had already joined the group chat for her freshman class, and kept making provocative comments under the initial S. Her profile picture was a cactus emoji.

She'd also started volunteering part-time for the local district judge, whose assistant had taken one look at her and promptly given her dozens of boxes' worth of backlogged papers to file. Sam understood she was being hazed, and did the work without complaint. After a few weeks, the office had begun to tolerate her, possibly even accept her. One of them had even leaked her volunteer work to the press. That, combined with photos of her shopping at the local Costco (she had her own membership card now), had tipped the scales in her public-relations turnaround. She was no longer Samcelled; she was now the People's Princess. The *relatable* Washington, the one who could navigate the metro and cook her own breakfast.

"You should raid the library before you go," Beatrice added. "Some of the books here might be useful in your history classes."

Sam cleared her throat. "Actually . . . I've been meaning to tell you, I'm taking some prelaw classes, too."

"You want to go to law school?" Beatrice asked, surprised.

Members of the royal family were prohibited from practicing law; it was a conflict of interest, not to mention too loud and opinionated. Princes and princesses could only study uncontroversial topics, like art history or classics. The sort of ornamental paths of study that would never threaten the Crown's standing.

But Sam didn't represent the Crown anymore; and it sounded kind of fun, arguing with people for a living.

"I might, now that it's actually possible."

Something like concern flickered over Beatrice's features, then she attempted a smile. "You have quite the history of rule-breaking for a future lawyer."

"The better you know the rules, the more easily you can break them," Sam teased.

Moving carefully in the weight of her gown, Beatrice shuffled to a small side table and grabbed a sealed folder. She handed it to Sam. "You may want to rethink law school once you see this."

Slowly, Sam opened it and began to read.

In the name of Her Majesty, Congress fully assembled declares and ordains that Samantha Washington shall be restored to her position as Her Royal Highness, the Princess Samantha. She shall undertake appointments and duties on behalf of Her Majesty and, as a result of such, shall enjoy the style, dignity, and income incumbent upon her position as a Royal Princess. . . .

Sam blinked as the meaning of the document registered. "You got my titles back?"

Beatrice was beaming. "*You* got your titles back. Everyone has been so impressed with the way you've handled things this year. I know you didn't start bargain-shopping and riding the metro because you wanted to help the Crown, but it helped anyway. You gave us a much-needed adjustment in the eyes of ordinary people. I see it, and so does Congress," Beatrice said softly. "And just in the nick of time! Now you can be the first to give me homage today, instead of Jeff. All you have to do is sign it," Beatrice added, holding out a fountain pen.

Sam stared down at the document, marked with the congressional seal at the top. She saw her old life unfurling before her again, a life she knew well—public appearances and galas, being curtsied to, wearing tiaras and gowns. Meeting so many people, yet never really knowing any of them. There were good parts of that life, undoubtedly.

And yet.

A different version of her life glimmered at the edge of her vision like a mirage. One where she could go to law school, date Marshall without complications. She didn't need to be part of the royal family to change lives, change prejudices, change the world.

All she needed to be was herself.

Her vision blurred with tears as she handed the congressional order back to Beatrice. "Thanks, but I'm okay."

Her sister stared at her in shock. Obviously, no one ever said *Thanks, but I'm okay* when offered the highest order of royal titles. "You don't want to be a princess?"

"I want to be myself, independent of my position and titles. And I'm still figuring out who that is."

"Sam—please." Her sister's eyes were bright; she blinked rapidly, wiping underneath her lashes to keep the mascara from running. "I can't do this without you."

"Oh, Bee. Of course you can." Sam stepped forward and pulled her sister into a hug. "Remember what you said last year when I wanted to run away to Hawaii? You told me that family comes before duty. That we would always be sisters, no matter where our paths led."

"I said that?" Beatrice sniffed. "Seems like I was very wise then."

"You are very wise now."

Beatrice's voice broke as she replied, "I'm going to miss you so much."

"I'm always here when you need me, I promise," Sam protested, but she knew what Beatrice meant.

For so long they had been on this journey together: the heir and the spare, and then, after their father died, the monarch and the heir. No one else could understand the strange idiosyncrasies of their lives.

Sam and Beatrice were bound by something much larger than them: by the skeins of history that had woven themselves around their lives and quietly tightened until the two sisters were gasping for air. Until they had learned to tear themselves free, each in her own way.

Beatrice stepped back, her expression a mix of regret and admiration. "I'm keeping this document in case you change your mind. Know that this door is always open to you."

"Maybe I'll change my mind and sign it someday," Sam assured her. "But for now, I'm going to do my own thing."

A new feeling was building in her chest, sending currents of excitement through her. She was Samantha, plain ordinary Samantha, and the whole world lay before her. It felt wild and unrestrained and utterly exhilarating—the taste of freedom.

BEATRICE

Beatrice stood before the double doors to the throne room, her ears still ringing with the shouts she'd heard from inside the carriage. It had taken most of the morning for her carriage to crawl the five miles from the old Alexandria lighthouse to the palace: a route that had been planned to mimic King George I's procession to his own coronation, though his march had been far longer and at the head of an army. She still couldn't believe all the thousands of people who had come to see her, screaming her name and waving flags, turning the city into a riot of noise and color.

Of course, not everyone was celebrating today. Some Americans still felt uncomfortable with the thought of a female head of state; they claimed that Beatrice had been deceptive and misleading, concealing the extent of her neurological damage after the accident, and what else could she be hiding? But her approval ratings among regular Americans had soared to eighty percent, higher than almost any monarch in the nation's history.

Beatrice knew her flash of vulnerability was the cause. All her life, she had cleaved her personal life from her public one, had maintained a pristine facade before the media. Now she'd given the world a glimpse of something *real*, and instead of turning on her, America had embraced her for it.

Samantha was right; they should have humanized the monarchy long ago.

The choir launched into a rendition of "Vivat Regina," and Beatrice startled. This was her cue. The pair of footmen grabbed the doors in a perfectly synchronized motion and swung them open.

It felt like her wedding all over again, and yet entirely different, because this commitment was far weightier and more severe than the promises she'd made to Teddy. That was a matter of the heart; this was a matter of history.

Even in her white satin dress, she didn't look like a bride; her gown was weighted down with too much gold embroidery, and was half covered by the ermine-trimmed robe of state, which Beatrice held folded over an arm. She let it drop, a bit dramatically, and the two footmen reached beneath it with gilded scepters to spread the cloak out behind her.

As she stepped forward, everyone in the throne room craned their necks. Beatrice felt the impact of all those gazes hitting her; felt her duty settling over her body, far heavier than the cloak around her shoulders.

She reached the front of the throne room amid a fanfare of trumpets. Slowly, she sank into four distinct curtsies, one in each of the cardinal directions—to represent the wide range of subjects she swore to govern, from north to south and east to west.

The Speaker of the House of Tribunes stepped forward.

"Americans here assembled: I present to you now Beatrice, your undoubted queen. Do you all swear to do her homage and service today and every day hereafter?"

A chorus of "God Save the Queen" rumbled through the room, echoed by the millions of people watching on television. The thought of all those voices raised at once sent shivers over Beatrice's skin.

When it came time for her to swear her oaths, the Chief Justice of the Supreme Court held out a Bible. Beatrice placed her hand over its leather cover, her heart picking up speed.

Then she felt a pair of steady blue eyes watching her from the front row of seats, and her nervousness calmed.

"Your Majesty. Do you solemnly swear to govern the United States of America according to its laws and principles?"

"I do," she replied.

"Do you swear to rely on law and justice, on mercy and care, in all your judgments?"

"I do."

"And will you protect and defend the Constitution of the United States, with your life itself, if need be?"

The *with your life itself* part of this oath had always struck Beatrice as a bit melodramatic. But caught up in the emotional crescendo of today's ceremony, she understood that her forefathers had done exactly that—and had expected her to do the same. She had always known that the Crown would ask her for everything, even her life.

Beatrice felt something like a hand on her shoulder, as if her father were here, telling her how proud he was. The sensation was gone as quickly as it had come, but Beatrice tipped her head up with new conviction.

"I will."

When the Imperial State Crown was held before her on

a velvet cushion, she reached out with shaking hands and lifted it onto her head—the way all eleven kings had done since King George I, because this was America, and no one, not even the Church, ranked higher than the monarch. She'd rehearsed this movement so many times, yet none of her practice sessions had captured what it would feel like in the moment. Terrifying and thrilling and sacred.

For an instant the crown seemed unstable, but she settled it with a slight movement and then it was done; church bells throughout the city were ringing and the artillery fired a twenty-one-gun salute. Even from inside the throne room Beatrice could hear the roar from outside, which felt shatteringly loud after the respectful stillness of her oath.

Jeff stood and came to kneel before her throne, bowing his head like an Arthurian knight. As the most senior peer in the realm, he was the first to pay her homage. Once upon a time that had been Beatrice's job—at her father's coronation, when she was eleven, she had been the first to approach the throne and lead the obeisance. She still remembered the girlish satin bow on her dress, which had been in the way when she knelt down. Beatrice had tugged at it futilely, then met her father's gaze, and he'd winked at her—just once, but the wink was unmistakable.

Somehow, that single gesture had calmed her enough to lower her head and recite the Oath of Vassal Homage, as Jeff was about to do.

"Your Majesty. I, Jefferson, Prince of America, solemnly swear that I am your liege man. I will honor and serve you in faith and in loyalty, from this day forward, and for all the days of my life. So help me God."

When Jeff looked up, Beatrice met his eyes, and understanding passed between them—as monarch and heir, yes, but also as brother and sister.

A part of Beatrice still wished that Sam were the one

kneeling before her. She adored her brother, but she and Sam had been in this together from the beginning.

She couldn't blame Sam for chasing her own dreams, instead of coming back to work for the Crown again. The royal establishment would call it selfish, but Beatrice didn't see it that way. Staying out in the world, without the cover of a title to protect you from the elements? It might be a little foolhardy, but it was also brave.

Jeff returned to his seat, and suddenly Teddy was walking up the steps, his face alight with unmistakable pride. Technically he shouldn't have been in the proceedings at all, given that he wasn't a duke—or even a future duke—anymore, but Beatrice had insisted upon it.

As he knelt before her and swore the same oath, she realized—Teddy had said these words to her before. That long-ago day when she'd proposed to him, he had knelt before her and sworn the same vow. To honor and serve her in faith and loyalty for all the days of her life.

Looking at him now, Beatrice felt her heart burst with love. How foolish she had been to think that getting married before her coronation would weaken her. Love could only ever strengthen you; it lifted you up and made you a better version of yourself.

As Teddy stood, and the opening notes of the national anthem reverberated through the throne room, Beatrice realized what it meant.

The reign of America's first queen had officially begun, at last.

ACKNOWLEDGMENTS

The end of a series is always bittersweet, and this one more than most, as I have lived with the American royals in my head for nearly a decade. I still can't believe we're at the end of it all! I'm really going to miss these books, in large part because of the brilliant and talented people I've gotten to work with along the way.

Caroline Abbey, I can't imagine American Royals without you—your unflagging patience, your thoughtful editorial notes, and the sheer force of your brainpower. (I love nerding out with you on royal history!) Thank you for being the fiercest champion of this series from day one.

Joelle Hobeika, can you believe this is our seventh book together? Thank you for your creativity, for your willingness to take a chance on me, and for the thousands of hours we have spent debating story beats. (I know there will be thousands more to come.) I am so lucky to have you in my corner.

I'm grateful to the entire publishing team at Random House, especially Michelle Nagler, Mallory Loehr, Kelly McGauley, Kate Keating, Elizabeth Ward, Jenn Inzetta, Meredith Wagner, Adrienne Waintraub, Tricia Lin, Jasmine Hodge, Katie Halata, Lauren Stewart, Morgan Maple, Barbara Bakowski, and Karen Sherman. Special thanks are due to Noreen Herits and Cynthia Lliguichuzhca, for constantly thinking of new ways to publicize American Royals, and to Trisha Previte and Carolina Melis, for yet another breathtaking cover.

I am incredibly grateful to everyone at Alloy Entertainment: Josh Bank, Sara Shandler, Les Morgenstein, Gina Girolamo, Kate Imel, Kendyll Boucher, Romy Golan, Matt Bloomgarden, Josephine McKenna, and Kat Jagai.

Thanks also to my foreign sales team at Rights People: Charlotte Bodman, Alexandra Devlin, Harim Yim, Claudia Galluzzi, Hannah Whitaker, Jodie O'Toole, and Amy Threadgold. Thank you for helping American Royals reach readers around the world.

I am lucky to work with a fantastic team on the American Royals audiobooks: Orli Moscowitz, Joseph Ward, and Brittany Pressley, who brings my characters to life with such talented narration.

I don't know how I would do this job without the support of my friends. Eliza, Alexandra, Biz, Stacy, Emily, Julia, Sarah—I owe each of you a massive debt of gratitude, for all the reasons you know so well. Sarah Mlynowski, I'm always grateful for your support and mentorship.

None of this would be possible without my parents, who have supported me in more ways than I could ever begin to count. (Though if I were trying to count, I would start with my mom, who effectively became the general contractor on our home renovation this year and never complained. Moms truly are the best.) John Ed, Lizzy, and MK—thank you for making our family so special. I love you all higher than the sky!

Alex, thank you for everything. You are my anchor amid the chaos, a source of laughter when I need it most, and my best friend. William and I are so lucky to have you.

Finally, to the readers: you have made this series a joy to work on! Thank you to everyone who has reviewed, recommended, or simply enjoyed American Royals—it means so much to me. I have loved sharing these characters with you, and I hope you'll stick around for what comes next.

Ever wonder how the future queen
Beatrice first fell for her bodyguard?
Or how Prince Jefferson and his sister's
best friend became entangled in a
love triangle for the ages? Read about
the infamous night when it all began.

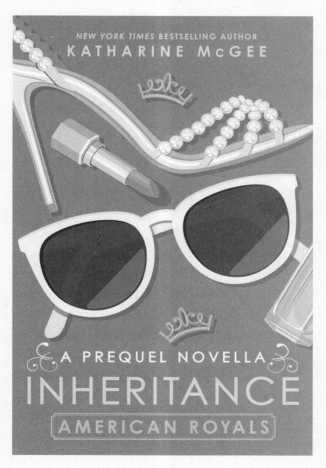